Josh, instinctively loosening the knot of his tie, dragged his gaze from Ann's dust-caked, averted face and looked around. It was as if none present dared trust their ears, look at each other, or even breathe. They stood as if literally petrified, staring in the same direction. He glanced back across the road and saw the lines of figures stiffen in unison, but could not hear the whispers of 'Something's happening' rippling along that far pavement, or see the only reporter amongst them, a cub from a London local paper, nudge his photographer away from the sports page of yesterday's *Daily Mirror*.

In a few minutes the first small gap was made, and Mr Wesley, lying on his face, called down, 'This is the SSO speaking. If you can hear me, please answer.'

The reply was immediate, distant, but clear. 'This is Sister Preliminary Training School speaking, Mr Wesley. Thank you, we can hear you. We are all well down here. All quite well. What do you wish us to do to help?'

Lucilla Andrews is the author of twenty-nine novels, including *The Lights of London*, *The Phoenix Syndrome* and *The African Run*. Her books have been translated into eleven languages and most have a hospital setting. She trained as a nurse at St Thomas's Hospital, London, during the Second World War, and has been a full-time writer since 1953. She lives in Edinburgh.

LUCILLA ANDREWS

– *Front Line* –
1940

Mandarin

A Mandarin Paperback
FRONT LINE 1940

First published in Great Britain 1990
by William Heinemann Ltd
This edition published 1993
by Mandarin Paperbacks
an imprint of Reed Consumer Books Ltd
Michelin House, 81 Fulham Road, London SW3 6RB
and Auckland, Melbourne and Singapore

Copyright © 1990 Lucilla Andrews

A CIP catalogue record for this title
is available from the British Library

ISBN 0 7493 1619 5

Printed and bound in Great Britain
by BPCC Paperbacks Ltd
Member of BPCC Ltd

– One –

The English sun didn't know what time it was either, Josh Adams reflected, turning his attention from the picnickers in Green Park to check his watch. It was 3.30 p.m. by British wartime double summer time, but only 1.30 for the sun, and though this was the first Saturday of September, hot as high summer.

He backed into the shade of the nearest sandbag wall, tilted forward the brim of his brown trilby, and wondered where Hitler would stand to take the Victory Parade. The Mall? No. The balcony of Buckingham Palace. Hitler was too smart an operator to miss out on that picture on the world's front pages, or to back out of the show at the last minute as he had done in Paris in July. With his luck this weather would hold for him. 'Dunkirk weather' the English called it here in London, and in the little pubs in Kent and Sussex where he and the other neutral correspondents sharing a car had stopped off for beer on their way back to town after another day spent on the white cliffs of Dover or the Downs watching the dogfights between the Luftwaffe and the RAF. These had been going on daily since mid-August, and most days from around mid-July. Goering had promised Hitler and Germany that his boys would finish off the RAF in two weeks. This was 7 September, and it was a fair assumption that right now the fat man's blood-pressure was not too good.

Josh took off and slung over one shoulder the jacket of his light grey suit, loosened the knot of his darker grey tie, and felt the heat of the sandbags through his white cotton shirt. They guarded the entrance to his hotel, which like just about every public building in London had sandbags heaped against the ground-floor windows, and every visible pane elsewhere criss-crossed with strips of anti-blast paper. And as ubiquitous as sandbags and papered panes were the Government posters warning the civilian population to obey the blackout laws, avoid careless talk, save water and electricity, carry gasmasks, dig for victory, and advising them of what to do when the imminent German invasion occurred. From what he had seen of London's attitude to the posters, they were one hell of a waste of good trees.

On the dry yellow grass of Green Park, Londoners in shirtsleeves and summer dresses lounged in couples or little groups. People were opening vacuum flasks or soft-drink bottles filled with tea, handing round brown paper bags of crusted sandwiches and rock cakes, and smiling and chatting as placidly as the queues for theatre matinées that he had seen in the Haymarket and Shaftesbury Avenue earlier this afternoon. Only about half the people in the queues, as now in the Park, had with them the small brown cardboard boxes containing civilian gasmasks. No one bothered to glance up at the Armada of grey barrage balloons poised above Greater London, or towards the distant south-east where all day the clear blue sky had been streaked by the appearing and disappearing wispy white vapour trails of today's dogfights. So what if there was a war on? Time for tea. But for once, no uniforms in the Park and the number of children down to single figures. His face hardened. One was too many.

His full name was Joshua George Adams. He was

a fifth-generation Bostonian of Anglo-Saxon ancestry, the second of his parents' two sons, and the first male member of his family to work outside the family business. He was thirty and had had his first European assignment for his newspaper, the *New York Banner*, in Paris in 1935. He had never known personal want or grief, but underneath the conditioned reserve of his upbringing and the detachment of a good reporter he had the imagination and sensitivity that turned sympathy into compassion when he encountered want or grief in others. But his compassion ran short when confronted by what seemed to him criminal stupidity. From his arrival in London in late July, the sight of a baby, a child or a pregnant woman had had him inwardly seething with anger.

Last September he had seen the Luftwaffe in action in Poland and, before the month ended, the stinking, smouldering ruins of Warsaw. This May, in Paris, he had had an eye-witness account from the *Banner*'s man in Holland of what the Luftwaffe had done to Rotterdam – 'You heard me, Josh – thirty thousand killed in two hours – three zero zero zero zero . . .' – and in 1936, in a war that now seemed as distant as the Great War, he had reached Guernica a few hours after the Luftwaffe's dress rehearsal for this one. Until this May, he had spent two years in the Berlin office, then New York suddenly shifted him back to Paris where, three weeks later, sick at heart and tasting bile, he had watched the first arrival of the victorious German Army and the hoisting of the Nazi swastika on the Eiffel Tower. Shortly afterwards he had been in one of the small groups of neutral press taken by the Germans to see the miles of military equipment abandoned by the British Expeditionary Force in their retreat to Dunkirk, where hundreds of thousands of men were stranded, floundering and dying upon the open beaches for ten days under continuous bombardment with only two days' respite provided by heavy fog.

In Germany earlier this year, he had interviewed military personnel of all ranks and, whilst their answers to his pre-censored questions had been patently pre-scribed, their training, equipment, physique and morale had been uniformly impressive and made them a superb fighting machine – arguably the best the world had ever known. Which is why, he reflected on that Piccadilly pavement, right now Germany has swept up Czechoslovakia, Poland, Norway, Denmark, Holland, Belgium and France, and kicked the British into their own Channel. And no excuses for not knowing Hitler's next move. Up to my quitting Berlin, each time the German radio announced another victory for the Wehrmacht, they topped it up with a chorus of the Berliners' favourite ditty, 'We March On England'.

The code message from New York telling him to join Pete Burness in London arrived in the Paris office in early July. The journey took fifteen days. He had had to travel down by bus through unoccupied France, then through Spain and Portugal to Lisbon. He had travelled light, with just his old portable and a small grip. He had bought his present suit off-the-peg in London, and its quality and low price had astonished him after the poor quality and exorbitant cost of civilian clothes in Germany during the whole of his time there. But Germany had been getting ready for this war long before his move to Berlin, whilst England, from all he had read and heard, had washed its hands and looked the other way – and not just once.

The Portuguese trawler that had disembarked him at Southampton in late July had been crammed with just about every other US newspaperman on the Euro-pean mainland making for London and elderly British expatriates from the South of France. The latter had been querulous with fatigue as well as financial and

4

other anxieties over their uncertain future in their home-
land, but unconvinced that 'that fellow Hitler really
means to have a go at England . . .' Josh Adams had
sympathised with their anxieties, but not their myopia.
When they reached Southampton, the Luftwaffe had
been attacking British convoys in the Channel from
its new French airfields for the previous two weeks,
and making probing raids into southern England to
test the strength of the coastal defences and, in particular,
that of the RAF. The continuation of these tactics into
August had given Pete Burness, the *Banner*'s only man
in London for the past eight years, time to steer his
new colleague through the throttling red tape surrounding the acquisition of official accreditation as a war
correspondent from the War Office, and the permits from
the Ministries of Home Security and Information, and
from Scotland Yard, without which he could not move
freely around London, much less travel down to Kent
and Sussex.

'Brother, was your timing great. Can we use the
double gas-rations now the good old Battle of Britain
has gotten going for real,' Pete Burness had reiterated
since mid-August, when the Luftwaffe switched tactics
and turned its full force upon the south-eastern and
southern English airfields. These had to be destroyed
before the German paratroops could fly over to take
specific targets all over the country, and then the
Wehrmacht could sail over.

Three weeks hard at it, thought Josh Adams, watching
the picnickers, and whatever Goebbels is giving out,
Berlin knows the RAF isn't finished off yet. One night
two weeks back the first German bombs had fallen on
the outskirts of London. The next night the RAF dropped
their first bombs on Berlin. Since then, every night
had been two-way traffic with no let-up in the daytime
attacks. There had not been much damage to London
itself: all the nightly targets had been on its periphery

5

and either factories or real or supposed military targets. Just how much – if any – serious damage the RAF were doing to Berlin, he couldn't judge. Inevitably the British and German official reports differed widely; but whilst he generally distrusted all such reports, he tended to believe that the British were only sending small forces of bombers to Berlin, simply because the RAF had fewer aircraft. How many fighter aircraft and pilots they had left was anyone's guess, for the RAF played its cards close to its chest. It was the common view of the international press corps in London that the Luftwaffe had started the Battle of Britain with probably a five-to-one and certainly a three-to-one advantage in aircraft and pilots, and that the RAF must be running dangerously short of both in view of the fact that the RAF fighter pilots were having to fly several sorties every day. No Commander-in-Chief of any Fighter Command would so wear out his pilots unless he had no alternative. Possibly Goering could still give his boys an occasional rest-day; not Air Chief Marshal Dowding.

On the night of 24 August, from the roof of the late Regency terraced house, a short walk from his hotel, that housed the *Banner*'s office on the second floor, Josh Adams and Peter Burness had watched the raid on the outskirts and decided to alternate their days in the country so that one of them would always be in London. The arrangement suited Josh, who preferred working alone to running with the pack and wanted the time to take a closer look at London. The look had not impressed him. He had never liked the place: this was his longest stay in England, and all his previous visits had been too long.

Today Pete Burness had gone down to Beacon Rise, one of the RAF's key fighter stations. Last night 'Lord Haw-Haw', broadcasting in English from Germany, had announced that it had been wiped off the map of

Kent. The RAF had retaliated by arranging for a posse of the neutral press to see for themselves the station that, though badly bombed twice in this last week, remained operational. Burness hoped to spend tonight in some country pub. 'No bets, brother,' he said. 'The RAF may have the edge on the British Army – and sure as hell on the Royal Navy – when it comes to playing ball with us nosy aliens, but they will not be too happy to have us moseying around on our own in the blackout. My guess is they will have us right back well before nightfall. I'm off. London is all yours.'

Josh could do without it in this steamy, stuffy heat. The beer was too warm, the streets were too small, and Londoners' cheerful indifference to their predicament was as infuriating as their voices and attitudes were incomprehensible. He was fluent in French, German and Spanish, and could get by in Polish and Russian without the difficulty in translation he was experiencing in London, and not only from the spoken word.

Once he asked Burness, 'How long did it take you to figure out the English?'

'When I do just that you will be the first to know.'

'After eight years and marrying an English girl?'

'Where's the guy that hand on heart figures out any dame? What's with eight years? This is one old country that kind of likes to take time before the "howdy, stranger".'

'And with fighting this war.'

'Ain't that so, brother? This right little, tight little isle only got around to taking it a mite seriously when they had to get their guys out from under at Dunkirk.'

'Much panic then?'

'Panic?' Burness' large, red, ginger-browed face creased into a wide grin. 'You should have been right there with me at Dover watching the crowds cheering their heads off whilst their guys were hauled out the

7

boats filthy tired, filthy dirty, and more than a few filthy mad at what they had been pushed through and the buddies they had had to leave behind. The crowds carried on like it was the Fourth of July, Christmas Day and "Hail to the Chief" Day rolled up in one. You could not hear yourself think for the cheering, back-slapping and folks telling each other wasn't it just great to know we were on our own and where we are! I kid you not, Brother Adams. Do not ask me why their greatest military defeat should send their morale sky high or why having invaders breathing down their necks should take it way over the top. I just report the facts. My Joan is as crazy. She was fit to be tied last month when I insisted she and the baby hightail it back to her folks down in Exeter. I tell you this – and not one word to my Joan or am I in the doghouse! – but after these eight years I have not yet figured out what makes the English tick. Arrogance? Stupidity? No imagination? The security of being islanders? Just a blind crazy faith in themselves? The lot? Or, whatever. Whatever, there is nothing – repeat, nothing – that boosts their morale like having their backs to the wall, and that is where they stand right now they have just – repeat, just – cottoned on. Like I said, they kind of like to take their time.'

No visible consciousness of backs to the wall in the theatre queues, over in Green Park, or in their office typist, Miss Dewly, when her working week ended at 12.30 p.m. today. Miss Dewly was a large, fairish, fresh-faced, youngish woman living with her Great War-widowed mother in Blackheath and 'let's face it, Mr Adams, positively potty about tennis'. This afternoon she was playing in the finals of the tournament at her local club. 'Let's face it, Mr Adams,' she announced before bouncing off, 'if That Man invades this afternoon I shall be positively peeved. Byee!'

8

His attention was diverted by the first cruising taxi he had seen all afternoon. He hailed it, reluctantly, solely to please his mother. As he climbed in he thought of the letter from her that had arrived this morning, and again he felt uneasy. Chances were that by doing as she asked he would eventually cause her more pain than pleasure; but she had asked, and for once he had the time and was in the right place. He gave the driver the address.

The man nodded. 'Across the river, sir. Might get a bit of air, crossing over. Do with it. Too hot by half in these parts. Which block, sir?'

'Block? Sorry, I can't say.' He produced his mother's letter. 'All I have is Room 1, Private Patients Ward, Saint Martha's Hospital.'

The middle-aged driver's abstracted gaze rested on the nearest invasion poster. 'Top floor, Block 1, that'll be. I'll drop you off at the bridge end. No call for you to take the long walk from the main entrance. Block 1's back of the Junior Nurses' Home, so you just got to take the path by the Home and go in the hospital by the side door. You'll see the arrows to Block 1's stairs. Tidy step you'll have. Private Patients is five flights up.'

'Thanks very much. You certainly know your London hospitals.'

'Not all same as old Martha's, seeing I been born not two good spits off.' He wagged his head at the poster. 'I don't know why old Hitler don't get his skates on. Maybe he don't like getting his feet wet.'

'The RAF are holding him up, wouldn't you say?'

'Aye.' The man smiled dourly. 'High time them Brylcreem boys got theirselves on the job. Like my young lad and his mates says, where was they when they was wanted over Dunkirk, eh?' On that rhetorical note he drove off, and completed the shortish journey in silence.

*

9

'Bloody hell! Pranged another stitch – oh, sorry, Mrs B.S.,' exclaimed Flying Officer Green, who occupied Bed 3, Room 2, of the currently misnamed Private Patients Ward. He was addressing a greying-blonde VAD, who was refilling with tea the china-spouted feeding cup of Flying Officer Daws in Bed 2.

Mrs Brigham-Smythe smiled graciously. 'Not to worry, Mr Green. One heard far worse in the last show.' She glanced at the several inches of mangled blue knitting suspended from thick wooden needles. 'One'll cope after Mr Daws' second cuppa.'

'Third, please, Mrs B.S.,' corrected Mr Daws, who was lying flat on his back in a spinal plaster with a white cotton cranial cap covering the healing scars that seamed his shaven head.

'Panic over. Got the form, thanks.' Mr Green, similarly capped, scarred and shaven, began laboriously unpicking to the dropped stitch. He was twenty-three and sat propped up in bed wearing blue poplin pyjamas. Having finished the tea he could now drink unaided, he had returned to his knitting. His wife had taught him to knit last week, to the joy of Mr Daws and the two Army sergeants in Room 7 and two privates in Room 6, when their individual turns coincided with Mr Green's on the ward's balcony rota. A wartime rule allowed only two bedpatients at any time on the hospital's riverside balconies. The mixing of officers and other ranks would have been unlikely in Service hospitals, but as Sister Private Patients frequently observed, St Martha's Hospital, London, was a civilian voluntary hospital – a circumstance that caused even greater joy to both pilots and the four soldiers, none of whom were regulars.

Mr Green had sustained severe head injuries in July when a Messerschmitt shot down his Spitfire into a Kentish hop-garden. Another Me. had shot down Mr Daws' Hurricane on to a village green in Suffolk, and he had been cut out of the wreck unconscious, with severe head and spinal injuries. He was twenty-one and single, and it was still uncertain whether he would walk again, but his head injuries were improving steadily.

Both men had been transferred from the same RAF hospital to be under the care of Mr Hamilton Joiner, Martha's honorary consultant cranial surgeon, generally acknowledged as one of the best in England. It was Mr Hamilton Joiner's expertise that had caused the reopening of the Private Patients Ward in late May as a temporary expedient to take a fraction of the head injury cases flooding into Army and RAF hospitals owing to their prevalence amongst dispatch riders and aircrew, especially fighter pilots. To deal with this apparently unforeseen situation that was bound to increase with the war, a Combined Services Head Injuries Hospital, medically staffed by civilian specialists in service uniforms, had now been opened in an inland university city, and Mr Hamilton Joiner was due to go there in the first week of October as a major in the Royal Army Medical Corps. Last week seven servicemen patients from the PPW had been transferred there, and Messrs Green and Daws, Sergeants Alcott and Weaver, and Privates Begg and Miller were expected to join them by the end of September. There were no expectations of this nature for Flight Lieutenant E. J. Laurings, Royal Canadian Air Force, alone in Room 1 and on the Dangerously Ill List.

Exactly one year ago Martha's had stopped admitting private patients and the PPW, like every top- and fourth-floor ward, had been closed. With the exception of Sister PPW, who was nearing retirement, the entire PPW nursing staff of senior staff nurses had gone either into the Services, or to the vast Emergency Medical Services Hospitals that the Government was opening in rural areas all over the country to take the thousands of civilian patients being evacuated from London and other large cities, and to await the officially anticipated thousands of civilian air raid casualties. Sister PPW had remained in London as the most senior, by twenty years, of the Office Sisters who presided over Matron's outer offices. She had been as automatic a choice to take charge of her reopened ward as the ward had been for its conversion into a temporary Cranial Unit. It was the one ward in Martha's whose position could provide the essential quiet for head injuries that was almost impossible to achieve in all the others, which were thirty-six-bedded long wards. The ward directly underneath was empty, and lower down were Faith, Hope, then Charity Ward on the ground floor.

Block 1 started the line of eight blocks, of identical height and size, that backed on to the long terrace over-looking the southern embankment and Westminster across the river. In August last year, Martha's had eleven hundred general beds, ninety-eight maternity beds, and twelve private rooms. The week following the declaration of war on 3 September had seen a massive evacuation of bedpatients to country hospitals, the exodus of younger Sisters, staff nurses, honoraries, registrars and housemen to the Services, the closing of upper wards, and the removal of the whole Medical School to a small country town well south of London. And then, as the expected air raids had not happened and the months of the 'phoney war' limped by, Martha's had slowly begun reverting to semi-normal. Third-floor wards had reopened; those lower down were more often full than half-filled; batches of senior medical students had returned on rota; small teaching rounds restarted; and Casualty, which never closed, had continued to treat an average of one thousand out-patients on Mondays, always the heaviest day of the Casualty week. On that first Saturday of September 1940, Martha's had 323 bedpatients.

Nurse Fenner glanced apprehensively at the scarlet DIL* and NO VISITORS, PLEASE notices on the door of Room 1 as she went by carrying the used teatrays of Sergeant Weaver and Private Begg from the balcony. She was thankful pros weren't allowed to nurse DILs, because just glimpsing Mr Laurings from the corridor always made her want to cry. She was the ward's only probationer† and three months out of the Preliminary Training School that her set had been the first to enter after the lowering of the minimum entry age from twenty-one to nineteen. She was a pretty, auburn-haired girl who had not yet lost her puppy-fat nor learnt to control her cap.

'Why must the child invariably look as if she had been pulled through a bush?' Sister PPW demanded regularly of her staff nurse. 'Really, Nurse Marlowe, why Matron now allows chits of gels into St Martha's is beyond me. We had to be at least twenty-five when I started. The lowering to twenty-one was quite young enough. A hospital is no place for children! Frankly, I dare not contemplate what we may be presented with next.'

Sister's venerability rather than her own training stifled Nurse Marlowe's instinctive retort – How about a Panzer division rumbling towards us from Parliament Square, Sister? She looked decorously downwards to conceal the amusement in her eyes. 'I think Nurse Fenner's main problem is her naturally curly hair, Sister.'

'That would have been no problem had Matron not permitted short hair in 1938.'

'You're quite right, Sister,' said Nurse Marlowe soothingly – to soothe Sister was one of her jobs as her

---

* Dangerously Ill List.   † First-year student nurse.

13

deputy. She had been offered this post under a year's contract when her general training ended in May. She was twenty-five, of medium height and slender build, and she wore her long, light-brown hair swept up into the high bun with centre parting that had been statutory for Martha's nurses up to 1938. The style suited her delicately pretty face, and it also saved a hairdresser's bill. She had no income beyond her staff nurse's pay of five pounds a month, all found.

Nurse Fenner's cap had become the concern of all the patients she was allowed to attend. 'Slipping down left, nurse,' cautioned Private Miller of the Arumchester Yeomanry, who was temporarily alone in Room 6.

'Thanks awfully, Mr Miller.' She put down on his bedtable the tray she had just picked up, and reskewered the cap pins anchoring the large bow on the back of her small starched muslin cap. 'Okay?'

'Smashing, nurse.'

'Mr Miller, you're a poppet!'

Private Miller's wizened boyish face flushed with pleasure. He was twenty, had been in the ward longer than the other patients, and his hair was beginning to grow again beneath his cranial cap. He had been an apprentice carpenter when he was called up as a conscripted Militiaman the previous summer, and he had loathed every aspect of the Army but his mates. He was just starting to recall dimly some of the mates he had made before his forage-capped head hit a French road in early May. He had hazy recollections of being carried off some boat somewhere, and of a woman's voice somewhere else saying she had needed six changes of water to wash him clean of oil, sand and salt. He had no memory of the five days and nights he had spent on a stretcher at Dunkirk.

Private Begg, of the Sherwood Foresters, said he was lucky. 'Proper noisy, mucky do, that was. Best forgot. Best not to remember nothing same as me, from coming off me bike down Tidworth to coming out me anaesthetic, seeing Nurse Marlowe's face close and thinking her cap's an halo and I'd had it proper. Mind you, Dusty, if angels don't match up, I'm not stopping.'

'Me neither, Robin Hood.'

Room 6 faced Room 1 across the long wide corridor that ran from the ward entrance at the landing backed by stairs and liftshaft, to the balcony at the far end. At both ends the double doors were hooked open, and against both long walls between the doors were ranged the fire buckets of sand and of water and the manually operated stirrup pumps that the Government insisted should be on every floor of every building in the land. As Nurse Fenner backed out with Miller's tray, Nurse Marlowe came silently from Room 1. 'Why aren't you at tea, Nurse Fenner? Five past and I told you to go at four,' she said.

'Terribly sorry, nurse. I got a bit behind. I know I shouldn't, but—'

'You shouldn't, but everyone does as a pro.'

Nurse Marlowe flicked out the watch pinned by its strap into a bib pocket of her long-sleeved, tight-waisted, long and voluminously skirted grey cotton uniform dress whose hem matched that of her starched white apron. Her white dogcollar, belt and cuffs were even more stiffly starched and, unlike Nurse Fenner's, looked impervious to today's heat. 'As we're so quiet, don't come back till twenty-five to. As soon as you get back, if I'm with Mr Laurings, gather up Mrs Brigham-Smythe and get in the balcony beds, so that Nurse Denton and Nurse Wood can get straight on with their washings when they come back at five. Both balcony men are expecting visitors this evening, and as it's Saturday, and the extra hour, they'll show up on the dot of six.'

Nurse Fenner beamed. She had forgotten it was Saturday. 'Honestly, nurse, I can get back by half-past.'

Nurse Marlowe smiled. 'Not without acute indigestion. Takes a good ten minutes from here to the dining-room. That your last tray? Good. Get weaving.' She went quietly back into Room 1, leaving the door just ajar on mufflered handles.

Nurse Fenner shot joyfully into the ward kitchen, the last door on the right and directly opposite the always open dutyroom door that was the last on the left. Sister had been on this morning, so she had forgotten that this was Half-Bliss Saturday and tomorrow *All*-Bliss Sunday! She now recalled Agnes, the wardmaid, telling her as they cleared the patients' breakfasts, that this afternoon Sister was off to Basingstoke to spend the night with some aged bod she had nursed with in the Great War or the Boer War or the Crimean or some other war. She could never remember when old wars happened, or understand why that one should matter or this one had started. She had no brothers or male relatives of military age, and her father, a country solicitor, was too old for call-up. She knew few young men and had never had a boyfriend: at home her mother did not approve of that sort of thing, and in Martha's she had had neither the time nor the opportunity to meet any young men socially. This had bothered her, but the war had not. She had ignored it until the last two weeks, when she and the rest of her set had been infuriated by their ability to sleep through the nocturnal 'nuisance raids' on the outskirts of London. They had decided inter-set that one of the snags of being civvy nurses in a civvy hospital was that they missed all the fun of the war.

Not to worry, thought Nurse Fenner. PPW minus Sister was always fun, and the new rule Matron had brought in this year that gave student nurses one day off *every* week instead of the old one day a month, and Sisters and staff nurses alternate half-Saturdays and all Sundays, was bliss unparalleled! She charged happily out of the ward, across the stone landing, and on the first flight down nearly knocked over a tall, thin, fair young man in grey coming up from the fourth landing.

'Terribly sorry – er – doctor,' she gasped breathlessly, having been taught so to address any unknown man around the hospital. (Martha's admitted no women to the Medical School or men to the Nurses Training School.)

'I guess it was my fault, nurse – and I am not a doctor, just visiting.' Josh Adams gestured with the hat in his hand to the large, gilt-lettered name board over the big mahogany-panelled entrance doors which stood open. 'Maybe you can advise me?'

Nurse Fenner was enchanted. She loved directing visitors: it made her feel – almost – a second year. He was much too early, she reflected, but even that old so-and-so Sister was good about letting in visitors who arrived at the wrong time. And that this one was more a fascinating monster than an oil painting was in his favour. Give her James Stewart over Robert Taylor every time! And he had such a wizard sort of American voice. Was he American, or Canadian? Her enchantment vanished. 'Please, who have you come to see?' she asked.

'Flight Lieutenant Edward J. Laurings, Royal Canadian Air Force. I am told that he is in Room 1. May I go right in?'

She looked distressed. 'I'm terribly sorry, but I've got to ask my staff nurse. I'll just show you – this way, please.' She ushered him into the dutyroom. 'If you'll wait in here, please – oh – yes – please, what is your name, and are you a relative of Mr Laurings or on leave from his squadron?'

He shook his head, smiling kindly. She looked so young and anxious and hot in all that starch. 'No relation, and a civilian. My name is Adams. I am not

17

acquainted with Mr Laurings, but our mothers are old friends, and my mother has written asking me to visit with him.'

'Oh. Thank you, Mr Adams.' She scurried out and a couple of seconds later knocked quietly on the next door. When Nurse Marlowe appeared she murmured an explanation and asked anxiously, 'Was I right, nurse?'

'Quite. Thanks. I'll cope. Come back at twenty to.'

'Thanks awfully, nurse.' She hurried away, looking ahead fixedly.

Josh saw her go by the open door and wondered momentarily what the staff nurse had said to scare the poor kid to hell. Then he returned to wondering what he could say to this wounded Canadian whose parents, according to his mother's letter, were worried sick: 'Frances Laurings called me long-distance after receiving my letter for her birthday this morning. She had not known that you are now in London. She said they had never wished Ed to volunteer, but one day last spring he drove into Winnipeg and that was that. He was twenty-two and had always wanted to fly. He gained his wings before war broke out and has done so well they are rightly very proud of him. His squadron flew to England last fall, served in France and was then returned to England in late May or early June – Frances is not too sure which. On 8 August, he was shot down over England. Frances was too distressed to tell me much of this, but I am afraid the poor boy has been badly injured. The RCAF has kept them informed, and they have had two very kind letters from Ed's Commanding Officer, and two short cables from this St Martha's Hospital. Could you possibly visit with him? Frances has asked me to say she is sure he would much appreciate a visitor from "home" . . .'

He turned to stare unseeingly at the high paper-stripped window with the lower sash pushed right up.

The hot afternoon air was too still for more than faint traces of tar and salt to intermingle with the inescapable hospital aroma of carbolic, iodiform, wax polish and scrubbing-soap, and the strong smell of must that had clung to the back of his throat since he came up the five flights of stone stairs that even on this hot day had been chilly enough to make him replace his jacket. He was so lost in thought that he did not hear the soft rustle of starch behind him.

'Good afternoon, Mr Adams. I'm Nurse Marlowe, the staff nurse in charge of this ward this weekend. I understand you wish to see Mr Laurings.'

He turned and did a mental double-take. Knowing nothing of English hospitals and having just heard the title 'staff nurse', he had expected the type of toughish, no-nonsense head nurse in early middle age that he recalled from occasional visits to classmates in hospital whilst at Harvard. He was unprepared for this impression of a lifesize Victorian porcelain figurine of a pretty young woman younger than himself, with cool grey-blue eyes and a polite little smile on her unpainted lips. 'Good afternoon, Nurse Marlowe. If I may, please,' he said.

She hesitated, covertly assessing his clever eyes and tanned face that at first sight struck her as all brow, nose and chin, and speculated rapidly he'd got the brains but had he got the guts? In theory, she should refuse his request, but in practice she had the latitude – and responsibility – of being in charge. The right visitor might help Ed Laurings, and to help him she would bend any rule. But could this stranger take it – and keep up the essential act? There was a lot of strength in his face, but she had to be sure. To give herself more time, she asked, unnecessarily, 'Are you related to Mr Laurings, Mr Adams?'

He shook his head impatiently. More British red tape. 'I'm American not Canadian.' Again, he explained his mother's letter, then added, 'I only heard this morning he was in this hospital. Does this help?' He took his Scotland Yard permit from his wallet and handed it to her. 'I have more if you wish to be sure I am not a fifth columnist.'

'I didn't think you were, and I don't need this. Thanks for showing it.' She returned the permit, her mind made up. 'I'm hesitating because Mr Laurings is a very ill man and, officially, only allowed to be visited by his CO, his proxy acting-next-of-kin as he has no relatives in England nor, as far as we knew till now, any friends in London. But all patients, even the most ill, love being visited, if only for a few minutes. I'm afraid that's all I can allow you with him, but before I take you in I have to ask, how much do you know about his condition?'

'Not too much. Quote badly injured unquote. That why he's in this and not some military hospital?'

'One of several reasons.' She moved to the small, flat-topped desk facing the corridor and the entrance to the ward and gestured to the opposite chair. 'Please sit down for a few minutes, Mr Adams,' she said, then she sat down herself and briefly explained the PPW's conversion to a Cranial Unit.

He had sat down slowly, fascinated despite himself by the crystal clarity of her diction and her English accent, and repulsed by the impersonality in her quiet voice and face. 'How bad is he?' he asked. She pushed the desk ashtray towards him and his eyes narrowed. 'That bad?'

She met his eyes blankly. 'I'm afraid so.' She waved aside the offered cigarette, saying, 'Not on duty, thanks,' then waited until he lit one before she went on, sounding to him as if she were discussing the weather. 'He's lost both legs from above the knee, his left arm from four inches below the shoulder, and a large part of his skull. He was a very strong young man and has a very strong will, which is fundamentally why he is still with us. He's still having coherent spells. He's in one now. When in one, he can talk and see to a limited extent, but he can hear and understand exactly what's going on. He's very intelligent and tremendously co-operative. He's a marvellous patient.'

He took a deep breath, dismissing the compliment as professional patter. 'What are his chances?'

She shook her head. 'I'm so sorry.'

He didn't believe her sorrow. Just a job. He stubbed out his cigarette and lit another, giving no other outward sign of the confusion of his emotions. He had seen wounded and dying men in Spanish hospitals and other places, but never before with even this indirect measure of personal involvement. He dreaded the pain his reply must cause his mother and Laurings' parents in Manitoba, and was suffused with an angry despair at this wreck of another young man's life. Price tag on war, he thought, and was then sickened by his habit of thinking in corny headlines.

Nurse Marlowe watched his downcast face with an empathy she had learnt, and had had to conceal, since the reopening of the PPW. Her only and twin brother was a Flight Lieutenant in a Spitfire squadron stationed at Beacon Rise. Each time a wounded pilot had been admitted she had thought – as now – this could be Michael, and how do I know that at this minute he isn't being lifted into another hospital bed, or dead? Late last night, when he got through a trunk-call to her at the Home to say Haw-Haw's broadcast had been its usual rubbish, he said he'd been up six times yesterday. How many today? She glanced at the open window and ran a finger under the rim of her dogcollar. When Josh looked up, her hands were back in her lap.

'How long?' he asked.

'I'm sorry, but I'm not qualified to answer that. I'm not a doctor. If I were, I don't think I could answer truthfully. But as I've been nursing for over four years, and with Mr

Laurings since he came in, I can say that I think you've come just in time and that he will appreciate your visit possibly more than you may find credible. I can also tell you he is not and never has been in pain. That, at least, we can do for him.'

He believed that last. She might be cold-blooded, but she had about her the unselfconscious assurance of an expert pronouncing on her own subject. 'That's good to know. Does – er– he know?'

She gave him another long blank look. 'No. He wants to live.'

Momentarily speechless, he just shook his head. Then he said accusingly, 'Maybe I should tell you, Nurse Marlowe, that from my mother's letter I am not too sure his parents realise there is no hope.'

'This hospital has cabled them, and I know his CO's written – he told me so on his last visit. But there's so little you can put in a cable, and when hope's all you've got you've got to hope.'

' "Your son is dying" takes only four words.'

'That's true.' She recognised his hostility as a symptom of acute anxiety, but she knew too, having nursed the Canadian, that it could owe something to the width of the Atlantic. 'But most English hospitals, and certainly Martha's, never use the word "dying" in medical bulletins. We do stick to the truth. When we tell next-of-kin their relative is on our Dangerously Ill List, it means that patient is dangerously ill. When anyone is that, the biggest and most obvious danger is that he or she will die. But I have to admit we do take cover in euphemisms that mean one thing in English English, but another in Canadian English, and possibly American English. I'll give you a couple; when we say "not too well" it means "very ill". "Very ill" means "dying".'

'Is that so?'

'Yes. Ready?' He nodded and they rose together. 'I'll just go in ahead to explain you. You're Joshua – '

'Josh Adams, Beth Adams' second son.'

'Thanks. Oh, I'm sorry, but you can't smoke in his room. He's on oxygen.'

'Sure.' He got rid of his cigarette and followed her, forgetting the hat on the floor by his chair and glad of his jacket. She left him standing in the corridor. He didn't notice how long he waited there; nor did he notice Mrs Brigham-Smythe's curious glance as she went by to the kitchen, or the sunshine streaming through the open balcony doors and the distant murmur of men's voices. Though normally an acute observer of his immediate surroundings, especially when they were unfamiliar, and so accustomed to making mental notes that the exercise had become mechanical, he was too preoccupied even to notice that the machine had switched off. And what most preoccupied him was the sense of foreboding that he was trying to rationalise as the only intelligent reaction to a disturbing situation.

'Please come in, Mr Adams,' Nurse Marlowe said.

There were pinkish floral curtains half-drawn over the high sash window open a few inches at the top, and the pink softened the whiteness of the high hospital bed and the fitted washbasin that had ordinary and not elbow taps, having being installed in the 1920s. Ed Laurings lay propped up high against a mound of white pillows carefully cradled to protect his bandaged head, which was grotesquely enlarged by the layers of cotton wool protecting the dressings that had to be changed every four hours. The foot of his bed was raised upon eight-inch wooden bedblocks, and the top sheet, single light blanket, and white cotton quilt embossed with the arms of Martha's covered the huge iron bedcradle which kept their weight off his mid-thigh stumps; the foot of the cradle was tied with gauze bandages to the footrail of the bed to keep it from slipping downwards. To the left of the bedhead stood a tall, black iron oxygen cylinder in a taller, low-wheeled, black iron stand, and beside this,

23

on a low wooden stool, stood a rounded glass flowmeter half-filled with sterile distilled water through which the green rubber tubing from the cylinder ran before reaching the bulbous green rubber mask with, at its base, a small green rubber bag. The bag rose and fell rhythmically, but too shallowly and rapidly. The thin material of the white cotton split-backed hospital night-gown, with the left sleeve empty below the bandaged stump, exposed the strength of the young shoulders and right arm, and the fading tan on the right hand that lay limply on the turned-down top sheet.

Josh moved to the right-hand side of the bed.

'Hi there, Ed. Beth Adams' wandering Number 2 son, Josh,' he said. He glanced at Nurse Marlowe across the bed, then gently gripped the right hand, which felt as cold as a dead man's.

A small but coherent smile lit the sunken brown eyes, and the slow, slurred voice was just audible through the mask and above the gentle hissing of the oxygen and the bubbling of the flowmeter. 'Glad – to – know – you – Jh-Jhosh. Th-thanks – for – coming – along.'

'I just wish I had known sooner you were right here. I guess Nurse Marlowe has explained that I only heard it from home this morning. My mother asks me to give you love from your folks and from her and to tell you they are all rooting for you in Manitoba and Boston.'

'Th-thanks – J-Josh. G-g-great.'

Nurse Marlowe put in quietly, but with a warmth in her voice and smile that startled Josh, 'Mr Laurings, I'm going to leave you two for a few minutes, but do me a favour and don't overdo your side of the nattering.' Her eyes laughed into his. 'I'm happy to stick out my neck for you, ducky, but I'd rather not chop it off.'

Laurings' chuckle came clearly through the mask. 'R-Roger, nurse. D-d-ducky, out.'

She backed to the door smiling, and only when she knew she was out of Laurings' tunnel vision did she

24

catch the American's eye and mouth, 'I'll be just outside.' He nodded imperceptibly and she went out, leaving the door sufficiently ajar for her to watch Laurings through the opening.

Josh talked for the next few minutes without knowing what he said. Ann Marlowe caught every word and liked what she heard. He's managing to be interesting and amusing without sounding insincere, she thought, and Ed's loving it. He's loving this tangible proof that somewhere he's got parents, a home, and old friends, and being a stranger in a strange country, this is something he has desperately needed. She had always understood this need, for she had never wholly forgotten her first few years in a strange, cold country called England that her parents had called 'home', and to which she and her brother had been brought from Egypt by their mother, to separate English boarding schools, shortly after their sixth birthday. Their father was in the Colonial Service, and after their mother left England to rejoin him they never saw their parents again. A year later both parents died of typhoid within days of each other and the elder sister of the twins' father became their legal guardian.

Ann Marlowe was still standing by that door when Nurse Fenner returned from tea. At her nod Nurse Fenner went into the kitchen, then she reappeared with Mrs Brigham-Smythe and both of them went by on to the balcony. They had just gone outside when the sirens down river began wailing the air raid Alert.

Damn the idiots! Ed can't take this row! thought Ann Marlowe, going quickly back to his bedside, smiling and saying, 'Sorry, gentlemen, have to break this up. Bound to be another false alarm. We only get "nuisance raids" at night.' She caught the American's eye and saw that he had taken the cue, though what sounded like every siren in London had joined the wailing chorus. 'I'll bet the All Clear goes in a few minutes, but I've got to follow form.' She patted Laurings' shoulder. 'We've all

had air raid drills up to our back teeth, Mr Adams.'
She switched on the red-bulbed bedhead light, closed
the window, fixed up the blackout screen and drew the
curtains. 'Mr Laurings, I'll just show Mr Adams where
to go, cope with this and that, and be back in two ticks.
I'll leave your door open. Okay?'

'S-s-sure.' Laurings' eyes had narrowed to slits with
the pain of the noise.

Josh said, 'I'll be right back Monday, Ed. All the best.'

'This way, Mr Adams.' Her voice was calm, but once
clear of the open doorway she shot ahead to the dutyroom, returning at once with his hat and her civilian
gasmask box slung by a crepe bandage sling over one
shoulder. 'I'm afraid you'll be stuck in the hospital till
the All Clear. Please go down those stairs as far as they
go. You'll be directed in the basement. Thanks for
coming. Sorry, must go.' She raced across the corridor
and disappeared into Room 6.

The sirens were still wailing and a new chorus of shrill
whistles was echoing up the stairwell. Josh stood in the
corridor looking up and down, weighing the chances of
this being another of the frequent false alarms, against
the possibility of the Luftwaffe's first daytime attack on
London. He guessed from the non-appearance of a squad
of ARP* personnel that this mausoleum of a hospital was
assuming the former, but from the continuing wailing
he wouldn't bet on it. He suspected that Nurse Marlowe
just might agree with him, but not the helpful kid and a
Red Cross nurse who were slowly wheeling in from the
balcony the bed of a hefty-shouldered white-capped boy
with an Army greatcoat, service respirator and attached
tin hat lying across the foot of his quilt. They were all
laughing. He went quickly towards them, flinging his
hat against the wall by some fire buckets, and heard
the Red Cross nurse saying, 'If it isn't a false alarm one

* Air Raid Precautions.

26

will be thoroughly browned-off. One's due out to dinner tonight.'

'Need any help, ladies?' he enquired.

Nurse Fenner said, 'Thanks awfully, Mr Adams, but we've only got to bring in Sergeant Weaver and – ' but he had vanished, and Nurse Marlowe emerged from Room 6.

'Treat as an "Orange", nurses,' she called calmly, going swiftly back to Laurings for a moment then on to Room 2. 'Sorry about this row, gentlemen.' She dealt with their blackout screen, curtains, and was laying the second greatcoat, respirator and tin hat over the foot of Daws' bed when the ward's only telephone rang in the dutyroom. 'Back in two ticks to get your beds into the corridor.' She raced for the telephone.

On the balcony Sergeant Weaver of the Royal Army Service Corps carefully turned his capped head from the east. 'Out of luck if you've come out for air, sir. All in once Moaning Minnie starts up. Standing orders.'

'Is that so?' Josh hastily scanned the south-eastern sky and had consciously to ignore the exquisite view of the sparkling greenish river and the Houses of Parliament glowing like fawn stone lace in the brilliant sunshine. 'Let's get you in,' he said.

'Have to give those front castors a kick for 'em to roll, sir.' The siren chorus was fading, and just audible was a distant, deep droning. 'You hear what I hears, sir?'

'I guess.' He freed the castors and gripped the top footrail. 'Hang on for the buggy-ride, sergeant.'

In the dutyroom Ann Marlowe grabbed the earpiece from its hook and said calmly, 'Private Patients Ward. Nurse Marlowe speaking.'

'Internal switchboard. Message from Casualty, nurse.' The girl's voice had a faint tremor. She was one of the operators presently ringing every ward, department, professional and lay, administration office open on Saturday afternoons and residential staff Home with the

27

message from Casualty that had the hospital's only direct line to the police. '*Red* Alert. I repeat, *Red* Alert.'

Ann Marlowe's heart seemed to hit her ribs. The 'nuisance raids' rated as 'Orange'. This was Martha's first 'Red' of the war, and it announced that the hospital was in imminent danger of direct air attack and that all movable patients and junior staff must immediately be evacuated to the basement. ' "Red" received in Private Patients by staff nurse in charge. Thanks, operator.' She hung up.

The bed was proving surprisingly unwieldy for a single mover. Josh had the foot castors off the balcony when Sergeant Weaver, his head again turned eastwards, observed laconically, 'Don't reckon this looks like a false alarm, sir.'

Josh looked up eastwards. A great black umbrella was opening in the sky. Opening and moving forward fast. 'I reckon you're not far wrong, sergeant.'

Nurse Fenner now rushed up saying, 'Thanks awfully, Mr Adams. I'll take the head.' When the bed was in the corridor she turned back to close both hardboard-battened glass doors, and had dealt with the first before she looked up. 'Oh, look!' she exclaimed, standing transfixed in the opening, her upraised face alight with delighted excitement. 'Look! They really do have big black crosses on their wings! I can see them quite clearly now!'

– *Two* –

Less than a quarter of an hour later Josh was back on that balcony, Laurings and Daws were the only patients left in the PPW, another formation of heavily fighter-escorted German bombers had flown up from the Thames Estuary and were passing directly over the hospital, and the first gigantic flames were shooting up from the docks down river.

Six minutes after the 'Red' message, Green, the four soldiers, Mrs Brigham-Smythe and Nurse Fenner reached the basement. They went down together in the block's only lift that, like all the block lifts, was elderly and slow, with bare wooden walls and floors, and, to a prearranged plan, were running a shuttle service from wards to basement in descending order of priority for movable bedpatients too weak to manage the stairs with help. Normally the lifts were strictly reserved for stretcher and wheelchair patients, heavy medical and maintenance equipment, electric food trolleys, and their various escorts. Nurse Fenner had never been in a Martha's lift before, nor, even temporarily, in charge of patients. Her patent delight in the occasion and oblivion to its realities helped to divert even the most apprehensive of her companions so that they shared her regret when Nurse Wood arrived to take over whilst the five men were still being lifted from the wheelchairs on

29

to mattresses on the floor of an alcove Mr Green promptly named PPW Mark 2.

Nurse Denton, a fourth-year student nurse, already State Registered, and Nurse Wood, a third-year, were at tea when the Alert cleared the communal professional and lay staff dining-rooms in seconds. They jog-trotted as fast as they could – and being senior students this was very fast – along the broad main corridor that connected all the blocks at ground-floor level and ran straight for half a mile, but only realised this was a 'Red' when they reached Block 1's stairs.

After an 'Orange' warning, as in air raid drills, every door had to be closed, every window blackout-screened whatever the hour to minimise the danger of flying glass. In the general wards, all the occupied beds were pulled well away from outer walls and lined up parallel down the middle of the ward, and every bed was covered with a spare mattress. In the PPW the patients' beds were pulled into the corridor, similarly protected by spare mattresses, and ranged against the walls as close as possible to the kitchen door, as all the iron fire escapes had landings outside the kitchen windows. But to lessen the disturbance to bedpatients – and since the outbreak of war up-patients had been an extreme rarity – none were moved to the basement.

Now coming down from Faith and Hope, both women's acute medical wards, was a single, unsteady file of pale-faced women in hospital dressing-gowns, clutching gasmask boxes, handbags and knitting, and telling the nurses and medical students supporting them that a change was good as a tonic and never a dull moment. Those particular medical students were following preplanned orders that had delegated others to the hospital basement, and the most senior to assemble with every qualified man on or off duty on hospital territory when the Alert sounded, in Central Hall, the ancient former main entrance to Martha's. This could hold hundreds more than the forty-odd young men gathering to await Casualty's warning of the first in-coming ambulances with air raid casualties. As this was the hospital's first 'Red', it was automatically assumed that such casualties would only arrive in ambulances.

Nurses Denton and Wood exchanged glances and went up the first two flights pressed sideways against the outermost wall, then raced up the remaining flights. It needed four people to move Laurings' bed and oxygen apparatus in one piece. When they let themselves in through the now closed mahogany entrance doors, the two beds were aligned facing the entrance against the wall on either side of the kitchen door. Daws' was ahead, with Nurse Marlowe adjusting his covering mattress. Laurings' protective mattress was draped over his footrail and bedcradle to midchest, his bed was off blocks to avoid the agonising jolt should it be blown off, and standing at his exposed side were two men in navy serge battledress and black tin hats, and Josh Adams. The two nurses recognised that the trio had helped move Laurings, and that two were hospital firemen and the third a stranger, without interest in his provenance. The noise was frighteningly louder than on the ground floor, and as they came up the stairs their concentration had been focused on the need to reach the ward.

Ann Marlowe joined them, and her encompassing glance registered the heightened tension in Nurse Denton's normally tense, sallow, slightly older face and the mixture of fear and exhilaration in Nurse Wood's younger eyes. Without moving her lips, she murmured ' "Red". Know?' They nodded. 'Thanks for coming back early. Wood, basement. Gone down:

Green, Alcott, Weaver, Begg, Miller, Mrs B. S., Fenner. Take over, stat.'*

'Yes, nurse.' Nurse Wood hurried away, profoundly grateful that she was a year Denton's junior in hospital time – and ten in age – and for Matron's rule that only the two most senior nursing staff in any ward remain with their immovable bedpatients. Nurse Wood was twenty-four, a fairly attractive and efficient nurse who enjoyed responsibility and life. She went down the stairs as rapidly as she had come up the last three flights.

Ann's attention was on Laurings. The firemen had moved up the corridor to check the windows in the empty rooms; the American, still by Laurings, was bending to say something to him. In these last ten minutes Laurings' eyes had sunk to deep holes and the rhythm of his respirations had kept altering disturbingly. He can't, and I'm not letting him, take much more of this, she thought, fighting down her surging anger at the raid, to prevent it clouding her clinical judgement, and in the process ignoring personal danger for the simple reason that she literally had no time for it. 'Here, Denton –' she unpinned the Dangerous Drug cupboard keys from her dress bib and handed them over – 'quarter, stat, for Laurings. We've got it written up in hand.' She hesitated, sympathising with Denton's terror, but knowing she would only increase Denton's chronic lack of self-confidence if she said so. 'I'll give, you witness.'

'Yes, nurse.' Nurse Denton vanished into the duty-room as another incoming formation passed directly overhead.

Daws squeezed his eyes shut. Ann moved to his side and looked down in secret anguish at his pleasant young face, now ashen and tight-lipped. He's so young, he's

* Medical abbreviation of the Latin *statim*. English, 'at once'.

been through so much, she thought. He's so helpless, and what is sheer agony is that he knows it. I can't give him a shot, but I've got to think of some way of getting some of his mind off this. She touched his arm gently. 'Sorry about the row, Mr Daws.'

He opened his eyes. 'Hellish noisy machines, bombers. Can't hear our chaps. Must be up. No ack-ack.'*

'Nor there is. Hadn't noticed,' she lied, smiling and pulling off and pocketing her cuffs and rolling up her sleeves. Nurse Denton had returned with the hypodermic tray, Dangerous Drug book, a small glass phial of quarter-grain morphine tablets in her bib pocket, and was removing Laurings' bedticket† from the hook on his lower front footrail. 'Look, Mr Daws, I'm just going to give Mr Laurings a shot then I'll be back for a natter.'

He forced a smile. 'I'll hang around for you, nurse.'

'It's a date.' She moved on to take Laurings' wrist pulse under the covering mattress and smile into his eyes. 'Just going to give you something to give you a little kip.' She stroked his hand then straightened and smiled up at Josh. 'Thanks again, Mr Adams. You've been a wonderful help. Now I must throw you out.'

He shrugged amiably. 'The story of my life, Nurse Marlowe.'

'Down the stairs as far as they go, Mr Adams. Just going to scrub up, Mr Laurings.' She disappeared into the dutyroom leaving the door temporarily ajar so she could kick it open and shut when she returned with wet hands. The dutyroom had elbow-taps.

'Be right back, Ed.' Josh raised a hand in farewell, then drifted across the corridor to pick up his hat. The firemen were still checking rooms, Nurse Denton was setting out the injection, and no one saw him go quickly up the corridor and cautiously out on to the balcony.

---

* Anti-aircraft gunfire.   † Notes.

Nurse Denton had set the white enamel, white-dressing-towel-covered tray on the high wooden stool placed for this purpose against the wall behind Laurings' bed. Her terror was accentuated by her terror of showing it. It took all her self-control to stop her hands from shaking before, carefully, by one corner, she removed the towel and then the glass lids of the containers severally holding in sterilising solution the metal and glass barrels, metal plungers, and steel needles in assorted sizes. She was pathetically thankful to be the witness and not donor of this injection, but it did not occur to her that this might be intentional, for she valued herself too little to expect consideration from others. A tallish, thin brunette, she had been a late entry to Martha's because, until her mother's death and her father's remarriage two years later when she was twenty-nine, she had never been free to make her own decisions. She had always longed to train and loved nursing, but though she was a far better nurse than she herself, or many of her superiors, if not Sister PPW and Ann Marlowe, appreciated, her lack of self-confidence made it doubtful whether she would achieve her burning ambition to be offered a Martha's staff nurse's post when her contract ended this November, and, later, a ward. It was that ambition that really stopped her hands shaking.

The firemen were leaving when Ann returned, her wet hands upheld. 'Thank you very much for your help, gentlemen.'

'All part of the service, nurse. We'll be back.' They stopped for a few words with Daws then ambled off.

On the balcony Josh stood flattened against the closed doors, shielding his eyes with hands and hat brim from the glare of the sun and the flames now shooting up from both sides of the river. He counted twenty-five bombers in the V-formation passing over-head, identifying Dorniers, Heinkels and, he thought but was not sure, a few Junker 88s. He lost count of

34

the infinitely more numerous Messerschmitt fighters guarding their bombers like worker bees guarding a multiplicity of queens. From the absence of ack-ack, he assumed that the RAF must be up, somewhere, but he could not see one Spitfire or Hurricane. Why not? Were they still on the way, having been caught off-balance by this switch of the Luftwaffe's tactics whilst guarding their own airfields? Or was this the start of the invasion, and were the RAF too busy fighting over the coast to spare fighters to defend London? No answering those questions yet, he thought rapidly, but one fact was very clear. London was getting it hard in the south, the east, the west, and up in the City on his far right where just visible through rising smoke was the dome of St Paul's. He watched one circling formation dropping sticks of bombs on what he judged to be the West End. The thought of the theatre queues and the picnickers in Green Park made him taste bile for the first time since Paris.

The sudden opening of both doors made him stumble backwards into the corridor, and before he regained his balance Ann closed the doors and stood with her back to them. 'Sorry, Mr Adams, out-of-bounds till the All Clear. I suspect it's your job to risk your neck. It's certainly mine to stop you.'

'I can appreciate that, but I still have a job – '

'So do I!' Her eyes blazed with anger. 'Jerry's giving me damn all help with it. Head injuries need quiet surroundings and minds. Presumably this is kicking-off the invasion, but whatever it is it's monstrous – wicked – to do this to patients and unarmed civvies, but I daren't think of London. I've got to concentrate on my two men and I can't waste time on a healthy man determined to risk his neck. Job or no job' – she jerked a thumb over one shoulder – 'out there you're a sitting target for any trigger-happy Jerry wanting to test his guns.'

He was shaken by the strength of her anger and her

35

common sense. He suddenly sensed that beneath the disciplined veneer that he had mistaken for cold-blooded impersonality lay tremendous and intriguing reserves of emotions and intelligence that, professionally, he was prepared to find interesting, but he neither wanted nor intended to do so personally. 'I guess you're right. The chance seemed too hot to miss. But a crazy chance. I am no hero.' He glanced back down the corridor at the two beds and knew, with an intentionally unreasoned certainty, that he had no alternative to the request he was about to make. 'I prefer to stay up here. May I? Or will that get you in trouble?'

She looked down the corridor before answering, and saw Nurse Denton, smiling painfully brightly, setting a high stool by Daws' exposed bedside. An idea that had occurred to her before Daws had told her the American had not left the ward, the thought of his previous and present behaviour, and the comfort the presence of a strong, able-bodied man would afford Daws, Denton, and herself, combined to overcome her reluctance to let him take this risk without lessening her appreciation of what it could involve. 'Possibly,' she said. 'But as you're neither patient nor staff, if you insist on staying at your own risk because being underground gives you claustrophobia I expect – '

He cut her short. 'You took the words right out of my mouth, Nurse Marlowe. Deal?'

She looked straight into his face. 'Yes. Thanks a lot – no – ' she frowned dismissively – 'no time for kidding. Just listen as – ' but she had to stop until the roar of a nearer explosion had faded that made the lights flicker. She went on quickly. 'If you're going to chance it up here there are things you must know. That's the kitchen door between the beds. The fire escape landing is at the kitchen window. Our first emergency exit is the stairs; second, fire escape; third, balcony. To lift Mr Laurings out of bed off oxygen and carry him down'll probably kill him. That shouldn't kill Flying Officer Daws, but it'll probably wreck his chances of walking again. He's twenty-one. Got that?' He nodded, watching her closely. 'Play poker?'

'Huh?'

'Poker,' she repeated as he stared bemused. 'Surely? In American flicks reporters are always sitting round in hats playing poker and swigging whisky. No whisky – and for matches, as gambling's forbidden in Martha's. Laurings' shot'll have him under in minutes. I can't give Daws one and he adores poker. We were going to play three-handed.'

'Deal me in.'

'Thanks. Let's join the party.'

She walked on ahead. He followed more slowly noting her straight-backed, graceful carriage, small waist, the gently seductive swaying of her voluminous skirts, and mentally juxtaposing her attitude and all she had just said and left unsaid with the panic-stricken terror of Paris in the final days before the German Army marched in. He watched her speed up to say something to the skinny, schoolmarmish brunette, then return to check Laurings' pulse, the gauges on the oxygen cylinder and the rate of the bubbles in the flowmeter. The machine in his head had switched back on and was recording as permanently as in a notebook all he had just seen from the balcony and was seeing and hearing in this top-floor ward in a civilian hospital in the heart of a city under air attack.

He looked down at the white-capped, shaven-templed, taut white young face peering like that of a helpless upturned turtle above the spare mattress brushing his chin. 'How do you do, Flying Officer? Josh Adams. Here for the poker game.'

'I say, bang on! Oh – how do you do? Peter Daws. This is Nurse Denton, or have you met?'

'Not yet, Mr Daws.' Her painfully bright voice only shook a little. 'Just going to get you something to sit on, Mr Adams.' She set down a second high stool and hurried to the dutyroom for a third. She had just closed the door when, like every door in the ward, it was nearly blown off its hinges by the thunderclap high in the air directly overhead. Neither nurse recognised its cause, never having heard a mid-air collision of two aircraft before.

Daws muttered, 'Poor sods.'

Josh nodded impassively.

And another incoming formation roared over the hospital.

One after another, for the next two hours, the formations flew up the river then circled over the docks, the East End, the West End, the City, and over main and side streets, squares and crescents, alleys and backyards, public parks and playing fields. All of these had initially emptied slowly in an atmosphere of bemused disbelief that was shortly replaced by the general conviction that the invasion had begun – a conviction that evoked more indignation than terror, though terror was there. But as the raid went on, the indignation was altered to a terrible anger that for many, but not all, extinguished terror.

One after another the sticks of bombs rained down on the docks, on Woolwich Arsenal, Beckton gasworks, West Ham power station, Westminster, Knightsbridge, the City. Whilst the sun was high in the western sky, the flames from the docks and other buildings down river from Martha's turned the eastern sky bright orange. On the roofs of the hospital the pairs of firemen working in relays, crawling on their elbows or lying prone on the flattened portions of the block roofs facing the river, peered through the stone pillars of the edging balustrades and agreed grimly that it would take all the water in the Thames to put this lot out.

*

'Two cards, please, Mr Adams.'

'Coming right up, Nurse Marlowe . . . Nurse Denton?'

'I'm not – er – sure, Mr Adams. Not having played poker before, I'm a bit muddled. I mean, I've got four tens – oh, shouldn't I've said that?' And when the laughter subsided, 'Oh, gracious! Nothing, thank you, Mr Adams.'

'Haven't woken old Ed, have we, nurse?'

'Not a stir, Mr Daws. Having a lovely kip.'

'Bang on.'

They sat in line at the exposed bedside, Ann Marlowe at the head, then Nurse Denton, then Josh Adams. He had noted that there was nothing fortuitous in this arrangement. Nurse Marlowe was best placed to watch and reach Laurings, Nurse Denton to heave the spare mattress over Daws' head, and he to complete the human guarding wall.

'How about you, Peter?'

'Stick as I am, thanks, sir.'

'The name is Josh.'

'Bang on!'

By six o'clock nothing had fallen close to the hospital, but it had no gas supply and was using its own emergency electricity generators. And despite solid stone walls, closed doors and screened windows, the only area of Martha's free of the smell of distant burning was the deep basement running underneath and extending beyond the sprawling buildings. Parts of the basement were centuries old, and it was a rabbit-warren of large and small storerooms, some in use, many more empty. Through a maze of narrow side passages there threaded and wound the slightly less narrow main corridor. Like the side passages it was low-ceilinged, with walls and floor of uneven rough stone. It was lined with pipes along its whole length, which hospital legend insisted was one mile, though no one had ever been known to measure it. Keeping that corridor whitewashed was the responsibility of Repairs and Works, and was regarded as a more permanent job than painting the Forth Bridge.

'Not just time to start again as soon as it's done, but afore it's even half done the new job looks like it's not had a fresh lick in years,' observed Mr Billings, the foreman of Repairs and Works, to Mr Jenkins of Accounts as, in their other roles as air raid wardens Basement, they patrolled their domain with measured tread.

'I believe you, George,' said Mr Jenkins, after a slight pause to collect his thoughts, which had been on his wife, his sixteen-year-old daughter and their small semi-detached in Lewisham. Last autumn he had sacrificed his cherished lawn in the little back garden to dig in and bury a corrugated-iron 'Anderson' air raid shelter. He could trust Doris to use the Anderson and get Janet there – if she was home. But the dress shop up the High Street where she worked was shut on Saturday afternoons, and war or no war a young girl on her half-day wanted to be out with her pals. Doris would take on if Janet was out. She'd be worrying about him, too, though he'd told her often enough that this basement was tough as Old Harry – it needed to be, being so close to the river. But Doris was a worrier. He just hoped she'd have her friend Mrs Welby, from over the road, down in the Anderson to provide a bit of company.

He eased further back on his head his black-painted tin hat with a large white W up front and told himself that next time he must take off his business suit waistcoat before getting on the navy serge battledress. 'Warming up down here, George,' he remarked.

'This Dunkirk weather, that's what, Reg.'

There were now over two hundred patients in the basement. They lay or sat on bare mattresses, using bare bolsters as pillows, and old yellowish-white or fading red or grey blankets as bedclothes. The mattresses were set

40

lengthways against the innermost wall along stretches of the corridor floor, and parallel in the innermost alcoves, with just enough room between them for one of the attendant nurses to stand sideways. All the bedding was old, discarded stock that had been in storage for years. Martha's was one of the best-endowed voluntary hospitals in London, but it was dependent upon voluntary contributions and legacies and it was a hospital rule that nothing was thrown away until it fell to pieces from old age. 'Does this not demonstrate the wisdom of thrift and foresight, gentlemen?' the Assistant Matron was in the habit of asking the sweating, shirtsleeved medical students emptying storerooms and layering bedding. The Ass. Mat. was off duty this weekend, but had still been in uniform and having tea with Senior Sister Tutor in her room in the Sisters' Home when the Alert sounded. She had promptly reported herself back on duty to Matron, then gone down the nearest basement stairs to take overall charge of the evacuated patients and nurses, as prearranged for a 'Red'. Assisting her were two Office Sisters and two Junior House-Physicians. The JHPs were growing bored and browned-off. None of the patients were showing any signs of panic or hysteria, having to make non-stop rounds meant their feet were killing them, and they longed to be up with the chaps in Central Hall where one could sit on the floor and have the odd fag before the real rush started. No one on the staff knew why no casualties had arrived, but according to the inter-staff grapevine, whose source was the firemen on the roofs, other London hospitals must be packing them in.

Shortly after six, the buzz of conversations echoing up and down the corridor reminded Nurse Fenner of the chatter of birds after a thunderstorm. She was again in temporary charge. A few minutes earlier Nurse Wood, with all the most senior student nurses from the wards, had been summoned to hear from the Ass. Mat. the new arrangements for their patients' suppers, customarily

41

served at 6.30 p.m. Nurse Fenner confided her impression to PPW Mark 2. 'Only this one hasn't stopped,' she added artlessly.

Mrs Brigham-Smythe smiled wearily. One did not know which hurt more, one's back or one's feet, and though one only came in three days a week from nine to five and was happy to do one's bit in dear old Martha's, where one had met one's husband in the last show, one had to admit one was getting a bit long in the tooth. One simply didn't dare contemplate what was happening up in the ward, outside, or to one's house in Ebury Street. One could only thank God Gerald had been posted to a hospital near Edinburgh since he got back from Dunkirk, that the boy's school had been evacuated to the wilds of Wales, and that one had a good coal cellar and such sensible servants. Cook and Ellen were bound to be sitting on rugs on the coal having a cuppa – and couldn't one do with one! Or just something to sit on . . . Oh, well, not to worry. Press on regardless.

She said, 'Very like birds, my dear.'

Mr Green lowered his knitting. 'Frankly, ladies, I'd have said more like the monkey house at the Zoo.' He glanced up at the low ceiling. He had spent a little of the last hour calculating its strength and that of Block 1 above. He had spent far more time reflecting with relief that his wife was spending this weekend with her parents in Devizes, and not with her married sister in Wimbledon, where she had been staying since his admission to Martha's. 'I'll be back Monday, darling,' she had promised yesterday. 'No, Tommy, don't panic! Of course I'll get a seat on the train. Everyone's marvellous when one's so preggers.'

Face Monday on Monday, thought Mr Green, trying not to listen to the distant thunder or to think of the chaps up for this show, and Peter, poor old Ed, and the two nurses up top. No future in banging the old pranged nut against that lot, he reminded himself yet again, knitting on. He was glad he'd brought his knitting down. It had given the boys a good belly-laugh when the lanky, black-haired Irish medical student who had helped little Fenner lower his undercarriage from the wheelchair had handed it over. 'Mother of God, good sir, why didn't I think to bring down my tatting? What've I to do but tote mattresses, bolsters, blankets, lift that stretcher, shove that wheelchair, and no chance at all of getting a little drunk. Angels and ministers of grace defend us – I spy the Ass. Mat.'s stockwhip! Empty wheelchairs back at the double, Sister!' the boy yelled down the corridor, charging off pushing one and pulling another, followed by another shirtsleeved student doing the same and Nurse Fenner racing behind with the last. Each ward had six wheelchairs in stock, and whilst the lifts were still considered safe every chair was needed again as soon as it was emptied. For the past fifty minutes all the lifts had been grounded in the basement.

The boys had needed that laugh, thought Mr Green, eyeing the privates on his left and the sergeants on his right. Young Dusty and Alcott had been dirty shades of green, Begg had lost his toothy grin, and only Weaver remained his habitual imperturbable self. 'Reckon we got ourselves a nice cushy little billet, sir,' he said when they had all touched down on the mattresses.

The boys had settled now. Little Fenner was too dewy to recognise a flap if it shook her by the hand, and Wood too busy pulling rank to let it bother her, but poor old Mrs B.S. was looking as old as his granny. He dropped several stitches, intentionally. 'Packet gone for a Burton! Mayday, Mrs B.S., Mayday!'

'Not to worry, Mr Green. One'll cope.'

'Let me give your bolster a shake whilst you're sitting forward, Mr Green.' Nurse Fenner squeezed in sideways to bend down eagerly. 'How's that?'

'Great, thanks, nurse.'

'Goody. How about yours, Sergeant Weaver? Looks awfully sandbaggy.'

43

'Wouldn't say no, nurse,' said Sergeant Weaver, glancing behind her. His bolster was comfortable, but the impeccably uniformed figure of Matron and two elderly civvies in black jackets and pinstriped trousers had suddenly appeared in the entrance of their alcove. He had never seen the men before but he recognised them immediately as brass hats, and he knew the value of being discovered working by an unexpected CO's inspection. 'Ta, Nurse Fenner. Feels good, that does.'

'Goody – oh – ' Nurse Fenner had seen her audience and turned scarlet. 'Er – good evening, Matron – er – gentlemen.'

'Good evening, Nurse Fenner – gentlemen – Mrs Brigham-Smythe. All quite comfortable? Good.' The Matron smiled, and the Dean and the Hospital Secretary bowed. Then Matron said, 'We hope you will all be back in your wards shortly. I'm afraid your suppers will be a little late this evening and that the food will be cold, but the cocoa will be hot – yes, we were sure you would all understand. Thank you, Nurse Fenner.' The trio moved on down the corridor and out of sight.

Nurse Fenner flopped in ecstasy against the nearest wall. Matron had smiled at her and thanked her by name.

'Nurse! What is your name?' The demand came from an Office Sister patrolling in the Matron's wake.

Nurse Fenner jerked from the wall clutching her hands behind her back. 'Nurse Fenner, Sister.'

'Well, Nurse Fenner, will you please remember in future that the walls of this hospital are in place to support the building and not the backs of slovenly probationers.' Having reduced the girl almost to tears, the Office Sister smiled professionally on the five patients. 'Quite comfortable, gentlemen?'

Mr Green said icily, 'Yes, thanks, Sister.'

Mrs Brigham-Smythe looked down her neat nose with an expression of well-bred distaste that was far more recognisable – and offensive – to the Office Sister than the expression now on all the soldiers' faces, which was what the Army termed 'dumb insolence'. She moved on reflecting that doctors' wives were trials in peace and war and leaving six of the occupants of PPW Mark 2 so incensed on Nurse Fenner's behalf that for a good thirty seconds they forgot the air raid.

Above ground it was impossible to forget for three seconds. The noise echoed and re-echoed up and down the unnaturally empty main corridor, lift-shafts, stairwells, and around the huge oblong Casualty Hall, the largest department in the hospital. The long mahogany benches set like pews on either side of the wide aisle which ran from the Casualty Yard entrance to the main corridor were empty, as were the twin lines of waiting stretcher trolleys ranged in single file. 'Why haven't they come to us?' the waiting nurses mouthed to each other (Sister Casualty, the most formidable member of Martha's, was on duty this weekend). But in Central Hall the question was openly voiced, and the voices vibrated with anger and frustration: 'What the devil's going on?' 'Why in hell haven't we got 'em?' 'Must be hundreds, probably thousands, injured . . .' 'Why are we hanging around doing damn all?' And between the questions, the news from the roof: 'London Docks . . . Surrey Commercial . . . West India . . . Millwall . . . Isle of Dogs . . . Royal Victoria . . . Royal Albert . . . Whole bloody lot blazing, and Silvertown such a bloody torch they're having to be evacuated by the river . . . And we're just sitting here on our bloody backsides doing Sweet Fanny Adams . . .'

'Frightfully sorry, one and all. Three queens.'
'You've just broken the bank and my heart, Peter.'

'Cleaned out, old chap? Bloody bad luck – oh – frightfully sorry, nurses.'

'We'll forgive you, Mr Daws.' Ann delighted him, again startled Josh, but only mildly shocked Nurse Denton by blowing the boy a kiss.

A little short of two hours ago Nurse Denton would have been deeply shocked, but until these last one-hundred-odd minutes she had never played cards with young men or spent two seconds in the reasonable anticipation that the next second could be the last for her and her companions. That two were patients had, by heightening her fear for them, lessened her fear for herself, and though she would never have believed this possible she was – almost – enjoying the game. But, as she kept telling herself, it really was helping this poor brave boy, Nurse Marlowe was really being such fun, and that nice Mr Adams was being so – well – very nice, that though she dreaded what Sister PPW would say, somehow it no longer seemed to matter very much.

After every hand, Ann Marlowe checked Laurings' pulse, respiration and apparatus, and Nurse Denton gave Daws a drink of glucose-lemonade from a china-spouted feeding cup. Just as regularly, they were visited by a solitary air raid warden or two firemen, from whom they heard when the gas had been cut off, before the speakers strolled into the kitchen to check that all gas taps were off. Then, a little later, 'Going on our own generators now, Nurse Marlowe. Might be as well to go slow where you can. The electricians say our generators aren't as young as they might be, but you know those lads – always looking on the black side.'

Only Daws asked, 'What's burning?'

'Nothing in the hospital, sir – not had more than a few slates off. It's coming from outside. Bound to have started one or two fires, but none close.'

Josh noticed that none gave any real news of the raid,

46

nor did the nurses ask for it. And every time, the men came in quietly, nodded affably at the card players, tiptoed on heavy boots past the sleeping Laurings, cast laconic glances at his oxygen before going on up to check the empty rooms. On their return they grinned at Daws, said, 'Much obliged, Nurse Marlowe,' and after she thanked them by name, left quietly.

In another interval, he asked, 'Do you know every guy in London's ARP, Nurse Marlowe?'

She smiled. 'None, Mr Adams. The ones we've had in aren't London's ARP. Martha's Own – capital O. They're all volunteers from our lay staff. Our block warden yo-yoing in and out is Mr Henty, the charge hand in Repairs and Works. Those last two firemen were Mr Stacey from the Dean's Office, and Mr Davis from Medical Records.' She looked at Nurse Denton. 'Remember him in Cas last winter?'

'That's why I know his face!' Nurse Denton read the message to keep talking to give Daws a rest. He was getting very tired, but was still wide awake and needed a new diversion. 'He's Mr Just-a-drop-of-Mag-Trisil-please-nurse that kept popping in when Sister Cas was at lunch.'

'He nearly drove anyone on the medical side round the bend, and has had our last two SMOs and the present one clean round! Dr White – our present SMO, Mr Adams – said it was far less dangerous for him to swig Mag Trisil than pints of milk for the ulcer that no physician, X-ray or barium has managed to find. Oh, sorry, I'll translate – SMO is Senior Medical Officer and Mag Trisil – '

'Magnesium Trisilicate?'

'Nice work.' She laughed quietly. 'You pick up a language fast. How many do you speak?'

He hesitated, feeling as disorientated by her laughing face as by the trouble he was having in reversing so many of his previous lines of thought. 'Not many.'

She looked at him as she had at Nurse Denton. 'Just how many?'

He took the cue. 'Just French, Spanish, German, and I can just about get by in Polish, Russian and English English.'

Daws' laugh was tired but genuine. 'I say, Josh, why didn't you pay more attention to your language masters at school?' he asked.

Ann added, 'And why is your paper wasting a man with your languages in London? Why aren't you in France or Germany?'

'Kind of a long story,' he said slowly, looking from one to the other and recognising that all three needed the break. He gave them a brief account of his last three years, censoring the ugly, accentuating the absurd, and was describing the two-berthed cabin he had shared with six on the voyage from Lisbon when the telephone rang for the first time in an hour.

'I'll take it, Denton. Do go on, Mr Adams, and when I'm back I'll demand a repeat.' Ann left her seat without undue haste, but when she had closed the dutyroom door she dived for the telephone. 'Private Patients Ward. Nurse Marlowe speaking.'

'SSO from Central Hall.' The Senior Surgical Officer's tenor drawl could have been coming over a bad line from John o'Groats. 'How are things up there?'

She flattened a hand over one ear and clamped the trumpet earpiece against the other. 'Well, thank you, Mr Wesley –'

'Speak up, nurse. Can't hear you.'

'Sorry.' She pitched her voice higher to give brief medical reports on both patients.

'Right. How are you two nurses?'

'As well as can be expected.'

'Skip the placebos, nurse! I'm in no mood for 'em after hanging round this damned hall doing damn all.'

She blinked. 'None in?'

48

'Why else have I been doing damn all? Don't ask me why we haven't had any customers. I can only presume nothing much has hit our zone. Dacey' – the senior Casualty porter – 'has heard from the cops that joints elsewhere are bursting at the seams. God only knows why some haven't been shifted to us. Possibly the powers that be have decided Martha's is too well-endowed to need the ten-and-six* per night the Government intends forking out for air raid casualties. Matron's as much in the dark as we are. The SMO and I have just had another session with her that *inter alia* affects PPW. Took too damn long to evacuate today – that's got to be changed – but doesn't matter now. What does is that, directly the All Clear goes and we've cleared the basement, we're closing PPW. Your two chaps must go down in their beds, Laurings to Luke, Daws to Stanley Parker – both ground floor – and Stanley Parker will take all your five straight from the basement. They'll go into emergency beds down the middle for tonight – and tomorrow, somehow, I'm getting all six out of London. I've just been round the basement. Your five are in reasonably good shape and I've told them they're going to Stanley Parker. Matron's Office will tell you about the nursing side. Got all that?'

'Yes, thanks, Mr Wesley.' She was too relieved for her patients to have time yet for her sadness at having to hand them over and the closure of her ward. 'I'm glad they'll all be on the ground tonight. This is so bad for them. Laurings was very shaken till we got him under. Daws is putting up a good front, but it's upsetting him too much.'

'Inevitably. I hear you've had him playing cards.'

Knowing the hospital grapevine, she was unsurprised, and guessed what was coming.

'He loves cards, Mr Wesley.'

* 52½ pence.

'Handy therapy. Henty from Repairs and Works says you've some civvy chap not on his list. Who is he, and why the devil isn't he in the basement?'

She told him the truth, and added, 'He's being a great help.'

The SSO snorted. 'Man must be a damned fool. Not his war. What was his name and paper again?'

She gave this, then asked, 'Mr Wesley, what's the real gen? What's burning?'

'London.' He rang off.

She needed both hands to replace the earpiece. For a second or so she looked down at her shaking hands as if they didn't belong to her, then she dried the palms on the back of her skirt. There was a slightly different loud droning overhead, but she was suddenly too deathly tired to care. She leant against the desk, her shoulders drooping, head bent forward, too tired to move another step or force another smile. Slowly it dawned on her what the reclosure entailed for Denton and herself after the All Clear and the transfer of Laurings and Daws. All the remaining beds would have to be stripped, and their mattresses rolled up and left on the landing for collection and re-storing in the morning; all the ward files, X-rays, the log, Dangerous Drug and Ward Address books and DD keys would have to be handed in to Matron's Office, and every other item of ward equipment left clean and tidy for the inventory she would have to take with the Assistant Matron tomorrow morning. Nothing to be done till the All Clear, she thought, exhausted – if it ever goes – if – *if!* Her head jerked upwards. Still more droning above but – *but* – going down not coming up river. She leapt for the door, and as soon as she opened it Josh put a finger to his lips. He was standing by Daws, who was fast asleep, and Nurse Denton had her back to the dutyroom as she took the sleeping Laurings' pulse.

Ann mouthed, 'Returning to base?'

Josh nodded slowly, and they exchanged a long look of mutual incredulity at the survival of all five and this top-floor ward.

The sky was growing quieter. The nurses and Josh leant together against a wall, watching the sleepers, whilst Ann quietly explained the forthcoming transfers and reclosure.

Nurse Denton sighed: 'Sister Luke's sweet.'

Ann looked at her quickly. 'I know. Hell having to hand them over, but better for them to be down and for PPW to shut. Too high.' She looked up and down the corridor. 'Pity,' she added briskly. Then, in another voice, 'Thank God. All Clear.'

The sirens were still blaring in single-noted chorus when she left Nurse Denton sitting on a high stool watching both patients, and with Josh walked up the corridor to open the balcony doors. They went slowly out on to the stone balcony and stood side by side at the flat-topped stone balustrade that reached to a few inches above Ann's waist. The outside air was hotter than that on a Piccadilly pavement this afternoon. Hotter, and reeking of cordite, burning and smoke. The sun was a red ball glowing through a smoke haze that covered the western sky; in the east the upper half of the sky was a brilliant orange, the lower a shimmering mosaic of orange, scarlet, blue and black. Down river on both sides the gigantic flames from the land licked the sky and looked from that balcony like uncontrollable forest fires. Across the river, Ann, who knew the skyline so well, noted strange new gaps, with behind them more, slightly smaller fires and others on the far right. The curtain of flames from London Docks obscured the flames from Wapping, the Isle of Dogs and Silvertown, and on the other side of the river the flames from Surrey Commercial Docks hid the blazing Woolwich Arsenal. They were standing just high enough to glimpse one of the stretches where the Thames itself appeared to be on fire being almost blocked by blazing barges set alight by sparks from the land. They could not pick out the fire-boats, their hoses flailing like octopi, desperately trying to edge through to the blazing land. But they could hear the hissing of countless thousands of tons of water on flames, the crackling of burning timber, warehouses, wooden paving blocks, factories, old tenement buildings, new council flats, and two-up, two-down workmen's terraced houses. And backing the hissing and crackling they could hear the jangling chorus of fire engine bells, the rumble of heavy lorries rushing in firemen from all over the Home Counties, and now that a black pall of smoke was beginning to rise, the slower rumble of real and makeshift ambulances nosing their way to hospitals down and across the river.

They stood in silence at the balustrade looking all around slowly, and breathing consciously and carefully. And below, on the hospital's riverside terrace, stood other silent figures in uniform, white coats and navy battledresses, looking around slowly, breathing consciously and carefully.

Josh had not looked at Ann since they came outside, to spare her – and himself – by avoiding the sight of her grief, despair, and, he was convinced, her silent tears. He was disturbingly conscious of the stirring of emotions that he did not want and was determined to withstand. He wanted no personal involvements during his stay in England, which, on this evening's showing, would be very short. Once the Germans took over, if New York didn't shift him out in days, he would resign and somehow get himself back to the States and a new job. He would have done this in Paris last July had he not been shifted to London. He loved Paris too much to have tolerated being a neutral observer of her prolonged humiliation. He didn't love London, but he knew now that he could not bear to see the same thing happening here. Though he had been expecting this widespread devastation, the shock of seeing it was ripping off layers of Anglophobia and exposing the unsuspected depth of his ancestral roots. He wasn't staying around to watch his distant forefathers' country reduced, like Poland, to stinking ruins and semi-starvation, echoing with the rattle of cattle-trucks filled with young men being taken to work as slaves in German factories, and still more crammed with Jewish men, women and children, and thousands of non-Jews, destined for the concentration camps that neither he nor any neutral correspondent he had met had been allowed to visit. Hitler made no secret of the fact that he planned to reduce England as he had Poland, but he, Joshua G. Adams, did not intend to stick around to watch the process or leave any part of himself behind when he left England.

It was then that the insatiable curiosity of a good journalist overpowered personal reticence and he looked down at Ann and breathed in sharply. She stood straightbacked, her softly rounded chin raised, and in her dry eyes and white set face neither grief nor despair, but an implacable anger. Sensing his gaze she looked straight up into his face. 'Jerry's had it now,' she said quietly, between her teeth.

He stared. 'He's – had it?'

She mistook the nature of his incredulity. 'Sorry. Slang. "Had it" means either that you've had all you can take of something or that you'll never get it. I meant the second. Not that this'll be his last try.' She gestured towards the east. 'Once it's dark he couldn't have a more marvellous flare-path up river.'

He was too confused to rise above inessentials. 'You know about flare-paths?'

'My twin's in Spits.' She turned from the balustrade. 'I must go back in. In a few more minutes the stairs should be cleared for you to leave. Thanks again for all your help. Good luck.'

'And to you – all of you. I'll be back to see Ed Monday if – '

She cut him short. 'Luke Ward, ground floor, Block 4. Cheers, Mr Adams.'

She went in briskly and was halfway down the corridor when the telephone rang. 'I'll get it, Denton,' she called, racing to answer it. 'Private Patients Ward, Nurse Marlowe speaking.'

'Assistant Matron from the Office, nurse. I will be up to take your ward inventory with you at eight-thirty tomorrow morning. Now, about the nursing staff . . .'

She was still on the telephone when Josh went past the open door, and they exchanged unsmiling waves. He had already said goodbye to Nurse Denton, and at the now open entrance he turned to look back first at Laurings, then Daws, before walking on across the stone landing and down the five stone flights of stairs. A few minutes later he left the hospital by the way he had come in. Exactly an hour later, the Alert resounded as the first heavily fighter-escorted formation of the two-hundred-odd German bombers deployed in that night's raid flew up the river from the Thames Estuary. All night the red glow in the sky over London was visible from Oxford, and when the All Clear went at 4 a.m. the pall of black smoke rising from London stretched to the Wash.

– Three –

Josh spent that night in a public air raid shelter near Trafalgar Square; Mrs Brigham-Smythe, and other trapped non-residents, on old mattresses in the hospital's basement; Nurses Denton, Wood and Fenner on their own mattresses in the basements of their Nurses' Homes; Ann Marlowe on hers on the floor of the ballroom in the Staff Nurses' Home. This last, the most modern of the four Homes for nursing staff, had been built in the 1930s and was a red-brick, steel-structured five-storey squarish building with a large, glass-roofed swimming pool in the basement. The pool had been drained since the outbreak of war, and the roof made it unusable as a shelter, but the ballroom directly above had been pronounced by experts, called in for this purpose, the safest part of the building, and strong enough to withstand all but a direct hit upon its ceiling by a five-hundred-pound high explosive bomb – which was generally assumed to be the largest aerial weapon that Germany possessed. In the Sisters' Home, as the Nurses' Homes, the staff carried down their own bedding and mattresses, and Ann's were placed between those of Mary Cavendor and Jill de Grey, her particular friends in her old set, which was now depleted to five.

When the second raid started, Laurings and Daws had been transferred to their new wards, Nurse Denton was at supper, and Ann was clearing the PPW alone. She heard the wailing sirens with a sensation not dissimilar to the feeling one has when hearing a banging door finally slam shut. Thank God they're all down, she thought, reclosing the balcony doors, angry at what she was closing out and could hear returning up river. Her mind flew to the American, to her brother, then back to Laurings and her other patients now in other hands.

The swift return of Mr Henty, from Repairs and Works, and two firemen was a welcome interruption, and they were still with her when an Office Sister rang from Matron's Office to say Nurse Denton was being told to finish her supper and then help in the basement. 'How is your clearing progressing, Nurse Marlowe? . . . Yes, presently, they do seem to be just passing overhead, but Matron wishes you just to deal with the dutyroom tonight, bring down the essentials and leave the rest till morning . . . No, thank you, nurse, we have enough staff helping in the basement. Matron wishes you to go straight to supper and off duty, as soon as you're done up there. Don't dilly-dally, nurse.'

'I won't, Sister,' Ann bellowed over the roar of an incoming formation. Hanging up, she smiled at the men. 'Sister says not to dilly-dally.'

They grinned, and Mr Henty said, 'She's not far wrong, nurse. Not nice to think of you up here alone.'

'Quite honestly, Mr Henty, I haven't had time to think of it.'

'Best not to think,' he said and the firemen agreed; but as they all insisted on helping her clear the dutyroom, they left her no alternative to thought as they proceeded to tell her all they had seen and heard of the first raid. 'Hundreds of fires out of control all over London,' one fireman said, 'and like as not he'll

56

start up more now he's back. AFS* lads have got their hands full, and from what's being said, too many got dry hands.'

'Dry? You mean water's short?'

'That's what's being said, nurse. Hoses running dry all over the shop. Not that you want to believe all you hear these days, though you've got to believe what your own ears don't hear and your own eyes don't see. Where's our ack-ack? And our fighters, eh?'

She shrugged tensely. 'I'd assumed our guns were laying off as our fighters are up.'

'That may be what some are hoping Jerry'll reckon, nurse. Doesn't look much like it from the roof. Jerry's having it all his own way – right, mates?' His colleagues nodded and all three faces tightened with anger. 'Not right, this isn't, nurse.'

'No. It certainly isn't.'

Now as she lay on her mattress at the far end of the ballroom, her body longing for sleep and her ears aching with the continuous droning of aircraft punctuated by semi-distant explosions, her too-active mind kept returning to this afternoon's raid, its immediate aftermath, the three men in the dutyroom tonight and to Michael. She kept fingering the gold signet ring she wore on a silver chain round her neck: it had been their father's, and Michael had inherited it on their twenty-first birthday.

Michael had left that ring in her keeping last July during his first forty-eight hours' leave after his squadron's withdrawal from France. By lucky chance this had coincided with one of her alternate free weekends – Saturday afternoon and Sunday. They spent the Saturday night with old friends in the Sussex village where the unmarried aunt who had been their legal guardian had lived until she closed her house and moved in with

* Auxiliary Fire Service.

friends in Yorkshire this May. After tea on Saturday they walked up the lane and through the woods to sit on the long, sloping southern side of a hill on the Kent–Sussex border. The hillside was thick with timothy grass, buttercups and dandelions, the earth beneath warm, and the clear sky was the Mediterranean blue it had been all this summer and alive with birds.

'Hang on to this for me until this show's over, Ann,' Michael had said. 'Rather you than Aunt Maud or Dolly. No future in starting up flaps or giving a popsy ideas. Okay?'

'Sure.' She managed to sound casual, though she was deeply distressed by the gesture. There was a bleak bitterness she had never seen before in Michael's attractive face, which had her well-set grey-blue eyes, short straight nose and generous mouth, but his own square chin. They had the mental accord of most twins, and she knew precisely why he had left the ring with her and not with his WAAF girlfriend (he had fallen seriously for Dolly and never before referred to her to Ann as a 'popsy'). 'Only two types of pilots now,' he said as they came up through the woods. 'The type that marries the first available popsy, and the type that stays single, single-minded and alive. Damned tough on the married types. Tougher still on their widows. Let's skip the war talk. Tell me about this new job.'

For the first time with him, she had to censor what she told him, and sensed he knew this and was doing the same for her. After giving her the ring he was silent for some time, and she stayed silent, hugging her knees, waiting for him to break the silence as she knew he would when he was ready, and inhaling the warm, sweet country air and the smoke of the cigarettes he was chain-smoking. He lay on his back beside her, his eyes half-closed and the cigarette clamped in his lips spilling ash over the new service dress uniform delivered only last week. When ordered back from France his squadron

58

had had to fly out in the flying-kit they had on, leaving behind all their other kit and personal possessions, and had touched down in England with near-empty fuel tanks.

'God, it was a bloody shambles,' he said.

'The withdrawal from France?'

'Whole bloody show in France. Waste of time from square one. The bloody Frogs didn't want to fight – and did we waste chaps and aircraft! We'd give our right arms now for all the chaps and machines we lost. Lost? Chucked away.' He then horrified her by listing names of dead pilots whom she had met as his friends, or knew to have been his friends, and by giving the true figures of the remnants of his squadron and Group. 'Thank God for Stuffy Dowding!' He went on, 'The inside gen is that he finally flatly refused to let us chuck away more – if he hadn't we'd have nothing left for the show that must come now Jerry's got France in the bag and he could just paddle over.' He glared up at the sky. 'And all the bloody BEF do is beef about where was the something RAF at Dunkirk?' He glared at her. 'I'll tell you where. Those of us that could make it, got there; and most that couldn't, didn't show up because they had either been burnt to a crisp or scattered in small pieces over the fair land of France whilst all the bloody Frogs were bleating "Il faut en finir." '

She had heard too much of the terrible, disfiguring and often blinding burns suffered by pilots to control her wince, but she kept her voice dry. 'Must have made a change from "Ils ne passeront pas." '

He grinned derisively at that reminder of the vainglorious maxim of the useless Maginot Line. 'You can say that again. Talk about being caught with their pants down and – God, I'm getting bawdy! Too many stag parties.'

'Poor Dolly.'

The look he gave her was identical with the one she

used when others stepped out of line. 'And how's *your* love life?' he enquired.

'Non-existent as ever. No time. No temptation.'

He distressed her further by looking concerned instead of amused by this, as he usually did. 'Not one Martha's man with SA?'

'Lots. Some are dreamboats – if you don't happen to work with them. Not that most aren't splendid chaps, and a few are good doctors. Snag is, Martha's men are still so closeted in the monastery and have to be to keep their jobs, that they tend, mentally, to be still in prep school. To be fair, it works both ways. We're still closeted in the convent, so lots of us are still in boarding school and never really leave it. I've a hunch those that have gone into the Services are suddenly growing up fast.'

'I wouldn't say that applied to you,' he said.

'But we had to grow up a bit faster than usual.'

'That's true. Will you go into the Services?'

'Let's face that when my contract ends next June,' she said thoughtlessly, as her mind was back in her early childhood. Then she heard herself and blushed in dismay. The future was a forbidden subject.

He said quickly, kindly, 'Not to worry. You'll make the right choice whatever the turn-up. You always have. Remember when we were kids and you decided you were the brain and I was the brawn?'

She laughed. 'And we were still fighting it out in the kitchen garden when Aunt Maud heaved us apart, torn between her suffragette youth and Edwardian upbringing, and gave you hell for fighting with a girl because no gentleman ever raised his hand to a lady, and gave me hell for kicking you because no nice girl ever kicked a boy's bare knees and "if you ever have to kick a man, child, for goodness' sake kick harder and higher!" '

Michael shouted with laughter. 'No wonder I found school bullyboys a piece of cake after the hols with you toughs!'

At their last meeting, just over a week ago, the bleak bitterness had gone, but his face looked years older and deathly tired. The previous night he had got a trunk-call through to tell her he had to be in London in the morning, thought he could swing a couple of free hours in the early afternoon, and any chance? Again, luck was with them. She had a two-to-five next day and they spent some of it sitting on a bench in St James's Park that afforded more privacy for conversation than a table for tea in a restaurant, their only alternative after closing time. Michael looked remarkably spruce, and seeing the blinding shine of his buttons she jerked her head towards Whitehall and the Air Ministry. 'Date? Or can't you say?'

Deadpan, he lowered one eyelid. 'Old kite can use the odd mothball.'

Her eyes darkened. 'Badly shot up, yesterday?'

He grinned. 'God, no. Just the odd nibble. Spits don't encourage moths – too nifty, as Jerry's twigged. His "Achtung, Spitfeuer!" ain't his "Horst Wessel Song".'

'Thank God for that. You're putting up a marvellous show.'

The grin vanished. 'So's Jerry. He's a damned good fighting man. We're putting up all we've got, but he's got more and he's dead nifty at fishing his chaps out of the drink.'

'Aren't we?'

'No flies on Air Sea Rescue, and better not be.'

It was another glorious summer's day, but suddenly she felt ice-cold. 'Michael. We're still losing so many?' she asked.

'Don't you read the morning papers?'

'Never in the morning. No time.' She didn't add that at night she was too tired for more than the casualty lists and headlines, in that order. 'You are getting replacements?'

'Some. Not enough. Takes more than the odd week to train a pilot, and already we're down to taking chaps straight from operational training. Chaps? Boys. They certainly make me feel an old man. At twenty-five that's what I am to them. Most haven't hit twenty – and won't.' He stood up. 'I need a drink and know a low dive where we can get one. Mind?'

She had never before known him drink in mid-afternoon. 'Not if you don't offer me beer. I still loathe it,' she replied.

'Who wants beer? I'm not flying today. Whisky.'

Just in time she stopped herself from saying 'But you've always loathed spirits.' She stood up, smiling. 'Let's go.'

Until last night's trunk-call she had never before heard his voice slurred with alcohol; it had loosened his tongue enough for him to tell her he had flown six sorties yesterday. Day after day, she thought, so held in her own thoughts that she barely heard the raid; day after day, and every day fewer left to go up the next day, so they have to go up more often. No man – no woman – no matter how young and strong, could keep up this pace, this strain, without enough sleep. But from the look of Michael in St James's Park, and from what he had let out later in the seedy little club whose name she had forgotten, his whole group was short of sleep. 'What we all need, aside from more pilots and aircraft, is a twenty-four-hour kip. Not a hope in hell. But we do manage the odd kip between scrambles. Remember how revoltingly fussy I've always been about sleeping in strange beds? Talk about hoist with my own whatsit. I can now kip down in seconds in a deckchair or on the grass up against the dispersal hut.'

Chronic fatigue slows even the fastest reactions, she thought, but on the speed of our pilots' reactions depend not just their own lives and aircraft but all our lives, all our futures. These last few hours have shown what Jerry can do when there's no one to stop them. I can understand why we don't seem to have put up anyone to stop him – our fighter-pilots can't fly non-stop day and night – but not why our guns aren't doing their stuff. London's supposed to be ringed with ack-ack guns. Why aren't they in action? A mounting wave of anger hit her tired mind like strong drink. Then within seconds she was so deeply asleep that she slept through the rest of the raid and the All Clear. When the 6.30 a.m. 'getting-up' bell roused her, for a few moments she thought she was still in her third-floor bedroom until she heard the authoritative voice of Nurse Francis, the senior Casualty staff nurse and most senior in the Home. 'All Clear went hours ago, girls. Nothing dropped close to the hospital but we've had some in. We can use our own rooms and floor bathrooms but must leave our bedding down here, pro tem. Incidentally, the invasion doesn't seem to have started, as the church bells haven't rung.'

The Staff Nurses' Home stood beside the much older Doctors' House on the far side of the broad main road, with its double row of tramlines, that ran parallel with the hospital's frontage. Ann's room overlooked the road, and when she took down the blackout screen the paper-stripped uncracked panes of her window seemed to have turned opaque. She pushed up the lower sash, then slammed it down again to keep out the billows of thick, foul-smelling smoke. By pressing her face against the glass she could just make out the ghostly but intact outlines of the sprawling hospital and glimpsed a portion of the low black cloud capping London like a lid on a simmering saucepan. Day nurses' breakfast was served at 7 a.m. and it was already 6.40, but she stayed staring at her window, mechanically undoing her long plaits and brushing out her hair. Her mind shot back to this time yesterday. Before the day had ended, she thought, so had her appointed job. No

63

ward, no patients of my own, so after the inventory, jobbing,* and like every nurse I've always detested jobbing. Yet now that prospect couldn't bother me less. Why? Simple. Because I know I'm lucky to be alive this morning. Odd, the difference that makes. Odd sort of feeling that Michael must get every time he touches down. It explains still more clearly why he's backing off from Dolly, which I'm afraid is hurting her badly: though she's sweet, and bright enough to be a Section Officer, she hasn't much imagination, so she probably can't see that he's backing off more to protect her than himself. Poor pretty Dolly – poor Michael – and damn Jerry for messing up their – all our – lives – for all the lives he's killed or wrecked since yesterday in London – for pitching my dear brave Ed into hell yesterday afternoon and, I'm afraid, last night. Luke can't keep him under non-stop. I hope to God he's come through the night – and that my others got some sleep – and that American's come through it – and Michael . . .

She closed her eyes in an attempt to close her mind and stood still by the window, her arms at her sides, the hairbrush dangling from her right hand.

'Ann! Five to!' Tall, dark-haired Mary Cavendor and smaller, fair Jill de Grey stood uniformed in the open doorway. 'Wakey, wakey!'

She blinked open wet eyes. 'Go ahead. I'll make it.'

'Okay,' said Mary, closing the door and exchanging guarded glances with Jill. Having shared each other's lives for over four years they had come to know each other better than did many sisters and regarded each other's families as their own.

Going down the stairs Mary said, 'Aunt Maud'll be

* On loan.

still more round the bend. She's awfully fond of Ann, but her sun rises on Michael's head.'

'Yes.' Jill de Grey's deceptively childish face was troubled. Her only brother, younger than her, a Gunner in a training camp in Yorkshire, had visited Miss Marlowe recently. 'I wonder if they were right to leave their next-of-kinship with her.'

'Dead right, especially now Jerry's going for London,' said Mary firmly. She was the Stanley Parker staff nurse, and an immensely practical young woman. She opened the front door. 'Oh, blast! This muck'll wreck our clean caps and lungs before we've crossed the road.' They yashmaked their faces with their cloaks and went down the five front steps at the same moment that Josh Adams pulled down the handkerchief he was wearing as a mask and went back into the hotel he had left at 3.30 p.m. yesterday.

He was too weary, and too irritated by the frustrating attitudes of the police and ARP wardens since the All Clear, to be more than mildly amazed by the normality of the foyer aside from the wisps of black smoke infiltrating the hardboard-battened revolving glass doors and hovering like filthy cobwebs. The night porter looked his usual morning self, pale and red-eyed, as he greeted Josh as if he were just returning from posting a letter.

'Mr Burness has just come in and gone up to wait in your room same as always, sir, and gas is off, electricity too low for the lifts and no telephones working. But we only lost a few windows, and none on your floor, though cracked, mind, so best not to try opening – not as you'd want to let in more of this nasty smoke.'

'No.' Josh felt slightly lightheaded with relief for Burness. 'Radios working?'

'A few, sir. Nothing much on the BBC about the invasion. Not that that means much.' The man's face hardened. 'Never tell us nothing till they have to, do they, sir? What I'd like them to tell us is where were our guns last night? And the RAF?'

Josh responded as he had had to frequently in the public shelter. 'Sorry. I wouldn't know.' He looked around. 'None hurt in here?'

'Oh, no, sir. All went down our shelter. Mr Burness, too. Just stepped in to ask for you last night afore Jerry come back, and seeing as he couldn't leave went down below. Had a fairish sleep he said on his way out after the All Clear. Not been back in long. Be a weight off his mind to see you, I reckon. Breakfast for two in the dining-room will it be?'

Josh looked at him for a moment that recalled to him Nurse Marlowe's 'Play poker?' 'Breakfasts as usual?' he asked.

'On Sundays, sir. Seven-forty-five to ten. Kitchen and waiting staff are coming in. Not all here yet. Got to expect some to be on the late side this morning. Nasty night, you might say.'

'You might at that.'

'Fires still burning all over, I hear.'

'So I've heard.' He liked the porter, so he didn't add that hearing had been just about all he had been able to do since the All Clear. And the least of the obstacles to his doing the job he was here to do had been the fires, smoke, blackout, chunks of fallen masonry, layers of rubble, broken glass and the craters. Wherever he had gone, or tried to go, an official figure had loomed in his path. 'No closer', 'not this way', 'get back', 'not that way', 'no loitering, please', 'move along there', 'get right back . . .' had been the message again and again.

'Right, Charlie. Thanks. Yes, please, breakfast for two – say eight?'

'Much obliged, sir.'

Josh hesitated. 'Live far away?'

'I've had lodgings with the wife's cousin in Brixton,

sir, since the wife passed on and I come on the night shift three years back.' Charlie smiled grimly. 'If I still got the lodgings, that is, sir.'

'Sure. I hope so. Be seeing you.' He walked slowly to the stairs and up to the first floor, which now accommodated all the hotel's few residents. When he opened the unlocked door of his room the burly figure slumped in one armchair, with feet on another, raised one hand and with the other reached for the half-empty whisky bottle beside two glasses, an overflowing ashtray and Josh's portable, battery-powered wireless. Josh was oddly touched. He knew Burness' capacity for whisky.

'Land's sakes, brother!' The small, shrewd, hot eyes of a hard drinker appraised Josh's crumpled, smoke-smeared suit and shirt front, and his unshaven face. 'What kept you?'

Josh took the offered glass and kicked free the armchair. 'City lights.'

Over breakfast in the only lighted corner of the otherwise empty dining-room they decided to check their office first then spend the day separately in London. Burness would use the influence and popularity he had built up during his eight years' residence in order to contact as many people as he could in high places in the War Office, the Air Ministry and the Ministries of Information and Home Security. At some point, he would check if he still had an apartment. Josh, meanwhile, would pick up what he could, where he could, at ground level. After coughing and stumbling the short distance, they found the Regency terraced house had lost all its windows but otherwise seemed structurally intact, and their office blackened with smoke and strewn with typing paper, carbons, files, newspaper clippings, strips of blackout curtains and broken glass. The two telephones, ticker-tape machine and electricity were useless.

'My oh my!' Burness thumbed his grey fedora to the back of his red head. 'Back to the good old carrier pigeon.'

'I'll get down to Trafalgar Square with my net after the chores.' Josh slung his hat on to a filing cabinet and took off his jacket.

'You do that, brother.' Burness scowled at the telephones. 'If I can't find me a phone fit to call her fast my Joan'll be fit to be tied. One'll get you ten her first words are "Why in hell didn't you call sooner, you lazy slob?" '

'No take, Pete, I play to win.'

'Skinflint puritan,' grunted Burness, much pleased. He adored his wife and infant son and was tremendously proud of his remarkably happy marriage.

Josh shovelled glass into a wastepaper basket, then used dustpan and brush on Miss Dewly's desk. Glancing at Burness, he was conscious of an uncharacteristic pang that was so akin to envy that it perturbed him. From the outbreak of this war he had cherished his freedom from domestic ties and their concomitant anxieties. He had been belatedly relieved that, unlike many of his expatriate colleagues, he had not married a European: the one woman he had ever wanted to marry had turned him down in Paris in early 1938. 'You are too young,' she had said. 'You are like all American men – too young – older than me, yes, but still too young. You are not a serious man. When I marry it will be with a serious man who will make me very comfortable. You would not make me comfortable. You are too young and you like too much to be free . . .' Two months later she had married a wealthy French lawyer twenty years her senior and moved to Marseilles and Josh had been moved to Berlin. He had not seen her again nor thought he could ever forget her. Last night in the shelter, to drag his mind from what might be happening across the river, from Ed Laurings, and from Nurse Marlowe's face on the balcony, he had tried to picture the lovely face of the French girl who had been his mistress for the happiest year of his life. He had loved her with the overwhelming passion of a generous-hearted, rather lonely young man, hungry for love, in an alien, if enchanting city, and seriously in love for the first time; but now he found he could no longer recall her face with clarity. In an attempt to erase that failure he had concentrated his anxieties upon Miss Dewly and her mother. This had worked for about ten minutes.

Miss Dewly's typewriter cover had been sliced by the glass splinters now embedded in the keys. He cleared the machine with particular care to atone for not worrying about her longer. He tested it. 'Okay for tomorrow,' he said.

'Great,' muttered Burness, clearing his own desk, and their mutually unvoiced 'if she's still around to show up tomorrow' was audible to both. Being Sunday, neither Miss Dewly nor Mrs Harding, their office cleaner, came in.

So many 'ifs', reflected Josh, moving to his own desk, but something of a break – he refused to put it higher – to have crossed one off, if only for this morning. During his frustrating peregrinations after the All Clear he had eventually encountered in the Haymarket a solitary air raid warden willing to stop and talk for a minute. 'St Martha's Hospital?' the man said. 'No, no damage as far as I've heard, and I'd have heard if she'd copped any. Just over the river. Word gets round London pretty fast, blackout or no blackout . . .'

Long before that Sunday ended, Josh learnt how right that warden had been. All that day, relatively unimpeded as officialdom was too busy to notice, he spoke to hundreds of Londoners. The accents and the grammar varied, but not the attitudes, the rumours, the tones: 'If old Hitler thinks this'll have us cap in hand asking for our cards, he'd best think again, sir . . .'

'. . . If Jerry thinks this'll have us packing it in, he's barking up the wrong tree, old boy! . . .' '. . . What I wants, guv, what I wants is for just one Jerry to bale out and come down in our street. Know what I'll do, guv? Lynch him, that's what, and I'll have help – and you can bung that down on your bit of paper! . . .' '. . . Young man, I have always disapproved of blood sports and violent behaviour and I am old enough to be your mother, but if you were a German and I now had a rifle I would use it on you with particular pleasure if it had a fixed bayonet! . . .' '. . . Oy, mister! This bloke here says as he's heard Jerry's had a bash at landing down in Sussex – Pevensey way, he says – and you can't see the beach for dead Jerries, and more are being washed up every tide. Talk about a sight for sore eyes . . .' '. . . I say, old chap, just had the latest gen. I gather Jerry's tried to land in Kent – some spot called St Mary's Bay – apparently you can't see the beach for dead Jerries, and more bodies are being washed in with every tide. Jolly good show, eh? . . .' '. . . Want to know what I thinks, guv? Tell you straight, I will. Not right, that's what I thinks. Why didn't we hear no guns yesterday teatime and last night? Why didn't our fighters do nothing? . . .' '. . . Actually, old boy, I reckon drains to our ack-ack. Not a cheep. Damned poor show . . .' '. . . What we wants to know mister, is where was our guns? Got guns all over, they told us. Why didn't we hear none? . . .' '. . . Was we down our public shelter, guv? You got to be joking! Not room for more than a few hundred down our nearest. Room needed for thousands! What's old Winnie doing about that, eh? And what's he doing about our water? You heard right, guv. *Water*. Hoses and hydrants ran dry all over, they says. We wants to know for why? Got the Thames, haven't we? And what's old Winnie doing about our guns? *Why didn't we hear no guns?* . . .' '. . . Er, yes, now you mention it, old boy, I have heard that water's been running short. Not clear why.

Damned bad show, and damned hard on the firemen – they're putting up a magnificent show . . .'

All that day he watched London's firemen, police, Civil Defence, Special Constables and hundreds of civilians fighting the fires in the heat, stench and smoke that were as omnipresent as the broken glass carpeting roads and pavements, the heaps of masonry and rubble partly or wholly blocking main and side streets. 'What you mean, who are all these civvies lending a hand?' demanded one red-eyed fireman with a blackened face. 'Volunteers, that's what they are, and why not? London's theirs, ain't it? Same as mine. You'll pardon my not stopping. I got work to do.'

All that day he watched, nosing through smoke and flames, over broken glass, around and between the heaps and mounds. He saw the convoys of ambulances, their white sides blackened by smoke; of private cars either volunteered or commandeered; of London taxis volunteered on the spot by their drivers, and packed with the injured; of heavily tarpaulined lorries filled with the bodies, or remains of the bodies, of the dead. No one he asked that day could – or would – give him any figures on how many had been killed and injured since 5 p.m. yesterday. (Though casualties were considerably fewer than had been officially anticipated, the known dead numbered five hundred, and the seriously injured two thousand. Neither then, nor for the duration of the war, were the figures for the walking wounded with minor injuries officially announced.)

He was watching an unusual convoy of red London buses crawl by, when a Special Constable paused near him to mop his streaming eyes. 'This lot, sir? They've been specially commandeered by the Government to ferry the homeless to Rest Centres. Running all round London today,' he said.

Not running, but crawling, to temporary sanctuaries in local town halls, schools, drill and church halls, and

71

other buildings with enough space and the minimum essential sanitation. And filling those buses were men, women, and often children, all their faces uniformly grey and aged from shock and fatigue, their shabby civilian clothes grimy with soot and plaster-dust. On their laps, in cheap brown cardboard suitcases, or brown paper bags, or bundled in shawls, they clutched the few possessions they had managed to save from their destroyed homes. As he glanced from the buses to the people watching the convoy go by, Josh saw in every face the same grim sympathy and an ugly anger. He scribbled in shorthand in his notebook, 'The Battle of Britain stays wide open and I guess goes on right now, but the Battle of London is the new front line, and holding the line are several million amateur, unarmed civilians.'

'Amateurs at fighting wars, maybe,' said Pete Burness when they compared notes in their office that evening. 'Not in the survival business, after being raised in the meanest, toughest slums these old eyes have seen any place Stateside or in good old civilised Europe. Old hands at survival they have had to be.' He paused to replenish his glass and watched Josh hammer a final nail to fix the hardboard now blocking both windows, and then start to hang the first of the four curtains decorated with Mickey Mouse and Donald Duck and lined with blackout material. Burness had taken those curtains – to please his wife he had stopped calling them 'drapes' – from his son's empty nursery in their apartment in a newish block in Knightsbridge that was only slightly damaged though the buildings on both sides were down. He had said nothing about the neighbours to his wife when, late this afternoon, he had managed to get a trunkcall through to her from the office of an English friend on a London national paper. The memory of his reactions on seeing his block standing like a tooth in a broken mouth, haunted his eyes. He took another gulp. 'And real old hands at spinning a yarn. No landings down in

Kent, Sussex or any other location, from what I could dig out. It is on the record that the whole British Army and Home Guard have been on stand-by from mid-afternoon yesterday. Not that that was any surprise to me after the number of roadblocks we had to clear on the detour we had to make on our return last evening. It surely was Birmingham by way of Beachy Head. We could only make it back in up the Great West Road, then we had a real problem getting as far as Notting Hill Gate, when it was – take a walk, brothers.'

Josh hung a second curtain. 'Invasion rumours just hot air, huh?'

'That is the official version.' They looked at each other in the flickering shadows of the two candles Burness had lighted. 'I guess there is some truth in it – I would not care to say just how much. I will say that I have more than a hunch little old Adolf has opened himself more than one can of beans. If he aims to terrorise London I would not say he is going about the job any too well. Sure he has terrified a good few, but he has made a whole lot more real mean mad, and not just with his boys. You heard.'

'I heard.'

They fell silent, thinking their own thoughts, and when the curtains were all up and closed Josh lit the two candles in jam jars on his desk, flopped into his chair, his feet on the desk top, sipping his first drink of the evening and looking back over the day.

It seemed to him that in the small hours of this morning, from cupboards under stairs, coal cellars, domestic basements, little metal Andersons in small back gardens, the vaults of churches and public shelters, had emerged millions of civilians forged into a single entity – London. London in an ocean of anger directed near equally at the Luftwaffe and its own authorities. And underpinning the anger there was already apparent an indomitable determination not just to survive but to win the war that had come to London's backyard. Not once today had one Londoner suggested to him that England should now sue for peace. On every occasion that he had tentatively suggested this possibility it had been rejected with one voice, and sooner or later with the four words that he had heard today for the first time and that his professional instincts now informed him would ring round the world like a gloriously defiant trumpet-blast: 'London can take it.'

Could it? Could any city? After what had already been suffered in just two raids, with the innumerable fires still blazing out of control making perfect markers from the sky once night fell?

An unwanted face rose to the forefront of his mind and he heard mentally the unwanted voice saying, 'Once it's dark he couldn't have a more marvellous flare-path up river,' as the sirens began wailing.

'Here we go again,' grunted Burness.

Before Josh could answer, the telephone on his desk rang shrilly. He grabbed it. 'Yeah?'

'Operator speaking, caller,' announced an impersonal female voice. 'Just to let you know this line is now in order. Sorry you've been troubled.' She rang off before he could thank her.

– Four –

'On Underground platforms, Mr Adams?' Ann set down her coffee cup in surprise. 'The Government's forbidden its use as a public shelter. How did they swing it?'

'By sticking to the law and buying the twopenny platform tickets that gave them the legal right to enter the platforms. Once there they sat down until the All Clear and then went back up and handed in their tickets, quote, in good order, unquote.' He was so disquietingly pleased to have made her smile that he had to look away. He looked round the little restaurant, smelling agreeably of fresh coffee and baking, which was in a side street near Martha's. They were having coffee at eleven fifteen on the following morning. 'Only a few hundred went down last night, but I think it probable that thousands will follow their lead when Jerry next shows up,' he said.

'I'm sure they will. It's such plain common sense that I can't understand why the Government's ruled this out. Or can I?' She thought for a moment, then grimaced derisively. 'Yes, I'm sure I've got it! I'll bet the Government thought that if this was allowed it would start up panics in the general public's rush to get down. Panic? Hah! The public bought platform tickets. Thanks, I'd love one,' she said, accepting a cigarette. She looked up at him across his lighter flame, from under the small, slanting brim of her cream straw boater. 'Our Government's trouble is that it doesn't really know us, but thinks that it does and that it knows best.'

'Is that so?'

She gave him a long, appraising look. 'Relax, Mr Adams, she said drily. 'I know you have to sit on the fence, but I don't – and, in case you haven't caught on to this yet, binding at our Government, binding at everything, is a cherished English custom and a good sign. The bad sign is when we stop binding. Bad round you last night?'

'Pretty hot.'

'As elsewhere, I gather. Not round here. We had no casualties in last night, but when I was going on this morning our senior Cas porter told me other hospitals were again inundated. Presumably you've heard.'

'I've caught the official version. No figures. Do you have any? Off the record.'

'Not official figures. Dacey, that Cas porter, said he'd heard – and, sorry, but even off the record I can't tell you how – that last night's known dead were nearing four hundred, seriously injured a thousand, and though he'd no figures for the minor injured his guess was thousands. I expect he's right. During Saturday night and yesterday morning we had in a hundred and fourteen minors, but officially only our forty-seven seriously injured admissions. And that description was an understatement for most. Thirty were on the Dangerously Ill List before they reached their ground-floor-ward beds.' She hesitated. 'Nine went to Luke. They were the patients behind the open red screens you must have seen this morning.' He nodded. 'Hope Ward, where I'm working today, took none as it's on the first floor. That's how I've this ten-to-one off.' She hesitated again and looked at him blankly. 'I haven't yet told you that most of yesterday I worked in Luke. I was with him.'

He inclined his head. 'That intern told me. Dr – or is it Mr Wesley?'

'Mister. More than an intern. The Senior Surgical Officer. Did he also tell you, KEA* from all angles?'

'He did,' he said, and for some little time they smoked in silence, sitting a little apart on the faded red plush wall settle.

When last night's Alert was fading and Ann was layering on Laurings' spare mattress, a sudden brain haemorrhage killed him in seconds. An hour later she performed his Last Offices and then escorted his body to the morgue, too numbed with distress to notice the raid or her own tiredness. Like all the trained and qualified staff, she had been on duty all day, and when she finally got to her mattress she was too tired to sleep. She lay awake for hours listening to the growling of aircraft and the semi-distant thunder of explosions with a sense of weary familiarity that had begun to breed a stoic acceptance. And constantly in her mind was the face of a pretty, plump woman in youngish middle age that she had only seen in the snapshot she had taken from Laurings' blood-stiffened wallet on the day of his admission to the PPW, carefully mopped clean of dried blood, and propped on the bedside locker to face him. A few hours back she had removed that snapshot from his locker in Luke, put it in a clean envelope, and packed it with his few possessions for eventual return to Canada. The face in the snapshot was smiling, but not the face in her mind reading the cable that might reach Manitoba in the next twenty-four hours, but more probably the next forty-eight. She did not remember the American's intention of returning today until woken by the All Clear. Then, unable to get back to sleep, she got up silently before the bell, and after it rang went over to the hospital in the hope of finding a usable telephone

* Killed by Enemy Action.

box and getting a message to his hotel. The telephone in the box in her Home had been useless since Saturday evening. During her search she met Dacey in Central Hall, and he told her that the only functioning outside line in Martha's was Casualty's to the police. 'Nasty night again, nurse,' he said.

'Very. I suppose he'll be back tonight.'

Dacey's face was as expressionless as those on the stone busts of long-gone physicians and surgeons set on waist-high stone pedestals along Central Hall's left-hand wall, behind which was the Out-Patients Department, and along the first half of the right, behind which was the main Dispensary. The three public telephone boxes were lined against the second half of the right-hand wall, over which curved the impressive marble front stairs with their red carpet. 'I wouldn't lay a wooden tanner against it, Nurse Marlowe,' he said. 'Still, your six from PPW got away in their Army ambulance in good time to be clear of London afore last night's do.'

'Thank goodness, yes. But, Dacey, how did the SMO manage to scrounge that ambulance in yesterday's shortage?'

'No names, no pack drill, nurse.' He jerked his neat greying head in the direction of the Governor's Boardroom that lay off the open, semi-circular, ornately balustraded first-floor landing. 'Dr White's not one to let the grass grow under his feet when he's got a job to do. He told me as he'd told Mr Wesley he'd get those six lads shifted out yesterday, and shift 'em he did. Relief for Mr Wesley, and needed, I reckon. He was operating for twenty-one hours yesterday, and Prof Surgery, he was at it for nineteen. Never a dull moment, is there, nurse?'

'No, Dacey.'

Nor between seven-thirty and ten in Hope this morning. Yesterday all Faith's immovable patients had been moved down in their beds, giving Hope thirty-two patients, four of whom were on the DIL and all the rest on the less grave Seriously Ill List. Later today fifteen were due to be transferred to an Emergency Medical Services Hospital in Surrey, if the ambulances from that hospital arrived.

'Dr White has been promised them,' said Sister Hope this morning, 'but with ambulances in such demand all over London again today, we can only be sure they will reach us when they do. If they do, I would say this will be in early afternoon. Now, about off-duty.' She looked from her permanent staff nurse to Ann. 'For obvious reasons I want my whole day staff on from five, so you will take two-to-five, Nurse Standing, and Nurse Marlowe ten-to-one.'

'What about you, Sister?' Nurse Standing protested. 'Yesterday was your free Sunday but you were on all day.'

'Hope is my ward, Nurse Standing,' said Sister Hope, as other women said, 'This is my home.' Sister Hope was fifty-two, but looked older. She had entered Martha's Nurses' Training School in 1905, and had been Sister Hope for the last twenty years. During the Great War she had nursed for two years in France, where she had often slept on a damp camp bed or on a ground-sheet on wet earth without ill-effects; but these last two nights on a mattress on a basement floor had left her very conscious of her age, and of the youth of all her nurses and so many of her patients. She was an inspired medical nurse and a kind, gentle woman. She recalled the Great War with dreadful clarity and reflected that all wars were predominantly killers of youth in every sense. 'I hope you have a pleasant off-duty, Nurse Marlowe,' she said as she dismissed Ann at 10 a.m.

As she went slowly down the one flight of stairs to the ground floor Ann's thoughts returned to Laurings, his parents, and the American. As the American came into her mind, she suddenly saw him standing a few yards away by the side exit door, accepting a cigarette from Mr Wesley, whose back was to her. From the set expression on the American's face it was obvious to her that the SSO had just completed the particular explanation that in Martha's invariably ended with the offer of a cigarette to a man and a cup of tea to a woman. She stopped involuntarily, the American glanced in her direction, and the relief that illuminated his face made the SSO glance round.

'Nurse Marlowe. Most opportune.' Mr Wesley glanced at the cloak over her arm and the gasmask slung from her shoulder that denoted her off-duty. 'Forgive me, Mr Adams, must push off. Pro with a query appendix, Nurse Marlowe,' he added over his shoulder with the first note of personal apology she had heard in his voice. He went out quickly, shutting the door behind him.

Josh glanced at the closed door as Ann joined him. He was as disturbed, in a different way, by the depth of his relief on seeing her, as by the news he had received, first from Sister Luke and then in greater detail from the tall fair intern. 'I've just heard,' he said.

'Yes. I'm so sorry. Was Mr Wesley in Luke when you arrived?'

'Yes. He said he had to come this way and would show me out and so forth.'

'That's what I thought. I am so sorry, Mr Adams.'

'Tough break.'

'Very.' She sounded and looked as composed as she had at their first meeting, but now he recognised her need for the camouflage – if not the additional, and far more trivial, reason for it that had just caused the SSO's unspoken apology. The main corridor was its customary Monday morning two-way stream of staff and out-patients going to and from the blocks and departments. For a uniformed nurse to be seen standing talking to a young man, in or out of a white coat, at best resulted in grapevine rumours, and at worst a report of unseemly conduct to Matron. And an Office Sister had just left the alcove to Matron's Office roughly two hundred yards away and was coming towards them.

Ann altered her stance slightly to avert her face from the approaching Sister. 'I wish I could talk to you, Mr Adams. I'm afraid I can't here.'

'I appreciate you're very busy and – '

'I'm not. I'm off duty. It's just not allowed here.'

He frowned a trifle incredulously. 'Not right here?' She nodded and the look in her eyes took him back to Saturday. 'Can we go somewhere else?'

Saturday was in her mind too. 'How long have you got?'

'An hour or so, only this morning. That's why I came early. Where?'

'It'll have to be off hospital territory. How well do you know this part of London?'

'Not well. I'll find it.'

'Right.' She opened the side door. 'Go down that path, over that main road, take the right fork then first right, and on the same side about forty yards down there's a small place called the Three Pigeons that does morning coffee. It'll take you about seven and me twenty minutes, as I've got to change,' she said very quickly without moving her lips. Then more audibly, 'Think you can find your way, Mr Adams?'

'Sure.' He had seen the large woman in the navy dress, white apron and lace-frilled cap eyeing them as she drew abreast. 'Thanks for all your help, Nurse Marlowe.' He went out on to the cement path, slapping on his trilby as she shut the door.

'Who was that young man, Nurse Marlowe?'

'A Mr Adams, Sister. An American friend of my patient from the Private Patients Ward, Flight Lieutenant E. J. Laurings, who died in Luke Ward at 7.39 p.m. yesterday. Mr Adams had not heard until he came to see his friend this morning.'

'Oh.' The Office Sister mellowed. She greatly admired President Roosevelt. 'So sad. So worrying for Americans trying to find their way round London in these rather trying times. Thank you, nurse.' She went on up the stairs of Block 1.

Josh paused in the entrance to the hospital grounds that was closest to the Junior Home and to the bridge end of the road. Like the others, it had lost its gates in one of this summer's national collections of scrap metal. He turned back to look up at the tall, grey, ugly Home, and then up and down the sprawling frontage that had every internal entrance and ground-floor window sandbagged. It was festooned with giant notices directing out-patients to departments, and ambulances to the entrance and exits of Casualty Yard, that was large enough to be a smallish parade ground. Outside the main entrance to Casualty were twin ten-foot-high sandbag walls set just wide enough apart to allow a single ambulance to back up to the open doors above which was another large notice: ST MARTHA'S CASUALTY DEPARTMENT NEVER CLOSES. OPEN TO ALL PATIENTS DAY AND NIGHT.

His gaze moved on, noting the height of the eight identical blocks and the strength of the stonework. He calculated that it would take at least one direct hit from a five-hundred-pound high explosive to bring down a whole block, and, even so, it would probably not do much damage to the nearest blocks, as they were all set so far apart. He wished he had taken a better look on his way in on Saturday, then recollected how many five-hundred-pounders had fallen on London since then and turned back to the wide main road with its tramlines that was one of the few he had seen free of glass, rubble, craters, holes and cordoning ropes, since yesterday morning. On the far side a line of dirty grey buildings jostled each other on either side of the double break made by a square, red-brick building that was tall for London, and an Edwardian monstrosity similar to the one behind him. On both sides of the road every visible window was paper-stripped, but few looked cracked, none gaped, and here the stench and smoke were infinitely lighter than on the other side of the river and there was enough breeze to raise the charcoal haze and give him his first glimpse of a barrage balloon since going down to the public shelter on Saturday night. He had to resist the urge to raise his hat to the bulbous grey outline. He had just crossed the road when the scream of a tram turning down from the bridge to run past the hospital was so akin to that of a dive-bombing Stuka that he grinned after the tram's swaying back. Goering's Stukas had terrorised the European mainland, but after one attack upon England no more had come over. He recalled, with far greater amusement in retrospect than he had felt at the time, an RAF briefing to the International Press Corps about ten days ago, by a disarmingly apologetic one-armed Squadron Leader. 'Actually, chaps, according to our chaps, yesterday's show was the nearest they've had to a clay-pigeon shoot. Enemy losses, thirty-three. Ours – actually – nil, chaps. Got to be fair. Stukas haven't the speed or manoeuvrability of our Spitfires and Hurricanes or their Messerschmitts. Piece of cake for our chaps . . .'

There were a few broken windows and some scattered glass in the side street, but the little restaurant seemed undamaged. A stout, handsome, black-haired woman, who could have been Italian until she spoke, ushered him on to one of the faded red plush wall settles, adjusted the position of the clean white-damask-covered table, and told him she was keeping the business going with her hubby gone for a soldier and the nippers gone for evacuees down in Somerset.

'Missing 'em cruel, I am, sir, and proper miserable they are, the poor little mites, what with the lady what's took 'em in being ever so fussy and nothing but all that grass and nasty cows and not understanding what's said. Talk ever so queer down Taunton way, seemingly. Bad as foreigners, they says. Coffee and cakes, sir? . . . Waiting for a young lady? That's nice . . . Last night, sir? Saturday night? Well, I mean, proper noisy and nasty, what with all the fires and the horrible smoke, and all those poor souls done in or hurt bad or packed off to the Rest Centres, but didn't trouble us much round here. Like my hubby's old mum says, could've done with a bit more noise. Where was our guns, eh? I dunno. Plain or fancies, sir? . . . Cakes, sir. Plain or fancy? . . . Wait for your young lady to choose? That's nice. You'll pardon the liberty, sir, but would you be Canadian?'

'American.'

'There! Should've known, shouldn't I, seeing as you've not got a uniform. Canadian gentlemen all got uniforms – and would have, wouldn't they, seeing as they're on our side. Coffee ready when you says, sir.' She bustled off to attend to another of her few customers.

Josh lit a cigarette, and the normality of the mingling aroma of nicotine, coffee and baking, and his sitting there waiting for a girl, accentuated the abnormality of the whole present. On the surface just a casual first date, he thought, but in reality an unpremeditated, unexpected arrangement. Beneath the surface swirled undercurrents that had to be disturbing, and even dangerous, for within all danger was the inevitable element of excitement. He wondered how she would look out of uniform, and was then so perturbed by his dread of disappointment, that he refused to dwell upon it. Instead he turned his mind to the proprietress' penultimate remark, and then to the continuing frustrations he and Burness had experienced after this morning's All Clear.

They had spent last night in his hotel's shelter, which they had been allowed to use because he was a resident.

After the All Clear they went out separately, having arranged to meet in their office – if it still existed – at around 9 a.m. They reached their office building within a few minutes of each other and found it relatively intact. Although the hardboard in their office windows had been pockmarked with holes, it had held; but again the electricity, tickers and telephone were dead, and the office was powdered with plaster from its cracked ceiling.

Burness was purple with fury. 'Why can't the bloody British appreciate we can help by telling the world just what is being done to London, and that to do the job we have to take a look! We're on their side, goddammit!'

'Maybe they can't be too sure we are, Pete.' He drew back the curtains to let in some light through the pockmarks. 'It's not too long since Joe Kennedy was our Ambassador here. What did he give them? Two or three weeks before they would have to pack it in? Thereabouts. They won't have forgotten, nor, I'd imagine, be in too much of a hurry to trust any ally after France.'

Burness nearly exploded. 'Kind of a new attitude for you, brother!'

'Confused attitude, Pete.'

'You don't – ' He broke off, beaming, his anger evaporated. 'Land's sakes, Miss Dewly honey! Are you one really happy sight for these sore old eyes! How've you been? And Momma?'

Miss Dewly's large, sunburnt face beamed from the open doorway. She wore an unbecoming puce headscarf and an old fawn Edwardian duster-coat of her mother's over the neat navy cotton shirtwaister she always wore on summer Mondays. 'Positively fine, thanks, Mr Burness, and how jolly nice to see you and Mr Adams! Mother and I have been rather anxious about you both. I kept trying to ring. Couldn't get through at all. Oh, my goodness, what a mess! But what pretty curtains! Both windows gone? Not to worry! I know just the glazier! Soon have it all shipshape and Bristol fashion. No sign of Mrs Harding?' She rattled on allowing them no time to answer. 'Probably having to walk from Tottenham Court Road, poor dear, as nothing seems to be running round here. Oh, the mess in poor old London, and all those poor people – doesn't bear thinking about, does it? I simply daren't trust my eyes when I saw this building still here. How's your flat, Mr Burness? Your hotel, Mr Adams?'

After they had reassured her, Josh asked, 'Did you play the tournament Saturday, Miss Dewly?'

'Actually, not quite all, Mr Adams. The men's doubles had to be postponed till next Saturday.' From her tone, play had been stopped by rain. 'But we played the mixed and ladies' doubles, and actually' – she flushed – 'my partner and I won the ladies'.'

Burness yelled, 'Miss Dewly, you are the tops!'

Josh bowed. 'Congratulations.'

'I say, thanks awfully. Actually, it was great fun, and so lucky we'd finished in time for me to horse home before things got too rowdy. Mother and I just tucked ourselves into the cosy little nook we've made under the stairs and were frightfully lucky. Not even one window cracked. But, oh, the flames from the docks! I can't tell you how it looked all Saturday night! Do tell me, has the invasion started? I left home before seven, so I missed the Home Service news, and the only train I could get on took ages and kept stopping and was jam-packed, but no one seemed to know or have today's paper. Half said it had and half that it hadn't, but no one actually knew and – oh! Sounds like Mrs Harding! Must take a peep!' She charged back to the landing to look over the banisters, pulling off the puce scarf and smoothing her short fairish pageboy bob. 'It is! Good morning, Mrs Harding! What a weekend, eh? But how jolly nice to see you, though I'm afraid there's

86

a bit of a mess waiting up here. Did you have to walk? Poor you! Not to worry. Press on regardless!'

The two Americans looked at each other and shrugged.

Ann said, 'I tried to ring your hotel before breakfast. I remembered the name from that permit you showed me. I hoped it was still around. I couldn't find out as no phones were working. Is it?'

'It is. It was good of you to try and call.'

'It was good of you to stay up with us on Saturday.'

'You and Nurse Denton were there.'

'Of course. They were our patients, we were their nurses.' She dismissed the subject and went on to tell him that Daws and the others had been evacuated. 'Because of the U/S* phones no one's yet heard if they've got there – or if they have I haven't heard.'

'Understandably.' He told her of Burness' difficulty in calling his wife. 'Right now it's easier to get through to New York than round England. Makes it tough on the married guys. Luckily that's not one of my problems,' he added to remind himself of this.

Ann looked into her coffee cup and heard Michael's voice. 'Nor mine, thanks to Martha's rules. If we want to marry we have to resign first. But this being so cut-off from the family is beginning to get me down.'

Watching her downcast face, Josh thought she was even prettier with lipstick outlining her soft, generous lips, accentuating the clearness of her flawless complexion and brightening her eyes, which her French-blue linen dress made more blue than grey. She looked younger, more vulnerable and approachable without the starch, and surprisingly and enchantingly elegant. His time in pre-war Paris had taught him to appreciate women's fashions, and one of the many things

* Unserviceable.

87

he disliked about London was English women's lack of elegance. When she first walked into the restaurant, as he had risen he had seen the flags flying and heard the trumpets. The flags had been lowered and the trumpets were silent when earlier she had talked of Ed Laurings, and he had stored much of what she said to put in the letter to his mother and the one he now knew he must write to Laurings' parents. Now he saw again the lowering of the flags in her downcast face.

'Worrying for your folks too,' he said.

She looked up. 'And yours.'

He nodded. 'Where do your folks live?'

'There's just our aunt.' She explained this briefly, and saw his eyes narrow, and was grateful that he asked no more questions and for the sympathy of his silence. 'Now, from London, Yorkshire could be on the moon. I don't know what's happening up there or down in Kent. I don't even know if the Battle of Britain's still on. Is it?'

'As ever.'

'I thought it must be.' She looked back into her cup.

Josh stayed silent. He was disturbed by all she had just said, and by his burning interest in this slight raising of the curtain on her personal life, which, incredibly, appeared to conceal no man aside from her brother.

Without looking up, Ann went on, 'It's the waiting that gets one down. The waiting, the longing and the dreading for news that's always there, at the back of one's mind. All this long, endless summer – waiting. God knows, I'm not alone. All over the country – wives, mothers, sisters, girlfriends – same set-up – the same in every war.' She glanced up, and the pain in her eyes hurt his heart. 'I don't know if at this minute Michael's alive.'

He had to help her. 'I could ask around,' he said.

She turned to him desperately. 'Would you? Could

you? No! This isn't fair. It could have someone somewhere thinking you a fifth columnist.'

'If that's so it will not be for the first time in London, and this is no crack at you. Just about every cop and warden around this weekend has had some such notion every time I've opened my mouth.'

'We're as bad as that?' she asked, very concerned.

Now he had to appease her. 'I'm exaggerating.' He produced his notebook. 'Can I have his full name, rank and number?'

She gave these, and the Squadron and Group numbers. 'He's stationed at Beacon Rise, Kent.'

He gave no sign of having recognised this from the last two numbers, and keeping his gaze on his notebook asked, 'Am I right in assuming you'd care to have me hold a watching brief?'

She studied his face before answering. On Saturday she had done so, as for years she had learnt to study patients' faces – looking for the character beneath, on which depended so much of the eventual outcome of all illness. Now she studied his bony face, that at first sight had struck her as all brow, nose and chin, and saw an oddly attractive and likeable young man. Her twinship with Michael and the particular circumstances of their childhood meant that, despite her cloistered years in Martha's, she knew far more about young men than most of her contemporaries, irrespective of whether they had brothers – as she had discovered since entering the Preliminary Training School. As she listened to the conversations on men that were her set's – as most young women's – favourite subject when they were alone together, it had seemed to her that they were talking, not of fellow human beings of a different sex, but of a rare, incomprehensible and potentially dangerous species that had always to be treated with deference and never with honesty. She had kept this to herself, even from Mary and Jill, having been disciplined into self-containment before her milk teeth had been replaced: 'Now then, Ann dearie, no more tears. Try and remember that lots of little girls have no mummies and daddies, and that you are a very lucky little girl to have kind Aunt Maud coming to take you out again at half-term. Won't that be nice! That's right, dearie. Dry your eyes – sunshine after rain – we won't talk about this any more . . .'

'It's a lot to ask, Mr Adams. We hardly know each other.'

He glanced up. 'You didn't ask. I offered. And doesn't our not being too well acquainted make it easier for the two of us?'

Ann nodded and thought, yes, you want to help me, just as you wanted to help Ed. Like everyone, you want to feel wanted – and one of the few good things Jerry's done for England is to make us all absolutely certain we are wanted, whoever we are, whatever we're doing, to 'keep the home fires burning' and put the damned things out. Only, being neutral, you feel out of it, and – as Ed was – a long way from home.

She said, 'Then, yes, please. And as you're being so kind I think I should explain that till now there's been no one I could ask. We've no RAF connections. Michael joined the RAF in '38 with a Short Service Commission. He wanted to be an airline pilot, and an RAF training was considered the best way into civil aviation. He'd worked in a bank since leaving school. Not his line. Neither of us thought this war would happen till the summer of last year. I know now that was wishful thinking, but that was how we thought. I knew some of his RAF friends, but none are – are around now. But, please, don't risk getting in a spot over this.'

'I guess that can be avoided. I have a good RAF contact who happens to be a very nice guy. He should keep me informed without getting me up against a wall facing a firing squad. Any news, I'll pass straight on to you.'

'Any. Any type. Please.'

'Sure. How do I contact you? Call you or write?'

'We aren't allowed phone calls on duty, but a message to my Home or Matron's Office with a number I can ring back will reach me as soon as I'm off – when the phones work.' She gave both numbers. 'Letters should be care of Matron's Office, St Martha's, London. I'm A. L. Marlowe.' She watched him scribbling shorthand. 'The truth, Mr Adams.'

'That's our deal, Miss Marlowe.'

She leant against the settle back. 'Thank you very much.'

He inclined his head in acknowledgement rather than voice some conventional response which events might prove to be unforgettable and even unforgivable. He knew too little about her, and about young Englishwomen in general, to tell whether she realised there was more to this offer than altruism. Had she been American or French, he would have known she expected – and was willing for – a pass when they fixed this date. But all he really knew now was that he had just chosen to embark upon a course over very thin ice. At the same time, as his emotions were clouding his judgement, he ignored the powerful emotional effect that the events of this last weekend and the approaching prospect of tonight were exerting on both of them.

Ann looked at him thoughtfully. She recognised the expression he was trying to keep out of his eyes and knew that it was releasing within her sensations no other young man had yet managed to arouse. I could fall for him, she thought, but there'd be no future in it, for we live and work in, and come from, different worlds. And then she thought, how much future have either of us got? Who in their senses would bet tuppence on our being alive tomorrow?

'My name's Ann,' she said.

'Josh.'

'From Boston, Mass.,' she said absently, and then asked eagerly, 'Was Henry James right, Josh?'

That he suddenly liked her immensely, made the ice thinner by edging sexual attraction towards intriguingly complex dimensions that were new to him. 'I'll answer that shortly when you have nine hours to spare, Ann. You go for Henry James?'

'In a big way. You?'

'Kindred spirit.'

She sat up straight. 'You're not telling me you know your *Anne of Green Gables*?'

He smiled. 'Time was.'

The unexpected pleasure that invariably accompanies the discovery of an affinity in literary tastes, their mutual longing for even a temporary escape from reality, heightening interest in each other, and the great resilience of their youth, enabled them to forget the war for the next half-hour. They were just agreeing that *The Great Gatsby* was one of the finest of twentieth-century novels when she remembered the time. 'Ten past. I'm due in uniform at twelve-thirty lunch and must fly! Terribly sorry, Josh, and thanks very much for the coffee and everything.'

He had risen with her. 'I'm due back at the Min. of Inf. at half-twelve. I'll just get the check and walk you – '

'No need, thanks. Take care. Cheerio.'

'And you take care. I'll be in touch.'

She smiled from the doorway, then vanished behind the hardboard-battened glass door and papered windows. There was no sign of her when he followed a few minutes later. On the far side of the main road he stopped for another look at the ugly grey Nurses' Home over the way, which his photographic memory imprinted in his memory for life, though he never saw it again. In the small hours of the next morning and fifteen minutes before the next All Clear, a five-hundred-pound high explosive sliced through the roof, exploded somewhere between the third and second floors, and in seconds reduced the building to a mound of rubble. At one side the cement path caved in, blocking the only underground passage connecting the House to the hospital basement.

The roar of the explosion and the collapsing building, and the reverberation of the blast, shook buildings and basements on both sides of the road. But by one of the freaks of sound and blast that were becoming common, the area least affected was immediately under the point of impact, and the overwhelming majority of the probationers slept on undisturbed.

Ann was jolted from a nightmare about Laurings with Michael's face, Josh Adams in a long white coat talking in the SSO's Oxford English tenor, and Nurse Denton wailing, 'I can't find the cards, nurse, I can't find the cards!' Fumbling for the torch under her pillow she felt the Home sway gently as Mary Cavendor gasped, 'He's got the hospital!' All round the darkened ballroom throat and pocket torches flickered on like fireflies, while down river roared the last formation of German aircraft returning to base.

Nurse Francis called from the end nearest the hall, 'Stay put, all of you, till I get back!' She rushed out, switching on one pair of wall lights and leaving the hall doors open. Just audible was the ringing of the telephone in Home Sister's office, which lay off the hall and was now fitted with her camp bed. The iron discipline of their training kept all the staff nurses on their mattresses. Like a well-drilled chorus they sat up and did their hair, for the swiftest method of getting into uniform was to put the cap on first. When Nurse Francis returned with Miss Merton, the Home Sister, Ann's hair was unplaited, combed out, and coiled up in a high, thick, tidy bun.

93

The Home Sisters' posts were reserved for former ward Sisters who were nearing retirement. Miss Merton's elderly face was pinched with shock. She wore a dressing-gown, a long flannel nightgown, and bedroom slippers, and her grey hair was plaited in a thin untidy pigtail. Despite the shock her voice was steady as she said, 'Nurses, I am sorry to tell you the Junior Home has had a direct hit.' She ignored the communal sharp intake of breath, and went on, 'As far as can be ascertained the whole building is down and all approaches to the Junior basement are blocked, so we have no means of knowing the condition of those inside. Matron, the police, the Fire Brigade and the ARP have been alerted, all the residents called up, and Matron is asking for eight volunteer staff nurses to help in the rescue work.' Every right arm shot up. 'Thank you, nurses, just eight – and Matron will accept none from Casualty, the theatres, Mary* and Florence.'† She looked swiftly around as some arms dropped reluctantly. 'Nurses Evans – Blore – Dawton – de Grey – Marlowe – Cavendor – Ash – Hartley.' Each leapt up at her name. 'Wait, nurses! Give your names and wards to Nurse Francis, then go up to your rooms in pairs for civilian clothes and bring them down here to dress unless the All Clear goes first, as it may now that it seems quiet above. Matron particularly said warm clothes, your thickest gloves and shoes, unless you have boots, and, if you possess any, trousers.' The enormity of that last dispensation went unnoticed in the urgency of the moment.

As the eight vanished, a chorus demanded, 'How many down there, Sister?'

'One hundred, in all, nurses. Miss Hamilton' – the Junior Home Sister – 'Sister Preliminary Training School, seventy-eight first-year and twenty Preliminary Training School probationers.'

* Maternity, Block 2.   † The sick nurses' ward.

94

No one in the ballroom asked more nor spoke again until the All Clear sounded. As it did so, the eight nurses were beginning to cross the road in the blackout. The darkness was made more impenetrable by the cloud of dust rising from what, at ground level, looked like a small mountain of rubble that only a miracle could save from proving to be a massive communal grave.

Jill de Grey grabbed Ann. 'Can't see a damn inch and don't dare think of those poor little pros.'

'Nor me,' lied Ann, haunted by the memory of Fenner's childish delight in spotting her first aircraft with big black crosses. 'No – I think I see Matron.' She moved ahead, Jill clutched her shoulder and the others followed in single file, each holding the shoulder ahead like blinded walking-wounded, for the closer they drew to the ruins the more blinding the dust became.

In the several roomy cellars converted into dormitories in the Junior basement, Nurse Fenner and the majority of the occupants slept on. It was a little while after the All Clear before the few who were awake realised what had occurred. Even then their knowledge was limited, for they had no electricity and the beams of their torches were too weak to expose the depths of the new multiple cracks in the walls and ceiling.

'Quiet, please, nurse. Don't wake the others. Just go back to sleep,' whispered Miss Hamilton and Sister PTS, who were going separately from dormitory to dormitory by torchlight. 'No, nurse, no one's hurt, all quite well. Try and go back to sleep . . .". . . No, dear, we can't get out just yet . . .". . . Yes, dear, our stairs are blocked . . .". . . Well, yes, dear, the tunnel is blocked, but nothing to worry about. Help will reach us soon, and we've air down here for at least twenty-four hours.' This last was an invention decided upon between the Sisters as neither knew the truth. 'We'll be helped out soon. Just go back to sleep, nurse.'

Their reassurances comforted some more than others,

but as no one had been hurt, it was still the small hours, and they were all very tired, with rare exceptions the probationers went back to sleep. The unimaginative, thankfully; the imaginative, praying silently.

Taking turns the Sisters got into uniform, and between torchlit rounds they retreated to confer in their shared bedroom, a former housemaid's cupboard. Miss Hamilton, considerably the older and frailer, shook her white, lace-frilled head. 'They are being so good, but they are all so young. Most are not more than children. I am so thankful so many are sleeping so soundly.'

Sister PTS looked with covert anxiety at her senior's shadowy face. 'Healthy children are generally sound sleepers, Sister. Won't you sit down for a little rest?'

'Not just now, thank you, Sister. I must get back to my gels. Yours still behaving well?'

'Very. Most sleeping their heads off. My present set are a sensible bunch. Several are ex-VADs in their early twenties, and their being older helps to steady the younger ones.'

'No doubt. How – er – how long do you think it may be before we are released, Sister?'

'Perhaps an hour or two.' Sister PTS was firmly cheerful. She had just returned from another private inspection of the rubble blocking both sets of basement stairs and the tunnel to the hospital. 'I just hope the hospital has been spared.'

'Indeed, Sister. Indeed!'

They stopped talking to listen for sounds from above, but they were too deeply buried to hear any. The voice speaking through a police megaphone some forty feet above their ceiling was heard only by the small army of rescuers and observers standing momentarily motionless around the mass of rubble and masonry.

'This is the SSO speaking . . . This is the SSO speaking . . . If you can hear me, please call or tap in answer . . . If you can hear me, please call or tap in

96

answer . . . If you are hurt, please try and lie still . . . If you are hurt, please lie still . . . If you are not hurt, lie down if you can . . . If you are not hurt, lie down if you can . . . We are working to get you out . . . Help will reach you soon . . . The hospital is undamaged and the All Clear has gone . . . We will reach you soon and get you all out . . . Can you hear me? . . . This is the SSO speaking . . . I will repeat all I have just said . . .'

Three times came long, slow repetition; three times, the long silence. Then the SSO threw the megaphone down to the nearest Special Constable and climbed down carefully. He wore a sweater and slacks over pyjamas, riding gloves, and on his bare feet Wellington boots – the last three nights had taught him that these were the safest civilian footwear after air attacks. He had left his white coat with Matron before climbing to the position most likely to be audible from below, in the opinion of the officials from the Auxiliary Fire Service, the ARP, and the police, all of whom were fast becoming experts in these matters. They had reluctantly allowed him to do the talking when he insisted that the voice of one of the hospital staff would be less alarming than a stranger's to any nurses still alive.

Immediately he reached the ground the work went on, as before, in silence. The slowly returning dawn light was penetrating the dust cloud to reveal that the mound was precariously based on huge chunks of masonry that any untoward noise or vibration might cause to slide deeper. The police had cordoned off a stretch of the main road, from the approach to the bridge to just past the hospital's far end, and were stopping unauthorised pedestrians from using the nearside pavement. The only sounds were the quickly stifled dust-induced coughs of the rescue workers, and the incessant soft clinks as stones, slates and broken glass were added to the growing heaps behind the last members of the human chains running like the spokes of a rimless wheel from the inner chain encircling the mound. The work had to be done by hand until the experts forming the inner chain considered it safe to use pickaxes and spades. The spokes were formed by Martha's 'own': firemen, wardens and fire watchers on the night-shift; the eight day staff nurses; ten junior housemen; and eight of the ten final-year medical students in temporary residence on the non-stop fortnightly rota worked by their year. All the residents and medical students had volunteered, but only a limited number had been given permission to join the SSO at the site by Dr White, the senior resident, as professionally physicians took precedence over surgeons. He had had to keep back medical staff for the hospital and, like Miss Merton, had picked the youngest and strongest volunteers to help in the rescue work. Mr Yeo, the senior of the two surgical registrars, was temporary acting SSO in the hospital under the preplanned arrangements for coping with an incident (the official term) of this nature. Matron's consent was needed before day staff nurses could volunteer, and no volunteers were permitted from among the day Sisters, day student nurses or night nurses. None of the day Sisters or night nurses protested at this decision, the former fully appreciating it, and the latter being too busy to think upon it, because the night raids were doubling the work in their invariably heavy eleven-hour shifts. But it caused the Home Sister in the Senior (Student) Nurses' Home to be confronted by the first near-mutiny of Martha's nurses.

The Senior Home backed on to the terrace on the bridge side of Block 1. It easily housed the three most senior student years, as at any time one-third of the fourth years and half of the third and second years were on nights, and approximately 10 per cent of all student nurses were either sick or on sick-leave. (When days off had been allocated at the rate of one a month, the sick-leave had been 25 per cent in the Senior Home and

40 per cent in the Junior. Several months of allowing one day free each week had reduced that 40 per cent to 15 per cent.) After the All Clear, the large front hall was crammed with furiously protesting young women in pyjamas and nighties. The Home Sister had to shout to be heard.

'Nurses! Please! Listen! Of course I understand your feelings, but you must understand Matron's position! Matron has first of all to think of our patients, and so must you! Think of your patients, nurses! Those in now, and those who may come in later today or not improbably in what is left of tonight! You have all to be on duty at seven-thirty, and your patients – your wards – are going to need you. Whatever the outcome of this – this distressing incident, no probationers will be allowed on duty today, and you will have to do their work and your own! You need your rest. You have a heavy day ahead of you. Go back to your dormitories. I promise to give you any news immediately I receive it. Go back to bed, nurses!' No one moved. The Home Sister looked for the nearest fourth-year and directly addressed Nurse Denton. 'Please, nurses. Now!'

Nurse Denton, in pink cotton pyjamas and her hair in shortish pigtails, glanced around at the motionless, sullen crowd, and for the first time at Martha's recognised the advantage of her seniority in age. She clapped her hands exactly as had, at some time, a schoolmistress of every nurse present. 'Come along, girls! Back to bed! Standing here creating is helping no one. Back to bed till the getting-up bell, and if you can't sleep just rest the poor old feet. Come along! All of you! Bed!' She was too upset about the pros to hear the authority in her voice, and too relieved at seeing the crowd dispersing angrily – but dispersing nevertheless – to notice the way Home Sister was watching her or to suspect that she had just cemented the previously precarious foundations of her future at Martha's.

The basement lights went out, but the mutiny lingered in the angry, restless silence. At the first jangle of the bell, like an avalanche in reverse, the student nurses swept up the stairs to crowd those bedrooms facing the main road. It was just light enough for the blackout screens to be hauled down from cracked or gaping windows, and just visible through the dust-haze were the empty road and the growing line of spectators on the far pavement. The angle of Block 1 hid ruins and rescuers, but they could hear the soft clinking and recognise its implications. It was only then that they properly appreciated the nearness of their own near-miss.

Mutiny went out like a light and took with it the comfort of 'it can't happen to me' that for the majority had been their most powerful support since Saturday evening. As young women born either during, or in the shadow of, the Great War, they had absorbed from infancy their parents' or war-widowed mothers' memories of the millions of men killed in that war, and the traditional belief, still extant, that wars were fought by men against men. They knew that since Saturday in London hundreds of women had been killed and thousands injured, but the air war was too new for them to be able yet to think of these casualties as other than 'patients'. They had had to accept that sometimes patients died and, to varying degrees, they found this distressing. But the pros weren't patients. Just pros – *us*. Only, being pros – the lucky little so-and-so's – they only worked till eight and not nine, then went off to supper, then chapel, then bed and lights-off at ten-thirty. No chapel last night as the raid had started, but they'd all been sent off at eight as usual. Now they could all be dead. Just ordinary pros, now buried alive or dead, those student nurses thought as they crowded into the front bedrooms. Now they learned for life the ugly truth that air raid casualties in cities, towns, villages, were just ordinary people living their ordinary lives until hit by the bombs, and that the bombs did not discriminate between men, women, children, active servicemen or civvy nurses.

They washed and dressed rapidly, and until ten to seven, when they could leave for breakfast, broke into little groups of special friends. Companionship was as necessary as breathing. They sat huddled together on bared bedsprings, sharing subdued conversations and cigarettes, and though smoking in uniform and in their bedrooms was forbidden the Home Sister, smelling the nicotine smoke, ignored it. Then in little groups they streamed from their Home and silently skirted the front of the towering mass of rubble encircled by the human chain and spokes, under the hovering dust cloud. Their eyes searched for familiar faces that, even so, were barely recognisable owing to the dust greying heads and caking faces and clothes. A few noticed without interest that two women wore slacks, garments normally forbidden to female staff in Martha's or its immediate vicinity as women in trousers were regarded with anathema by the general public of both sexes. It was only with difficulty that anyone recognised one tall man as the SSO, though he was currently regarded in the Senior Home as the most glamorous man in Martha's.

Nurse Denton's urgently searching eyes belatedly recognised one of the two women in slacks as Nurse Marlowe, and catching her eye mouthed, 'Any news?' At the shake of the greyed head she walked on with her two friends, hugging her cloak around her, inclining her neat, capped head to Matron, who was standing to one side of the nearest gateless entrance, as they went by to cross Casualty Yard and go into the hospital through Central Hall. Going up the twenty-two stone steps to the portico that the Victorians had flanked with lifesize stone figures of ragged, crippled children on makeshift crutches, she said, 'Marlowe looks like an old woman, but at least she's doing something.

Far worse for Matron having to stand and watch and wait.'

One of her friends said, 'And face their parents.'

'Yes. Especially those of the minors for whom she's legally in loco parentis until they're twenty-one. Little Fenner's only nineteen.'

'Fenner? Who's – oh yes. That pretty, untidy kid in PPW who'll be a knock-out glamour girl when she –' The speaker stopped abruptly.

They walked on in silence, through Central Hall, down the main corridor to the dining-room and the most silent day nurses' breakfast in Martha's history. The fact that it was, unusually, attended by all the day Sisters evoked only occasional, incurious glances.

Matron had refused the offer that a chair be brought out for her and had been standing in the entrance that Josh had used, and that gave the widest view of the scene, for the past three hours. Neatly piled on a red rubber mackintosh sheet by her feet were the residents' white coats. She was seldom alone. Constantly changing officials kept appearing at her side. Senior police and fire officers, the Night Sister, the Professors, the Dean, the Hospital Secretary, Dr White, Mr Yeo, and as time dragged on, singly or in pairs, black-jacketed, pinstriped honoraries who had heard the news in Harley or Wimpole Street and driven as close as they could then left their cars and walked on. From time to time the Matron broke off a murmured conversation as the work was suddenly halted as someone thought he or she had heard sounds from below. Each time after 'This is the SSO speaking . . .' there was nothing but silence and the work went on, and under the folds of her long cloak the knuckles of Matron's clasped, cold hands were white.

'I am so sorry, Commander . . . Chief Inspector . . . Dr – . . . Mr – , you were saying?'

'Ah – yes, Matron. In connection with . . .'

Ann worked in a spoke a few yards from Matron that was headed by a hospital fireman, with Hugh Dixon, a medical student, in second place, Mary in third, Ann fourth, and the last in line, Paddy Brown, Dixon's 'pair'. (All Martha's medical students working anywhere in the hospital were 'paired'.) Ann and Mary had worked with the two students in Casualty at different times earlier this year, and all four had formed themselves into a quartet for the same reason that the student nurses had huddled together before breakfast. Ann had lost all sense of time, and all awareness of her stinging eyes and aching arms, shoulders and back, but not of what must surely be at the end of this living nightmare, when Big Ben struck seven as she handed Paddy Brown another load of broken slates.

Unwittingly, he thought aloud. 'Mother of God – but whose side is God on?'

Her warning glance was too late. The SSO, returning from talking to Matron, was just behind him. He tapped the gangling boy's shoulder and jerked his head then backed a couple of yards. Paddy Brown lowered the slates gently, then hurried to him. 'Sorry, sir. Forgot.'

Mr Wesley's face was too caked with dust to have any expression but his bloodshot eyes were furious. 'If you can't keep your big mouth shut, Brown, get the hell out of it or I'll – ' Suddenly diverted by something behind the student, he shot off. Paddy Brown glanced back. The SSO was making for a senior police officer and a tall young man in a belted mackintosh and brown trilby who stood on the pavement just to the left of the entrance. Paddy shrugged thankfully and went back to his post. Taking the next chunk from Ann he breathed into her ear, 'Saved by the bell before he had me out for the count.'

Ann glanced round, momentarily froze with a new apprehension, then savagely reminded herself of Josh's job and that he couldn't have known he would see her

103

now. Nor did he appear to be looking for her or anyone in particular. He was looking slowly, detachedly, all around, and his gaze rested upon her then moved on without recognition. She was raising a hand to attract his attention when Mary passed the next load.

Half an hour ago in Whitehall, whilst discussing the night's events with a grey-haired and unusually forthcoming warden, who was a City accountant by day, Josh said, 'So the same targets.'

'You could say that. Usual targets had the usual plastering, though nothing worth mentioning dropped close to this side of the river in my patch.'

Josh's eyes flickered. 'Close on the other side?'

'Afraid so, old chap. Nasty business. One got St Martha's. Nurses' Home.'

Josh felt as if he had been kicked in the stomach. 'Direct hit?'

'Slap on target. All down. Damn bad show. Pack of girls doing a damned fine job.'

'I guess I'll take a look.' He strode off.

The warden eyed his back with distaste. Chap in his job had to be a cool customer, but there was something rather unpleasant about his eagerness to be in at the kill. Of course, one had to remember he was just another of those damned neutrals getting under everyone's feet. But a fast mover. Chap had passed the sandbagged Cenotaph already and actually remembered to raise his hat.

Josh strode on, broken glass, bomb splinters and strewn rubble crunching beneath his feet. He was oblivious to his surroundings until he was over the bridge and was stopped by the policeman guarding the cordoning rope. Then he was able to get a look through the dust at the ruins of the building he had looked at yesterday and see the ant-like figures shifting the rubble with their hands.

The policeman returned his credentials. 'All Press on the far pavement only, sir.'

'Thanks.' He stepped over the rope and began walking towards the far side, then wheeled round to shadow the police officer who was crossing the road and making for the entrance facing the ruins. The officer reached the nearside pavement before discovering he had a shadow and waved aside the offered permits. 'All Press the other side of the road.'

Playing for time, Josh dropped his wallet, which spilled its contents on the pavement.

'After a good story, Mr Adams?' The quiet query had an icy undertone that stung like a whiplash.

Josh straightened, shuffling permits, and in the couple of seconds it took him to place the speaker, the police officer demanded, 'Gentleman a friend of yours, Mr Wesley?'

'We've met. As far as I'm concerned he can stay put, providing he doesn't move or open his mouth.' He swung away, knowing he'd only spoken up for the damned chap because he'd been Laurings' pal and put up rather a decent show on Saturday. Turning into a soft touch, thought Mr Wesley furiously – fury was his only defence to the unaccustomed turbulence of his emotions. He was justly proud that he possessed the unemotional temperament essential to good surgery. He was a very good surgeon who many, including himself, were convinced would rise to the top of his profession. But the thought of what he was certain must lie under this rubble not only aroused all his humane instincts, but cracked open all his young male Anglo-Saxon attitudes to young women and war. Bloody monstrous set-up, he fumed mentally, returning to his place in a spoke. Women and girls had no place in war. If he could swing it, he'd have every woman and girl out of London in the next twenty-four hours, he decided, forgetting – as he had more prudently since qualifying twelve years ago – that nurses were women and girls; forgetting too the consequences to any hospital which might attempt to function without them for five minutes.

The police officer gave Josh a hard look and without further comment moved away to talk to Matron. The officer was not too sorry the American bloke had a friend at court. Though a keen disciplinarian who normally had no time for reporters, he harboured a never-voiced and deep-rooted dislike of censorship. And in the early editions of the morning papers he had glanced at shortened accounts of the reports of this weekend's raids that had appeared in yesterday's American papers. He thought the American reporters in London had written some very nice things about Londoners, and more than a bit that wasn't nice but needed to be said. 'Good morning, Matron. Bit warmer than yesterday.'

'Good morning, Chief Inspector. Yes, quite a bit warmer.'

Josh, overhearing, shot them a bemused glance, then again quartered the scene with his eyes. Belatedly, he recognised Ann. Relief so drained the colour from his face that Matron, happening to glance in his direction, beckoned him to her. 'Are you feeling quite well, young man?'

He raised his hat. 'Surely, ma'am. Thank you so – ' He was silenced by her upraised hand. All work had suddenly stopped, and all the rescuers stood poised and staring in the same direction. A small, still intact portion of the basement ceiling had been exposed.

The amateurs were waved back to leave pickaxes and spades to experts, and as they backed away, only their bodies, not their eyes, moved. Matron, the Chief Inspector, and Dr White, racing from Casualty to join them, moved closer; the Head Porter and Dacey, following as swiftly, stopped dead, to watch from Casualty Yard; and Josh remained unnoticed just inside the gateless entrance. And then, after the first two blows of a pickaxe, there came from below a distant fusillade of tapping. Josh, instinctively loosening the knot of his tie, dragged his gaze from Ann's dust-caked, averted face and looked around. It was as if none present dared trust their ears, look at each other, or even breathe. They stood as if literally petrified, staring in the same direction. He glanced back across the road and saw the lines of figures stiffen in unison, but could not hear the whispers of 'Something's happening' rippling along that far pavement, or see the only reporter amongst them, a cub from a London local paper, nudge his photographer away from the sports page of yesterday's *Daily Mirror*.

In a few minutes the first small gap was made, and Mr Wesley, lying on his face, called down, 'This is the SSO speaking. If you can hear me, please answer.'

The reply was immediate, distant, but clear. 'This is Sister Preliminary Training School speaking, Mr Wesley. Thank you, we can hear you. We are all well down here. All quite well. What do you wish us to do to help?'

– Five –

'What annoys me about this war, Mrs Harris,' observed Sister Hope to the patient whose bed she and Ann were making at seven-forty the following Sunday morning, 'is the way it has made us temporarily abandon evening Visitors.'

Mrs Harris, darkly jaundiced by an advanced, incurable renal condition that had had her in and out of Hope for years, said she didn't mind missing evenings so long as it was still two-to-four Sundays. 'My Mabel and my neighbour Mrs Pinker'll be up s' afternoon, Sister. Mrs Pinker'll lend Mabel an arm seeing she's carrying her third and there's all the muck and holes about. Ever so kind is Mrs Pinker. Couldn't have a better neighbour.'

'How very fortunate, my dear. But I thought your daughter had been evacuated with her children?'

'That's right, Sister, only can't abide it down the country, Mabel can't. Been fretting cruel for her dad and me all week she has, so seeing the nippers have taken to the lady as took 'em in, Mabel's just popped back for a visit. Not as I holds with it, and I'll tell her so, Sister! She's got no cause to fret, what with me looked after lovely in here and her dad not able to do more than wet his whistle afore Mrs Pinker fetches him out the pub and down the shelter of a night. I'll say this for Jerry, he's always on time.'

'Yes, his nightly raids are punctual. Comfortable,

Mrs Harris? Good.' Sister Hope, sleeves up, cuffs in pocket, whisked the hardbacked chair for the neatly stripped bedclothes to the foot of the next bed, whilst Ann cantered alongside with the double-shelved metal trolley stacked with clean bedlinen. All the patients had to have been washed, their beds remade, and the ward swept, dusted and tidied before 8 a.m. ward prayers that immediately preceded the patients' breakfasts, and on Sunday mornings all the patients' bedlinen was changed. This routine, on this particular morning of Sunday, 15 September, was regarded by the student nurses in every ward as a further turn of the rack. The subsequent sorting of dirty linen, and where necessary 'mopping',* was part of the pros' routine work, and from last Tuesday Martha's had been pro-less.

Ann, bed-making at the double – Sister Hope's age did not impair her speed – noticed the martyred expressions of the second-years doing the pros' early morning cleaning. She reflected that the milk of human kindness now flowing round Martha's was no longer extended to the pros by their immediate seniors. A few days had transformed them from 'the poor little pros' to 'those lucky leadswingers on a week's buckshee hols'. Just now at breakfast, which, since Tuesday, had been attended by the day Sisters, the latter had discreetly averted their eyes from the outraged faces at the second- and third-year tables when Night Sister announced that when the week's leave granted to all the probationers ended, only those in the Preliminary Training School would return to London to finish their term. The whole first year would be transferred to Emergency Medical Services Hospitals in the country, and for the duration of the war Matron would allow

* Rinsing dirty linen clean of blood and other stains before depositing it in the wet-linen bin.

no probationers, nor any student nurse or VAD under twenty-one, to work in Martha's.

Sister Hope, with the same discretion, had delayed her arrival on duty by a couple of minutes. When Ann arrived ahead of her, the student nurses were giving their views in the clinical[†] room that doubled as the nurses' cloakroom. Pre-Tuesday the four student nurses would have vanished when Ann appeared. Now they turned to her for sympathy, leaving the floor to Nurse Sellars, the third-year now promoted senior day student nurse in Hope. Nurse Sellars was twenty-three, sharply pretty and very angry. 'Honestly, Nurse Marlowe, what we could do to Jerry! We can take this blitzing and having all days off cancelled and not knowing till we come on in the morning if we've got a ten-to-one or two-to-five and having all our DILs scrounged by the basement wards and half the day staff scrounged by the night and breaking our backs with the Rope Trick! But life without pros and having to go back to all the skivvying and bedpan rounds is more than flesh and blood can stand – and if I wasn't taking Finals in November I wouldn't stand it! I'd blow out my lamp this morning and join the ATS even if they have the most hideous uniform invented! Wouldn't you feel the same?'

'Exactly. Only I'd pick the WRNS. Smashing caps. That sounds like Sister,' she added under her breath, hanging on her peg her cloak, gasmask, and 'shelter-bag'. The latter was another of the numerous innovations since Tuesday, and had to be carried by every member of the nursing staff going on or off duty to their mattresses, day or night. The receptacles were their spare clean laundry bags that had always to be embroidered with their names in large letters, and contained a full change of uniform, a minimum of three spare clean aprons, nightwear, washing things, towel, brush, comb and any small,

[†] Urine-testing.

110

especially precious personal possessions. In Ann's were leather-framed photographs of her aunt and Michael, and the smallish, flat leather writing-case in which were the five letters she had had since Tuesday. The shortest, from Josh Adams, had come on Wednesday; the longest, from Michael, yesterday; those from her aunt, Mrs Brigham-Smythe and Nurse Fenner on Friday. She had not yet answered the last two, and had replied to Michael's in the ballroom during the early part of last night's raid and posted it in the box in Central Hall on her way to breakfast.

On Tuesday morning, once it was certain all the occupants of the Junior basement were unharmed and could be safely brought out, Ann had had no time to exchange more than a strained smile with Josh before racing back to her Home to bath, wash her hair, get into uniform, and breakfast before going on duty. All eight staff nurses reached their wards or departments by 8.45 a.m., and the SSO, ten housemen and eight medical students, damp-haired and freshly shaven, started their official working day as usual at 9 a.m. The eight staff nurses were given two-to-fives that afternoon to make up lost sleep, and when they returned to duty all the probationers had been sent home in civilian clothes loaned by the Senior Home.

'We looked,' wrote Nurse Fenner to Ann, 'just like all those school kids evacuated from London when the war started, only we didn't have labels tied on us. We had to wear our own black uniform stockings and shoes – we nearly died of shame! I'm livid about sleeping through all the fun. I didn't wake till one of my set shook me to tell me a fireman was about to come through our ceiling. I thought she was so mean not to wake me sooner. What's worse is that Daddy's just had a letter from Matron saying my set are moving to some huge place in Hampshire – Daddy says it used to be a loony-bin till the EMS took it over – and that I can't work in London till I'm twenty-one. Nearly two years! The war's bound to be over by then, so I thought I'd write to say goodbye to you as I don't expect you'll still be in Martha's then. I hope you don't mind my writing, but I was terribly sorry the PPW closed . . .'

Last Tuesday marked a turning point in Martha's war. During the day the whole of Mary* was evacuated to the country; the wards' night staff were doubled and Casualty's trebled; the first four fourteen-bedded basement wards opened to take every DIL in the hospital, staffed by senior staff nurses as acting Sisters, fourth-years as acting staff nurses – one of these was Nurse Denton – with the remaining nursing staff solely composed of third-years. In the widespread general post, Ann replaced Nurse Standing in Hope, and Nurse Sellars moved up. Before that night's Alert, a new, infinitely swifter method of evacuating above-ground wards was evolved – no one seemed to know by whom – and the grapevine's choice varied hourly and ranged from Sir Joshua Levy, the senior honorary general surgeon, Matron, the SSO, Mr Billings of Repairs and Works, to Dacey. The new method used that night, and every night since, was known throughout Martha's as the Rope Trick before Tuesday's Alert faded, and accounted for the ten-foot lengths of rope now looped around the lower footrails of Hope's eighteen occupied beds.

It was not just Martha's war which changed course that day. On the previous night, as Josh and Ann had anticipated, a few thousand Londoners copied the example of the first few hundred and bought platform tickets and spent the raid on Underground platforms. On Tuesday night around ten thousand streamed down in orderly queues. All round London joyous cheers greeted the tremendous barrage of ack-ack fire that met the first incoming formation of German aircraft.

* The Maternity Block.

The barrage was kept up during the whole of that night's raid, and on the following nights. By that night of Tuesday, 10 September, the tidal wave of London's indignation at the guns' silence had swept through the highest places and the Officer Commanding London's Anti-Aircraft Command had ordered every gun to fire every possible round and regard every aircraft as an enemy target, as no RAF would be operational over London. (This demonstration of the weight of public opinion was shortly followed by another when people were officially allowed to use Underground platforms as public shelters without the need for platform tickets.)

'When at last we heard our guns on our last night,' Mrs Brigham-Smythe wrote to Ann from Edinburgh, 'we were even sadder to be leaving dear old London. But my husband's telegram insisted. I had to see his angle and think of our boys, and Cook and Ellen, who have been with us years, are far from young and have no homes but ours. Matron could not have been more understanding, but I feel so guilty at leaving you all without even an *au'voir* to you and dear old Sister PPW, now banished to the EMS! We left home earlyish yesterday – just locked up and left – and I will draw a veil over our cramped, sixteen-hour train journey to this austerely lovely grey city where, as Cook has just remarked, "Wouldn't say as they've heard there's a war on, madam" . . .'

Ann passed on this remark in her reply to Michael. 'Aunt Maud', she continued, 'is meeting it in Yorkshire. She says she can't wait to get back amongst those that know it's on and if Jerry doesn't get cracking and invade, arthritis or no arthritis, she's going back home. She's terribly grateful for your postcards, and so am I for your letter that came in today's second post.' She stopped writing to listen to another barrage of ack-ack and stare again at the postscript to Michael's three scribbled pages that he had explained were written between scrambles sitting on the grass in front of the dispersal hut.

The PS read: '1910 hrs. As the Yanks say, another day another buck. Ref./Yanks: A chap called Lefty Smith I hadn't run into since he was one of our instructors in FTS* dropped in today. He says the one you have in tow is a good type. *Why no gen?* Love. M.'

She had already briefly explained Josh, and what mesmerised her in that PS was the first line. Today's been another day, she thought tensely, glancing at her watch, which showed 11.10 p.m., then round the still lighted ballroom. Mary, on her right, was already asleep, as were half the others. Only she and Jill de Grey were sitting up writing letters; the rest were reading. Unusually since Tuesday night, all were present. Martha's zone had remained outside the main targets, but for the past four nights the hospital had taken some of the casualties from other zones, and always the theatre nurses, and twice the Casualty, had been called up.

She went back to her letter: 'Our outside phones still keep going U/S, and presumably will whilst what everyone in London's now calling "our blitz" lasts. I expect you've heard our ack-ack's now doing its stuff, and if you've got the inside gen on why, do tell me. I haven't a clue, but their ghastly row is hitting us like shots in the arm. Literally. Works just like a sweet lullaby, I expect because there's something gloriously satisfying and relaxing in the feeling that at last we're hitting back.

'Another thing hitting Martha's is a universal attack of sweetness and light that's making us all terribly matey and putting a hideous strain on old arch enemies and all who till this last week have regarded etiquette as Holy Writ. We're so all-girls-together in this ballroom that we're using Christian names – just like being back at school.'

She didn't mention the Junior Home to Michael,

* Flying Training School.

nor had she in her reply to Aunt Maud last night. I'll bet Jill isn't telling Dick Lofthouse, she thought, glancing at her friend. Jill, in a fluffy pink bedjacket, with her short straight flaxen hair falling forward to brush her engagingly youthful pink cheeks, was writing to a former Senior House Physician who was now a Surgeon-Lieutenant RNVR in a battle cruiser in the Far East Fleet.

Jill looked up, her blue eyes smiling. 'I've just decided to nurse the Navy when my OPD* job ends next summer. Dick says there's a smashing naval hospital in Hong Kong. I think Hong Kong'll be a wizard spot for our wedding.'

Ann was entranced. 'You never told us Dick had proposed.'

Jill smiled serenely. 'He hasn't. He will. I'll fix him then gladden his manly heart by falling into his arms crying girlishly, "Dick, darling, this is so sudden!" '

'Blushing girlishly, of course!'

'Ducks, I'll be puce from holding my breath till he spits it out.'

Ann's yelp of laughter evoked a deep sigh from Nurse Standing at the other end. Then, torn between her sense of dignity as an acting Sister and her conviction that we should all pull together in the lifeboat, she said in a stage-whisper, 'I'm all for your laughing like a drain, Ann, but do remember the sleepers – and it is after eleven.'

'Sorry, Nancy.'

Nurse Francis lowered her book. 'So it is. Who's ready for lights-out?' All those still awake raised their hands, except Ann and Jill. 'Sorry, kids, outvoted. I'll give you three minutes.'

'Thanks, Judy,' they chorused softly.

When the lights were out Jill leaned towards Ann

* Out-Patients Department.

to murmur, 'Worse than school dorms. No midnight feasts. I'll have to cure my night starvation with impure thoughts of Dick. 'Night.'

''Night,' murmured Ann, smiling in the darkness at Jill's unfailing ability to retreat into sexual fantasies that had been the particular envy of their set during their first year. The rest of us wept on the clean blankets in linen-cupboards, she reflected, but Jill just rested her face on the blankets, closed her eyes, and was in some man's arms. There were – and are – worse counter-irritants, she decided, listening to the gunfire and droning growing louder, though the explosions remained distant. She thought again of Michael's letter, and then of Josh's that she answered by return on a postcard, and how he had nearly reduced her to tears of relief on Wednesday morning. I hope to God he's not one of Jerry's targets for tonight, she thought, more anxiously than she realised, for she was very sleepy. A few minutes later she was asleep, and so deeply and dreamlessly that Mary had to shake her awake after the six-thirty bell.

Josh spent a far more restless night in his hotel's shelter. That day he had gone down to Kent with three of his oldest friends in London – Charles Dubois, Gus Mackinlay and Steven Karminski, respectively of New Orleans, Los Angeles and Chicago papers – with whom he had played poker and drunk in bars around Europe. Today's outing had been arranged after a Press-briefing on Thursday by the one-armed Squadron Leader, now one of Josh's new friends. 'Sorry I can't fix this for tomorrow, chaps, but show up here at 0900 hours Saturday, and I'll have car, driver and bumf laid on. You'll need 'em. It's getting even dodgier to clear the roadblocks now the Army's thoroughly browned-off with hanging around to repel non-existent boarders and letting off steam hunting for Jerry paratroops. Do yourselves a favour and don't come dressed as nuns.'

This morning they had just piled into the small

Ford saloon when the slight, dapper Squadron Leader bounded from the heavily sandbagged and guarded doorway calling, 'Hold it, corporal! Mr Adams aboard? A word in your shell-like, Josh – pipe down, you chaps! Purely personal matter concerning popsy's phone number for the use of.' And after Josh left his window seat, the Squadron Leader backed behind sandbags. 'Bit of cover in order, old chap. Nothing like being chairborne for discovering all you chaps have outsize ears and cats' eyes in light or dark.' He looked up at Josh and tugged one corner of his neat, golden moustache. 'Yesterday I chanced to bump into the chap you're doing the reccy on. Remember my saying the name rang a bell but I couldn't fix on a face? Knew the chap soon as I spotted him. Good type. We had the odd natter and later a beer, after he'd knocked off for the day.'

Josh relaxed imperceptibly. 'Busy day?'

'Chap's got to earn his pay, old boy,' he protested mildly. 'Keen type, Jerry. No accounting for tastes. Thought I'd slip you the gen.'

'Thanks, Lefty. Next round's mine.'

'Good show.' He gave his moustache another tug and studied the sandbags. 'Good-looking chap Marlowe. Twin sister, you said?'

'Yeah.'

'Bit of a smasher, I imagine?'

'Uh-huh.'

They looked at each other without expression for a few moments then walked in silence back to the car. Lefty slammed the door after Josh. 'Chocks away, corporal,' he said.

Josh had lost his window seat, and squeezing into the back seat between Dubois and Mackinlay he wondered if he should wait until his return to write, or ask the driver to stop at the first undamaged public telephone box in the hope of getting through to Martha's and leaving a message that Ann could immediately decode. But then, like the other correspondents, he was asleep before their car crossed Vauxhall Bridge. They had all been up since the pre-dawn All Clear and spent a large portion of the raid playing poker together in the basement boiler-room of a block behind Oxford Street where Dubois and Mackinlay shared a studio flat. They slept through the roadblocks until their driver woke them on the outskirts of Dover. 'Wakey, wakey, gentlemen! Rise and shine! Wakey, wakey!'

The unclouded sun shone down on the fading warm green grass on top of the white cliffs and glinted on the lenses of binoculars, the metal cups of vacuum flasks filled with black coffee, and the blue silk English Channel. All day the wide blue sky was empty of natural clouds, but again and again streaked with white vapour trails, pockmarked with white puffs, black puffs, alive with screaming, wheeling, weaving aircraft, and bright balls of fire diving into the calm sea. And each time the quietness returned to the sky, the cries of the disturbed sea-birds sounded like nature's requiem. The mood of all four young men had altered since he had last sprawled with them on that grass nine days ago.

Too many lifetimes back for counting, he thought. Looking at his friends, he recalled how previously he had watched the dogfights with a carefully nurtured detachment, whilst Karminski, the grandson of Polish immigrants, had grinned in delight when a German plane went down, and tightened his lips when a British one did. Dubois, who had distant French and Spanish ancestry, had shrugged off both events with equanimity. Mackinlay, the grandson of Irish immigrants on both sides of the family, had kept up a running 'Tough, Limey, but I guess you had it coming!' and 'Not even you can win 'em all, Fritz!' Now, Mackinlay too watched tight-lipped and mostly in silence.

Another deadly air battle was tearing across the sky when Mackinlay thumped the grass with a clenched fist.

'Jeez, but never did I think – never in hell did I think the day would come when I would find myself thinking of the bloody Limeys as the game little guy taking on the big guy. But ain't that the truth, fellars? Yeah, sure, they still have the Great British Empire, but from where I sit' – he gestured with both arms towards the Channel – 'said Great British Empire is one hell of a long ways from little old England.' Suddenly he leapt up, waving his arms above his head and yelling. 'Watch your butt, Limey! Watch it, bud! Holy Jesus!' The Spitfire he was addressing exploded in mid-air only seconds before a second one shot down the Messerschmitt responsible. He crossed himself instinctively, then dropped his arms to his sides as the spinning, smoking Me. dived into the sea, sending up a great plume of spray, whilst the burning remnants of the first Spitfire floated gently down like a handful of sparkling confetti, which for a few seconds rested upon the surface of the water and then fizzled out and sank.

No one spoke. Mackinlay flopped down on to the grass, mopping his face. Silently he accepted the cigarette Josh passed him, then shook out two matches before lighting it with a third.

Josh lay stretched out on his back, his rolled-up jacket under his head, his tie loosened, one hand holding his trilby so as to shield the sun from the binoculars clamped to his eyes. They brought the aerial battles so close that it seemed as if he could reach up and pluck an aircraft from the sky – if his arm could move as fast as his eyes could blink once. The speed of the dogfights transformed them into nightmarishly beautiful, split-second ballets. Dancing to death, he thought, struggling to maintain detachment and ignore the probability that the pilot of one of the Spits he had seen go down was Ann's twin. Her postcard in his wallet weighed heavier than lead, and he was disturbingly relieved that he had fallen asleep on the drive down. He decided that he would make no attempt to call or write her when he got back to London. Not tonight. Maybe tomorrow after checking with Lefty. Not tonight, he thought, as once more the sky was quiet.

His emotions had taken such a hammering that he was profoundly thankful they had to leave earlier than usual, and did not stop for a beer, so as to get back to London before darkness brought the now uniformly expected night raid. He was equally thankful to get back to his hotel and be on his own.

Saturday was the one night in the week when the *Banner* men had no deadline for New York, and Burness was spending the night with friends in Esher. Waiting for Josh in his hotel were three invitations to parties tonight. Two were from compatriots living nearby, the third from an Englishwoman renowned as a party-giver, whom he had met once when Burness took him to one in her house in Park Lane, shortly after his arrival in London. Her hand-written invitation urged him to drop in any time as the party would be going on all night: now the blitz had closed all the theatres and cinemas, she just had to do her bit 'for all you brave Americans sticking it out with us'. As the sirens sounded Josh tore up all three invitations and dropped them in the wastepaper basket in Reception, without bothering to ask if the telephones were working. (They were, for another two hours.)

He avoided being drawn into the party in progress amongst his fellow residents in the newly opened underground bar, and no one objected to his asking the dining-room for a supper tray and then taking it up to his room. After eight consecutive night raids the initial strict enforcement of air raid precautions was slackening in the hotel and elsewhere. If he had wanted to attend any of tonight's parties, the police and ARP would have let him through with little more than 'Keep your head down and watch how you go.' Just as now after the All Clear it was generally, 'If you must, just watch your step.'

He needed to be alone to sort out his troubled thoughts. Despite the events of the last eight days, his opinion as to the eventual outcome remained the same. Nothing he had seen today changed that. He knew the RAF would keep up the fight to the death and die hard, but experience and intelligence continued to insist that courage was not enough to win this war, and that no matter how game the little guy, if the big guy was equally game – as he was – in the end he had to win. He had known since Tuesday morning that he was nearing the point of no return where Ann was concerned, and recognised the enormity of his folly in offering this watching brief and not backing out of her life on Monday. The realisation that nothing would now persuade him to back out of that brief, and the strong chance that it was already superfluous, added to his despair – a despair that encompassed Ann, London, civilisation, and himself. When he eventually went down to his reserved bunk in the hotel shelter that despair gave him a restless night without any assistance from the continuous thunder of guns, aircraft and explosions.

'What annoys me about this war, Nurse Marlowe,' said Sister Hope as she signed Sunday's Dispensary order-list, 'is the way it is increasing an unhealthy dependence on nocturnal sedation and other forms of medication.' She tapped with the heel of her fountain pen the request for ninety-six tablets of M and B 693. 'When we began using these earlier this year it was only for pneumonias and bronchitics. Now half my patients are on four-hourly courses, and very ill it makes them feel.'

'But it does seem more effective than Prontosil, Sister.'

'Be that as it may, when administering Prontosil I

disremember any necessity to enquire before starting courses if my patients have recently eaten onions or taken Epsom salts, nor to observe them carefully for subsequent signs of cyanosis. Not that I've ever seen one patient on 693 turn blue. Have you, nurse?'

'No, Sister.'

'We must be grateful, nurse. However, as the Senior Medical Officer has seen fit to start three more patients on 693 during the night and we've only enough in stock for the 10 a.m. round, I refuse to contemplate the prospect of running out before our order is returned at midday. Please take down the basket yourself and return with the M and B. I'm sure the dispenser on Sunday duty will understand.'

I'm not, thought Ann cheerfully. Mr Maxton the Head Dispenser's on today and he loathes rush orders. She smiled. She was feeling extraordinarily happy this morning. 'May I go down now, Sister?' she asked.

'Please, nurse.' Sister Hope nodded approvingly. Happy nurses made happy patients and a happy ward. Sister Hope loved her patients and ward with the devotion of a woman with a great capacity for love that she had willingly channelled into her long career. 'Before you go, do you agree that between us Nurse Sellars, you and I can manage the mid-morning work and patients' lunches?'

'Oh, yes, Sister. And we'll have Alice' – the wardmaid – 'till one as this is her alternate half-Sunday.'

'Indeed we will. A tower of strength, our Alice.'

Ann quickly collected the empty Dispensary basket and left the ward, enjoying this latest manifestation of the all-in-the-same-boat syndrome. Normally Sister Hope was too good an administrator to allow, much less invite, the views of others upon her decisions. As she walked along the main corridor Ann enjoyed exchanging gallant smiles with all she passed. We few, we happy few, she mused, reaching the only open staff hatch of the main Dispensary. 'Good morning, Mr Maxton.'

Mr Maxton, tall, thin, greying and chronically disgruntled, demanded, 'What is it now, Nurse Marlowe?'

She fluttered her eyelashes. 'I'm afraid Hope's having a bit of a crisis and – '

'When isn't it, nurse? Well?'

She turned up the voltage of her smile to explain and, as attack was the best form of defence, added, 'If I go back without the M and B, Sister Hope'll do to me what Jerry did to the Junior Home.'

Mr Maxton softened visibly. The nasty corn on the little toe of his left foot had made him forget the blitz. 'Wouldn't want that, nurse. Oh, well, I expect I can fit it in now.' He looked over her head. ''Morning, Mr Wesley. What'll you be wanting?'

'A word after you've dealt with Nurse Marlowe's request, Mr Maxton. Musn't queue-jump.' The SSO smiled and bowed gallantly to Ann, then leant his white-coated back against the counter as Mr Maxton disappeared into his vast department. 'What's so urgent that you've had to turn on the charm and kick under the belt, nurse?' Her answer evoked another gallant smile. 'Useful stuff, 693 – though, alas, it makes the patients feel hellish.' He glanced up and down the otherwise empty corridor running from Central Hall to Casualty. 'Damned quiet.'

'Sunday morning and for once no casualties in last night, Mr Wesley.'

'True.' He lit a cigarette. 'Odd turn-up, none in last night. What's even odder, not one acute abdo's come in since Jerry's kicked off blitzing. Do you know this has been the first week in Martha's recorded history without the admission of one emergency abdo? Even that pro – apples.'

'Apples?'

'Apples. Poor kid had a hellish belly-ache. She

123

told me she'd felt hungry in the night and eaten three pounds. I advised her to go easy on the apples in future. But eight days – ' He shook his head. 'Eight days and nights and not one acute abdo! Admittedly the customers have had other matters on their minds, but one would not have expected Jerry to cure every bit of twisting or thinning gut in our zone. And that's not all he's cured. Neuros.'

'I've heard the new psychiatric clinics in OPDs have been empty all week.'

'Shaken the trick-cyclists rigid. They'd expected the bombs would inundate them with every neurosis in the book. Poor chaps are having to psychoanalyse each other. Distressing to watch their sufferings, Nurse Marlowe.'

'The very thought tugs the heart-strings, Mr Wesley.'

He laughed, and was rather glad he had never before noticed she had quite a spot of oomph. He needed intelligent women in his professional life, but in his private life, he reflected, like a hole in the head. 'We think as one, nurse.'

Only till Jerry lays off and we all climb out of the boat, she thought, smiling – she hoped – coyly. 'I suppose Jerry still hasn't invaded?'

'Don't ask me. No one tells me anything, and how in my state of ignorance I am to win this war single-handed, is beyond me. But the Government's nauseating posters insist upon it. IT ALL DEPENDS ON YOU, they keep informing me. The strain is killing me. Ah.' Mr Maxton was back. 'Very nice running into you, Nurse Marlowe,' Mr Wesley added, bowing and smiling as before.

'And you, Mr Wesley.' She had to resist the desire to curtsy. 'Thanks awfully, Mr Maxton.'

Ann walked away vastly amused until she suddenly recalled exactly when the SSO had told her he was going to look at a pro with a query appendix. This evening it would be only a week since Ed Laurings died. Only one week? Years have seemed shorter, she thought incredulously, not realising that since the blitz started she had lived every waking second more intensely than ever before, and how many seconds there were in eight days. The sound of Big Ben striking ten speeded up her pace. Though the ward was half-empty, all eighteen were bed-patients, and for the next three hours there would be only three nurses to do the work of six.

Two hours later, when Big Ben began the chime before twelve, Nurse Sellars and Alice had pushed the heavy electric food-trolley into mid-ward, Alice was plugging it in, Sister standing poised to start serving, Ann and Nurse Sellars waiting with trays to take round the plates to the patients, who sat propped up, napkins outspread, and individual trays laid with cutlery and drinking water on their pulled up bedtables. Twelve was striking when, from down and up river, on both banks, the sirens chorused the Alert.

'How tiresome,' murmured Sister Hope, replacing the trolley lids. Pulling off her cuffs she raised her voice. 'I am so sorry, ladies, but lunches will be a little delayed.'

In unison, Ann and Nurse Sellars deposited their trays on the trolley and charged up opposite sides of the ward pulling off cuffs, putting up blackout screens, closing the balcony doors. Nurse Sellars muttered 'I'll kill Jerry if he mucks up my two-to-five,' and Ann, just catching the sound of fast-approaching aircraft engines, thought, something different – Spits! She raced back, rolling up her sleeves, to hand to the patients on her side the dressing-gowns, slippers, gasmasks and handbags from their bedside lockers, whilst Sister released ropes from footrails and laid them across the beds. Alice, unplugging and pushing the heavy trolley back to the ward kitchen, narrowly avoided knocking down the posse of young men racing in from the stairs. Some folks have got no

125

consideration, thought Alice. Sunday dinners having to stand would ruin the Yorkshire puds.

Mrs Harris called, 'Back to the Rope Trick, eh, doctors?'

The assortment of junior housemen and medical students whose first responsibility under the new order was the evacuation of Hope, grinned in reply to save breath and time. Three paired with the nursing staff, the rest with each other, to double and slide the individual lengths of rope under the mattress and tie patient, bedding and mattress in a kind of cat's-cradle, which, together, they gently lowered to the floor, slid along ward, corridor and landing, then carried down the stairs, across the main corridor, and down the basement stairs to the waiting bared beds – brought down in the past few days from the permanently emptied wards – ranged lengthways along the portion of the basement corridor reserved for Hope. Throughout the move the sick women kept up encouraging cries of 'Any more for the *Skylark*!' and 'Move along down the car, please!' and then sighed in private relief when they were gently lowered onto the bared bedsprings. In the five minutes it had taken to empty Hope, the roaring and screaming of aircraft and bursts of machine-gun-fire were so deafening that those patients were in the basement before they realised that once again London's guns were silent.

When all were down, leaving Nurse Sellars in temporary charge with Alice in support, Sister Hope and Ann raced back to Hope for the essential additions in this new order: the patients' bedtickets and X-rays; the ward log, Dangerous Drug and Address books; the small locked tin of Dangerous Drugs and cardiac stimulants; the smallish, oblong sterile tins containing, respectively, emergency blood transfusion and drip-infusions settings, hypodermic syringes and needles, the basic surgical setting for major first-aid, and sterile dry dressings.

'Manage those tins, nurse? Good. Just the 693, our

shelter-bags and cloaks. Bother!' An explosion high above jerked books and X-rays from Sister Hope's grasp and blew outwards the blackout screen and glass in the window between Beds 29 and 30, directly opposite the ward desk. That sudden exposure of just a fraction of the massive air battle now being fought above Greater London – and in a roughly twenty-mile wide air corridor to the Channel – was so literally breathtaking that for several seconds they both stared transfixed. The sky was a maddened hornet's nest of aircraft, the German bombers breaking formation, diving or climbing to avoid colliding with their Messerschmitts as much as the guns of the Spitfires and Hurricanes; the opposing fighters on each other's tails, in each other's sights, their guns spitting fire and their machines flying so fast that from that window every blink of the eyes exposed another aspect of the battle.

'This won't do. Get the rest, nurse.' Sister Hope scrambled for books and X-rays as Ann ran from the ward. Sister Hope took one last look at her emptied ward, then rushed after Ann. On the stairs she said breathlessly, 'Our delay'll worry the patients. What annoys me about this war is the way it worries them so!'

When they reached the ground floor, streams of young men in short white coats or shirtsleeves, their ties buttoned inside their shirts, were coming up from the several sets of basement stairs opening along the length of the inner wall. Sister Hope called to the nearest, 'Thank you, gentlemen.'

'All part of the service, Sister,' they retorted, turning towards their assembly point in Central Hall.

All part of hospital routine now, thought Ann, following Sister down the basement stairs. Then she thought, but this is different. Jerry must be sure of himself to make another daylight attack on London, but this time he's got the RAF at his throat and – *No! Stop thinking! Stop it!*

'There you are, Sister dear. Better late than never.'

'How right you are, Mrs Harris. All quite comfortable, my dears? Good.' Sister Hope moved on to deposit her load on the card-table in the alcove presently designated Hope's dutyroom, then clicked her tongue against her teeth. 'I am so peeved with myself, Nurse Marlowe. I've left our DD book behind.'

'I'll nip back for it, Sister. It'll worry the patients if you leave now.'

Sister nodded reluctantly. 'Just slip away. Be careful, nurse.'

'I will, Sister.'

She walked slowly past the patients, exchanging smiles and agreeing that it didn't sound as if Jerry was having it all his own way today, which certainly made a nice change. Once out of their sight she ran the rest of the way and was picking the DD book off the floor under Bed 10 when Mr Henty from Repairs and Works rushed in, tightening the chinstrap of his tin hat. 'You shouldn't be here, nurse. Whole block's cleared. Best get down. Hotting up upstairs.'

Ann had to swallow to answer. She had just glimpsed through the gaping window a Hurricane going down in flames. She held up the book. 'I came back for this.'

'Aye. Got to keep the books straight.' He glanced upwards. 'Time to scarper, nurse.'

They left together, running down the stairs. When they reached the foot the SSO, who was talking to the Block 1 firemen about to go up to the roof, glanced round and said, 'All out, Mr Henty? Nice work. All blocks cleared in record – ' His voice was cut out by the roaring of a sharply diving bomber that was immediately followed by the shrill whistle of falling bombs.

'All down!' Mr Henty bellowed down the corridor, and along its length and in Central Hall every standing figure dropped to the floor and lay flattened, face down, arms folded over the backs of unprotected heads, or the napes of the necks of those with tin hats.

The first high explosive to go through the roof of Block 1 exploded in the PPW, the second in Faith, ripping off the ceiling of Hope. In seconds the roof and three upper floors had cascaded on to the hospital terrace, and every remaining window in Block 1, and all those on the near sides of Block 2 and the Senior Home, had been blown out, and the ground corridor ceiling under the points of impact rained plaster. Ann, lying between Mr Henty and the SSO, felt the corridor floor shake as if a maddened giant was trying to tear it from its foundations, and her ears, teeth and every bone in her body ached under the onslaught of noise. When at last the floor was still and the noise of the explosions and falling masonry faded away, for another thirty seconds she and the four men lay gasping like landed fishes.

Very slowly she lowered her arms, and raising her head saw the four men doing the same, and she thought vaguely, we should be dead but aren't. Her shocked eyes recognised that same thought in the dazed eyes of the SSO and Mr Henty as other hands helped them up. 'Thank you,' she said vaguely, and with the four men leant against the inner wall to brush plaster from her face and uniform and straighten her hair and her flattened cap.

On seeing they were unharmed, only Mr Yeo, the Senior Surgical Registrar, stayed with them when the would-be rescuers who had raced from Central Hall rushed away to peer over the shoulders and heads of those now crowding around the doorway of the one fire exit door in the riverside wall to see the damage to Block 1. Far far away, and of as little concern to her as the continuing uproar of the air battle, Ann heard the Senior Medical Officer's voice calling, 'No one hurt, Matron. All safely out.'

The Senior Surgical Officer, straightening his tie, asked absently, 'What did Roger White say, Bill?'

Mr Yeo, repeating the SMO's words, surreptitiously loosened the knot of his tie. Mr Yeo was twenty-seven, stocky, dark-haired, and the son and grandson of Royal Navy captains. He was daily expecting his call-up by the Navy, and up to a few minutes ago he had dreaded this prospect because he was seasick in a rowing boat on flat calm water. But when he was lying on the floor of Central Hall and heard Block 1 coming down, knowing Piers Wesley was up this end and that, if he had bought it, he, Bill Yeo, would immediately have to take over the whole surgical side, which almost certainly would result in Martha's requesting for him the two-year deferment from active service already granted Wesley and Roger White, he had cursed the Navy's delay. He was a conscientious young man and he knew he had neither Wesley's experience nor an especial talent for surgery, and too exactly what the SSO's job entailed. He was too modest to appreciate that what he might lack in brilliance was made up for by his infinite capacity for hard work and taking pains that had endeared him to patients and staff.

Mr Billings, the Repairs and Works foreman, edged from the crowd to join them. 'Bit of a near-miss, eh, Mr Wesley, sir?'

The SSO's faint smile was a trifle euphoric. 'What's the score, Mr Billings?'

'Block 1's fetched off down to Hope that'll need a new lid if what's left up don't come down first. Blast'll not have done it much good.'

Ann's mind was still working in slow-motion. 'Faith, Beatrice and the PPW gone?'

Mr Billings nodded sympathetically. Pretty as a picture she was, for all she was white as a sheet, same as the SSO, Bert Henty, Sam Jeavers and Dick Toms. Young Mr Yeo knew what he was doing, keeping an eye on 'em. 'That's about it, nurse. Don't you worry. Still got the seven nice wardblocks on the river wall, haven't we?' He exchanged glances with Mr Yeo, then turned to his charge hand. 'You could do with a bit of a sit-down and a cuppa in our restroom, Bert. And you two lads.'

'Good idea,' said Mr Yeo, and after Mr Billings removed the three men, 'Mightn't hurt to apply that therapy to Nurse Marlowe and yourself, sir.'

'Perish the thought, Bill!' The SSO suddenly grinned euphorically. 'I don't need it. No one's hurt. Personally, never felt better! How about you, nurse?'

As suddenly, the full force of shock-induced euphoria hit Ann. She grinned. 'I'm fine, thanks, Mr Wesley.'

He laughed. 'What else? Takes more than a block dropping on her to deter a Martha! And as the chap says, we still have seven nice wardblocks – '

Ann broke in wildly, 'On the river wall.' Then, without thought and to the tune of 'Nine Green Bottles' she sang softly,

'Seven nice wardblocks, on the river wall,
Seven nice wardblocks, on the river wall,
And if another nice wardblock should accidentally
    fall
We'll have six nice wardblocks on the river –

Oh!' She stopped singing. 'The DD book! Where – there!' She dived for the book, now jammed between two fire buckets. 'Do excuse me, but if I don't get cracking what'll annoy Sister Hope about this war is having her staff nurse go AWOL.' She shot down the nearest basement stairs leaving Mr Wesley smiling and singing to himself an amended version of her improvisation, Mr Yeo clinically speculating on how long it would be before delayed-action shock caught up with both, and neither surgeon nor Ann realising that

she had just replaced 'You'll Be Far Better Off In a Home'
as Martha's most popular war song. Long before that
afternoon's All Clear, the SSO's version was all round
Central Hall. This began with the eight original Blocks
and ended:

> And if the last bloody wardblock should
>   accidentally fall,
> Poor bloody Martha's will then have
>   bugger-all.

When the All Clear sounded at three-forty-five, three
more basement caverns had been swept, walls and
ceilings washed down, emergency lighted and installed
with the beds of the patients from Faith, Hope and
Charity, as temporary expedients until transfers to the
EMS could be arranged. No raid casualties had come
in, nor, according to Casualty, were any expected,
as London's other hospitals were 'coping'. What had
already come in were the rumours flashing from Casualty
and the rooftop firemen, that the air battle had been
the greatest ever fought between the Luftwaffe and
the RAF, and the RAF had given Jerry hell and won
hands down. The wave of euphoria that swept through
the hospital was followed between five and six o'clock
by a human wave, composed of the patients' relatives,
friends and neighbours living within walking distance
who had decided, separately or collectively, that as Jerry
done them out of their two-to-four, five-to-six would
do nicely to set the poor souls' (the patients') minds at
rest, and would do no harm to their own, seeing they'd
heard Block 1 had copped it, and though it was said no
one was hurt it didn't do to credit all you heard these
times, not by a long chalk it didn't.

'Best to see for yourself, Sister,' Mrs Harris' neighbour,
Mrs Pinker, told Sister Hope. 'And talk about a mercy! All
safe and not a scratch, same as when your young nurses'

Home copped it! It was Meant, that's what, Sister, and like I says to Mabel coming up, if we steps in around five the poor souls'll have had time for a nice cup of tea and we'll have time to get back for our tea afore packing up to go down the shelter for the night. But, Sister, have you heard – ' Her worn, kindly face glowed with delight at the item that she was bursting to impart. 'He got the Palace! That's right, Sister, Buckingham Palace – but not bad, mind, just knocked it about a bit, and the King and Queen's not hurt, bless 'em! They says it was this Dornier as drops it, and he's got this Hurricane on his tail and the Hurricane keeps after him and shoots the Jerry down over Victoria – that's right, Sister, Victoria Station – and the Dornier he comes down out the front, and that's his lot and good riddance! But the Hurricane – he's got this Me. after him and he gets shot down, but the Hurricane pilot he bails out lovely, they says, and comes down nice and safe not two good spits from Sloane Square! Bless him! But what a day, Sister! Jerries coming down all over, they says, and our lads done lovely! What a day!'

'A day indeed, Nurse Marlowe,' Sister Hope observed later when they were sitting together at the card-table, now moved into the middle of the improvised ward, in the few minutes between Sister's return from handing in her written day report to Matron and reading eight o'clock ward prayers. 'Of course, today's official figures still have to be confirmed, but Matron has just told me that it appears over a hundred and fifty enemy aircraft were shot down, our own losses were small in comparison, and there is no question that our young men won a famous victory. So well deserved!'

'Yes, Sister,' said Ann politely. She was still in the grip of a kind of selective mental anaesthesia that had replaced her euphoria within a few minutes of her return to the basement with the DD book, and had left her incapable of personal thoughts and emotions, whilst allowing her to work efficiently and tirelessly. For though, like Sister and Nurse Sellars, she had had no off-duty, she could not feel the fatigue now evident in her pale face and bruised eyes. But the active, trained part of her mind noticed that, whilst Sister Hope had simply looked very tired when she left to hand in her report, she had returned looking a very old and sad woman. 'Did Matron have any more news concerning Hope's future, Sister?' she asked.

'I was just coming to that, nurse.' Sister Hope paused for Nurse Sellars to replace with a red night-bulb the last bare white bulb, which hung from the ceiling a couple of feet from the desk. The muffled waves of the Alert filtered down to that deep basement under Block 7. 'I expected this.' Sister looked swiftly around the faces of her eighteen patients, their beds tinted pink by the night-lights, along each longish side of the rough-stone-walled, low-ceilinged cavern that, despite the strong solution of raw carbolic used to wash it down and the small, carefully positioned electric fan keeping the air circulating, reeked of centuries of must. 'The last war taught me that, whatever their faults, the Germans are brave fighters, and far more likely to launch a counter-attack than lick their wounds after today's defeat.' She blinked. 'What was I about to say, nurse?'

'It concerned Hope's future, Sister,' prompted Ann against a muffled barrage of distant ack-ack fire that stirred the numbed areas of her mind into the purely academic reflection, no RAF up now.

'Yes. Well, providing transport is available, tomorrow all Block 1's patients will be transferred to Garden East Emergency Medical Services Hospital in Hampshire, where we already have a Nursing Unit, as, indeed, do several other London hospitals. Garden East has two thousand beds. Ample room for us all, I understand. Sisters Faith, Charity and I will accompany our own patients and take with us three fourth-years and a larger number of second-years. You and Nurse Sellars will remain here. Matron has not yet decided where you will be working, but I shall be sorry to lose you both.'

'Thank you, Sister. We'll be very sorry to leave Hope.'

'These things happen in wartime, nurse. There's no question that it will greatly benefit our patients to be nursed in peaceful surroundings and clean country air, though I fear they will sadly miss being so available to the visits of their families and friends.' She paused again to look all round her improvised ward, and Ann, watching the old, tired face, glimpsed Sister Hope's recognition that her age made it improbable that she would ever again work in her beloved Martha's. Then Sister Hope faced Ann, straightening her back and the starched lace bow under her chin. 'We shall all look forward very much to the reopening of Faith, Hope and Charity Wards in our rebuilt Block 1, after we have won the war.'

Momentarily, Ann was speechless. Her recognition of what this meant to Sister Hope had suddenly released the post-shock grip on her emotions. Her eyes filled with tears and she looked down quickly. 'We will, Sister. We certainly will!'

At the same time, across London, Josh, not long back from the Air Ministry, was uncharacteristically yelling into a mouthpiece and down the transatlantic cable, 'What the hell do you mean, you require verification of the goddam British figures I have just given you? I have just received them and I go right along with them! I was right here and I goddam saw it!' He slammed the earpiece back on the hook and reached for the glass held out by the hugely grinning Burness.

'Brother, brother, have you just made the grade – or had it!' Burness said.

Josh, grinning, raised his glass. 'Puts me in pretty good company, wouldn't you say, Pete?'

– Six –

'This may be the second week in October but summer isn't over yet. The swallows are still here.' Ann put the basket of blackberries on the battered roof of Burness' black Morris Oxford saloon and leant against it to watch the swallows swooping to perch on the telegraph wires along the Surrey lane where she and Josh had stopped to pick blackberries. 'They'll be off soon. They always line up like this just before taking off for Africa.' She looked around the country sky that in the south and west was clear blue and in the north and east smudged grey by last night's new fires in London. 'Doesn't the air smell wonderful?'

'It surely does.' Josh reached for another high handful and trickled the berries into the basket, grudging the momentary distraction of his attention from her. This was their first time alone together, and their first meeting since seeing each other in the early morning of 10 September, and he was hoarding the moments like a miser uncertain of another chance to look upon his gold.

They had spent most of the drive from London, and the stop for an early tea in Chertsey, telling each other of their childhoods. Their recollections had been gilded by nostalgia, and, especially in the car, prolonged by the strain of the convention that kept them sitting carefully apart and imposed new strains in the rare silences both had been anxious to break. They were in Surrey – their nearest open country, and Josh had only managed to get enough petrol for a fifty-mile round trip. Two miles further on from that lane was an Emergency Medical Services Hospital with a Martha's nursing unit which, when stopped at roadblocks, they had used to explain Ann's presence in the car of an American correspondent gathering material for a feature on the peaceful beauty of the English countryside in the aftermath of the Battle of Britain.

Ann turned from the sky to look at the dented and scratched car, involuntarily fingering under her blue cashmere jumper her father's signet ring that Michael had insisted she keep 'till your show's over'.

'Twice dug out in working order?'

'Started straight off, both times.' He slapped the bonnet affectionately. 'Big break for Pete's blood-pressure. He was spitting mad when Jerry got the second garage. He really loves this old jalopy. Treats it so like a horse it's a wonder he feeds it gas not a bran mash. He's given it a name now.' He switched into Burness' Kentuckian drawl. 'I would have you know, ma'am, this automobile is known as the Old Grey Mare – and guess what? – she ain't what she used to be.'

Ann laughed. 'Corn is the staff of life.'

He shrugged, laughing. 'Even Homer sometimes nods.'

'And many a true word spoken in jest.'

'But every cloud has a silver lining and – '

'And one swallow doesn't make a summer – No, Josh! We must stop this or we'll keep it up all night,' she protested, swooping back to reality. 'And the sun's dropping. We must get weaving.'

He sighed, waking from the dream. 'I guess so. Do you have enough blackberries?'

'Masses.' She took down the basket to examine the fruit with purple-stained fingers. 'They're wizard.'

'What'll you do with them?'

'I think we should give them to your Miss Dewly. From what you've told me, I'll bet she and her mother have saved or can scrounge sugar for jam. If not, for pies, tarts, fools and – '

'Fools?'

'A sort of mousse.'

'Won't that require eggs?'

She looked at him quizzically. 'Don't ask me. I can't cook proper food. All I've learned is invalid cookery as a pro. Egg custard, calf's foot jelly and everything else minced to mush. You seem to know your stuff. Where did you pick it up? Paris?'

'Uh-huh.' He hitched up one side of the bonnet to replace the rotor-arm. It was one of the most strictly enforced wartime laws that in all circumstances the rotor-arms must be immediately removed from engines to immobilise parked cars.

Ann sensed his sudden change of mood, though there was no sign of it in his outward manner. This afternoon he looked so English, in sports jacket, slacks, Fair Isle pullover, white shirt and grey tie, that when he spoke, at every roadblock, the interrogating soldier had done a double-take. If he were Michael or one of Michael's friends, she thought, I'd now be sure I'd strayed on to some other girl's territory, and that he would tell me about her in time. But he's American – No, this is stupid! Being American doesn't alter the fact that he's a young man, and I can't risk wasting time on tact or patience. If he's still in love with her, I'd better know it, stat.

'Did you love her very much, Josh?' she asked.

He closed the bonnet, and faced her. 'I did.'

'Why on earth didn't she marry you?'

He flushed faintly, then grinned. 'She preferred the other guy.'

'So you went big-game hunting in Berlin?'

'I did just that.'

138

'Poor Josh. Tough.'

'In the event. Why haven't you married, Ann?'

She smiled quickly. 'No one's asked me, no temptation, no time, and no wish to risk losing my job. Martha's sticks to the book on this. If we let one of our men date us, we'd better marry him, or he'll risk his job too. Not that marriage would help his career at Martha's. Hospital medicine, like hospital nursing, is strictly for the celibate, and I mean strictly. So, I play by Martha's book. No one asked me to train at Martha's, I chose to – and as, up to this year, we only had one day off a month, there wasn't much time for playing outside. Josh – time. We must move.' She looked away from his watchful eyes at the gentle green fields on either side of the lane, and the swallows on the telegraph wires, as if she too were storing the moments. Josh saw in her pretty, pale, tired face that she was saying farewell to the swallows. She raised a hand to them, and without saying more got into the front seat of the car, put the basket on the back seat, and laid across the lap of her navy tweed skirt the fawn swagger coat she had left on the floor. He closed her door and walked round and got into the driving seat.

'Credentials and spiel at the ready, Ann?'

'All set.' She smiled a little too brightly. 'We're a smashing pair of liars.'

'Comes with my territory.'

'And mine. Michael's a lousy liar, so for that reason only I'm glad he's having to spend this forty-eight up north and London's still off-limits to servicemen in transit unless they have homes there. Aunt Maud never flaps over herself, but she flaps like mad over us and can always see through Michael.'

'Not you?'

'In person. Not at a distance.'

'Figures.' He started the car, watching himself carefully, trying to subdue his joyous relief at all that had just passed between them, and not to think upon what might lie at this immediate journey's end. The evenings were shortening, the nights lengthening, and this was the night of the full moon. The bombers' moon, London calls it now, he thought, driving off the grass on to the lane.

The great air battle on 15 September had swung the Battle of Britain in the RAF's favour; by last week the Luftwaffe's daytime attacks on English airfields had finally tapered off, and, if only for this year, the threat of an invasion had passed. The Germans were dismantling the invasion barges in the French Channel ports, and moving back to Germany the crack divisions intended to spearhead the Wehrmacht's attack on England. But still, nightly, London was attacked by an average of two hundred German bombers, and still every morning the millions of civilian nocturnal troglodytes emerged to new smoke, new devastation, and the new figures of the night's known dead and seriously injured.

Driving along the lane that ran for a few miles alongside a little river, Josh sought comfort in the innumerable recorded and inexplicable instances of twins whose lives, even when long-parted, had run on parallel lines. Michael Marlowe was one of the handful of RAF pilots to have fought through the Battle of Britain and survived uninjured. One swallow didn't make a summer. One victory – though vital for Britain's survival – wasn't enough to win this war. Somehow, England had survived this summer; somehow, London was still surviving the blitz; somehow, he thought, glancing guardedly at Ann watching the little river through her side window. During the last four weeks Martha's zone had often been one of the main targets; the hospital had been hit again and now had a seventy-by-forty yard crater caused by the explosion of the main Dispensary, shut for the night when hit. From 16 September Ann had been moved to Casualty as an extra day staff nurse: every night Martha's had taken in increasing numbers of casualties, and each day seldom discharged the last of them more than a few hours before the next night's casualties began coming in. Every few days Josh had sent her his latest news of Michael, and she had replied by return on postcards. Twice he had asked if there was any chance of their meeting for lunch, tea, morning coffee, and had had the same reply: 'Thanks. Wish I could, but, sorry, can't make it. All the best. A.'

He still knew so little about her, and though his common sense insisted that Ann meant what she wrote, the memory of the former rejection made him disproportionately sensitive, and unhappier than he, but not his colleagues, appreciated, until yesterday when Ann rang his office.

Burness was out, and Miss Dewly took the call. She covered the mouthpiece. 'A Miss Marlowe for you, Mr Adams. Are you here or shall I take a message?'

His tired face, thinner now, lit up. 'I'll take it, thanks.'

Miss Dewly handed over the telephone, congratulating herself. I knew it! I told Mother more than tiredness was making him look so peaky and I was sure he was sweet on some girl! I do hope she's a nice girl. Ladylike voice – but with all these little tarty types dressing up in uniforms and giving themselves airs these days, who can tell?

'Josh here, Ann. How are you?'

'Fine, thanks.' Ann, in the front hall box that for once was working, closed her eyes in relief at the sound of his voice. 'How about you?'

'Just fine.'

'Good. So tell me something. Why have you never told me you wrote to Mrs Laurings and sent that lovely piece on Ed to his hometown newspaper?'

Josh further delighted Miss Dewly by blushing. 'Hasn't been too much time. She's written you?'

'I had a sweet letter this morning with a copy of your piece. Josh, it's so good and obviously meant a lot to his parents. Mrs Laurings says they've framed it and she's sent a copy to your mother. It was copied in Ottawa and Toronto papers, and the Laurings have had letters of sympathy from all over Canada. I know nothing can help their pain, but you've helped them feel less terribly alone, and so right to be so proud of Ed. It was sweet of you, and don't tell me you were just doing your job. You weren't and I know it. Have you seen it in print?'

His heart leapt. 'Not yet. I'd like to. Any chance you could show it me? Or – post it?'

'I can't make today – I'm due back on in an hour. I should make it tomorrow afternoon as something splendid's happening this week. Because none of us in Cas have had days off since we can't remember when, Matron's put her foot down and insists we get a half-day. One-to-eight, owing to night calls. I've got tomorrow. Any use?'

'Sure!' He had a full schedule tomorrow afternoon, but nothing short of a direct hit would keep him from her. 'Can we meet for lunch at the Three Pigeons?'

Ann closed her eyes for another reason. 'Sorry, no. Had it, night before last. No survivors.'

He winced involuntarily at the recollection of the handsome black-haired woman . . . hubby gone for a soldier . . . nippers gone for evacuees . . . hubby's old mum. 'That's too bad. HE?'

'One of these new land-mines. Took down half their street.'

He didn't tell her he had spent most of that particular night at an ARP post in Deptford that had had a direct hit only a few minutes after he and all the occupants had gone across the street to help dig out two women and an elderly man buried in their own coal cellar. Only the women had been brought out alive. 'I hadn't heard.' He paused a moment. 'When and where can I call for you?'

'Hold on a tick.' Ann suddenly felt sick. I didn't know, she thought. I didn't know how much I've been flapping about him and want to see him. 'Listen – better not fix lunch in case I'm off late. Let's say two, and I'll wait for you outside our Home. It's the red-brick building directly opposite the Out-Patients Department, just beyond the huge wooden palisade blocking part of the hospital front.'

He didn't tell her of the several times he had seen that palisade and the wooden boarding now in every remaining window in Martha's frontage. Nor did he let himself recall his reaction upon hearing that the main Dispensary, and the oxygen store directly beneath, had exploded through the roof between Central Hall and Casualty on a late September morning after possibly the heaviest night raid yet. Burness had been with him when he had this news from a Special Constable just back over the river after five hours in Martha's. 'Bad enough, but could've been a lot worse. Just the six gone, poor blokes. Two young doctors, and the others hospital firemen and fire-watchers. No patients, no nurses hurt . . . Yes, I'm sure. Just come from the hospital, haven't I?' Burness had been watching Josh, and when their informant moved he pulled out his hip flask. 'Take a real good slug, kid. You can use it.'

Josh said into the mouthpiece, 'I'll find it, Ann. Two'll be great. What would you like to do?'

She sighed. 'That's impossible.'

'Tell me anyway.'

'What I'd most like would be to get right out and into the country and do something gloriously normal like blackberrying. They'll be ripe now. I adored blackberrying as a kid.'

He thought quickly. 'Why don't we do that? Pete'll loan me his jalopy. I'll scrounge the gas somehow.'

'Could you? It would be wonderful! Hang on – can we get through the roadblocks?'

'Why don't we try?'

'Let's! They can only shoot us.' The delight in her voice hit him like a pint of champagne. 'Thanks awfully and let's not say more. You never know who's listening.' She rang off.

He hung up smiling, and looking so much younger that Miss Dewly smiled maternally and stored the tit-bit for Mother under the stairs tonight. Mother loved a cosy little natter with her mug of Ovaltine.

'This is where we came in.' He slowed the car then saw that Ann was asleep with her face turned to her window. He drew up a few yards from the crossroads of two lanes sheltered by blackberry hedges and golden brown oaks, and three khaki figures rose languidly from the patch of long grass round an armless signpost crowned with a tin hat. The three wore ill-fitting battledresses, forage caps, LDV (Local Defence Volunteers, now renamed Home Guard) armbands, and left their civilian gasmask boxes half-buried in the grass. One had a corporal's stripes and an Army rifle Josh recognised as early Great War issue; the older of the two privates, a middle-aged man, had a shotgun, the younger, a boy of around sixteen, a sporting rifle.

'Sorry, Ann. Roadblock.' He had to shake her gently. 'Block. Bumf wanted.'

She stirred, and without opening her eyes or turning her head felt for the National Identity card and Martha's badge in her coat pocket. He took them from her hand and held them out of his window with his sheaf of permits.

The corporal ambled up, smiling apologetically and sketching an unmilitary salute. He was well-built, roughly Josh's age, with an attractive tanned face and bleached streaks in his fair hair. 'Sorry to hold you up and all that.' He had a pleasant voice and the accent Josh identified as Oxford English. 'I have to ask, is your journey really necessary? How did you come by the petrol to make it? Who are you and have you proof of identity? Oh, thanks, sir.' He cast a perfunctory glance inside the car, being far more interested in Josh's credentials. 'American correspondent? I say!' He looked up eagerly. 'Are you the chap they were talking about on – what was it – yes – "In Town Tonight" on the Home Service last Saturday – or was it the Saturday before? Anyway it was about this chap making all those broadcasts to America whilst bombs are dropping around London.' Josh was shaking his head. 'Not you?'

'No. That guy is Edward R. Murrow of the Columbia Broadcasting System. I am not a radio reporter. Newspaperman.'

'So you are! Says so in the bumf. Sorry and all that, Mr Adams, but what are you doing in this part of the world?'

Ann had woken up and now stared at the speaker. Before Josh could reply, she leant across him smiling. 'Amongst other things, David, giving me a lift back to town. I'm on duty at 8 p.m. How are your mother and Joy and the boys?'

'Good God!' The corporal stooped to peer in. 'Ann Marlowe! Long time no see!' He grinned broadly and pulled off his cap. 'Still nursing in London? Where was it? Thomas's, Guy's, Bart's?'

'Do me a favour and look at that bronze star in your hand. Martha's. My name and training dates are on the back.'

'You're right! "Ann Laura Marlowe, 1936–1940." And still at it.' He looked more closely at the brooch in the palm of his hand. 'There was something about St Martha's in *The Times* a week or two back. Haven't you copped it a bit?'

'A bit. Let me introduce – David Wadhurst – Josh Adams. When David's not playing soldiers, Josh,' she added as the men shook hands, 'he farms on the Sussex side of the county border, and his mother and my aunt were at school together. How's the farm, David, and what's a Sussex man doing guarding a foreign county?'

'My captain's not too hot on map-reading. Rome wasn't built in a day,' he allowed cheerfully. 'Family's fine and farm's not too bad after all the sun. We'd a decent hay harvest and the clover's healthy, but the beans need rain. Black and shrivelled as hell. But our Land Girls are getting the hang of things nicely. Took 'em a bit of time,' he explained to Josh, 'as, coming from London, they thought milk came from bottles till I introduced them to cows, and when they first joined us they had the devil of a time finding their way around with all the signs gone from the signposts.'

'Quite a problem.'

'And how. Poor girls kept getting lost till the recent spot of activity above made life much easier. Now instead of having to draw maps and warn the girls to eat 'em if they run into Jerry paratroops, all one has to say is turn left by the burnt-out Me. up the lane to the tail of the Dornier, carry on to first right after the nose of the Hurricane and you've hit the five-acre field, and if you pass the Spit in the hedge you've gone too far. Works like a charm.' He paused, looking at Josh. 'Some party, that show. See much of it?'

'Some.'

'We had a grandstand view. Made harvesting a shade dodgy as we had to keep downing scythes and diving into ditches. Our Land Girls never turned a hair, but it turned my offspring into bloodthirsty little savages. Yells of glee every time a Jerry bit the dust. Upset their mother a bit on their behalf, but as it didn't affect their appetites or sleep I said I'd prefer them as little monsters rather than nervous wrecks, and as my mother says, when haven't small boys been bloodthirsty little savages?'

Smiling, Ann put in, 'Josh, Mrs Wadhurst, senior, and my Aunt Maud are kindred spirits.'

He smiled back, warmed by her private reference, and by the additional insight this chance encounter was providing into another unexpected affinity with her. It was obvious that her friendship with this Englishman had been rooted before either were born, in the friendship of two school-girls. This explained why Ann had immediately understood his calling on Ed Laurings, and had appreciated his writing to Mrs Laurings and unasked, sending Ed's obituary to his local editor. And listening to Ann giving Wadhurst news of her aunt for his mother, he was filled with admiration and gratitude towards the unmarried woman who had given her dead brother's small twins the measure of love and security that had healed the most devastating wounds any child could suffer and given Ann's nature its generosity and strength.

He nodded his thanks for his returned permits and sat back to let Wadhurst hand back Ann's. 'Great to hear Michael put up such a good show. DFC. Nice work. What is he now?'

'Squadron Leader.'

'Give him my congrats!'

'Thanks. I will.' Ann hesitated. 'Aunt Maud wrote to me about Paul Norman and George Stapely. Same day, she said.'

'The fifteenth of September.' Wadhurst hesitated. 'And Billy Carter.'

'Not little Billy? Oh, David – ' Her voice cracked. 'Was he old enough? I thought he was still at school.'

'He was nineteen. Sergeant Pilot, like Paul and George. Good chaps, those three.' He withdrew his head. 'Damned good seeing you again, Ann.'

'And you, David. Give my love to the family.'

'Will do! I'll let you push on now.' He replaced his cap, saluted a little more smartly, then dropped his rifle. He picked it up grinning. 'Just as well it's not loaded. Got a damned dodgy safety catch.'

Josh gazed into mid-air. Ann demanded, 'Haven't you any ammunition?'

'Not enough to waste shoving one up the spout till I'm sure I'll need it with this safety catch. Not to worry. Haven't needed one up the spout yet. All the best to you both and – er – watch it in London. Rather hot up there, one gathers.' He stepped back and took off his cap to wave them off. The privates too waved their caps, and Ann, winding down her window and putting out her arm to wave back, murmured, 'He's got one good lung. TB as a kid.'

'Uh-huh.' Josh waved, then started the engine. He wondered if, even after all Churchill had said on the subject, the British people – even Ann – realised what would have happened had the RAF lost the Battle of Britain. If the ill-equipped remains of their regular army, the similarly ill-equipped and still largely untrained conscripted army, and the hundreds of thousands of volunteer, amateur, grossly ill-equipped, part-time soldiers had had to take on the superbly trained, equipped and professional Wehrmacht, nothing could have saved the British mainland from German occupation this year.

Ann withdrew her arm, wound up her window swallowing a yawn, then looked at his carefully impassive profile. 'Yes,' she said as if he had spoken his thoughts out loud, 'thank God we've still got a navy.'

'Uh-huh' was the only response he dared make. When he risked glancing sideways a minute or so later, she had gone back to sleep, and did not wake till he shook her outside her Home.

'Oh, Josh, I'm so sorry – '

'No need. I'm glad you had a good kip.' He opened his door. 'I'll just see you – '

'No, wait.' She put a hand on his arm and felt the immediate tension of his arm muscles. 'You must get back. It's getting dark. It's been a glorious afternoon. Thanks for everything.' She leaned towards him, and before he realised what she was about to do, kissed his lips lightly. 'Take care. Cheerio.' She jumped out of the car before he recovered breath for speech, ran up the five stone steps to the open, polished oak front doors, then turned smiling to wave him off.

He waved back, smiling, and as he drove off he felt as if he were walking on air.

'Trust Jerry not to waste the bombers' moon. Not that you'd know it was up from here.' The speaker, a Special Constable, peered through the billowing smoke that was coming from over the river and blocked out the sky. He was standing against a sandbag wall in Trafalgar Square, on the corner of the Strand and Northumberland Avenue, and Josh had stumbled into the sandbags before stumbling into him. 'Now the wind's getting up it should fetch in a few clouds, and not before time for the south side. Their turn tonight. Turn and turn about, that's his motto.'

'It certainly is.' Josh turned up his mackintosh collar to nudge the back brim of his trilby. The south-east wind that had come in with the tide an hour ago hinted of winter, not autumn. 'Chilly,' he remarked.

'Proper parky. You're a long way from home, aren't you, sir?'

'You could say that.' Josh peered blindly through the smoke filling the black canyon into which Northumberland Avenue, like every street in London, was transformed every night. 'You're a Londoner, officer?'

'Not a proper one.' There was a smile in the South

London twang. 'Born and lived all me life down in Putney. You can't hear Bow bells in Putney, and you got to be born in the sound to be a Londoner proper.' He settled more comfortably against the sandbags and in the tone of a man settling down for a chat, asked 'How long you been over this side of the Atlantic?'

'A good few years.' He could, thought Josh, be a lonely cop on the night-beat in some small Midwestern town that regards a kid pitching a brick through a window as a crime to endanger civilisation. He's grown too accustomed to the barking of guns, the circling of aircraft growling like angry wolves, and the thunder of exploding bombs to pay heed unless they are directly overhead.

He stayed talking for a few more minutes then set off down Northumberland Avenue towards the Embankment, groping his way along the walls, testing the ground ahead at every step, bumping into invisible figures, chorusing 'Sorry!' and catching snatches of conversations from others passing unseen. A girl's voice: '. . . and a fat lot of use your saying blame Jerry! My mum'll blitz me something awful if I'm not home by midnight . . .' A woman's: '. . . "tonight and every night" same as the theatre placards used to say when theatres was open . . .' A man's: '. . . ever such a good picture that was we saw s'afternoon, Doris . . .'

The blitz has become a way of life to them, thought Josh, groping on. And they've adapted to that way of life with a stoicism that would have Hitler throwing one of his tantrums if anyone dared tell him and could get him to believe it. Every night they sleep underground, but if it's not 'their turn' first they go down the pub, or meet up for dates; every day those that can, show up for work on time; every afternoon those that can take the time off, fill to standing-room only the movie houses now reopened for afternoon performances and the National Gallery for the lunch-time concerts Myra Hess has started putting on. The theatres stay closed, but every department store and shop standing or semi-standing is back in business. Every afternoon orderly queues start forming for the Underground platforms that from four o'clock open as public shelters. And every morning, on the new ruins, new boards announcing DOWN BUT NOT OUT, OPEN FOR BUSINESS AS USUAL, LONDON CAN TAKE IT, and new rashes of tatty little Union Jacks stuck on the mounds of rubble, and drawing-pinned to the sills of gaping windows.

Last month he had asked Burness, 'Where do they get all these flags? I've seen none for sale.'

'Who needs to buy any after the Silver Jubilee of King George and Queen Mary back in '35 and the Coronation of George VI and his Elizabeth in '37? This old city kind of likes to hang on to its old bits and pieces, and sure as hell if there is one thing it likes above all it is putting out the flags and having a good old street party. So maybe the party has to wait – maybe the street has gone for a Burton? Not to worry! Put out the flags and press on regardless! My Joan is as crazy. She is hoarding real safe her flags for Victory Day – and that reminds me. When I managed to get the trunk-call to her yesterday she said again to be sure and tell you that any time you care to take a break you will be more than welcome in Exeter.'

'Do thank her, Pete. I am looking forward to it. May I take a raincheck?'

'Any time, Josh. You will be more than welcome.'

Some other time, thought Josh, groping on, the smoke making his eyes stream and his lungs tighten and the increasing noise hammering his eardrums. Once out of the smoke he saw, as through an undulating gauze curtain, the swirling dark shapes of aircraft, the long pale probing fingers of the searchlights, the flashes of the guns, the exploding stars of the ack-ack shells, and what looked like stationary airborne tiers of little tongues of flames and were the fires the incendiary bombs had started on unguarded roofs. 'It's raining incendiaries on the south side,' had said a warden to whom he had spoken before the Special Constable. 'Making for Millbank? You should be all right, but keep to the nearside pavement and keep your head down. What goes up must come down and this wind'll bring some our way.'

Not just raining incendiaries, but high explosives. At least, right now, there was no deep-throated roar of one of the new, deadly land-mines that floated down quietly, landed silently, and had already misled rescuers into the fatal assumption that they were unexploded bombs until their timers went off.

He couldn't see Martha's, but the knowledge that the hospital – and Ann – were in the heart of this attack suddenly ripped off his civilised layers and exposed the primitive. He was consumed with the ugly anger he had seen in so many English faces, and thought savagely – if he gets her – God, so help me I'll join the lynch mob first chance! Then he realised what he was thinking and was appalled, and the more so for recognising that he meant it.

At last he reached the sandbagged concrete pillbox that housed the warden's observation post he was making for. A few nights ago he had visited it by chance, and recognised one of the wardens as a middle-aged civil servant he had met at a cocktail party in Kensington in early August. He had remembered the carefully combed, thinning black hair, rather vacuous face and that the name was Nigel Something. He still didn't know the man's surname. On the first occasion he had greeted Josh warmly with 'Good to see you again, dear boy!' and when Josh left, 'Do drop in any time you're passing. No visitors more welcome than those that let us scrounge their fags.'

This time he had a similar reception. 'Delighted to

see you back, dear boy! Perfect timing. Just brewed up. Couldn't you sleep?' Nigel Something shouted through a burst of gunfire neither sandbags nor concrete could muffle.

'Felt like taking a walk.'

The men sitting drinking tea on the short, low benches against the walls agreed that they enjoyed stretching their legs before turning in, and those on the nearest bench edged up to make room for Josh. He was glad of the seat and the offered mug. Just before ducking under the low doorway he had seen a searchlight trap a Dornier like a fly on flypaper, in the reflection of other searchlights swinging up to form a cone, Martha's seven standing blocks and one half-ruined one. Only the latter was lapped by tongues of flame as on the roofs the hospital firemen were extinguishing the incendiaries as they landed. The relief made his bones feel as if they had turned to water, and he handed round cigarettes, then lit his own, hungrily, knowing that there was no chance of being allowed over any bridge until the All Clear, nor, until then, of any but Jerry shifting him from this outsize cement coffin reeking of pipe and cigarette smoke, cordite, sweat, damp sandbags and strong, sweet tea.

A bomber diving under searchlights screamed so low overhead that they all ducked. 'Bridge-hopper,' grumbled the man on Josh's left, mopping spilt tea from his dusty navy serge battledress. 'Thinks he's a Me.'

Nigel Something fitted the fallen cigarette back in to his long ivory holder. 'Some of these Jerries handle their bombers as if they were fighters for all they're so much heavier and less manoeuvrable. Dashed fine pilots – God bless my soul!' A tremendous roar echoed over the river. 'Sounds as if poor old Martha's has copped a land-mine this time. Frank?'

The man nearest the doorway ducked out, then returned grinning. 'Still got her seven-an'-a-tanner.' He

produced two greasy packs of cards and pulled forward
an old upturned tea chest. 'Who's in?'

'Play rummy, dear boy?'

'Gin? Sure.' Josh spoke without moving from his
clamped lips the outer portion of the cigarette he
had just bitten through. Surreptitiously removing the
piece in his mouth, he glanced at his watch. Five
before twelve. Hours to go now dawn was later.

Ann was smiling in her sleep when she woke without
knowing why, for the first time that night. She sur-
faced slowly to the crashing noise of man-made thunder
and hail, and the whispered argument between Jill
and Mary going on across her in the darkness. Near-
misses and physical exhaustion had become too common
for torches to flick on until their owners were called
up.

'It came from ahead. Must've got Martha's!'

'Phooey, ducks! It was behind us!'

Ann muttered, 'What's the time?'

'Five to twelve and will you three shut up! You're
worse than Jerry!' hissed Nancy Standing's voice.

Ann frowned and leant closer to Mary to murmur,
'Why's Nancy pulling rank? Judy up?'

Mary cupped her mouth to Ann's ear. 'Judy, Monica
Aitkin' – the Casualty nurse on first-call tonight with
Nurse Francis – 'and all the theatre girls an hour ago.
You've been flat out whilst we've been Jerry's bull's-eye.
He keeps coming back to us. I think he's got his lines
crossed and thinks this is Westminster and Martha's is
the House of Commons. He's just dropped a land-mine,
judging by the row. Jill's probably right about it falling
behind us as, if he'd got the hospital, by now Home Sister
would have come in. If he keeps this up and we end up
queueing at the pearly gates we'll just have to explain to
St Peter we're not MPs.'

'I'll leave that to you.' Ann lay back smiling sleepily at Mary's characteristic response. There was another barrage of ack-ack followed by what sounded like a cloudburst of hailstones. Mary's not kidding, she thought, struggling between the longing to sleep and the necessity to think clearly – she and Sue Hardy, the former Charity staff nurse transferred to Casualty on the same day as herself, were on tonight's second call. As two for Cas and all the theatre girls are up, obviously Cas is swamped already and in the Theatre Block at least four tables are in action, she thought wearily. And if a land-mine has just dropped behind us, it's hit one of the most populous parts of London, so by now the cops have warned Cas, and any minute now the first minors will start staggering in and the majors being carried in, though it'll be hours or tomorrow morning before the most deeply buried arrive. Oh, hell, the noise is getting worse – worst I've heard – Sue and me next – get my hair up.

She sighed and sat up in the darkness, too drugged by the urge to sleep to feel fear. She wondered if this afternoon with Josh had actually happened and not just been a lovely dream, and then recalled the difficulty she had had getting the blackberry stains off her hands before going over to supper. The recollection was no comfort, for by reminding her of her happiness with Josh it rewoke her nagging anxiety for him. *No! Stop it!* she thought, as automatically as she had done over Michael, and reached for the comb and hairpins under her pillow. She had her hair up and was asleep again when, several minutes later, Home Sister came in and switched on one pair of wall lights.

Miss Merton was in uniform. She had got dressed after calling up the first six staff nurses at the request of a handwritten note from Night Sister that included the words, 'All outside lines including Casualty's to police, down.' The note was delivered by Paddy Brown, now, with his pair, amongst the ten volunteer medical students on the reserve team also in temporary residence. Paddy wore a warden's tin hat and was in shirtsleeves. The limp mask round his throat and his shirt were smeared with soot and plaster.

'Mother of God, but it's a rowdy night, Sister,' he gasped, stumbling into the dark front hall when she unlocked the front doors in answer to his urgent ringing.

When he arrived with the second note, his attractive young face was white and glistening, his dark eyes bright with fear, excitement and anger. 'The swine's just got that Rest Centre down the road in Pilgrim Street, Sister! Slap on, kerplop! Crossing the road's murder! All but the kitchen sink coming down. I'd leave the tin lid for a nurse but I swore blind I'd – '

'You keep it on, Mr Brown! Night Sister's given me no figures? No idea how many?'

He shrugged wildly. 'Cas's message from the cops said between three hundred and fifty and four hundred in the Centre but – er – '

'Quite. Thank you. You must get back. Be careful, Mr Brown – be careful.'

Miss Merton now said to the ballroom, 'I'm sorry to disturb you, nurses. Second Casualty-call wanted and, please, four volunteers for Casualty.' Ann and Sue Hardy leapt up, and every other right arm was raised wearily, in conditioned habit. 'Nurses de Grey – Ashdown – Blore – Dawton. Thank you, nurses. I'll note your names, wards and departments.' Miss Merton paused momentarily. 'Sister Casualty is back on duty.'

The communal gasp was audible over the noise from above. She couldn't, thought Ann, have shaken us more had she said Hitler was goose-stepping through Central Hall. If old Sister Cas, the oldest and toughest upholder of Martha's traditions and etiquette, has cut through both and gone back on at night, Martha's *is* fighting for its life.

A chorus of voices demanded, 'What's he got now, Sister?'

'Unhappily, a direct on the Pilgrim Street Rest Centre. I'll be in the hall, nurses.' Miss Merton hurried away to unlock her lost-property cupboard, leaving behind an outbreak of outrage.

'God, how ghastly! Bombed out last night, then this . . .'

'They'll be barely out of last night's shock.'

'Those poor people! A direct! It's like a nightmare – '

'Not like! It *is* for them!'

The only silent voices belonged to the six stripping off and getting into uniform with a lack of conventional modesty that no longer offended even the few present who had not attended boarding schools. Ann and Sue Hardy reached the hall first, slinging gasmasks, shelter-bags and cloaks over their shoulders, and Miss Merton thrust at each one of the six old black umbrellas she had taken from her cupboard and just tested.

'Use them going over, nurses, and the patients' entrances to OPD. It's unlocked.'

Ann and Sue Hardy, who was three months Ann's senior in hospital time and age, exchanged glances just before Miss Merton switched out the hall lights. That entrance to the OPD was forbidden to all staff and always locked between 6.30 p.m. and 9 a.m.

'Now, nurses.' Miss Merton held aside the heavy floor-length blackout curtains hanging just inside the tall, polished oak front doors that had been unblemished when Ann waved Josh off. The darkness hid the multiple pockmarks and the shrapnel and glass splinters now embedded in the outer sides. 'Be careful crossing – a lot coming down – be careful, nurses – ' She quickly opened the front door then closed it behind them, adding mentally, 'Please, dear Lord – take care of them all.'

For the few seconds it took to acclimatise their eyes to night vision the two stood poised on the doorstep. The sudden full exposure to the noise, to the throttling, blinding, billowing smoke smelling of cordite, burning and gas from a sliced mains pipe in a nearby side street, to the rattle of invisible fragments of shrapnel hitting stone, macadam and metal, and the slow crunching of invisible wheels on broken glass, made those seconds the most terrifying they had ever experienced.

Ann felt terror tighten her throat like an iron band, and as she struggled with shaking hands to open her umbrella she thought helplessly – this is what blind panic feels like – we're going to be killed! And then, in an upsurge of rage that sent soaring her adrenalin – I'm damned if we will! Where's that damned moon?

Sue Hardy muttered through chattering teeth, 'I hear traffic – can't see – or can I?'

'Yes! Just getting it. Convoy for Cas.' Ann peered frantically through the smoke and blackness and just glimpsed the line of uneven, snail-like outlines crawling behind narrow beams of light from blackened-out head-lights along the far side of the road. 'No gap – yes! Hold-up now – gap just outside OPD.'

They ran down the steps and across the road between a private car with two stretcher-cases lashed to the roof luggage-rack and a third lying across the back seat, and an ambulance with four stretcher-cases in improvised tiered bunks and three on the floor between.

The ambulance driver, glimpsing headless, legless white streaks, rubbed her aching eyes. 'Am I seeing ghosts, Harry?'

'Ghosts don't carry open umbrellas, Diana. Nurses.'

The driver had had four hours' sleep in the last forty-eight. 'It's not raining.'

'Not rain it isn't.'

'Oh. That. Stopped noticing.' She leant on the wheel. 'Get a move on, you clot ahead! We've got to get straight back if you haven't!'

'Bound to be a bit of a hold-up unloading.' Her colleague wound down his window and cautiously stuck out his helmeted head to search for the first red glow of hurricane lamps. These were roofed to be invisible from the air, and were only put out to guide ambulances to and through Casualty Yard on nights when they were expected in convoys and not just pairs or singly.

Martha's had been without mains gas and electricity for over three hours, and to spare the emergency generators the empty Out-Patients Department was in darkness. The noise echoed and re-echoed through the innumerable large clinic rooms, small offices and maze of side corridors, and when Ann slammed behind them the unlocked door of what she had been regarding as a sanctuary, she was suddenly even more terrified than she had been on the doorstep opposite. Too terrified for coherent thought, she switched on her torch, flung her closed umbrella on to the nearest empty bench, and gasped, 'Run, Sue – run!'

'Hold it – no breath – '

'Run!' She grabbed Sue's hand, hauling her until they were running abreast down every short cut to the main corridor that provided the only internal entrance to Casualty since the side passage from Central Hall had vanished with the main Dispensary. Once in the empty, dimly lighted, long corridor the noise remained overwhelming, yet Ann, still running her fastest, was acutely conscious of an inexplicable sense of relief that was another aspect of that night that she was never to forget.

All the dimmed lights were on in Casualty Hall, and in all the surgical dressing-rooms and medical clinical-rooms that opened off it, and, as always when the rooms were in use, all the doors were hooked open. On the left the wall that had been backed by the Dispensary was now wooden-boarded from floor to ceiling. And now on the rows of long, low-backed, mahogany benches on the left of the centre aisle running from Casualty Yard to the main corridor were seated around two hundred minors who all night long had been staggering in unannounced and aided only by each other. They sat slumped with grey Casualty blankets over their shoulders and legs, their hair, faces and clothes powdered with soot and plaster, their bloodshot eyes glazed with shock, and clutching between their hands saucerless cups or mugs of sweet tea.

On the right, the inner half of the benches were filled by casualties lying prone under the layers of grey blankets covering the torn, matted, filthy clothes in which they had been carried in. Every stretcher-trolley and examination couch in the department was in use. Like all the majors, those on the benches had been given injections of morphia, made as comfortable as possible, and as none had obvious bleeding points, left temporarily to rest whilst attention was given to those in danger of bleeding to death. There were already twenty-one in the theatre queue; in the Theatre Block five tables were in action; and every professor in the hospital, every resident, all the pathologists, radiologists and X-ray technicians on call, and seven honoraries who had come in unasked, were working in Casualty or the theatres.

When Ann and Sue Hardy turned in from the corridor, stripping off cloaks, shelter-bags and gasmasks, three more stretcher-cases were being lowered on to a bench to the right. Dr White, masked, stethoscope up, his long white coat smeared with grime and spotted with blood, bent over the first newcomer, Nurse Aitkin the second, Sister Casualty the third, nearest the aisle. The stretcher bearers – two junior housemen and four medical students – gently eased out their poles from the canvas, leaving this under the patients, then raced back to the Yard. Sister Casualty, small, stout, white-haired and crackling with starch, kept one hand on her patient's pulse and with the other beckoned the incomers. As they hurried towards her, Ann's quick encompassing glance evoked the instinctive thought – this is what hell looks and smells like. She had no time to analyse that thought or identify any particular smell in the heavy atmosphere that mingled smoke, plaster, ether, surgical spirits, iodiform, carbolic, the sickly-sour smell of fresh-spilled blood, and human exhalations; but what in that moment she smelt most plainly was the dreadful smell of human fear. She had no time to reach Sister Casualty before the thunderclap of an explosion nearby put out every light and drowned the sounds of lotion bottles and enamel dressing dishes shooting off china shelves on to the floor.

Immediately she could be heard, Sister Casualty called in the stentorian voice she normally reserved for reprimanding the staff, 'Will all patients please stay where they are. Our emergency lights will be on directly. We will attend you all as soon as possible.'

Within seconds the first battery-powered lamp came on outside the porters' lodge that guarded the Yard entrance, and then others in the dressing-rooms and at the corners of the Hall. Nurse Francis, in charge of the theatre queue, raced to light the hurricane lamps in the medical rooms that contained neither ether nor other bottles of spirits. The emergency lamps gave a golden glow, and when they came on, all the benches on the left were empty and their former occupants lay flat, or crouched on the floor, between their own and the bench ahead, with their heads under one or the other.

And when those emergency lamps came on in Casualty, the ambulance driver called Diana, her colleague Harry, the seven grossly injured casualties in their ambulance – five women and two men – the two equally injured young women lashed to the roof of the car ahead, the youngish man dying on the back seat, the driver who had on-the-spot volunteered his car as an ambulance, two more hospital firemen, and Staff Nurses Elizabeth Ashdown, Janet Blore, Angela Dawton and Jill de Grey, were dead.

– Seven –

Two hours after the All Clear, when the official rescue services had left for more urgent calls, the first morning light enabled the men still searching the new ruins to put out their hooded torches. The wind had dropped, and the stench of death was as tangible as the dustcloud. Ann and Sue Hardy emerged slowly from the staff door to Central Hall. They had just been sent off by Matron in person, to have five hours' sleep then lunch, before returning to duty for the day.

The high explosive that had cut through the front of the roof of the OPD and exploded in the ceiling of the patients' entrance, had blown the whole frontage outwards. A mangled mass of masonry and metal blocked the width of the road like a sprawling, ill-made causeway that was about ten feet high, thirty feet wide in parts, and in others never less than fifteen. The men searching the causeway trod carefully and worked grim-faced and in silence. And in that same grim silence they watched the appearance of the two cloaked nurses on the portico the Victorians had flanked with lifesize stone statues of ragged, crippled children. Only three statues now stood, on the far side from the OPD, and the others either lay cracked and chipped at the foot of the twenty-two stone steps, or crushed under the causeway.

The nurses looked neither at watchers, statues nor new

ruins. They went slowly, in silence, down the steps, their heads and eyes lowered, their exhausted faces as frozen as their minds after last night's insatiable demands upon their emotions and the stamina and training that had enabled them to go on working efficiently and swiftly for hours after the first agonising rumours had begun flashing around the staff in Casualty at 12.20 a.m. No 'staff only' caution was given with the rumours, or needed. Had there been time, none could bear to think, much less talk about, the private information that all knew must be confirmed – as had happened by 4 a.m. This was the second time in this war that Martha's own had been killed in the hospital; the first time in any war that patients, and the ambulance crews bringing them in, had been killed literally in Martha's shadow; and the first time in five centuries that Martha's nurses had been killed within its walls. The four staff nurses had just reached the OPD when the whistle of the falling bomb flattened them on the floor just inside the patients' entrance.

Slowly, the two nurses began crossing the rubble-strewn road, skirting the causeway, when suddenly they stopped. Lying at their feet, as if dropped by an absent-minded owner, was an apparently undamaged, closed, old black umbrella. They stood looking down at the umbrella for about a minute, ignoring the tears suddenly pouring down their frozen faces, then one – it was Ann – stooped to pick up the umbrella and carried it under her cloak as they walked slowly on to the pockmarked front doors that were opened to them before they reached the top step.

The searchers watched until the doors closed, then went on with their work, as before in a silence that had no connection with saving lives. They had been searching those ruins for hours and knew and dreaded what they must still find. What they had found already filled several large black oilskin sacks. Their task was one that every policeman, fireman and Civil Defence worker in London most dreaded, and when it had to be done, it was done in a blinkered concentration that had become another form of blitz-acquired expertise. But for those particular searchers the sight of the two nurses had broken that concentration and rekindled the white-hot anger that fatigue had begun to dull. Most were hospital firemen; all were volunteers from the lay staff. The dead nurses had been 'their nurses', the dead firemen 'their mates', the dead incoming patients 'their patients', and the ambulance crews, whether official or volunteers, were to them, as to all London, 'everyone's mates'. None of those searchers voiced their anger or thoughts to each other, and their silence underlined the tragic truth under the humour in the song currently most popular among London's firemen: 'Please Don't Talk About Me When I'm Gone'.

The customary stream of officials had been coming and going to and from the hospital and along the road ahead for hours. Some ten minutes after the nurses disappeared, three more men came down the middle of the road from the direction of the bridge and stopped several yards away. The searchers noticed without interest that one was a Metropolitan police sergeant, one a warden and the third a tall young civvy.

'No closer.' The sergeant's blitz-experienced eyes appraised the causeway. 'Won't take much to bring that lot down.'

'Very decent of you to let us this close, sergeant.' Nigel, whose surname Josh now knew was Desmond, sounded as old and tired as he looked, and that was far too old to have fought in the Great War, as he had from 1915 to 1918. 'Nasty. Nineteen here, you said?'

'Known.' The sergeant glanced over his shoulder. 'Would have been hundreds had he got Casualty and not an empty department. From the figures I've had there were thirty-one staff, two hundred and forty-nine patients inside Casualty, and more queueing to come in when it dropped.'

Nigel Desmond looked at Josh's white-lipped, blue-chinned face, with the trilby brim shadowing his eyes and his head uptilted to watch the searchers. Poor boy knows precisely what those poor chaps are doing, he thought sadly. 'How about the Rest Centre?'

'Ninety-three known dead. Too soon for the total injured, but into three figures last I heard. Still digging them out and now going over the river. Martha's has had a bellyful for one night.'

Josh swung round to face him. 'You said four nurses killed outright here?'

'That's correct, Mr – '

'Adams. *New York Banner*.'

The sergeant nodded. He had checked the credentials, but he had too many names in his mind to have room for the living.

'Like I said, Mr Adams, no use asking for names. No names till the families have been informed.'

'Would you know them? Is one a Staff Nurse Ann Laura Marlowe? I have to know!'

The sergeant hesitated, recognising the look in the eyes of a man in hell. 'Your young lady?' Josh nodded briefly. 'No one of that name on my list.'

'You can't be sure! Those guys are still – '

'I am sure about the nurses. My guv'nor had a word with the Matron not an hour back. The Matron runs a big hospital and has to keep her records up to the mark. Day and night she knows the whereabouts of all her nurses working in the hospital and sleeping in their Homes. Only the four young staff nurses missing last night. Found since, and identified by the Matron herself.' He didn't add that identification had only been made possible by the four charred bronze badges with the owners' names engraved on the backs, or what he had been told of the Matron's expression when she looked down at the four charred badges lying on a clean strip of surgical gauze on her desk blotter. But he had to pause and look at his feet. He reckoned he had as strong a stomach as the next man – and needed it after fifteen years in the Force without help from Jerry – but there were some things he couldn't stomach and he wasn't ashamed of that neither. He took another deep breath, then looked up. 'Ta. Don't mind if I do.' He accepted one of the three last cigarettes in Josh's last crumpled packet, then quickly struck a match to forestall the difficulty Josh's trembling hand would have flicking a lighter. 'Time we got back. I got a day's work waiting, same as you both, I reckon.'

Josh had to have positive proof. He thanked the sergeant, glanced at the pockmarked front doors, then turned with the others and walked back in the direction of the bridge. Leaving his companions talking to the Special Constable guarding the rope, he walked on towards Waterloo. He knew what he must do.

York Road had just been reopened to pedestrians, bicycles and handcarts, but nothing larger, and slow human streams already flowed in both directions. Workmen going to early shifts in greasy caps, shabby jackets and dungarees with mufflers round the collarless necks of their shirts, either on foot, or occasionally riding but more often pushing their bicycles around or between heaps of rubble and over the inevitable early morning carpet of broken glass and shrapnel chips. Little groups of women of all ages, sometimes accompanied by an elderly man; women in dusty, shabby civilian clothes, headscarves, turbans, or with their untidy hair prematurely greyed with dust, pushing old perambulators or little handcarts laden with what they had managed to salvage from their bombed-out homes and were taking to the relatives or friends with whom they were moving in. Josh saw them all go by without seeing their faces. He saw them as figures in a recurring nightmare and moved amongst them like a sleepwalker motivated only by instinct.

He ducked down the York Road entrance to Waterloo, and when he reached the mainline station saw one small, packed suburban train pulling in slowly, but no other rolling stock. A railway guard who had just chalked on a huge blackboard WE APOLOGISE TO PASSENGERS FOR ANY INCONVENIENCE CAUSED BY THE FOLLOWING CANCELLATIONS CAUSED BY ENEMY ACTION lowered his chalk to nod in Josh's direction. "Morning! Noisy night,' he said, then continued chalking up a long list of trains. The yawning youth taking down sandbags and wooden shutters from the only book-stall open was too sleepy to say anything when he sold Josh a packet of envelopes and another of cigarettes.

Josh sat on the nearest bench and in his notebook wrote a short note to Ann that ended, 'I just wish I could help. Josh.' He tore out the page, folded it into the envelope he addressed only to 'Staff Nurse Ann L. Marlowe', then put it in his breast pocket and walked swiftly back the way he had come. Nigel Desmond and the sergeant had gone, but the Special at the cordon remembered him, and after his brief explanation let him through. 'So long as it's just to hand in the letter and come straight back, mind.'

'Just that, thanks.'

He had barely touched the bell when one of the pockmarked doors was opened by a tall, thin, elderly woman in a spotless starched Sister's uniform, her red-rimmed eyes dazed with grief. He pulled off his hat. 'I apologise for disturbing you so early, ma'am, but I am not too sure I have the right location. May I ask if Staff Nurse Ann L. Marlowe lives here?' He produced the envelope. 'If so, may I leave this for her?'

'You may, young man.' She took the envelope. 'Nurse Marlowe is now sleeping. I will see she has this when she wakes.'

For a few moments he could only stare at her. Then he said, 'Thank you – thank you, ma'am.'

'Not at all. Good morning.' She closed the door.

Two mornings and two night raids later, and after all the remaining day staff nurses had spent their second night in hospital beds in the basement cavern under Block 7 that had once temporarily housed Hope Ward, Josh had Ann's reply on a postcard:

'Thank you. You have. A.'

– Eight –

It was another three weeks, and early November, before they could meet again – another three weeks of nightly raids, and spasmodic daytime air attacks that were labelled 'tip-and- runs'. Londoners largely ignored them unless they were in the target areas or were professionally involved. 'You ever heard tell of Gipsy Corner, brother? . . . Me neither, after more than eight years. Jerry is sure as hell teaching us nosy aliens our London . . .' said Pete Burgess.

In Martha's the sound of men hammering up wooden boards had become as routine as the almost nightly incoming casualties and the almost daily evacuations of patients to the Emergency Medical Services. The traffic returned to the hastily repaired main road; a second vast palisade patched the hospital's frontage; and the undamaged rear of the Out-Patients Department was reopened for daytime clinics. When October ended, the Thames, which the previous week had reeked of the raw sewage flooding in from bombed main sewers, reeked as powerfully of the cleansing chemicals being poured in: the residents opened a book on whether cholera, typhoid or typhus would be the first epidemic to hit London this winter. None of Martha's staff ever referred to the night that had left Ann and many others emotionally scarred for life: they had all learnt one of the most vital rules when fighting for survival – never look back, but if you must, keep it to yourself.

Twice in the last two weeks of October Josh and Ann arranged by post dates that had to be cancelled. On the first occasion when Josh called at the Home for Ann he was given her verbal apology by the portress; on the second, Ann rushed back to change in her room, which was in-bounds during daylight when no Alert was on, only to find Josh's apology in an unstamped envelope delivered by a taximan. When writing to arrange their third attempt to attend one of Myra Hess's concerts, theoretically possible as the Casualty nurses' daily off-duty had been altered to twelve-to-four or four-to-eight, she wrote, 'Let's switch tactics. Let's meet on the steps of St Martin's as soon after twelve as we can make it. It shouldn't take me more than fifteen minutes to nip over the bridge and down to Northumberland Avenue . . .'

It was cold and drizzling when Josh arrived on the steps of St Martin-in-the-Fields after booking a table in a restaurant off St Martin's Lane that served lunches until mid-afternoon. There was no sign of Ann and, impatient for his first glimpse of her, he moved to a corner of Northumberland Avenue so that he could look down its whole length and also watch the church steps. He waited tensely, reminding himself he was early and of the odds against Ann being able to get away. So far today there had been no tip-and-runs; but last night two more hospitals had been badly damaged, and this morning their patients were being moved to other London hospitals to await the fleets of ambulances and ambulance coaches from the Home Counties running shuttle services between London and country hospitals. A Government order insisted that, whenever medically possible, all seriously injured air raid casualties must be moved out of London within twenty-four hours of admission, and from one of the letters he and Ann now exchanged regularly, he had a new insight into what this involved for the hospitals concerned. 'It's a sensible and kind order, but as all our young porters have vanished into the war, it's turning the rest of us into expert stretcher-bearers. Just about every early afternoon, medical staff, medical students and Cas nurses roll up their sleeves and tote stretchers. I've always admired ambulance crews, but never like now. Occupied stretchers weigh a ton and are hideously unwieldy . . .'

The drizzle was heavier. He tugged down his hat, turned up his mackintosh collar and backed into a doorway to check his watch again just as Ann turned into the avenue from the Embankment. She saw him first. She was too far away to see his lowered face clearly, but she saw him hold his watch to one ear, and that gesture and her upsurge of joy on seeing him pierced her with guilt at being alive and happy when Jill, Liz, Angie, Janet – and especially Jill – were dead. And then she almost heard Jill's high, amused voice saying, 'Ducks, don't be dumb! Would *you* hold it against *us*?' She blinked rapidly, grateful for the drizzle.

Josh had seen her. His face lit up with joyous wonder and he darted recklessly across the road. The driver of an Army lorry that had to swerve to avoid hitting him shouted, 'Blind, or blind drunk, mate?' Josh grinned apologetically and raced on, his heart thumping. He wished he had remembered the umbrella Miss Dewly had insisted on buying for him and putting on expenses. He had assumed Ann would have one, for every civilian woman in London now seemed to carry one far more habitually than she had carried her now discarded gasmask box. Ann had only a small navy leather sling handbag. She wore a powder-blue beret pulled stylishly forward, a matching soft woollen scarf tucked into the upturned collar of her navy, single-breasted, belted raincoat, flesh-coloured rayon stockings and the brogues she had worn blackberrying. He took in every detail of her appearance, the graceful walk, the sweetness of the smile on her darkly shadowed, visibly thinner wet face. He was suddenly acutely aware that for Ann this meeting must revive memories of what had come just after their last parting, and the carefully wrapped jar of blackberry jam in one of his mackintosh pockets felt like a grenade with the pin out. He didn't know how to greet her. He longed to ignore convention and take her in his arms, but seeing her again illuminated too plainly how much he loved and desired her, and revived the anguish he had felt the night he had thought her dead. It was the underscoring of that anguish by his vivid memories of these last fifty-seven consecutive night raids that clamped on the invisible straitjacket. He was preparing to take refuge in conventionalities when she forestalled him.

'Remember Peter Daws in the PPW, Josh?' she asked smiling, and as if they had parted five minutes ago.

'Sure.' He breathed out mentally, hearing the trumpets and seeing the flags flying. 'Good kid. How's he doing?'

'Fine. I had a letter from him this morning. He's out of plaster, up in a wheelchair two hours daily, has got engaged to one of his VADs, who's one year younger, looks like Alice Faye but can't sing, and being a VAD won't be automatically sacked for falling for a patient, and life is a bowl of cherries.'

'Great! So is seeing you, Ann.' He took both her hands. 'Just wish I hadn't forgotten my umbrella.'

Momentarily the smile left her eyes. 'I'm glad. I loathe umbrellas.' The smile returned. 'Have we made this one?'

'Let's take no chances.' He drew her arm through his, clasping her gloved in his bare wet hand, too dazed with joy to rise above the obvious. 'Would *you* be automatically sacked for falling for a patient?'

She laughed. 'Next to deliberately murdering one, quickest way out of Martha's.'

He laughed and they walked on together to join the crowd of office and shop workers and off-duty servicemen and women making for the concert in the National Gallery. In fine weather these were held with the piano just inside the open main entrance so the music could be heard by those unable to get inside who were sitting on the Gallery's balustrade and steps, and, when wet, indoors, with the packed audience standing or sitting on the floor.

Ann looked around. 'This is fun!'

'It certainly is.' He tore his enchanted gaze away from the happy anticipation in her face and saw it mirrored in all the surrounding faces. And instantly his mind began writing. London was following form as uniformly as it had done right from that first Saturday in September. First came the passionate anger and savage determination to survive, then the stoic adaptation to continuous danger, intolerable conditions, domestic disasters, personal tragedies. Those layers remain, just pushed deeper by the new top layer composed of Londoners' indomitable refusal to be defeated and their determination to enjoy, if only outwardly, every possible moment of pleasure, and for that moment to ignore all others in the past, present or future. So they still pack the movies in the afternoons; these concerts, at lunchtime; and they have started packing the performances of scenes from Shakespeare that Donald Wolfit's company are putting on at the Strand Theatre between one and two o'clock. So the dressing-rooms had a direct hit last week? The stage is okay. Who needs dressing-rooms when there's an improvised curtain handy? Who needs night-time theatres when every night provides more real dramas than could be seen in a long lifetime's theatregoing? The pubs open early in the evenings and are rowdy with voices and the sound of laughter that's as common as the coughing – the endless chorus of coughing echoing through every public shelter and up from every underground entrance from dusk to dawn. And every working morning Miss Dewly and Mrs Harding swop last night's bomb stories, trading a Dewly window for a Harding one, taking umbrage when one tops the other's near-misses, uniting on the problems of getting hold of glaziers 'when it's not that they haven't the glass!' and if That Man really thinks the blitz is doing him or anybody but the glaziers any good he must be positively potty! Every other morning Miss Dewly shows up with more chrysanthemums from her garden, and two days back she brought the homemade teddy bear Mrs Dewly knitted in the cupboard under the stairs for Pete junior's first birthday yesterday and which old Pete's taken down to Devon. Then this morning – and there his mind stopped writing and the pot of jam in his pocket all but ticked.

Not yet. Later. When she was sitting in the restaurant with a glass of something handy. It had to be 'something' as he didn't yet know what she liked as an aperitif. There's so much about her I don't know, he thought, but the so much I do know reduces what's left to the trivialities they have always been, though too often they have been distorted into priorities when there's been time to get these in the wrong sequence. With no time, they fix themselves good and clear in the right order. Much too clear, he reflected, thinking of Pete three nights back when finally agreeing to take this short vacation. 'I kid you not, Josh – not for all the good Kain-tuck whisky going would I have passed up hitching with my Joan and having the baby, but sure as hell this ain't the job for a married guy.'

When the concert ended the drizzle had stopped, and in the restaurant he left the jam in his mackintosh when he hung it on the hatstand. Ann did not remove hers as it had dried and the small restaurant was chilly, despite the illusion of warmth provided by the candles on the table that were lighted to save electricity until darkness fell, though the light of the November afternoon barely infiltrated the cracked, paper-stripped windows sandbagged on the outer sides. Josh took so long hanging up his mackintosh that Ann, glancing up from her powder compact mirror, wondered if he shared Michael's dislike of her solecism that would have appalled her aunt. ('Ann dear, please! No lady ever makes up in public.') She noticed from Josh's back that he wore a well-cut dark suit she had not seen before, and when he joined her, his I'm-a-neutral-and-don't-let's-forget-it expression she had often seen before.

She smiled and put away the compact. 'Sorry, but I refuse to eat lunch with a shiny nose.'

'It didn't look shiny to me. Just very cute.'

The uncharacteristically pat compliment worried her. She looked more closely at his tired, taut face that had aged years in the last few months, his neat, freshly cut fair hair that lack of sun had darkened to English mouse, and the nick in his bony, well-shaven chin. She was touched by his anxiety to look his best for her, but troubled by the wariness in his clever blue eyes and by his changed mood. 'Wasn't that Chopin heaven?' she asked.

'It certainly was.' He longed to add, especially sharing it with you knowing I should, that is, hope to have you with me for nearly two more hours. He longed to say so much he dared not risk speech in that moment, and silently offered his cigarettes.

'Thanks. Love one.'

She noticed now that he was trying not to look at her and was careful not to touch her when he offered his lighter flame, even though on the way from the concert he had again drawn her arm through his and held her hand. Was it something I said on the way here, she wondered, that strayed on to forbidden territory without my realising it? No. That's too trivial an explanation for the sensation I'm getting now that he's backing off. Does this tie up with his not kissing me when we met, though I saw he wanted to as much as I did? Or is that just wishful thinking? No – I don't think so – he's reminding me of – who? Of course! Michael with Dolly last July. That's it. He *is* backing off, and it makes sense to him, just as it did to Michael. Not to Dolly, though, so the inevitable's happened as she's so pretty, the RAF's full of men, Michael made her miserable, and someone else offered her a shoulder to cry on. She's now engaged on the rebound, and Michael's instructing in Scotland, miserable with the posting and miserable without her. He's bright, but he couldn't see this was bound to happen; and I couldn't tell him in July, he would not have listened. He was so determined to save Dolly from being hurt that he refused to entertain the thought that she did not want to be saved in that way. If I'd told him so, he wouldn't have believed me. No nice young man would. An older man, perhaps. Not the younger men with the touch of the Galahad that makes them so nice, and 'women and children, first' engrained since they were in short trousers. They're so determined to be heroic they forget that this time there are no lifeboats for the women and kids in London or in Beacon Rise last summer, when Dolly on the ground was often as much in danger as Michael in the air. But if I reminded Josh of this, and said today may be all we have so let's not waste it being noble, I think I'd only make things worse. Thank God, the waiter!

'What do you like to drink, Ann?'

'What I'd like is dry sherry, but as I'm on at four it'll have to be soft. Preferably fizzy lemonade if still available, please.'

'You have that? Good. Half of beer for me, please,' Josh said to the waiter.

She waited till the waiter left before raising amused eyebrows. 'I thought newspapermen only drank whisky.'

He smiled politely. 'Not this one this time of the

afternoon. I've to work later and I've gotten fond of warm beer.'

'All part of when in Rome?'

'Just so.'

'How's the office?'

'In good shape.' He told her of Burness' vacation. 'His first break since he took his family down to Devon in May.'

'How lovely for them.' She paused expectantly, then prompted, 'How's your Miss Dewly?'

'Just fine. Maybe we should take a look at the menu.'

'In a tick.' She waved it aside, looking at him, before asking intuitively, 'Blackberries?'

His eyes narrowed. He nodded and without saying more got up, went over to the hatstand, then set the wrapped pot on the table before her. 'She's the Brenda.'

Ann unwrapped the pot that was labelled 'To Miss Marlowe, with very many thanks from Helen and Brenda Dewly.' She held it up in both hands as if judging the jam's colour and consistency at a village fête, then turned to Josh so quickly that she saw the concern in Josh's face before he managed to contain it. She said briskly, 'How terribly kind. Do thank Miss Dewly.'

'I'll do just that.'

'You had some?'

'I have. Pete's awaits his return. Shall I put this away till after?' He did not wait for her assent, and when he sat down again he went on talking of Pete. He loved courage. The lovely virtue, Barrie called it, he reflected, looking at Ann, and he was so right. Lovely! 'He's due back Tuesday night and if he can't get back into London before the election results start coming in, will he be mad!'

'Election – ? Of course, yours! The patients in Cas have been talking about it for days. Is President Roosevelt going to be re-elected?'

He shrugged. 'Open question. Wendell Wilkie's had a good campaign, and getting the Selective Service Act passed last month can't be doing F.D.R. too much good.'

'Why not?' she demanded, grateful to him for diverting her with this genuinely interesting topic. 'I should know but I don't. What is this Act?'

'It requires the registration of all American males between twenty-one and thirty-five.'

She frowned. 'Registration? For conscription?' He nodded. 'Why? You're not at war. Or does this happen in the United States when Europe's in one?'

He shook his head. 'First time in peacetime in American history. And if F.D.R. gets back for a third term that'll be another first.'

The arrival of their drinks and the placing of their order gave her time to think this over. She left their choice to Josh, and whilst dealing with it he watched Ann with fresh anxiety. He was sure of so much about her, but she was very English and there was still much about England over which he was unsure and unhappy. And Ann, watching him, thought sadly that he looked too old to have to register and she too probably looked years older than when they first met, then she dismissed that second thought in her dismay at what this could mean for Josh. Directly the waiter left, she said, 'You'll have to register.'

'Uh-huh.'

'Musn't this mean America's preparing for war.'

'That's not how Franklin Delano Roosevelt tells it.'

'Naturally. He wants to get back and needs women's votes. I hope he does get back. I think he's marvellous and he's helping us tremendously, but were I American I'm not sure I'd now vote for him. Particularly after nursing Ed Laurings and watching him die for, and in, a country that wasn't his. But, at least, Ed was Canadian and Canada's part of the Empire. America isn't. This isn't America's war, the Atlantic's wide, and were I American I'd do everything I could to keep my young men my side of it.'

I guess we will do just that, my dearest, he thought heavily, uncomfortably relieved that she had not responded along the lines of 'And about time too!' Neither F.D.R. nor Wilkie will dare bring us in unless the United States is attacked, and Hitler's too smart an operator to risk that until long after he has swept up the British Isles. All of them. Eire's neutrality will stop him as little as did that of Norway, Holland and Denmark, and even when he has an Atlantic seaboard, neither he – nor the US – yet have bombers capable of flying across the Atlantic much less making the return trip. But I can't see him not getting that seaboard, and for all the great show London's putting up, England, now literally on her own, can't hold out much longer. There'll be no invasion till next spring or summer, but by then, on present showing, what'll be left of London? And in all your history, who takes London, takes England.

He said, 'You'd have a tough choice. Wilkie goes along with the Selective Service Act, but as he didn't pass it, it does not appear to be hurting him.'

She set down her lemonade so sharply that a few drops spilt over. 'That's an unhealthy symptom.'

'You think?'

'I know. So do you, so you can come off the fence on this one. This is the same as when the House of Commons stops shouting at each other and starts shouting with one voice, and every pundit called in for a consultation agrees on the prognosis.' She jerked one thumb down. 'Obviously both men think this war's going to go on for ages so America had better be ready for this and that. I'm afraid they're right about it lasting ages. It's bound to take us quite a few years to win. We will, of course. Eventually,' she added with a certainty that twisted the knife for him. 'How do you feel about registering?'

'Ambivalent.'

'I'll bet! This isn't your war, you don't like it – who does? – and certainly, since I've known you, you've been falling backwards in your determination to stay neutral. But it can't be easy to stay feeling neutral after being one of Jerry's nightly targets for – how many is it? I've lost count.'

'Up to this last, fifty-seven consecutive.'

'Only fifty-seven?' She was incredulous. 'Seems years since we taught Denton poker. "Four tens – oh, goodness, shouldn't I have said that?" '

They laughed and the waiter grabbed the chance to serve their soup whilst their eyes continued their unspoken conversation about the afternoon that had altered the course of their personal lives as violently as it had the course of London's war.

Josh had to break the spell or burst out of the straitjacket. 'I've heard tell Germany's none too pleased with the Selective Service Act.'

'Too bad,' said Ann drily. 'But as a charming old boy – a retired professor of something with a badly sprained ankle after slipping on rubble in Stamford Street – said this morning, "those that sow the wind must reap the whirl-wind." ' She paused reflectively. 'The snag about starting up wars and bombing other countries is that you can't be too sure you won't get hit back. When I was coping with the old prof's ankle he told me the gen we've been getting from our regulars about our bombing of the Ruhr, Berlin and some synthetic oilfields somewhere – '

'Western Germany.'

'Yes, that was it. He said it was correct. Is it?' He nodded. 'I thought it must be. I'd taken our regulars' gen with lashings of salt as they adore making a story better, but the old prof I believed. He was a sweetie with a lovely, kind, clever face and only needed the top hat, goatee, and stars and stripes waistcoat to be the dead spit of Uncle Sam.' She looked at him thoughtfully. 'Actually, he could have been your grandfather. He said we weren't doing much damage. Was he right about that too?'

He was so enchanted by her unexpected compliment that he sounded abrupt. 'Could be.'

'Makes sense. We must be very short of aircraft to put up so few night-fighters to defend London. I suppose we're as short of bombers. That's not a question – I know if you know the answer, you shouldn't and can't tell me,' she added quickly, then sighed. 'I'm as thrilled as Michael's livid about his Scottish posting, but with him out of range I've no hope of that kind of inside gen. I'm not mug enough to ask, nor he to answer those sort of questions in letters, and, anyway, we usually write postcards. I never have time to read the papers or hear the wireless news – but both are so censored and so often old history that I don't miss much. Particularly with our regulars on that job every morning.'

'Who are these regulars?'

'Our own patients. I mean, not the air raid casualties, ours from our zone, our backyard. Our Londoners.'

He loved the warmth in her voice, but his professional side demanded clarification. 'You mean those living in real estate owned by Saint Martha's?'

'What's real estate? Property? Yes, Martha's owns some, but this doesn't come into it.' She smiled. 'This is about old tribal customs.' And as their meal progressed she explained that, for generations, the Londoners in Martha's zone had regarded Casualty as their local doctor's surgery and brought themselves in for the treatment of every condition from carcinomatosis to a splinter in the finger. 'Cas is open to all, free to all, so in they all come as regularly as their mums and dads, nans and grandads before them (nan here is short for nanny, granny). They're "our Londoners", we're "their Martha's". This has been going on for centuries. Gives a nice matey feeling that works both ways. We get to know some of them very well, especially the kids bringing themselves in on their own.'

He stared. 'Kids? Coming into hospital alone?'

His incredulity reminded her of how frequently she had encountered in highly intelligent, educated outsiders, irrespective of nationality, an ignorance of so many common realities of which she too had been unaware, until exposed to them by her training. She remembered Michael's horrified incredulity when she had told him of having to remove the underwear – often sewn on for the winter – of patients alive with body and hair lice. 'They don't bath? All winter?' She had snapped back, 'Would you? If you'd no bathroom, had to share an outside lavatory with your tenement block, a cold tap on the landing with your floor, in the English winter when you've got to heat every drop of hot water, coal and gas costs money and you've only got a few bob a week to keep you and often your family?'

Now she said gently, 'Dickens still lives round Martha's, Josh. When Jerry finally lays off, one quiet night you should drop into Cas after 9 p.m. when Sister goes off-duty. Sit on any bench, and when asked what ails you say you've got a headache that a couple of aspirins always fixes but you haven't any on you and being American don't know the nearest all-night chemist. Then take a good look around.'

You really believe this, he thought in despair. You, my sweet, gallant, intelligent girl, can't – won't – see what must come. You really believe that one day Jerry'll pack in blitzing, head for home, and allow London to pick up the pieces and get right back to normal. Oh, my dearest, are you going to have to find out that you are so wrong and that Hitler goes along with Bismarck's 'leave to the conquered only their eyes to weep with'.

He needed all his experience in dissembling to interviewees to answer casually, 'I'll do just that. Maybe you'll come and see the office?'

'I'd like that, very much. I've never seen a newspaper office off the flicks.'

His grin was genuine. 'We must fix that, but I should warn you the *Banner*'s London office is no big city news-room, and right now could be taken for a movie star's dressing-room.' He explained the chrysanthemums. Then, to divert his despairing mind, he went on to talk of the daily routine of his job. Encouraged by her interest, and without realising it, he told her more about himself than he had previously revealed to another person. And as he talked, the comfort of her presence, and his own absorbed interest in his work, began imperceptibly loosening the straps of the straitjacket. He was still doing most of the talking when the bill arrived and they discovered it was half past three. Josh asked the waiter if there was any chance of getting a taxi.

'Won't be easy, sir. I'll have a try – oh, thank you very much, sir.'

'Can we fix now for you to come to the office, Ann?' Josh asked.

'Sorry, no. I doubt if I can make it this week. From yesterday our half-days have had to be postponed again as two more Cas staff nurses got shifted, one to a basement ward, the other to the EMS. This morning Sister Cas said she'd have the revised off-duty rota ready this evening. Okay if I write?'

'You know it is.' His eyes caressed her. 'As soon as you can, please?'

She returned his look. 'You know I will.'

'Sir!' The waiter was back, jubilant. 'Just stepped out and there he was, passing! Thank you, sir! Talk about luck for you and your young lady, seeing it's coming down cats and dogs. If you ask me, that's what's given old Moaning Minnie a sore throat. Not one moan all day!' (Indeed there had been no raid today.)

The downpour dimmed the fading light and the

taximan sighed gloomily. 'Martha's first if you says so, guv.' He twisted his head to Ann on the shadowy back seat. 'Nursing there, are you, miss? Huh. Can't say as you've picked the healthiest spot in London for your job.'

She smiled. She had nursed dozens of London taximen. 'You pays your money and you takes your pick, driver.'

'Still says rather you than me, miss. No use saying bombs don't strike the same spot twice.' He sniffed the drenched air. 'Not a peep out of Jerry all day. He's up to something. We'll pay for it, you mark my words.'

She said consolingly, 'I expect you're right,' and as they set off she murmured to Josh, 'What'll really cheer him up will be a good skid, crash and all three of us getting pneumonia before the ambulance shows up.'

The laughter in her shadowy face, her nearness, and the prospect of having to leave her in a few minutes, snapped the final restraints. He took her into his arms and kissed her for the first time as if it might have to be the last. And as he did so, he was conscious that this was a wholly new experience for him. An ecstatic sense of unity with her, of which he had been subconsciously aware from their very first meeting, transcended national differences.

He raised his face a couple of inches to whisper breathlessly, 'I just love you so much, Ann. I just love you so. Do you know that?'

All she knew was that she had been lifted to a plane of happiness she had never known existed. It had aroused instincts and emotions she had never known she possessed, and she rejoiced that she did, and that he was the one man in the world with whom she could share this glory. 'I didn't know. Just hoped, as – '

'You – love – me?'

'Of course I do and – ' She couldn't finish.

He was still kissing her when the driver coughed loudly before slowing to stop at her front steps.

Josh released her reluctantly. 'I'll just see you – '

'No!' She put her hands on his shoulders and lightly kissed his lips. 'Thanks for everything. Cheerio.'

He seized her hands. 'We have to talk – '

'We will.' She slid her hands from his grasp, leapt out into the rain, ran up the steps, waved, then went inside.

The driver had watched in gloomy interest. 'Knows her own mind, does your young lady, guv.' He turned his attention to the huge palisades on either side of Central Hall and the uncleared ruins of the Junior Home that made glistening black patches in the darkening shadows. 'It's a wonder to me old Martha's still standing. Won't take much more to bring her down.' He neatly turned the cab between the swaying backs of darkened trams going in opposite directions. 'Too close to the river, that's her trouble.'

'Uh-huh,' grunted Josh, too torn between ecstasy and the nightmarish memory of what had followed Ann's first farewell kiss to hear what the man said. But he heard in retrospect, and his mind kept returning to the thought during that endless evening when, long after dark, the sirens stayed silent. 'Only fifty-seven?' she had said. Only fifty-seven, he thought. Only fifty-seven consecutive nights of deadly danger . . . I have to get her out . . . I have to talk to her straight . . . Why in hell hasn't he shown up yet?

'This is as bad as waiting for a door to bang, Nurse Marlowe.' Mr Thane, the smaller and darker of the two junior house physicians doubling as junior casualty officers, did a little tapdance to ease his aching ankles.

'Maybe he's just overslept, Mr Thane.'

'Not Jerry, nurse. Far too methodical. He's up to something. What's your bet, Dacey?'

'I couldn't say, Mr Thane.' The senior Casualty Porter rested his elbows on the shelf of the half-open stable door of the lodge where the telephones were as unnaturally silent as the patientless hall and the sirens. He smiled at Ann, who was standing in the open dutyroom doorway. 'I shouldn't wonder if Jerry heard this was your first time in charge, nurse, and reckoned to ease you in gently.'

'Dacey, say no more, please! Still ten minutes to go,' she protested and the housemen grinned. Nurse Francis was off duty and Sister Cas at third supper, from which, by a tradition only broken by air raids, she would return as Big Ben struck the first note of eight o'clock.

Mr Bradley – large, fair and as quiet as his former student pair and great friend Mr Thane was talkative – said that what foxed him were the customers. 'Last out and no more in for twenty-five minutes. What ails them all to be so healthy?'

'Biding their time, Mr Bradley, same as us, not knowing what he's up to.' Dacey surveyed with a proprietary air the two housemen propping up the wall opposite, Ann in the doorway, the two student nurses sitting on high stools in the dutyroom making stock (dressings) on a towel-covered glass dressing-trolley, the four tweed-jacketed medical students sprawled in the front row of the wheelchairs ranked against one half of the wooden wall to the left, the empty stretcher-trolleys ranked against the other half, the darkened rooms opening off, the mahogany benches, and the stillness of the heavy blackout curtains concealing the open entrance to Casualty Yard where no lighted hurricane lamps had been put out. Suddenly he looked more closely at the curtains, put a finger to his lips, then ducked silently from the lodge, dived through the curtains and hauled back into the light a wriggling little boy in a grubby

186

threadbare jersey and grey shorts, his bare feet in too large, old wellington boots. 'You again, Tommy Benson! What's your mum thinking of to let you out the one night you could be in bed on time?'

'It's me mum as sent me over to ask what's what, Mr Dacey, that's what!' The child wriggled free, unabashed. He was nine, with the build of an undersized six-year-old, and had adult eyes in his small, pale, sharp face. He turned to Ann. 'It's her I wants. Where's Jerry, Nurse Marlowe?'

She crouched down so she was level with his face. 'Duckie, I honestly don't know. None of us here know more than you or your mum.'

'Cops not tipped you off nothing?'

'Nothing.'

'Straight up?'

'Straight up, Tommy.'

'Garn!' He was disgusted. 'Best tell me mum it's all clear to go back down the pub.' He nodded at the housemen. "Evening, all. Ta, nurse.' He dashed out through the curtains and they heard his footsteps running surely over the flags in the darkness.

Mr Thane flopped back against the wall. 'If that little sodling isn't Hitler's secret weapon, I'm a Chinaman.'

Mr Bradley murmured, 'Come off it, David. The kid's no more dangerous than an unexploded HE.'

They all laughed. Dacey returned to the lodge, and Ann, unthinkingly, leant against one jamb of the dutyroom doorway, her mind occupied by the uncanny silence over London, and by Josh. In the wheelchairs, Paddy Brown and Hugh Dixon, back from noon today for their last spell in official temporary residence before their final qualification examinations, split and surreptitiously lit their last Woodbine.

Paddy inhaled luxuriously. 'Isn't this the life – *cave*, chaps!' He catapulted to his feet, hiding the butt behind his back. Sister Cas had swept in from the main corridor five minutes early.

She stopped at the far end of the aisle to bellow, 'Nurse Marlowe! May I remind you you are a staff nurse in temporary charge of my Casualty Department, not a lackadaisical lily! I will have no lackadaisical lilies propping up doorways in my department!'

Ann apologised, keeping her eyes downcast to conceal the laughter in them. Dacey looked wooden. The housemen studied their feet, musing that the lily was dead on target. The same thought struck Paddy Brown, leading the students' stealthy retreat as Sister advanced upon the lodge. Once in the main corridor Paddy sang quietly the new words he had begun setting to 'Lily of Laguna', his friends offered suggestions, and the mutual completion of the new version, and their admiration of their own brilliance, took their thoughts off the sirens' silence for a good fifteen minutes.

'No patients in, Nurse Marlowe? . . . Nothing from the police, Dacey? Very well.' Sister Cas turned to the housemen. 'Whilst we're quiet I see no reason why you junior casualty officers should not both go to supper. Do you?'

'Er – no, Sister.'

'Very well. Bustle to. The dining-room staff will appreciate getting off on time for once.' Having dismissed them, she turned back to Ann. 'I have returned early for a private word with you, nurse.' She stomped off, then stopped in mid-aisle, and Ann, following her, felt more curious than apprehensive. Had this concerned a professional reprimand Sister would already have given it, and had it been a personal matter she would now be discussing it behind the closed dutyroom door.

'Yes, Sister?'

'What ideas have you in mind for our forthcoming Christmas Show, nurse?'

Ann blinked. 'I'm sorry, Sister, I haven't thought about it.'

'And why not? You are now my second staff nurse. You must be well aware that I have been Chairman of the Organising Committee since 1926 and am accustomed to expect my staff nurses to co-operate fully in the production, being better placed for this purpose than those in the wards. I have just been discussing the matter with the Senior Surgical Officer, who has kindly agreed to take over medical and surgical sides in this context as present circumstances render it essential that Dr White, as Senior Resident, remain free of extra-mural responsibilities. Mr Wesley anticipates no difficulty in obtaining volunteers to perform, scene-shift and write scripts. As he has just observed, St Martha's men are not renowned for underestimating their artistic talents.'

Ann smiled quickly. 'Indeed, droll,' admitted Sister Cas sternly. Then she went on, 'Just now at supper Senior Sister Tutor recalled to me how pleasantly you sang the solos in the probationers' annual carol service in your first year. A most pleasing soprano. Untrained but true and strong. Do you still sing?'

'Not since my first year, Sister.'

'You must practise in the bath, nurse. Which bathrooms are you staff nurses now using?'

'Albert's since it emptied, Sister.'

'Good acoustics there. I well remember hearing the patients singing in their baths when I was the staff nurse in Albert Ward in 1909.' She frowned. 'But why were you not in last year's show? You were eligible as a fourth-year?'

'I was on night-duty over Christmas, Sister.'

'Oh. Very well. You will volunteer to perform, nurse. The lists requesting the names of volunteers will go up outside Matron's and the Dean's offices tomorrow. Put your name down and put on your thinking cap! It's November already. Christmas round the corner.

Time's getting short. Bustle to!' Her sharp old eyes had seen Dacey using one telephone. 'Well, Dacey? What news?'

Dacey came out of the lodge brushing a speck from one cuff of his navy frock coat, which had pale blue lapels to differentiate it from the Head Porter's gold. 'No change since before you went to supper, Sister. I've just given the police a tinkle. All quiet over the coast, all quiet over south-east England, and no word of anything going on further inland or up north. No telling, is there, Sister?'

'No indeed, Dacey. Thank you.'

No indeed, thought Ann, struggling to ignore, until she got off duty, the glory she had found in Josh's arms, which had made this the happiest day of her life. She watched both Sister and Dacey looking around the empty hall and listening to the silence from the sky, as if they dared trust neither eyes nor ears. Then she found that she too was doing this, with the same incredulity. Is this because we just daren't believe the blitz is over, or because we sense this is only the calm before the storm? Because that, she thought, is what this feels like.

– Nine –

Ann stopped on the penultimate step up to Central Hall to peer through the foggy blackout. When she came out a few minutes ago there had been three little statues on the portico. Now she could just make out a fourth shadowy outline.

'Who is that?' She was amazed she sounded normal – she was absurdly scared.

The fourth outline sniggered. 'It's me, Nurse Marlowe.'

'Tommy! You nearly gave me a coronary!'

Delighted, but innately suspicious, he demanded, 'You're not having me on?'

'Cross my heart.' She joined him. 'Do you often do this?'

'Play statues? Sometimes.' He posed again, balancing on one foot, crooking the other knee, hunching his narrow little shoulders in the cut-down man's jacket, open and buttonless, that was his overcoat, dangling his arms over imaginary crutches. 'Dead spit, eh?'

'Dead spit, duckie.' And may God forgive us, she thought, putting a hand on his shoulder and feeling the dampness of the threadbare jacket. 'Does your mum know you're out?'

'Nah. Me mum's down the pub, me nan's kipping, me big sister's out snogging with her bloke, and I got fed up with me comics and come out. S'boring, that's what.' He gestured disparagingly in the direction of the shadowy traffic and the darkness of Casualty Yard.

'S'ever so boring now Jerry's scarpered. Reckon he'll be back, nurse?' he added eagerly.

She was thankful for the resilience of his tough little mind, but deeply concerned over the effects the damp, cold night air could have on his ill-nourished, ill-clothed little body. 'Don't ask me, duckie. I'm just so grateful for eleven raid-free nights in a row.'

'Softy!'

'That's me.' She crouched down to his level. 'Tommy, do me a favour and go home to your comics. You shouldn't hang about in this cold.'

'I'm not doing no harm. S'boring going back. Why should I?'

Knowing him, and having nursed numerous children, she was honest. She had never nursed one child who had failed to recognise or respond to the truth.

'You're not harming anyone, but you could harm yourself. Hang around like this and you'll pick up this bronchitis that's going round and that'll be terribly boring. Now we've no children's wards, we'd have to pack you off to a country hospital. All the hospitals we send patients are miles from anywhere. Not even a hope of one of the tip-and-runs Jerry's been making around since laying off us. Not one bomb's dropped anywhere near any of them.'

'Not none? Straight up?'

'Straight up.'

'Garn! But I got no cough and – '

'Hang around like this and you'll get one. I'm not kidding, Tommy. Please.' She reached for one of his skinny little hands and straightened up. 'You're freezing. Come on, home. I'll see you over the road – there's more traffic tonight.'

'Get away!' He snatched his hand free and ducked out of her reach. 'I can take care of meself. What do you think I am, a bleedin' nipper?' He ran down the steps as if in daylight. He lived across the road in two basement rooms with his mother, grandmother and older sister. He had been born in Mary (Block 2) a few days after his father was killed in a drunken brawl, and from around his fifth birthday had brought himself into Casualty with cut knees, slashed fingers, black eyes, or to see what was going on when he had nothing better to do. Twice in this last year he had been evacuated and within two days made his own way back to London, first from Bournemouth and then from Devizes.

Ann had come out in a hurry to collect from the staff nurses' sitting-room the music needed for the rehearsal she was due to attend. She waited until the running footsteps faded, braced against a sudden squeal of brakes, but none came. He's home by now, if he's gone home, she thought, gazing into the darkness made deeper by the low cloud hiding the almost full moon and by wisps of fog coming from the river, which no longer smelt of chemicals. Smelling the old familiar sourness of the fog at night, she thought of what she had told Josh about Dickens on their last date. Dickens would recognise Tommy and London tonight in this cold clammy blackness with the threat of cholera, typhoid and typhus hanging over the city. Miraculously, no cases had yet appeared, but the physicians were convinced all three were unavoidable; they were so obsessed with the prospect, that not even the Fleet Air Arm's sinking of half the Italian Navy in Taranto harbour a couple of nights ago had diverted their gloom and despondency, though they had little time for either with London coughing its lungs out. This morning in Cas the SMO had said that in these last ten days he had listened to more consolidated lungs than in any winter month since he qualified in 1929. 'And that, Nurse Marlowe, irrespective of the lamentable fact that London has the world's third highest rate of pulmonary tuberculosis. One can only be grateful to Jerry for piping down and allowing us space to deal with this onslaught of chests. Who's next?'

Piped down permanently or temporarily, she wondered, going through the dimly lit Central Hall that now had a wooden wall blocking the right side as far as the first-floor ceiling. The charred red carpet had been stripped from the marble stairs, the remains of all the busts and all the pedestals on the right removed in sacks. The three public telephone boxes had vanished when the Dispensary was hit, but on the left the pedestals and stone wall had withstood both that and the hit on the OPD. Ever since the explosion of the Dispensary had belatedly illustrated the possibility of the entire medical staff being killed simultaneously, the Hall had ceased to be their air raid assembly point. New, separated assembly points had been established in the basement near the rabbit warren of small storerooms under Block 6 that had been converted into the residents' and resident medical students' sleeping-quarters. The SMO and SSO shared the one with the emergency telephone set on the floor between their bunks; the others had either four, six or eight bunks.

Ann turned into the main corridor and down the nearest basement stairs, puzzling – as she had done repeatedly in these last eleven days – over why the Luftwaffe had switched tactics to make the series of tip-and-runs upon Channel coast and Midland English towns, which from Wednesday of last week had taken Josh from London. According to the patients in Cas, and Judy Francis who had received her mother's weekly letter from Coventry yesterday, they were causing more nuisance than damage. Josh never mentioned the war, nor where he had been or was going, in the long letters he was writing her daily, which were causing the Cas patients to tell her daily that it was easy to see she had caught up on kip since Jerry scarpered. 'Fresh as a daisy you looks, nurse, and always a lovely smile . . .' Today's letter had a Liverpool postmark. His first from outside London had been posted in Reading, and in it he explained that he was writing it in a train as New York wanted him out of town, that his views on this were unrepeatable, and he would let her know immediately he got back. The postscript read: 'F.D.R. has his third term, I have a hangover, and you have my heart. J.'

She walked quickly, quietly along the winding basement corridor with pipes running along it. Parts of it were lined with bared beds that now looked to her as unnatural as empty beds in a ward. She went past still unused dark alcoves and closed storerooms and the open entrances of basement wards transformed into glowing red caverns lined with shadowy white beds. The night nurses glanced after her incuriously. It was too early for her to have been either Night Sister or the Night Ass.: now the hospital had reverted to normal routine neither left their nocturnal base, Matron's Office, to start their separate rounds until ten o'clock, nor did the residents start theirs until ten-thirty. Consequently rehearsals for the Christmas Show were always held from nine-thirty to ten-thirty; the nurses involved were restricted to staff nurses and fourth-years on days; and, until the last couple of weeks before the performance, rehearsals were held on Thursdays, in peace-time the quietest night of the hospital week. (Friday was the local payday, and only physical collapse forced breadwinners to miss it or their wives to be absent when they brought home their pay packets.)

The previous Thursday night Judy Francis, the official producer for the past four years, and the SSO, as ex-officio producer, held the casting auditions for performers and musicians. The hilarity of that occasion had made even Nurse Denton, an accomplished amateur pianist, forget her nervousness. She was still the acting staff nurse in Basement Ward 2, and had been offered and had accepted a staff nurse's one-year contract from 1 December. This had so increased her self-confidence that when her acting Sister, Nancy Standing, bullied her into volunteering as a pianist, Phyllis Denton had only lost a couple of quiet nights' sleep. Formerly, from the opening of the Staff Nurses' Home, performance and rehearsals had been held in the ballroom. 'This year,' Sister Cas announced the previous Thursday afternoon, 'Matron and the Board of Governors have kindly given us permission to use the Antenatal Clinic under Mary that has had to be opened because our maternity patients refuse to leave London until within a few days of their expected delivery dates. It will be most convenient. It is always empty at night, already has the chairs, lighting, telephone and space for the piano Mr Wesley's young men are moving down from a closed upper ward this afternoon, and the stage they will put up for the dress rehearsal that the full Committee will attend. We never intrude earlier, but whenever possible Mr Wesley will be present to assist Nurse Francis. He cannot tie himself to taking a fixed part in the performance, but we very much hope circumstances will again allow him to entertain us with his guitar. He has a most pleasing tenor.'

If Jerry keeps out of our hair, I'll bet he will, thought Ann, smiling unkindly and turning into the last side passage. Martha's is back to normal, so he's back to the Right Little God Almighty and all RLGAs adore being one of the chaps – so long as you lot don't forget the Dr, Mr or sir! He'll give us the old 'Foggy, Foggy Dew', and 'Abdul Abulbul', and – as last Thursday – 'If you insist, Nurse Francis – bowdlerised and with suitable acknowledgements to Nurse Marlowe – "Eight Nice Wardblocks" . . .' No! Don't be bitchy, woman! Why shouldn't Piers Wesley enjoy being one of the chaps after working non-stop twenty-odd-hour days all through the blitz? He rates the break as much as Josh sightseeing round England and Michael cursing his embryo pilots in Scotland.

She took the music from her shelter-bag before opening the door labelled ANTENATAL CLINIC. PLEASE WALK IN. The huge former storeroom had been converted by ranging down one half rows of hard chairs, and blocking off the other with open, brown rexine, screens with fixed feet. Behind these were two similarly screened partitions each with an examination couch and the obstetric equipment on covered glass dressing-trolleys, and a third, slightly larger screened partition furnished with a small doctor-cum-midwives desk, three hard chairs, two large metal filing cabinets, an emergency telephone set, portable X-ray screen, and the fitted scrubbing-up sink Repairs and Works had installed after dismantling it from the ruins of Charity Ward.

During rehearsals the blocking screens were moved back to leave a space in front of the chairs that when Ann arrived was crowded by everyone present. When she joined them unnoticed Paddy Brown was saying to the SSO, 'Honest to God, sir, must be pukka for the cops to tip Cas.'

Ann looked quickly around at the uniformly tense faces. Judy Francis was staring at the floor. Ann glanced at the SSO. 'Jerry up to something, Mr Wesley?' she asked.

His face was professionally impassive. 'The gen we've just had is that he's pasting Coventry.'

Ann's mind flashed from Judy to Josh and then the map of England. Liverpool, yesterday. Where last night? Tonight? No tip-and-runs further north that she'd heard of, but Coventry had had a series.

She said, 'Thank you, Mr Wesley. Sorry I'm late with the music. Got a bit held up.'

He nodded, took the music and glanced at his watch.

Judy looked up slowly, her face so pale her brown curls looked black. 'Now we're all here, let's get cracking. Please sit down, everybody. Up front.'

Following indoctrinated custom, all the nurses moved to the right chairs, and all the young men but Paddy moved to the left. Paddy, whose lack of inhibitions was the envy of his peers, sat by Ann, and Phyllis Denton on her right. Paddy's quick dark eyes watched the SSO pick up his guitar, and leaning closer to Ann, he murmured, 'Just call him Nero.'

Ann looked at him blankly and without moving her lips, breathed, 'Francis' home Coventry. Parents in situ.'

Paddy looked ready to burst into tears. Ann turned away to look fixedly into mid-air. Phyllis Denton had just caught the exchange, and seeing the look on Ann's face was immediately reminded of the only time in her life when she had played cards with young men.

The next afternoon, Miss Dewly was alone in the office, and was drawing the blackout curtains across windows reglazed and paper-stripped for the fifth time since the blitz started, when one of the two telephones that had both been ringing all day rang again. The anxiety in her plain, kindly face, deepened. It was bound to be another of his friends, and what could she say but no news was good news?

'London office the *New York Banner*.'

The crackling line reduced the operator's distant voice to an indistinct mumble, then faintly came the unmistakable click of Button A being pushed in a public telephone box. Her eyes lit up in hope. Perhaps – ?

'Miss Dewly – Josh Adams. Can you hear me?'

She gasped. 'Only just, Mr Adams! Thank goodness! We've been so worried and – '

'Miss Dewly, get this down and to Pete.'

First things first, Brenda, she admonished herself, reaching for her open notebook and pencil. 'Ready, Mr Adams.'

'Sorry – hold, please.' Josh spat out the words angrily. The gash over his right eyebrow had begun bleeding into his right eye again, his left was blurring in sympathy making reading from his dirty, crumpled notebook impossible in the fading light. He had had no sleep since the night before last and was beyond feeling the soreness of the gash, or the aching of his head. He was emotionally stripped to the screaming nerve ends and at the pitch of fatigue that illuminated reality far more clearly than the small mirror fixed to the wall above the black metal coinbox reflected his haggard, unshaven face smeared with smoke and blood under the trilby pushed to the back of his dust encrusted head. Impatiently, he mopped the gash and his right eye with his last remaining, filthy handkerchief. He had started last night with four clean ones, but three had gone in the night, two for use as tourniquets, one to cover the face of a severed head that only the long hair had identified as female.

'Miss Dewly?'

'Here, Mr Adams. I can only just hear you. This line sounds about to go.'

'I'll talk up and fast. Punctuate from my voice, and after, then get it to Pete to use as he thinks fit and can get passed. Getting me any better?'

'A little. But are you all right?' He sounded so unlike himself – so angry. 'Are you?'

'Sure. Ready?'

'Yes, Mr Adams.'

' "Dateline, Friday, 15 November, England," Starts. "Last night I was in Coventry. Last night for eleven unbroken hours the Luftwaffe bombed Coventry, an English provincial city of around two, four, zero, zero, zero, zero citizens. Last evening the heart of Coventry was a quaint mass of narrow streets and half-timbered buildings centuries old when the Declaration of Independence was signed. The City of Three Spires the citizens called Coventry when their legendary Lady Godiva took her famous horseback ride on their behalf. Lady Godiva is one of their prides. Another was their fourteenth-century St Michael's Cathedral. This morning the heart of Coventry is a blazing ruin. St Michael's Cathedral is destroyed. Hundreds of civilian citizens are dead, thousands injured, many more thousands homeless. This eye witness estimates around four-fifths of Coventry was destroyed last night." Getting it, Miss Dewly?'

'Yes, Mr Adams, but faintly. Can you – '

'I'll speak up more. Continues. "The air raid sirens sounded the Alert 7.12 p.m. British time. The Luftwaffe attacked in waves. Wave after wave, dropping fire and death. First the incendiary bombs fell in thousands exploding in blue-white flames all over the city and the marker flares floated down like chandeliers brighter than moonlight. Then came the high explosive bombs. Down came the bombs, hour after hour, all through the night, pounding stone buildings to dust, melting lead, exploding on hospitals, schools, shops, offices, fire stations, police departments, air raid posts, factories, churches, homes, and men, women and children. It was just after 6 a.m. British time when the last aircraft turned back to base. No sirens sounded the All Clear over the burning, bleeding city, the shocked, stunned survivors, the injured and the dead. Coventry's air raid warning system had been destroyed. The air raid warden's shouts of 'It's all over!' had to be passed by mouth." Okay, Miss Dewly?'

'Yes, Mr Adams.'

'Continues. "I am calling this in nine miles from Coventry, and right here the smell of the burning city is so strong it could be in the next block." Ends. Got it, Miss Dewly?'

'Only just, Mr Adams. Your voice is fading. Where are you?'

'Leamington Spa. All okay your end?'

'Oh, yes, very quiet. You're sure you're all right?'

'Sure I'm sure. I'm aiming for London tonight.'

'Mr Burness will be so relieved! We've been so anxious – ' The line had gone dead. 'Mr Adams? Mr Adams?' There was no response: the damaged line had finally snapped.

Miss Dewly sighed and hung up. First things first, Brenda. She slid a carbon between two sheets of quarto, fed the paper into her typewriter, then looked at her shorthand notes and had to pause and fold her strong hands in her lap. Oh dear, she thought, oh dear. Who could have imagined this when he got through his trunk-call from Coventry this time yesterday with his piece about the tip-and-runs? He had said he so liked the look of the place that he was staying on overnight to take a closer look at some of the ancient buildings. And even though from the rumours coming into London all day it had been obvious that Coventry had had a dreadful night, who could have imagined it had been quite so dreadful? Eleven hours – and unlike London, Coventry wasn't used to it, and being so much smaller must have made an easier target for a concentrated air attack. Such a pretty little medieval city, even though it had so many factories. Mother and she had spent a weekend there a few years before the war and thought it so charming with all the little streets, the statues of Lady Godiva on her horse and Peeping Tom, the lovely old buildings, the beautiful Cathedral – oh dear! Mother would be so upset. Last night after Mr Burness rang, she hadn't dared tell Mother his real reason, and had said he had only rung to check where she had put something he couldn't find. Actually he had rung to check whether Mr Adams was staying overnight in Coventry; she had taken his trunk-call and Mr Burness hoped she might have somehow misunderstood what Mr Adams had said. She had been a little peeved about this until Mr Burness explained why he was so anxious, and then positively thankful they were sleeping in their own rooms again, as her restless night would have so disturbed Mother. Perhaps now she knew Mr Adams was safe she should just give Mother a tinkle to explain and say she might be late home? Mother would understand and now London was quiet she wouldn't worry . . .

Two minutes later she again hung up, then began

transcribing and typing with her customary speed and precision. She had just finished when Burness burst in.

'Any news, Miss Dewly?' he demanded.

She beamed. 'Oh, yes, Mr Burness! He's just called in this piece from Leamington Spa.' She handed him the top copy and a typewritten list. 'These calls came for you whilst you were out. And I'm afraid the mechanic still hasn't come to repair the tickers.'

'Who cares about tickers?' Burness' heavy red face smiled hugely and for the first time in over nineteen hours. He thumbed the grey fedora on the back of his head, unbuttoned and unbelted his camel-hair overcoat, and perched against one edge of her desk to glance through the listed calls and messages, then read the top copy whilst she read the carbon.

Neither was smiling when they lowered their copies.

'Sure as hell, some night.'

'Doesn't bear thinking about, Mr Burness.'

'It does not.' He scowled at his typescript. 'The censor'll chop this to hell, but I guess I can get by enough to have this under banners on tomorrow's front page. What's the time?' He looked at his watch. 'Land's sakes! I'm due at the Home Office in fifteen minutes. I'll take this piece along and get right on it, after. Oh my!' He slapped his forehead. 'What time are head office calling about accounts?'

'They hope six-fifteen our time.'

'Wouldn't you know it?' He thought for a moment. 'I do not see me making it back here on time. Would you hang on to do the job for me?'

'Of course, Mr Burness. Only, as head office particularly said they wanted to talk to you about our accounts, they may not like just talking to the typist.'

'Miss Dewly honey, you are not just the typist and you do not say so! You are the one person in this office that can figure out our accounts. You say, right out, that you are Miss Brenda Dewly, our London office manager, speaking for Peter D. Burness and Joshua G. Adams. You give it New York clear and hard, honey!'

She blushed. 'If you say so – '

'Sure I say so! Ain't it the truth?' He got off the desk, swept off his hat and held it against his heart. 'Neither Peter D. nor Joshua G. could get along without you for five minutes, Miss Dewly. You are the tops!'

She simpered archly. 'Oh, Mr Burness! The things you say!'

'The truth, the whole truth, and nothing but the truth, so help me God! Be seeing you, honey!' He slapped on the fedora and swaggered out of the office singing untunefully 'All the Things You Are' to vent his relief that Josh had bobbed back up, that Joan and Pete junior were way out of the Luftwaffe's range, and in his attempts to silence his thoughts of Coventry last night – and today. 'Strictly off the record, old boy, a dead city. Goering's chaps did a damned thorough job by first starting up more fires than any city's fire services could possibly control and then getting on to the job of concentrated pulverisation . . .' Sure as hell they did just that, thought Burness, slamming behind him the front door of the Regency terraced house.

Just like a little boy whistling in the dark, thought Miss Dewly, for whom clichés were a tremendous comfort as they so exactly expressed her feelings in words she understood. He always sang when upset – like the little girl with the little curl, in the nursery rhyme, though he was never really horrid. But she could always cope with him, and underneath he was so nice and kind – and as she'd so often told Mother – the things he said! She didn't know where to put her face! Oh – now who?

'London office, *New York Banner*.'

Ann, taut with anxiety, pushed Button A in the phone box in the front hall of her Home. It was her tea half-hour, and as no letter from Josh had come in this morning's post, she had rushed over in the hope that one had been delivered by hand. She had known this was a faint hope, for had one come either Home Sister or the portress would have taken it over to her post pigeonhole in the hospital. They were good about this on days when particular wards or departments were extra-heavy, and would have heard that all day Cas. had had a spate of major road accidents, this morning Judy Francis had left on compassionate leave, and Ann was her temporary replacement.

'Is that Miss Dewly?'

'Yes!' Miss Dewly had a quick ear and retentive memory. 'Isn't that Miss Marlowe?'

'Yes. Please, is it possible to speak to Mr Adams?'

Miss Dewly was delighted to have reassuring news. Mother and she had decided Miss Marlowe must be a nice girl from her charming thank-you letter for the jam and the fact that she was a St Martha's nurse, St Martha's was renowned for only training nice girls, and, anyway, nursing was such a nice, ladylike occupation.

'I'm afraid Mr Adams is still away, Miss Marlowe, but I've just been talking to him on the telephone and he's hoping to get back here tonight. It could be early tomorrow. Depends on you-know-who.'

'You've just spoken to him?' Ann's voice shook a little. 'He's all right?'

Miss Dewly had to hedge. The poor girl sounded so anxious. 'He called in his piece as usual. The line wasn't very good.'

Ann squeezed her eyes shut. If I'm right, it's a miracle he found a working line. Matron had to tell Judy the police say Coventry's totally cut off from the rest of the country. 'Where was he ringing from? Did he say?'

Miss Dewly hesitated. She disliked even white lies – but office rules were office rules. 'As I've just said, the line wasn't too good.'

Ann persisted. 'The last letter I had from him arrived yesterday and had a Liverpool postmark. Was he in Coventry last night? Or can't you tell me?'

Now Miss Dewly was confused. Surely Mr Adams was too professional – but, of course, as Mother said, when a young man was in love . . . 'Did Mr Adams tell you he might be?'

'No. He never tells me where he is. I just get the general idea from the postmarks. I – er – I just wondered last night if he was in Coventry. It's not that far from Liverpool, and as they'd been having tip-and-runs – I – er – wondered. But I'm so glad you've just spoken to him. When he gets back, please would you tell him I've rung and am looking forward to seeing him again?'

'With pleasure, Miss Marlowe. Thank you so much for calling and for your nice letter. Mother and I were delighted you enjoyed the jam. We were thrilled with the blackberries. It was so kind of you to give them to us.'

'Not at all. It was fun picking them and your jam was delicious. Thanks for everything, Miss Dewly. Cheerio.'

Ann hung up with shaking hands, and staring at her reflection in the little mirror above the telephone, saw she still looked as apprehensive as she felt, despite the intensity of her relief at Miss Dewly's news. She tried to persuade herself she was being neurotic, and that she still had no proof of her instinctive conviction, from hearing the rumours last night, that Josh was then in Coventry. The self-persuasion failed, because she knew that now, as all her life with Michael, some undefined area of her heart and mind was as much in instinctive accord with the man she loved as a man, as with the man she loved as a twin brother.

I always know when Michael's unhappy, she thought, leaving the box and hugging her cloak around her as she went out into the cold, darkling late afternoon. I always know when things are going terribly wrong for Michael. I've felt that about Josh all night and I can still feel it – but she *spoke* to him this afternoon! She *spoke* to him – he's coming back – he's alive! Thank God for that and leave it there, she thought, as the traffic on both sides stopped to let her cross the road for the last time that weekend.

In the *Banner* office Miss Dewly sat with her hands folded in the lap of her neat, navy pin-striped skirt. Oh dear, Mother was so right. This was no time to be young and in love . . . poor young people – and poor, poor Coventry . . . oh dear! But this wouldn't do! Look on the bright side! How nice to have Miss Marlowe's call as a pleasant tit-bit for Mother tonight on top of the very nice things Mr Burness said just now. It was so nice to be appreciated. She would never forget what he said.

She never did, though she never saw Pete Burness again. She had just reached her front gate that evening, which was colder and clearer and lit by the pale light of the rising full moon, when in Blackheath and throughout Greater London the sirens wailed the Alert for the first time in twelve nights to announce the onset of arguably the most savage night attack London had yet known.

When Josh next awoke the train had stopped again and the crowded compartment was lit only by the pinpoints of the cigarettes of the two sailors sitting on the floor. On both sides the armrests of the five seats had been pushed up to squeeze in six. Josh was the only civilian, the rest were soldiers, slumped shapes in the darkness, sleeping with the soundlessness of youth. He had no notion how long he had been asleep or how long this stop had lasted. He had slept through most of the other stops at darkened, unidentifiable stations thronged with servicemen in full kit in transit to postings, or to and from leave. No one had woken him, but his sleep had been infiltrated by the shouted orders of a Railway Transport Officer or NCO, and men's voices yelling that there was no room for another sardine in the corridor or the guard's van, or singing in chorus snatches of 'You'll Be Far Better Off in a Home' and 'Why Are We Waiting'.

Before he woke properly he recognised why the train had now stopped and all the lights were out despite the closed blackout blinds. He gently eased off the heads sagging against his shoulders and leant forward to flick his lighter to his watch. It was 9.50 p.m. and over four hours since he had boarded at Warwick this train that should have reached London nearly an hour ago. He whispered, 'Would you guys know where we are?'

A Scottish voice replied in a whisper, 'Anchored up aft of a tunnel, sir. My oppo's just stuck his head out.'

An Oxford English voice added, 'Couldn't get more than a shuftee of fields in moonlight up forward. Have a fag?'

'Thanks.'

The lighter flame exposed the congealed red scar over his right eyebrow, the purpling swelling around his right eye, and the dried blood on the upturned collar of his begrimed mackintosh.

'Canadian or American?'

'American. Newspaperman.'

'War correspondent?' The English voice was amused. 'Looks as if you've joined in, old chap. Who gave you the shiner?'

'Didn't catch his name. Any notion where we are?'

The Scotsman thought west of Swindon, the Englishman south of Reading. They told him they had got on at Northampton, but not where they had come from or where they were going. He didn't want to know. He didn't want to talk. He had to persist. 'Think London's getting it again?'

'I dinna ken.'

'Your guess is good as ours, old chap. Been in England long?'

'From last July.'

'Nice work picking our best summer in years. Sorry.' The speaker stifled a yawn. 'If London is getting a return match we'll be berthed here all night. May as well kip down. Shift your bloody feet, Jock – thanks.' Both sailors stubbed out their cigarettes and from the sounds were stretching out in opposite directions. 'Piece of cake now she's stopped rolling.'

'Aye, Mike. Flat calm.'

Josh grimaced painfully in the darkness, trod on his cigarette, and squeezed back between the sagging heads. He couldn't take that reminder of Ann. He didn't dare think of her. He didn't want to talk to another English man or woman, see another yard of England, write another line about their war. But he knew he would – must – do all these things and see this war to the end, unless it ended his life first, for even if he had never met and loved Ann, he was incapable of backing out of the greatest professional story of his life. He dreaded more than ever having to write that story. He knew it would have to be written. Remorselessly, the machine in his mind flicked out the headlines: DEATH OF ENGLAND – DEATH OF GREAT BRITAIN – DEATH OF THE GREAT BRITISH EMPIRE – DEATH OF EUROPEAN CIVILISATION. London's size and sheer blind guts had prolonged the dying, but last night in Coventry he had heard the death-rattle. Last night he had recognised the methodical ruthlessness of the Luftwaffe's attack for the carefully planned knock-out blow it had proved to be. In the first few hours of last night he had encountered in Coventry the same fury with the Luftwaffe, and with the RAF for 'letting Jerry have it all his own way', the same fierce determination to survive, that he had met in London since September. London was not yet finished, but couldn't take much more. Coventry had been finished off in just one night, and this morning was a blazing tomb from which unidentifiable dead were being dug out. A tomb without gas, electricity, telephones, public services, and either waterless or knee-deep in red, muddy water flooding from bombed pipes. Finished off, period.

How many more English cities would have to be finished off before the English faced the truth and stopped blinding themselves with the hypocrisy, arrogance and sheer infantile stupidity of 'we'll win in the end'? How many more before they accepted they had no chance and that all Churchill's talk of fighting on the beaches, in the streets and never surrendering was so much hot air? How many more before they realised that if they did not sue for peace, any day, any night, in a rain of fire and steel, some other guy could stumble over something in a blacked-out street and, stopping to see what it was, find himself holding between his hands Ann's faceless severed head?

That last thought made his stomach heave as violently as it had last night. This time he managed not to be sick, but he could not contain his imagination and his agonising fear for Ann. The sweat poured down his face in the darkness that was as bright daylight in comparison with the black hell in his mind. He did not know how he could ever again look at Ann's beloved, pretty, porcelain face, without seeing that ghastly head in the white brilliance of a falling flare. He had to get her out – right now – fast! He had to get her to the States – as his wife if she would marry him – if not, he'd fix it. He didn't know how. He just knew he would – must – fix it. If necessary, he'd take her over to Boston – Canada – anywhere she chose – but out! He'd have to leave her and come right back, but she would be safe. She had to be safe! So he had to get back to London fast to talk with Pete and the US Embassy, even though it was a dime to a buck that this time tomorrow he would be making for or already in the ruins of tonight's target. Unless – it was London? What did that guy say about fields in the moonlight? Of course. Full moon tonight. London again, he thought with an icy certainty, just before exhaustion blacked out his mind with dreamless sleep.

– Ten –

I'd forgotten the moon, thought Ann incredulously. Eleven nights – and I'd stopped watching what the moon was doing . . . Not Jerry . . . It's far too bright . . . He hasn't wasted a full moon in London since the blitz started . . . He's not wasting time now . . . Just laying waste . . . God help them over the river, and don't let Josh have got back before this started – why hasn't our phone rung?

She raised herself silently so as not to waken Mary on her right, and Peggy Butler on her left, who was with her on first Cas-call. It was nearly midnight, but not even the first pair of theatre nurses had been called up, and the emergency telephone set on a card-table in the alcove just opposite their curtained entrance that had once temporarily been Hope's dutyroom, had been silent since all the day staff nurses came off duty at the usual time.

The depth of the basement under Block 7 muffled the noise of the raid to a distant thunderstorm even when formations were passing directly over the hospital. Ann lay listening with the old mixture of weary familiarity and resignation, waiting for the telephone's shrill ring as formerly for Home Sister's arrival. She turned on her face to flick her torch on her watch under her pillow, when a sudden series of louder thunderclaps jerked her bed forward – she had forgotten to lock the castors. Instinctively hauling the pillows over the back of her head, she thought automatically, he's got another block. A couple of seconds later she flicked her torch on and off to show she was awake and briefly played the beam on Mary then Peggy. Neither had woken.

Nancy Standing enquired in a weary stage-whisper, 'Anyone else awake?' A few more torches flicked on and off in the routine established since their move from the ballroom and the installation of their telephone. 'I'm sure that got us.'

A theatre nurse whispered, 'I thought he'd go for a hat-trick tonight. Last full moon, the OPD; the one before, the Dispensary. God, how I hate the moon!'

'Shut up, Jean. Don't wake the others till we have to. I'll check our phone's working.' Nancy got up in the darkness, switching on her torch only when through the blue floral cretonne curtains covering the open entrance. The curtains had once hung from the new cubicle-rails in Mary (Block 2)'s first-stage room.

Ann lay back, pressing her right hand over her father's signet ring, which had become far more to her than Michael's inheritance in her keeping. She had been their father's favourite, as Michael had been their mother's, and it seemed to her a secret source of supernatural protection by her father. Unquestioningly she accepted the comfort this afforded her, knowing it to be as irrational and inexplicable as the instinct that had saved Sue Hardy's and her own life on the night of the last full moon. She had never referred to this to anyone but Sue, and then only once, on the evening before, at her own request, Sue was transferred to the EMS. Sue had asked, 'How did you know, Ann?' 'I don't know, Sue. I don't know,' she had replied.

Nancy was back, playing the torch on her slippered feet. 'Block 2. Right down.'

Someone muttered, 'Thank God Mary evacuated.'

Ann whispered urgently, 'Firemen, Nancy?'

'Four missing. Two fire-watchers on the ground floor got out in time, with only minor injuries. No others in.'

Ann sat up. 'Where were the firemen?'

'At the last report just changing over on the roof.'

'Know who?'

'Hughes, Stacey, Davis, Jenks. Mason and Gould got out.' Nancy switched off her torch and got back into bed, and from conditioned experience no one said more.

Ann lay back slowly, and the new pain – as new pain always does – revived the old for her other friends killed in the hospital, especially Jill de Grey. Ann now knew all the hospital firemen and other Civil Defence workers, not merely by name, but as old friends with whom in Casualty she had shared corny war jokes, grapevine gossip and grumbles, whilst dressing their innumerable cuts, grazes and sprains, taking multiple fragments of glass, shrapnel, stone and wooden splinters from their faces, arms and hands, dosing them with antacids for their indigestion and linctus for their coughs. Her top pillow was drenched when the release of tears slid her into a sleep so deep that she heard no more of that night's raid or the All Clear. It was only after the Night Ass. rang their getting-up handbell that she heard that at 4.20 a.m., another direct hit had blown off the roof and two upper floors of Block 8. 'Two firemen missing. Every riverside window gone again,' continued the Night Ass. as impersonally as if giving a medical report, 'and no casualties in yet. But the police have just warned us St Benedict's' (a voluntary hospital just over the river) 'is inundated and having to send us around fifty seriously injured and that we must expect more to follow.'

Peggy Butler and Ann leapt out of bed. Ann asked, 'Any news of Block 2's firemen, Sister?'

'Still missing, I'm afraid.'

Mary was half-awake. 'I thought you said Block 8, Sister?'

'He got 2 just before midnight, Cavendor. Not much else in our zone. Over and down river had the worst.' She hurried away.

Mary turned to Ann. 'Think Josh got back?'

'I don't dare think.'

Peggy Butler, her cap on her neat pale blonde head, stepped into her uniform dress and pulled it up. She had worked in the OPD until this was literally cut down to half-size, was one year junior to Ann's set, and today she and Ann were the only Casualty day staff nurses. She was very tall and thin, with a crisp manner and little imagination. 'If he is starting another blitz I can't think how Martha's'll cope,' she said.

'Don't be so damn silly, Peggy,' retorted Mary. 'We'll cope because we've got to.'

Mary's right, thought Ann, in the first few seconds of that long working day that were her only moments of private reflection until it was long over.

Once again the benches along the right-hand side were in use as improvised stretcher-trolleys, every room off Casualty Hall was in action, and a queue was growing for the five operating tables working simultaneously in the Theatre Block. Once again little processions of laden stretchers were being carried to the emergency beds put up down the middle of the ground-floor wards and in the basement wards overflowing into the pipe-lined corridor, and the atmosphere in Casualty Hall was thick with plaster dust and the mingled aroma of fresh-spilled blood, antiseptics, damp blankets, grime, sweat and human exhalations. But the ugly smell of human fear was missing, for the injured were mercifully drugged. All day the left-hand benches were empty. No walking-wounded 'minors' had had the strength to stagger the extra distance to Martha's, and the local patients who normally thronged in on Saturdays kept their ailments to themselves until 'Old Martha's gets a bit of a breather'. None of the staff had any off-duty, and by mid-morning the message was flashed round, 'Hughes found, identified . . . Stacey found, identified – no others.' Once again there was no time for grief. In relays the staff snatched hasty meals, and were too thankful to sit down to know what they were swallowing or talk to others. All day the hospital echoed with the old hammering as windows were boarded up and the new sounds of rumbling wheelbarrows and the clinking of the trowels beginning the bricking-in of all the usable ground-floor windows with bricks taken from new and old ruins.

No posts came into Martha's that day, but no one had time to notice this absence. And that night, the Luftwaffe came back. Again Martha's zone was outside the main targets. All that fell upon the hospital were spasmodic showers of incendiary bombs that the firemen and fire-watchers extinguished with the speed of experts in a white rage. The mutilated remnants of the body of a third fireman had been found; those of the three others were never found, having been blown into the Thames. From shortly after the pre-dawn All Clear the casualties from other zones began coming in, and all day, in every way, Casualty resembled yesterday and the uncountable yesterdays in October and September.

On Sunday night Ann had dropped into bed when she realised she had not thought of Josh since early yesterday morning. Last night she had fallen asleep immediately her head was on her pillow. I love him so much – how could I have forgotten him? she wondered, too exhausted for guilt, but not for the upsurge of anxiety that haunted her sleep. All night, in nightmares filled with huddled grey shapes and flames, she searched the grey, ageless, sexless faces for Josh's, unable to find him and obsessed with the conviction that she must, or she would never find him again.

She woke sweating in the darkness to find Mary gently shaking her and crooning, 'Only a nightmare, Ann. Only a nightmare. The All Clear's gone.'

She grabbed Mary's hand. 'I couldn't find him!'

'Good sign. You'll see. Go back to sleep. All quiet. Even the theatre girls are flat out.'

'Thanks. Sorry I woke you.'

'You didn't. It was the All Clear. Go back to sleep.'

Ann gave a long shuddering sigh and was asleep before Mary was back in her own bed.

Mary lay awake until the getting-up bell. She was too angry for sleep. Her equitable temperament was slow to anger, but once roused her anger was not easily quenched. She loved nursing, Martha's, and her ward – Stanley Parker – and this slow, steady destruction of the staff and the hospital had roused her to flashpoint. She was infuriated by the thought of being killed without doing something tangible about hitting back. Just taking it isn't enough for me, she thought. The Army. Yes. I'll ask Matron for an interview, tell her I want to apply to the QAs.* We can't win this war until our Army hits back where it really hurts – in Germany. One day we'll do that, and when it comes I want to be with our troops. Why wasn't I born a man? If I had been, even if qualified, I'd scrub the RAMC and non-combatant racket and join the infantry. They're the chaps that get the most chance to fix bayonets – and would I love to use one on Jerry! Would Ann join me? No. Not just because she's so smitten with her Josh that she's been mumbling his name all night. It's not her line. She could only use a bayonet in self-defence or to defend patients or those she loves . . . I hope to God her American's okay – in every sense. Probably he is. He's used to wars and keeping his head down . . . I wish Michael could get down and take a look at him. I'll bet he does too now

* Queen Alexandra's Imperial Military Nursing Service.

Ann's told him about Josh. Wonder how Michael's taken it? Brothers can be odd about these things, particularly twin brothers. Why wasn't I born a man? That's damned silly. I wasn't, and that's that. I'm joining the Army . . . Jill always said I should . . . oh, Jill – Jill . . .

Quietly, practically, Mary buried her face under the bedclothes so that her stifled weeping should not disturb the others.

That morning fewer casualties came in; a massive evacuation of the weekend's admission took place before noon; Matron insisted that every day nurse had three hours off duty; and the first post since Friday arrived a little before one o'clock. A few minutes later Matron received the telegram that Judy Francis had sent from Leamington Spa the previous afternoon, saying her parents had survived, shocked but unhurt, their house had been destroyed, offering to return at once if necessary, and giving an address of cousins in Leamington Spa for the reply. Matron replied by return: 'Greatly relieved stop no necessity curtail leave regards G. M. Lydiard, Matron.' Whilst Matron was dealing with this, posses of medical students under the supervision of Mr Billings of Repairs and Works were busy hanging old bedsheets nailed to wooden frames suspended from thick ropes along the embankment wall of the hospital terrace, and over the Yard entrance to Casualty. Painted on the sheets in huge black letters were the words: ST MARTHA'S HOSPITAL IS DOWN BUT NOT OUT. OPEN TO ALL PATIENTS AS USUAL.

Ann had a one-to-four. She left Casualty intending to check her pigeonhole on the way to lunch, and if there was no letter from Josh, directly after lunch she would go over to the Home. If there was nothing from him there, and as all the outside telephones were still down, she would write asking him to reply on a postcard by return, then she would go up to her floor to have a bath and an hour or so's sleep in her own room. As she left Casualty, Phyllis Denton came up the nearest basement steps and stopped on seeing her.

'Hi, Phyl. Lunching?'

'Yes. I hoped I'd run into you.' Phyllis' prim, tired face was troubled. 'What was the name of the American newspaper that awfully nice friend of poor Mr Laurings worked for?'

Ann's face froze. '*New York Banner*. Why?'

'I thought that was it. There's a bit about it in today's paper. I remembered he was a Mr Adams – that wasn't the name.' She flicked up her apron and read the note inked on the upturned hem: 'Peter D. Burness, 45. US cit. *NY Banner*. K.E.A. London, 15/11/40.' She smoothed down her apron skirt. 'It was in a patient's *Express* – or could've been *Mirror* – I saw it by chance when sitting him up for lunch. It said he'd been in London for several years and left an English wife and baby son somewhere in England. I thought it so sad. Not his war.'

Ann stared at her blankly. 'Yes. Terribly sad. You go on, Phyl. I must check my post.' She rushed on ahead, but found no letters had come for her. She stood for some seconds staring at her pigeonhole. Monday, she thought – the 15th was the first half of Friday night. Wherever Josh was then, he should now be back. He's always told me there were just the two of them. He's told me so much. Not this. Why? Letter still in the post or bombed? Can't bear to tell me? Or – can't?

She turned and discovered Phyllis waiting behind her. 'I'm skipping lunch. Something I must do, stat.'

Phyllis opened her mouth to protest that whatever this was could be done better after a meal, then closed it without saying anything. The discovery of her own powers of endurance had heightened her recognition not only of that same strength in others, but of the power of the human mind over the human body. She'll eat better when she has done what she wants to do, she thought, going on to the dining-room alone.

Ann raced back to the Home. 'Any letter or message for me, Miss Smithers?'

'Sorry, nurse, no. Do you wonder with posts haywire and phones U/S? What a weekend! Going up for a bath and nap?'

'No. I've got to go up west.'

'Best not, nurse. When Home Sister came back from Matron's Office just now she said most of the West End's still roped off. Craters all over – outside Swan and Edgar's – up Piccadilly – Regent Street – Oxford Street. Best not to try it, nurse.'

'I must. Two addresses for you.' She gave those of Josh's hotel and office and watched the portress write them in her log-book. 'I'll try the hotel first.'

'I'm not sure you'll be let through, nurse.'

'I'll get through,' said Ann quietly, between gritted teeth. 'On or off my bike.'

She ran on up the stairs and once in her room flung her cloak, shelter-bag and gasmask box on her unused bed, unpinned her Martha's badge from her apron bib and repinned it just below the front stud of her dogcollar. She took off her apron, replacing the white starched belt around the waist of her grey uniform dress, and leaving on starched cuffs, black uniform stockings and shoes. She put on her navy mackintosh, a navy beret at a sensible angle, and only a light dusting of powder on her unpainted face. She slung the gasmask and her navy shoulder bag over one shoulder, checked her appearance in the dressing-table mirror, then buttoned and turned up her mackintosh collar to conceal her uniform dress until she was well clear of Martha's. The wearing of indoor uniform off hospital territory was forbidden all nurses on the general side, but permitted to Sister and pupil-midwives under the navy serge outdoor uniform coats and pork-pie caps they wore when doing district midwifery. This outdoor uniform had, for generations, proved one of the quickest, safest passports around

London. Never in the hospital's long history, on the darkest nights in the roughest slums, had any Martha 'on district' been even verbally assaulted.

She ran down the stairs to the drained swimming pool in the basement that had become the bicycle shed, leaving the Home by the seldom used back door that was only locked at night. Traffic was running normally in the road passing the hospital, but the bridge was only open to bicycles, handcarts and pedestrians. When halfway over, she turned down the collar and undid the top button of her mackintosh.

Parliament Square and Whitehall, though covered with broken glass and rubble, were open to cyclists, and she only had to get off and push her bike between heaps of rubble twice. Trafalgar Square was roped off.

A policeman standing there asked, 'Where are you heading, nurse? Far end of Piccadilly? I'm sorry, nurse, you can't take that bike on from here.'

'May I leave it here and pick it up on my way back, officer?'

'You do that, nurse. I'll just shove it against these sandbags and keep an eye on it. How long do you reckon to be?'

'Not very long. I'm due back at the hospital at four.'

'Which one's that, nurse?'

'Martha's.'

'You've had your share. Under you come, nurse. Watch your footing and keep to the middle of the road where you can. This wind's shifted the smoke but it's shifting a lot down off the roofs.'

'Thank you very much, officer.'

On the far side of the square another policeman asked, 'Where you for, nurse? Haymarket? Watch your step on the duckboards over the craters. Touch of ice in this wind's making 'em slippery. Keep in the middle where you can.'

'Yes, officer. Thank you.'

At Piccadilly Circus she was asked, 'Piccadilly or Regent Street, nurse? Piccadilly? Just give you a hand over these duckboards. There we are. Not often we see the back half of a double-decker bus sticking out of a hole in Piccadilly Circus, is it, nurse? Watch your step up Piccadilly and give that second crater from here a wide berth. The sides are crumbling.'

'Yes, officer. Thank you.'

Mentally and physically blinkered by acute anxiety, she walked, slithered and clambered on, her eyes fixed on the next step ahead, her mind focused on the need to find Josh. She didn't feel the icy wind that pinched her nostrils so that, even without the anaesthesia of anxiety, she would not have detected the inevitable post-air attack smell of cordite, escaping gas and sewage, grime, wet clay, and death. She saw neither the new devastation nor the squads of civilian workmen, Gas, Electricity and Water engineers and soldiers, working against the clock to clear the chaos whilst the light lasted. The squads watched her go by, appreciating her pretty young face, slender figure and slim ankles but recognising the urgency with which she walked. Several touched their caps to her, but none wolf-whistled or cat-called after her.

She only looked up on reaching the hotel. The frontage was chipped and cracked, several windows gaped, but the front of the roof had only lost patches of slates. The sagging sandbag walls guarding the entrance were coated with grime and glass and were spilling sand in places, but the candle-lit foyer and lounge seemed undamaged.

The hall porter shook his head. 'I'm sorry, nurse. As soon as Mr Adams got back from Devon this morning he only stopped for a quick wash and breakfast, then went straight out. He said he'd go along to his office first to see how it had fared, and as he's not come in since, I'd say it's still standing. I'm sorry I can't give it a ring to find if he's still there. None of our telephones are in order yet. Would you know the address?'

The relief was so overwhelming that she had to swallow with difficulty before answering, 'Thanks, yes. I'll go there now.'

'You'll have to go the long way round, nurse. Third right's best. First right's quickest, but blocked.'

'Right. If I miss Mr Adams, could you please say Nurse Marlowe called and will be in touch.'

'Leave it to me, nurse. I – er – I take it you'll have heard – er – '

'Yes. I'm so sorry.'

'As are all of us here, nurse. Home from home for Mr Burness we've been since he first came to London. Ever such a pleasant gentleman – always a laugh – a bit of a card, you might say. He'll be missed.'

'I'm sure he will. Thank you for your help.'

'Only sorry not to have been more help, nurse. If you'll pardon the liberty, what hospital would you be from?'

'St Martha's.'

The man came round the desk. 'You've had your share, haven't you, miss?'

'Yes. Thank you, again. Good afternoon.'

'A very good afternoon to you, miss,' he said and ushered her out through the hardboard-battened swing doors.

Relief had ripped off the blinkers. Once round the sandbags she stopped on the pavement and looked around slowly, breathing carefully, as when she had watched London burning from that fifth-floor balcony and her face took on that same implacable anger. Her gaze moved slowly over the roofless buildings, the gaps, the buildings that had survived intact, the others that had only lost slates; the gaping windows; the jagged-edged craters exposing layers of broken terracotta and lead pipes half-choked by the surrounding yellowish-grey clay; the chunks of masonry and mounds of rubble blocking road and pavements; the carpet of broken glass. The wind was making the barrage balloons sway drunkenly on their ropes as if on long thin unsteady legs, and the small army of men working with wheelbarrows and shovels had to pause repeatedly to wipe the grit from their streaming eyes. And over in the empty Green Park, the last fallen leaves were dancing on the green grass.

This is Piccadilly on a Monday afternoon, she thought numbly, glancing at her watch before hurrying on. It was already two-fifteen.

In the first turning on the right workmen were shovelling into wheelbarrows the rubble blocking this end of the narrow street. One of the three workmen nearest to Ann leant on his shovel and said, 'Sorry, nurse, not this way. Not open to pedestrians.'

She smiled at him. 'Oh dear! I'm in a tearing hurry. Couldn't you just not notice me? Or will that have you on the mat?'

The man exchanged glances with his colleagues, then all three grinned and stuck their shovels into the rubble and dusted their hands. 'Best if the lads and me lend you a hand, nurse.'

They lent more than hands. They lifted, propelled and steadied her to the clearer end of the short street and the turning she sought, to shouts of encouragement from their colleagues.

'Thank you very much gentlemen,' she said.

'Any time, nurse. Shifters Limited, that's us!'

The Regency terraced houses had only lost chimneys, patches of slates, and unboarded windows. The street was littered with broken glass, slates and bricks, and slit by two long, narrow craters. One of these was directly parallel with and just outside the open front door of the house containing the *Banner* office. A glazier was fitting new glass to the ground-floor window just to the right of the doorway.

He touched his tweed cap and called, 'My guv'nor says if glass is wanted, glass we fits whiles we got the glass. Coming in here, miss? Hang on.' He ducked back then appeared in the doorway rubbing his palms on the seat of his dungarees. 'Give you a hand over. Slippery as a greasy pole, them boards.'

'Thanks.' Taking his outstretched hands, Ann glanced down at the exposed layers of gaping pipes and heavy clay. As jagged and deep as a human bomb-wound, she thought, oozing clay for blood.

'What floor you wanting, miss?'

'Second.'

'Stairs is sound but dark, seeing the electric's still had it.'

'Yes.' She glanced around the dark hallway. All the doors were closed and under some there were flickers of candle-light and under others the steady golden glow of hurricane lamps. Through all but the first door on the right came the rattle of typewriters. 'It's busy.'

'Monday, miss. All in for work this morning seeing they still got offices. Knew how to build, they did, when they put this terrace up.' He smiled dourly. 'Mind when we used to say, safe as houses?'

'I do. Thanks awfully for your help.'

'No trouble, miss.' He touched his cap again and went back to his glazing.

The wide mahogany stairs curved elegantly round the stairwell. The carved banisters, dark blue stair-carpet, dark brown linoleum on the landings, the badly cracked white walls and high ceilings, and every door but one, were thick with plaster dust. The exception was painted pale grey and newly washed, the brass plate engraved *New York Banner* newly polished.

Ann looked from door to plate then, using the latter as a mirror, adjusted her beret to a slant across her smooth white forehead. She could hear the noise of two typewriters, and pressed the bell in case it was clockwork. Hearing no ring, she knocked. One typewriter stopped and a woman's voice she recognised as Miss Dewly's called, 'Please come in.'

She opened the door and for a few seconds stayed in the doorway, registering, as if her eyes were a camera, yesterday's new boarding in the windows, the filing cabinets their tops laden with wire baskets stacked with newspapers and clippings, the wall shelves lined with reference books, the lifeless ticker-machine, the three desks set at differing angles, the lighted hurricane lamps on the two in use, the squat black paraffin heater on the floor, and the two overcoated figures rising slowly to their feet. Miss Dewly, large, fairish and sad-eyed, with a grey woollen shawl draped over her head. Josh with his black velour double-breasted overcoat open, the collar up, and its darkness accentuating the livid scar over his right eyebrow, the yellowish-brown bruising round both eyes, and the blueness of his chin in those first few seconds when the shock of her appearance drained what little colour remained in his drawn face.

She said quietly, 'Hello, Josh,' and went forward with her hand out. 'I'm Ann Marlowe, Miss Dewly. How do you do? I had to come. I only heard this morning Mr Burness was killed on Friday. I'm so sorry.' She looked from one to the other but only Miss Dewly met her look. 'I wish there was something I could say to help, but I know nothing anyone can say can do that. I just had to come. I hope you don't mind.'

Josh inclined his head, still not looking at her.

'Pleased to meet you, Miss Marlowe.' Miss Dewly's handshake numbed Ann's knuckles, and the grief in her eyes went to Ann's heart. 'It's most kind of you to come and express your sympathy. Such a sad loss – yes – ' Her unsteady voice paused momentarily. Then she added firmly, 'I must thank you again for those scrumptious blackberries!'

Recognising the cry for help, Ann said quickly, 'I must thank you again for that delicious jam.' She had nursed numerous Miss Dewlys and knew their unspoken language and tremendous courage.

'Do sit down, please.' Miss Dewly charged round her desk to clear a hard chair of stacked newspapers, but Josh, moving like a man in a trance, picked up his desk chair and set it in front of Miss Dewly's desk. 'Oh, thank you, Mr Adams. Please, Miss Marlowe,' she urged, profoundly thankful for this interruption and that Miss Marlowe looked pretty and ladylike as she and Mother had hoped. Just what poor Mr Adams needed after his sad time breaking the news to poor Mrs Burness and all the travelling. It was only after he had said how brave poor Mrs Burness had been, 'spunky as hell' he'd said, that he had told her he had heard in the train that St Martha's had been hit twice more and was this so? She had had to say she didn't know as so much more had come down from Friday night, and he had just nodded, and got on with all the work that had been piling up whilst Mr Mackinlay had been covering London for him, but looking so distressed that she positively hadn't known what to do for the best. Then this! Like the answer to a prayer, thought Miss Dewly guiltily. Yesterday as usual she had gone with Mother to Matins before coming in to the office to supervise the new boarding and see if Mr Mackinlay needed help, but since Saturday morning she hadn't been able to pray.

Josh folded his arms, leant against the front of his desk and addressed the wall behind Ann's head. 'Is it right you've two more blocks down?'

'One and a half. No patients involved.' She was desperately distressed by his refusal to look at her and by the appearance of his injured face. In the golden lamplight his hair was as grey and lifeless as his tone.

'That was a nasty knock. Left eye bruising in sympathy, isn't it?' He nodded at the wall. 'Any effects on your vision?' He shook his head. 'Good. Pity you didn't get that gash stitched, but as it looks to be healing by first intention you shouldn't have much of a scar. Few days old?' He nodded again at the wall. 'Lucky it missed your eye.'

Miss Dewly sighed. 'You don't know how lucky, Miss Marlowe!' she said, and as it was old history added, 'He got that in Coventry on Thursday night. Shrapnel.'

I knew it, thought Ann, slamming down the mental shutters on what-might-have-been, and seeing Josh's involuntary grimace. 'How is your mother, Miss Dewly?'

Miss Dewly responded gratefully. So much wiser to talk of something else! 'A little tired, naturally, but bearing up wonderfully, and so busy with all the rationing and queueing and keeping the house and the garden . . .'

She talked for the next few minutes with Ann putting in occasional remarks, as if chatting over a garden fence, and oblivious to Josh's silent presence. Ann, paying lip-service to the conversation, thought, Coventry, then all this. He's tough, but not tough enough for this. No one is. No one who hasn't been through this will ever know, or be able to imagine properly, what it's like to have crammed into weeks or days the kind of devastating emotional blows that in peacetime most people have spread over a whole lifetime. I know this isn't his war and he doesn't have to be here – but he is here and helping – not just me – but us – England. He, and the other neutral reporters, are telling the world what's being done to us, and as they are neutrals the world will believe them far more than anything we say. He'd say he was just doing his job – the job that's just killed his friend and could kill him, without a direct hit. He's young, strong, and has the enormous physical stamina of all wiry types; the physical strain won't kill him, but the mental could. In this and other wars, it's killed those with his imagination, sensitivity and intelligence. 'Happy are those without imagination,' wrote Wilfred Owen in the Great War that killed him at my age. Josh has far too much imagination, and he looks unhappier than anyone I've ever seen. Unhappiness is another killer. I've got to help him, I don't know how, but I've got to, she thought frantically, whilst agreeing with Miss Dewly that Woolton Pie was rather nice even though it only contained vegetables. Then she heard her own voice saying, 'I'm terribly sorry, but I have to leave and collect the bike I've left in Trafalgar Square. I'm due on at four. Only, before I go, now I'm here, I'd like to ask you both something I'd intended doing in a week or two.' And having realised the idea thrust up by her subconscious, she looked in appeal at Miss Dewly. 'I want to ask you both a straight favour.'

'I'm sure, if we can, we'll be only too happy, Miss Marlowe.'

Ann sensed Josh's glance in her direction but kept her gaze on Miss Dewly. 'Thanks. It's a bit complicated. The thing is, every year Martha's staff put on a revue for the staff and guests in the week after Christmas. This year's is on the late evening of Saturday, 28 December. I'm in it for the first time and the prospect scares me stiff. Every performer's allowed two guests – usually family – but I've none in range and would love you both to be mine for the show and the party after. If necessary, there'll be beds or mattresses for you in the basement for that night. So, if you could fix for a friend to spend that night with Mrs Dewly – please do come! I realise neither of you can promise to make it yet, but if you can, do come and clap like mad.' She turned quickly and met Josh's appalled eyes. 'I'd love to have you there.' She stood up quickly. 'I must get back. Be seeing you. Cheerio.' She backed to the door

227

before Miss Dewly could rise, but Josh had lunged to open it. 'Thanks.'

'I'll just see Miss Marlowe over our doorstep crater, Miss Dewly,' he said, following Ann out, and closing the door behind him he reached for her with both hands. He folded his arms around her and held her clamped against him, needing this physical proof that she was alive, as a man dying of thirst needs water. On Friday night he had thought he had reached the bottom of the pit; he had discovered that to have been a misconception in another dark, stationary train in a tunnel in the early hours of this morning, when the middle-aged civilian man sitting on his right on the floor of the corridor, woke for the first time since Exeter and began talking. 'Only left London yesterday morning. Chose the right weekend to see my first grandson, didn't I? Bad night Friday and from the news – if you can believe it – last night wasn't much better, and they're at it again tonight, I'll be bound. I'll see a few changes when I get back to my lodgings in Kennington – saw a good few afore I left. Poor old Martha's lost two more on the riverside and more of the staff gone, I heard . . . No, couldn't say if they was doctors, nurses or maintenance – but not many, I heard – not like other parts. Hundreds gone that night – same as every night . . . Ta, but if you don't mind, I prefer the pipe . . .'

Ann's beret had fallen off, and with his face buried in her hair he muttered, 'Till you showed up I didn't know if you were – ' He couldn't finish.

'Nor did I, till I went to your hotel, just now.' She managed to free her arms to lock them round his neck, clinging to him, as he to her. Then she asked softly, 'Why can't you look at my face?'

He shuddered violently, 'It's not your – I can't – I can't tell you – but I have to tell you you can't stay around till after Christmas – you have to let me get you out, fast. Marry me, please – say

228

you'll marry me – you have to let me get you to the States.'

She cupped his face in her hands and gently eased it up, tilting back her head. He still held her off the ground so that their faces were level. She looked searchingly into his distraught, bloodshot eyes. 'Someone's dead body reminded you of me?'

He closed his eyes. 'I can't talk of it.'

'You must, my love. I've got to leave you in a few minutes. I can't leave you in this hell. Tell me. Someone's body or –' her voice shook – 'head?'

Slowly his eyes opened and he looked at her in a long silence. Then he told her the truth.

'Oh, my God. My poor darling.' She buried her face in his shoulder.

His hold tightened. Another precious minute passed in silence before he was able to kiss her as he had never kissed her or any woman. Then, again, 'Will you marry me? Please – marry me,' he said.

She sighed, too disturbed for joy, but not the hope that flared in her eyes. 'I'd love to, and of course I will soon as – '

'Not soon – right off! I'll get a special licence – '

'Josh, we can't – '

'We have to! Once you are my wife I'll pull every string I can in our Embassy here, Washington – New York! I have to get you out! I love you too much to let you stay one day longer than I have to, and you must – '

'Josh, listen!' She dropped her hands on his shoulders and shook him. 'You must listen!' She looked straight into his urgent, passionate face. 'How much would you now love me if I'd run out on Ed Laurings and Peter Daws? How much would I now love you if you hadn't joined our poker game?'

He winced as if she had struck his scar. 'Don't play dirty!'

229

'I'm not playing! I'm fighting for the marriage I want us to have! But what I – you – any of us caught up in this war want, right now doesn't matter a damn! We're as helpless as seeds in a wind until the wind blows itself out. It will. We've just got to wait till – '

'We can't wait! You just do not appreciate what is happening – what must happen to England! My dearest – oh, my dearest – I hate to have to say this – '

'Don't!' She pressed one hand over his mouth. 'I know! I've always known you don't think England's got a hope, and as you know so much about what's actually going on, you've obviously got some pretty good reasons for thinking that way. I know you want me out because you love me, and I love you for that thought, particularly as you aren't running out.' She removed her hand. 'Are you?'

He couldn't lie. 'No. I have to stay. I can't even take you over – now.'

'Of course you can't. But if you could I wouldn't go with you. Were I fool enough to do so, it would be the finish for you and me. If I let myself chicken off to America knowing what I was running out on, knowing how much I – me, Ann Marlowe, SRN, young and healthy – am needed in my own country, I'd never forgive myself, or you, for it. Can you think of a better way of wrecking any marriage before it got off the ground?' He couldn't answer, and seeing the anguished defeat in his eyes she kissed him passionately. 'I have to go, my love.'

Never before had she, or any woman, kissed him like that. Never before had he dared to imagine that beneath her enchanting and disciplined exterior lay a passion as strong as his own, which by some undeserved miracle he had succeeded in tapping, and which held out the promise of a happiness he had never expected to know in this or any other world. His recognition of this lit within him the last sensation he had expected or wanted to harbour, but he could no more control it than he could the shaking of his own hands when he reluctantly set her down and picked up and returned her beret. That last sensation was a wild, unreasoned hope, which erased a little of the tension and returned a little of the youth to his face.

He thought aloud. 'Goddammit, I don't know which of us is the more crazy!'

Ann rested her back against the banisters, breathing deeply, seeing the life returning to his face, knowing she had won for today and refusing to think of tomorrow. 'So what if we are? Always been a lot of it around. I don't just mean now.' She hesitated. 'Adams is an English name. Where did your father's family come from before they went to America?'

His eyes narrowed. 'Holbeach, Lincolnshire. 1683.'

She smiled faintly. 'Chancing their lives and futures to crossing the Atlantic under sail, and landing in an unknown, dangerous new world. If that wasn't crazy, what was it? If the foundation of the American dream isn't hoping against all the odds, what is it? I must go! I'll cope with the crater.' She ran from him and down the stairs without looking back.

– *Eleven* –

During that night's raid, in a long letter to Ann, Josh wrote, 'Please may I give you an engagement ring? *Please* . . .' Next morning he posted the letter on the way to the US Embassy on Jean Burness's and his own behalf, but when it reached Ann the following day he and Gus Mackinlay had left London, Charles Dubois, down with flu, was covering the capital for both, and the first patients in Casualty had accurately deciphered the morning papers' announcement that last night enemy attacks on a fairly heavy scale had been made on a town in the Midlands.

'Birmingham, nurse. Fog gives us the night off, so up he nips to do the poor old Brummies.'

At tea-time Ann found in her pigeonhole an un-stamped short letter from Josh that included the telephone numbers of Miss Dewly's home, Dubois' office and flat. 'Just in case other lines U/S . . .'

Just in case, thought Ann, in the very few moments she had for private thought. The fog had sent Casualty's intake of road accident cases soaring.

'Birmingham again, nurse,' said next morning's first patients. 'Not as the papers are giving the name yet. I dunno. Must reckon we're as thick as our pea-souper.'

All day more road accident victims came in, and the two Surgical Registrars, and particularly the SSO, had repeated calls to Casualty. It was a Martha's rule that

232

all patients with obvious or suspected fractures must be examined on admission by Fellows of the Royal College of Surgeons, and only the SSO had the authority to admit to surgical beds. That evening Sister Cas had just gone to supper when the SSO swept back again, dangling from the hand of his outstretched left arm four sets of wet X-ray plates.

'By God, Nurse Marlowe, if it's not Jerry's bombs it's the blackout he's forced upon us. Do you know that more people have now been killed on UK roads in the blackout than by all he's dropped?'

'No, Mr Wesley.'

'Fact.' He thrust the wet plates at her. 'Chaps in 17, girl in 19? Right. Girl first.'

A little later, whilst they washed at neighbouring sinks, he went on, 'Only the third week of November, but already our road intake has peaked over all past records for the whole month. December'll be worse. Shorter, darker days, longer nights, icy road surfaces already cracked or hastily repaired, and traffic with only enough light to see a few yards ahead without this foul fog that's keeping Jerry out of our hair. Too bad Birmingham's clear. From the off-record gen trickling in it's taking a hell of a pasting.'

'Too bad.'

He glanced at her masked, downcast face. 'You from Birmingham?' She shook her head. 'Who's next?'

'John Anthony King. Thirty-seven. Messenger. Query fractured skull, compounds left femur and tib. and fib.'

'Push or motor?'

'Motor-bike.'

'Lethal contraptions. Ban 'em if I could.'

When he had examined the three men and signed their admission forms he said as they rewashed, 'I'll do the chaps tonight, the girl in the morning. She'll do better for a night's rest. Chaps can't wait or I'd leave them for the night.' He soaped his hands and forearms thoroughly.

'One of the few good turns Jerry's done is to force our appreciation of the medical benefits to patients attendant upon masterly inactivity. We have been swamped with such numbers that we had no alternative to plugging them with morph. and leaving them to recover from the shock without interference unless obviously vital, and this has proved by far the best form of treatment. From all the reports coming back to us from the EMS the majority are doing remarkably well.' He dried his hands, untied his mask and smiled self-derisively. 'When it comes to healing, in comparison with nature the whole medical profession's in its infancy. What do you really think Jerry's up to now?'

Amongst other things, thought Ann, blitzing Martha's into the twentieth century. Never pre-blitz would you have made this admission nor put this question to a nurse. 'I think he's trying to bomb, burn and starve us out as the alternative to the invasion he's had to postpone. We're an island. He's no mug. His U-boats are sinking tons and tons of our ships every month, his blitz kicked off on London docks, then London, now he's going for our other industrial cities, and I'm afraid our ports are the next stop.' She saw the expression that flickered through his vivid blue eyes. 'Where are you from, Mr Wesley?'

'Newcastle.'

She said quickly, 'I could be off-target. I'm no military expert.'

'If you were I wouldn't have bothered to ask your opinion. That bunch's prognostications have been as abysmal as the Government's. Know what our moronic legislators told our top brass just before the war started?' She shook her head. 'That once London was under air attack we should expect forty-five thousand casualties per week – per week! – plus wild panic of the entire civilian population.' Ann pulled down her mask and grimaced. 'Precisely. One would have thought that those mistakes would have taught them to stop treating civvies as so gormless and gutless that we can only swallow the censored pap they feed us in the papers and the wireless news. Doesn't seem to have struck them that if that was what we were, Jerry would have been goose-stepping down Whitehall since September.'

Ann nodded and her mind flashed to Josh. 'They still don't know us, and if they don't, it's not surprising that others get us wrong – especially after the way our leaders kowtowed to Hitler in the thirties, and all the peace-at-any-price rubbish then gushing out of our ancient universities. I'll bet Jerry and the rest of the world thought at the first stick of bombs on civvies we'd all be shouting "*Il faut en finir!*" if not in French.'

'Shouting what?'

Her explanation amused him. 'How's your gallant warrior brother getting along now? Doing his stuff in the Western Desert?'

'Thank God, no. Just fed up to the back teeth with instructing in Scotland, and the Scottish weather.'

'War is hell for warriors,' he said, and as they both laughed Ann thought how that remark would have infuriated her all last summer and how the war could change attitudes as swiftly as lives.

'Nurse Francis back from compassionate leave, nurse?'

'An hour ago.'

'Trust her to show up on time for tonight's rehearsal. I'm afraid she'll have to cope minus surgical thespians, but I'm glad she's back. A chance to hear the truth for once. Right. I'm pushing off for an early supper, should you want me in the next half-hour.'

'I hope we don't, Mr Wesley.'

'Hope like hell, nurse. Don't bet on it.'

He swept off as quickly as he had come in, and Ann, glancing after him, thought, the story of all our lives.

Only half the cast were able to attend that night's rehearsal, which began late as the first forty minutes

235

were taken up by Judy Francis' account of Coventry in
the last six days. Judy looked tired and sad, but from time
to time as she talked her eyes shone with a pride that was
mirrored in those of her listeners. None later mentioned
anything she had said to the patients, but as they all told
their friends the staff grapevine had it round Martha's
before midnight, and the patients' grapevine had picked
it up before the in-patients finished their first cups of
early morning tea. A few hours later, within minutes of
'Papers come out with the name this morning, nurse –
better late than never. Birmingham copped a third night
. . .' the news from Coventry was being avidly passed
along the benches filling up on both sides of the aisle
in Casualty Hall.

'Only five days after, missus – only five days after
Jerry done 'em, Coventry got some of the factories back
open, some of the shops still standing open for business
and some as lost their shops was opening up on stalls
on bomb-sites . . .' '. . . You heard right, mate! Only five
days after . . .' '. . . Well, no, not got their gas, electricity
and water to rights yet, and wouldn't expect it neither,
knowing what councils and Government's like. Oh, yes,
had to fetch in the Army for the clearing up and that. A
tidy bit of clearing needed after what he fetched down,
and water tanks and food got to be fetched in. Folk got
to eat – can't go long on empty bellies, and if you not
got no food, no oven and no kitchen, not much you can
put in your belly is there, and from what's said, the first
day or two after, more than a few didn't get so much
as one bite. Not right, that wasn't. But the WVS, they
got their sleeves up fetching in their canteen vans and
setting up their field kitchens in tents, and for handing
out clothes coming in from all over the country for them
as got no more than what they got on their backs – and
we knows about that, don't we? . . .' '. . . Looting? Well,
wouldn't expect none, would you? War's never stopped
a wrong 'un doing wrong same as we all knows been

236

happening in London – and what I says is, string 'em up! Shooting's too good for looters! String 'em up! . . .'
'. . . You heard right, dear. Only five days after and Coventry got its sleeves up and back on the job . . .'
'. . . That'll be Nurse Francis, dear – over there with the dark curls and the dimples, having a word with Dr White – him in the long white coat and glasses. SMO, he is, and Nurse Francis, she's second in line to the old Sister and from Coventry, and only got back last night from the special leave the Matron give her seeing her mum and dad was in it – both nicely, bless 'em – but their house copped it bad so they had to move in with family out Leamington way. You need family at times like this, and don't we know it? . . .' '. . . Funeral, dear? Oh, yes, they had the big municipal funeral out in the open – they had to, seeing the Cathedral and so many churches copped it – and had to bury hundreds of poor souls in one big grave, seeing there was no telling who was what, same as after he got the Pilgrim Street Rest Centre – but all done proper and the flowers was lovely . . .' '. . . Trekkers? Oh yes, thousands still going out of a night to sleep in any bit of shelter or just rough, seeing they got open country on their doorstep, then coming back of a morning for the day's work . . .' '. . . That's right, dear! Down but not out – same as London. Coventry's took it and Coventry can take it! . . .' '. . . You heard right! Only five days after . . .'

Ann had a one-to-four, and in the second post she received letters from her aunt, Michael and Miss Dewly. After lunch she groped her way over to the Home. 'Anything for me, Miss Smithers?'

The portress shook her head despondently. She was huddled in a shawl and overcoat and her ageing face was pinched with cold. 'You're the first to step in since Home Sister went over to the hospital at ten. Still over she is, and if you're wanting a bath you're out of luck. Heating's right down. Got to remember there's a war

237

on, says Home Sister, but I tell you, nurse, I don't mind the war, just this cold. Cruel for my chilblains. What's going on over at the hospital to keep Home Sister?'

'She's probably temporarily relieving an Office Sister. Nothing on the grapevine but Coventry.'

'He's not done 'em again, nurse? I thought as how it was Birmingham again.'

'It was.' Ann explained and then asked, 'Is our phone box working?'

Miss Smithers had brightened. 'A treat, when Home Sister used it before going over.'

'Thanks,' Ann said. One minute later, she said, 'Hello, Miss Dewly. Ann Marlowe. Thanks awfully for your letter. I'm delighted you're coming to our show.'

Miss Dewly was alone in the office and was feeling cold, anxious, lonely and desperately sad. Her voice was fiercely cheerful. 'How nice of you to ring, Miss Marlowe. Yes, all arranged! A dear friend will spend that night with Mother and I'm so looking forward to it. I've always heard hospital shows are positive hoots! I do so hope Mr Adams can join us, but as I said in my letter, when he managed to call in yesterday – hours of delay – he couldn't say when he'll be back. Naturally – er – now he's single-handed – he –' her voice suddenly quavered – 'he – er – has to keep his schedule open.'

'Of course,' Ann said gently. 'Having to cope without Mr Burness makes his job much heavier, but it must be far worse for you. After working years together, you must miss Mr Burness dreadfully.'

Miss Dewly's eyes filled with tears of grief and gratitude. Now Mr Adams was away, no one else coming to the office ever mentioned Mr Burness to spare her feelings, not realising how much she longed to talk about him. Mother said it had been the same after Father was killed on the Somme and that this was a form of misplaced kindness one just had to grin and bear. 'Oh, Miss Marlowe, I do. Mr Burness was such a tower of strength – so amusing – the things he said – had me in stitches! He was a positively wizard newspaperman! Head Office thought the world of him. Everyone liked him.'

And you, my dear, loved him, thought Ann sadly, though I am sure that even now you can't admit that to yourself, because he was married, and you could no more consciously harbour an immoral thought than commit an immoral action. Aloud she said, 'Mr Adams told me that and that Mr Burness thought the world of you. He once told Mr Adams, "Sure as hell did the *Banner* collect all the crackers in the barrel when we took on our Miss Dewly."'

'Did he really? Oh, Miss Marlowe, I can just hear him.' Miss Dewly mopped her streaming eyes. 'The things he used to say – ' and her words rushed out until stopped by the pips. 'Oh dear – '

'Hang on, please.' Ann pushed in two more pennies. 'I want to ask another favour.'

'Of course!'

'If Mr Adams manages to call in today or' – Ann closed her eyes – 'when he next does, could you give him my love and a couple of short messages?'

'Gladly. Pencil poised.'

'Thanks. First, "Yes, please." Second, "If you can, go back to Coventry."'

Miss Dewly scribbled shorthand, tightening her lips. How could this nice understanding girl not understand that this was the last place Mr Adams could bear to recall, much less revisit? 'If you say so.'

'Please. I'll tell you why.' She did so, rapidly. 'Had you heard?'

A little colour had returned to Miss Dewly's cold, sad face. 'Actually, no,' she said. 'I've seen nothing about it in the papers – on the tickers – and poor Mr Dubois is so poorly he barely opens his mouth when he comes in. Mother will be interested. Your friend just got back last night?'

'Yes. Heck! Pips! Thanks awfully, Miss Dewly. Be seeing you.' Ann hung up, then checked the change in her hand before calling the operator to ask about the delays on trunk-calls to Michael in Scotland and Aunt Maud in Yorkshire. The answer for both was roughly five hours. She had expected this, so though she longed particularly to talk to Michael, she shrugged, hung up and went up to her room reminding herself that the cliché 'bad news travels fast' was especially true in Josh's world. She had grown so accustomed to living with acute anxiety for Michael, Josh, Martha's, and to a lesser extent for herself, that she had come to accept it as inevitable, like trunk-call delays and chronic fatigue. But knowing that if she lay on her bed to write letters she would be asleep in seconds, she wrote in her armchair wrapped in her cloak, eiderdown and two blankets.

She wrote first to her aunt, then to Michael, and then to Josh. Normally when he was away she waited till she heard he was back before replying, but the shades of Pete Burness and Jill de Grey were too close to be ignored. 'This is something I know you will want to know . . .' she wrote, deeply relieved to put down on paper words she might not be able to say aloud to him. It was three-thirty when she stamped the letters, remade her unused bed, redid her hair, changed her apron, and groped her way back across the road and up the steps to Central Hall. When she posted the letters in the new wooden, locked box just inside the staff entrance, she wondered when she would next see the three people she loved most. She could not remember what it was like to take such meetings for granted. Now they were uncertainties so hedged with danger that they could only be anticipated with hedged thoughts.

'Can I scrounge your scissors, Ann? Better still, a sharp scalpel.'

She spun round, not having noticed Paddy Brown sitting on the lowest of the bare marble stairs at the other end of the dim, unlit hall. He rose languidly and sauntered towards her looking unrecognisably elegant. The medical qualification examinations were in progress in London, and he wore a dark suit, stiff white collar, white shirt, hospital tie, and his normally untidy longish black hair had been subjected to a neat short-back-and-sides.

She smiled at his pale, mournful face. 'No, Paddy, you can't cut your throat in Central Hall. Go and find an empty bathroom. How did today's medicine viva go?'

He groaned. ' "Tell me what you know of Pink Disease, Mr Brown." What do I know? Sweet bloody – sorry – Fanny Adams.'

'What did you say?'

'What could I say? That it's a disease that turns the patient pink.'

She laughed. 'That was on target. Gives a rash.'

He was furious. 'You're not telling me you've met the swine?'

'Occasionally in kids' wards. Hits in early childhood. It's a form of polyneuritis. Hang on – Erythroedema Polyneuritis.'

'Now she tells me.' He beat his breast. 'I've had it. Back to Dublin and no fatted calf. My old man wanted to kill me for qualifying in England. He'll bump me off for sure for crawling back with my tail between my legs. No hope of a Martha's house job for Brown.'

'Do you honestly want one?' He glared at her. 'Keep your hair on – but for weeks you've been telling me this war's none of your business. Fair enough. You're a neutral. It isn't.'

'And when's that ever stopped an Irishman sticking his neck out?'

Or an American? 'Not to worry, Paddy,' she said.

'Feeling suicidal during exams is a healthy sign. I'll bet you do well and land a medical house job.'

That only cheered him momentarily. 'If I do, it'll be in the sticks. "Shove him to the huts," they'll cry.'

She stared. 'What are you talking about? What huts?'

'You've not heard?' He flung up his hands. 'Mother of God, girl, the grapevine's been blowing all fuses this last hour! Martha's is for the old heave-ho!'

'*What?*'

'Not the whole joint, and that's what set the cat amongst the pigeons. The notices went up outside the Dean's and Matron's offices an hour back. This is the way of it' – He rushed on, his gloom forgotten in the joy of imparting bad news. 'Early in the New Year the main body of the hospital is shifting to some moth-eaten huts the Army doesn't want way down in the sticks. They've even given it a name. St Martha's-in-the-Country, no less! It'll take our London patients from here, gather back into the fold the Med. and Nurses' Training Schools, have branches of every professional and lay department in the old firm that'll carry on carrying on in London – if it survives this turn-up. Nothing Jerry's bunged on us has shaken it so rigid. The lot are at each other's throats. No one wants to go. Some must. And not one word out on that yet. Talk about best-kept secret of the war. The top brass have closed ranks and mouths.'

'Wow!' She was too angry to think clearly. 'Five hundred years we've been here! How dare Jerry push us out! I'm damned if I want to go – oh, blast!' Big Ben was beginning to chime the hour. 'I'm on. Good luck tomorrow, Paddy.' She raced to Casualty.

For once Paddy had not exaggerated, and throughout the remaining days of November the passions aroused in Martha's by that afternoon's news raged as continuously as the Luftwaffe.

'West of England town, nurse. Bristol, plain as the

nose you still can't see on your own face outside. Poor old Tiddy-Oggies . . .'

'Downright batty! How can we possibly staff two hospitals? We're stretched so thin up here that no one's had a day off since anyone can remember!'

Ann had a short letter from Josh with a two-day-old Solihull postmark: '. . . maybe tomorrow . . .'

Not today, nor tomorrow, thought Ann – *stop it!'*

'If Matron intends recalling our Sisters from the EMS to run the hut wards, how's she going to replace them? She can't leave our EMS Units without Sisters, and the whole country's desperately short of trained nurses and doctors now the Services are swiping our men immediately they've finished their six months from qualification – crazy!'

'South of England town, nurse. Southampton, you mark my words – when the papers come out with the name next week – next year . . .'

On that same day, at two hours' notice, Peggy Butler and four fourth-year SRNs were transferred to Garden East Emergency Medical Services Hospital in Hampshire, which was increasing with emergency beds its two-thousand-bed capacity to take some of Southampton's thousands of air raid casualties.

'Matron's doing *what*?'

'Rallying the OMs.* She's sent out a round robin asking for single, married or widowed ones under fifty

* Old Martha's trainees.

in good health to come back fulltime, living-in, in the EMS. She won't allow any married Marthas to work in London or at the new base, but she's got to use them in the EMS because they are her only reserves. Married Sisters! Talk about the end of civilisation – as if that hadn't ended on 3 September last year!'

'A town in the North, nurse, and no mention of it being done before. Liverpool, you'll see . . .'

'Nothing in the papers this morning, nurse, but word's out that Liverpool copped it again last night. Tidy sized port, Liverpool, and there's Birkenhead. Poor old Scousers . . .'

'Liverpool again, nurse – the name's given – and our fog's shifted lovely. He'll be back.'

He will, thought Ann, struggling to ignore her heightened awareness of the preciousness of her life now she had so much more to lose. And before she went off duty that night:

'Here he is again, Sister.'

'Indeed, Dacey. Nothing more from the police?'

'Not for us, Sister. Leastways, not yet.'

It was 29 November and that night's attack was one of London's heaviest for some time. But Martha's zone was outside the main targets and comparatively few casualties came in from other zones, so no day nursing staff were called up. By blitz standards the hospital had a quiet night.

The next afternoon, when Miss Smithers came over for four-thirty tea, she first handed in to an Office Sister a small, square, wrapped and sealing-waxed packet. 'Gentleman left this for Nurse Marlowe an hour back, Sister.'

'Thank you, Miss Smithers. Just sign my book, please.'

Ann had been off ten-to-one, Casualty was less busy, and the day seemed endless to her. She was sent to first tea, then first supper, and each time checked her pigeonhole. The second time she was just turning away wearily, when an Office Sister called through an open doorway, 'Packet for you to collect and sign for, Nurse Marlowe.'

She had to have privacy. She shut herself in the nearest hardboard-battened, unlit, out-of-order public telephone box in the main corridor, her back to the door and her lighted torch propped on the black metal coinbox fixed to the rear wall. Her hands shook as she cut off the wrapping and took out a folded page from Josh's notebook and a red velvet-covered ring box embossed in gold with the name of a Bond Street jeweller. She opened the note first:

> London, 30/11/'40. 1300 hours.
> Dearest – I am hoping for the chance to see you this afternoon and have your opinion on the enclosed. If you don't like it, it can be changed for whatever you prefer, or if the fit is wrong, that can be easily adjusted. I was only able to get it this morning, but as you will appreciate, I can't wait to give it to you – I would add with all my love did you not have the lot already. I am just writing this in case I can't meet with you today. I so hope I can. I do so want to see you.
> Yours. Period.
> J.
> P.S. I did. I have. Thank you. J.

She slid the note into her apron bib, opened the box, and gasped at the exquisite beauty and size of the solitaire diamond set in diamond shoulders and gold, sparkling like trapped fire in the torchlight. She took out the ring and laid it in the palm of her left hand, then stood very still looking down at it for a long time. She knew that it was far more than an immensely generous

245

engagement ring. Perhaps even more from Josh's letters than from him in person, she had learnt to follow the way his imaginative mind worked. She knew that what, fundamentally, he most feared for her, was that he might be killed before he could marry her and so give her the protection of US citizenship. If Michael were killed, and England defeated, she would be left alone, a displaced person in her own country under German occupation, unable or forbidden to work – and hungry. This is small enough for me to hide, she thought, valuable enough for me to sell to keep me from starving. It cost a fortune, and even if it could only raise a fraction of its value, in war or peace, if there is any to be had, diamonds can buy bread. Of course he couldn't wait to give it to me. Last night over the river was as bad as the night Pete Burness was killed. Tonight could be the same. Tomorrow's too far away. And now he's realised what I've known since we met – that we can't afford to stop hoping, or waste time. Even so, only he is putting this on my finger – and I'm wearing it as long as I live – starving or otherwise.

She unstudded the front of her dogcollar, pulled up and unclasped the chain and slid on the second ring on to it, almost mechanically. Her sudden overwhelming relief that Josh was alive and back in London this afternoon, and her wonder at this manifestation of the measure of his love, was numbing her feelings nearly as acutely as had the shock after the destruction of Block 1. This new numbness was shorter-lived, but it lasted for the rest of her working day. As before, she was able to work efficiently, but she heard the noise of the rising wind that had come in with the evening tide, and the wailing of the sirens, as if they were occurring in another world.

'Back he comes, Sister. And there I was hoping this wind would give us a night's breather.'

'Very droll, Dacey. Nothing for us yet?'

'No, Sister. Down west. Going for Battersea and Lots Road power stations, seemingly.'

By 9 p.m. the wind howled round the damaged hospital, rattling loosened boards, broken rafters and the huge tarpaulin sheets covering the gaps in the front roofs, distorting the roar of bomber formations passing over-head and the more distant growl of circling aircraft, and the sound of guns and explosions. By ten, all fifteen re-maining occupants of the day staff nurses' dormitory were off duty, and in their deep basement the noise was barely audible over the outraged voices continuing the dis-cussion. They all sat or lay on top of their beds, in uniform dresses under cloaks and dressing-gowns, their shoes on the floor, caps and clean aprons on the patients' bedside lockers now by their beds, shelter-bags and gasmasks hanging from the headrails. The raid was too young and their experience of raids too old for any to risk getting undressed yet. Only Ann, lying propped up on her bed writing to Josh, took no part in the conversation until Nancy Standing's voice rose above the others: 'Frankly, the prospect of being shifted from my nice basement ward to nurse in the wilds for the duration, just sticks in my throat!'

Mary suggested, 'If the worst happens, Nancy, why not join me in the Army? Shall I collect a QA application form for you when I go over to Millbank for my medical next Tuesday?'

Nancy sat up indignantly. 'I know you mean well, Mary, but, frankly, I don't want to join the Army. I mean – I'm a civilian. I want to stay in poor old battered London. I don't want to go to war.'

Ann joined in the general yells of laughter. 'You and me, both, Nancy,' she called. 'Simple civvy types, that's us.' Then, as before in delayed-action shock, she sang words that just came into her mind, but this time to the tune of 'I Don't Want to Join the Air Force' and at the full strength of her true, untrained, soprano.

'We don't want to join the Army,
We don't want to go to war,
We want to stay in Martha's,
In poor old battered London,
The civvy types we've always been before.'

Judy shouted over the vociferous applause, 'We're
using that in our finale, Ann! Do me a couple more
verses, get together with Phyl Den – ' Her voice was
cut off by what sounded exactly like an express train
rushing towards them, and as one they flung themselves
off and under their beds as the first of a series of close
explosions put out the lights, and shook the floor of even
that deepest part of the whole basement. The onslaught
of repetitive roars was over in under five seconds, but
when the noise died, as always, for a few more seconds
they stayed face down and gasping for the breath forced
from their lungs. Then slowly, in unison, they rolled clear
of their beds, hauling themselves up by their bedside
rails, their feet groping for shoes, unsteady hands for
torches under pillows or in shelter-bags. Before they had
breath for speech or the first torch flicked on, the blaring
single-note of the hospital's fire-alarm galvanised their
actions and steadied their hands. Swiftly, in darkness,
they laced shoes, pinned on caps, buttoned on aprons,
slung shelter-bags and gasmasks over their shoulders
and grabbed their cloaks whilst straining for the
moment when the single blaring would stop and the
staccato signal denoting the source of the fire begin.
Every department had its own – Casualty's, one short,
one long, one short; the blocks, short blasts of their
respective numbers – and the code was repeated at least
three times. Fire drill was well practised, and like every
member of the professional and lay staff they knew what
they must do. Their fire stations were their own wards
or departments, and as in raid drill, the order of saving
was patients, juniors, seniors, equipment; and in fire drill

(or where haemorrhage was involved) Martha's nurses were not merely permitted, but ordered, to run in the hospital.

The blaring stopped, the code began. They counted in breathless chorus the short blasts: 'One – two – three – four – five – six – ' A pause. 'Theatre Bl–' Again the voices were cut out by a different roar rushing towards them against the background of the first repetition that was incomplete when a wave of lukewarm water cascaded over their invisible feet. Their dormitory emptied in seconds, but already the water had risen to the hems of their voluminous skirts.

The first stick of bombs dropped by a German pilot emptying his load on being prematurely recalled to base owing to the increasingly stormy weather over south-east England, had hit and set alight one front corner of the roof of the Theatre Block (6); the others had landed and exploded on the wide inlet of terrace between Blocks 6 and 7 under which lay the main boiler-room, and had sliced all the mains pipes.

All the Casualty day nurses were immediately dispatched to help in the basement wards, four of which, together with the connecting stretches of corridor, were flooded. The lowest was Basement Ward 1, and when Ann and Nancy Standing hastily hauled out the last patient's bed the water was ten inches deep. They forced the bed along the winding corridor against the swiftly flowing water in the soft glow of the hurricane lamps now hanging from widely spaced hooks fixed to the rough stone walls lined with pipes. Under Block 5 the stream turned to a trickle, and under 4, which was at a higher level, the floor was dry.

'Fire and flood in the one night's a bit much for poor old Martha's, Sister,' observed the patient laconically. 'Oy, oy! All Clear. Jerry's knocking off early. What's he want to do that for?'

Nancy said brightly, breathlessly, 'I expect bad

weather stopped play, Mr Collins. Such a windy night. Must have tossed them about like cockleshells. Comfortable? Splendid! As soon as the urn boils on the primus you'll all have a nice cup of tea. Thank you, Nurse Marlowe. We can cope now.'

'Thank you, Sister. Goodnight, Mr Collins.'

Whilst they were helping empty the basement wards, Sister Cas had sent by her night junior a verbal message to her day staff: 'Once all patients evacuated to dry areas, volunteers only to Theatre Block, others report back to Casualty.'

Judy had already disappeared. Ann knew instinctively where she had gone, and where she herself must go. She felt no fear, nor noticed that her legs and feet were soaking – there was no time. She ran back to the basement stairs between Blocks 4 and 5, then up to and along the main corridor to join the small army of assorted professional and lay staff volunteers fighting to save as much surgical equipment as possible from the block that was now alight from the third floor upwards. Outside, on the hospital terrace and high above it, a larger army of London and hospital firemen were fighting to contain and control the fire. Below, in other parts of the basement, another small assorted army of staff was fighting to contain and control the flooding.

Matron was back on duty, seemingly omnipresent. More often than not she was flanked by the Dean and the Hospital Secretary, both of them too elderly to take part in the heavy manual work going on all around, and their recognition of this fact added years to their grave, lined faces. Sister Cas was back in Casualty Hall, once more lit by battery-powered lamps and, aside from Sister Cas, staffed only by the night nurses, who like all night nurses were forbidden to leave their departments or wards. But all members of the professional, lay and domestic day staff resident in Martha's that night, were up and working against time, fighting either fire or water. The urgency of the situation had forced Matron to abandon previous wartime rules and accept every female volunteer, and without exception the day Sisters, student nurses and wardmaids had volunteered their services.

The swirling pillars of flame soaring high above the burning block lit up the south bank of the river from Hungerford Bridge to Vauxhall, but by 1 a.m. the fire was under control; in the basement, the manually operated pumps had reduced to a few inches the water level that in the staff nurses' dormitory had risen to the springs of the high hospital beds; and under Block 3, a two-table emergency theatre was ready for use. An hour later, Mr Wesley, his eyebrows and front hair singed, operated in that theatre under battery-lamps, upon the two badly injured hospital firemen who had been on the roof when the bomb hit. No other London or hospital fireman suffered more than minor burns that were treated in Casualty, and no patients nor any other staff were injured. The residents and medical students spent what was left of the night on mattresses on the floor of the Antenatal Clinic; the day staff nurses, on their ballroom floor and the mattresses and bedding they carried down from their own bedrooms in the small hours. Too tired for any thought but relief, they all slept as if poleaxed, and it was only when they woke that they realised Martha's had neither gas, mains or emergency electricity, nor water.

The nurses' getting-up bells rang at the usual 6.30 a.m. and were followed by an identical announcement from the respective Home Sisters:

'Good morning, nurses. Matron wishes me to thank you all for your help last night and to express her great regret that, as breakfasts will be late, she must request you to go on duty as soon as you are ready. You will be informed of the arrangements for your breakfasts later. Thank you, nurses.'

It was 7.10 a.m. when Ann and Judy reported

to Casualty in clean caps, uniforms and stockings, and soaking shoes, just as the first convoy of empty ambulances crawled into the Yard. The ambulances had come to transfer as many as could be moved of the 248 bedpatients to other London hospitals to await the arrival of the ambulances from the Home Counties that would take them to country hospitals later in the day. The list of transfers and collation of the patients' notes and X-rays had been made by the SMO, the SSO, the Assistant Matron and two Office Sisters, all, like Matron, working through the night and still on duty. Only the two badly injured firemen and six other DILs were too ill to move from their beds, which were now in either Male Basement Ward 5 or Female Basement Ward 6, the only underground wards unaffected by the flooding. 'When they have all gone, Matron,' said Dr White, 'our total bedstate will be eight. Cut us down a bit, has friend Jerry.'

'Temporarily, Dr White. Temporarily.'

The main road passing the hospital had been cordoned off for hours to all but fire appliances, ambulances and official cars and motor-bikes. But from 6.45 a.m. the WVS canteen vans were allowed through. It was still dark when the first two arrived. They parked at the far end of Casualty Yard, close to the steps to Central Hall, then began piling the offered trays with the patients' breakfasts – the individual ration was one mug of scalding tea and two large sandwiches. It was growing light when two more vans arrived, parking in the same line, well away from the ambulances still coming and going. The second pair began serving breakfast to the combined staff who came out in turn, in pairs, the juniors first. The faces of the night staff were grey, and those of the day staff white with fatigue, and all their eyes smarted in the icy wind that was clearing the smoke but not the smell of smouldering from the Theatre Block that was now a burnt-out shell.

None of the staff who came out in the first hour noticed the thin line of spectators on the far pavement, among them a strangely subdued Tommy Benson, the little groups of officials standing around the Yard, and smaller group of pressmen, including Josh and Gus Mackinlay, on the nearside pavement. The observers watched in silence the pairs of figures wearing uniform, white coats, navy battle dress or dungarees, coming and going as continuously as the ambulances. The watchers' faces, professionally impassive or grimly sympathetic, were stung by the wind that was trying to tear down the defiant notice on the now filthy sheets nailed to thin wooden frames swinging over the entrance to Casualty. They had all heard what had happened to the hospital during the night, and it seemed to many, apart from Josh, that they were watching its dying moments.

Big Ben was striking 9 a.m. when Judy and Ann came swiftly from Casualty, hooking the collars of the long navy cloaks which the wind hurled back over their shoulders, exposing the scarlet linings and broad scarlet cross-straps. They walked swiftly to the nearest WVS van, where Judy stood back for Ann to be served first.

'There you are, staff nurse. I expect you can do with a hot cuppa. Pilchards with, or without?' (tomato sauce) 'Or one of each?'

'With, please, and thanks most awfully.'

Ann stepped back to wait for Judy, and then she saw Josh standing about twenty yards away, his trilby jammed down on his head, his hands in the pockets of his mackintosh, his haggard face as grey as the faces of the night nurses. He was staring at her as if she were a mirage.

She smiled joyfully straight at him and, raising her mug to him, she thought, he's always there.

– Twelve –

'Oh yes, sir, I'll see Nurse Marlowe gets it. Mind you – '
Miss Smithers hesitated, not wanting to disappoint the
tall young American she had greeted like an old friend
– 'if you got the time, you might be able to give it her
yourself.'

Josh's pulse-rate soared. 'Nurse Marlowe's off this
afternoon?'

'Well, sir, to tell you the truth I can't say for sure,
but seeing I've not set eyes on her today, this is the
first Saturday in December, she's second staff in Cas
and we had the last night quiet, she's most like to
have the two-to-six for Christmas shopping. Sister Cas
always gives her two staff nurses the extra shopping
hour on the first two Saturdays in December – second
first, like.'

He nodded with an understanding that would have
been beyond him three months ago. Last night had
been London's only raid-free night this week, and Miss
Smithers had just told him Martha's had reopened all the
basement and three above-ground wards. 'Customary
routine.'

'That's right, sir. Can you wait?'

'Surely, thanks. I'll just step out – '

'Not in this cold, sir! We've got the smoking-room
for gentlemen callers to wait in. This way, sir.' She
ushered him to a room directly across the hall. 'If

254

Nurse Marlowe is off I'm sure she'll be over to see if anything's come for her here, specially with Jerry back, and phones and posts haywire again. And not just back to us, neither,' she added chattily, as she didn't mind admitting to herself that it made a rare treat to talk to a nice young gentleman as sounded like he stepped straight out of the talkies. 'Birmingham and Bristol and all the tip-and-runs we had till yesterday. But not none today, have we, sir?'

'Not that I've heard.'

'Not one cheep from Minnie round here. Makes you wonder what he's after, but I expect we'll know soon enough. Would you like me to fetch you Home Sister's *Times* to pass the time? She's over at the hospital but I know she's done with it.'

'Thanks, but I have today's.' He gestured to the folded copy sticking out of one pocket of his black velour overcoat.

'There! Never spotted! Not that I bother reading the papers myself, sir. Never nothing in them that's not old news, and precious little of that. Home Sister says not been nothing of our night raids this week, nor what happened over the hospital last Sunday night. Mustn't give helpful information to the enemy, she says, but what I says is, Jerry must know where he's bombed and those that copped it know well enough, so why can't the papers say? But I'd best get back to my lodge. Please smoke in here if you wish, sir. Can you give it ten minutes or so, sir?'

He smiled. 'Gladly, Miss Smithers. Thanks very much.'

'No trouble, sir.' She backed out, warmed by his smile, and left the door on the latch.

He dropped his trilby in the nearest armchair, lit a cigarette, and stood looking around the room. It was about ten foot square, unheated, lit by a solitary ceiling light with a white glass shade, decorated in drab greens and browns, and furnished with three small brown-rexined armchairs, a little bamboo table holding three glass ashtrays, and a gunmetal clock with a loud tick on the greenish-marbled mantelshelf over an ancient, unlit gasfire. It had the atmosphere of a vestibule overlooked by a convent grille. The atmosphere in particular transported him back to his first visit to Martha's three months ago to the day and date, for it was 7 December. He looked thoughtfully at the boarded front windows and, as if they were glass, visualised across the road the massive, ugly wooden palisades on either side of the steps to Central Hall, the still uncleared ruins of the Junior Home (there had been neither the men nor the time to spare for the job), the gaps at both ends of the line of blocks, the roofless, windowless, blackened shell of the penultimate block at this end, and the ambulance he had just seen backing between the sandbag walls outside the entrance to Casualty above which was suspended the scrubbed and repainted notice, ST MARTHA'S HOSPITAL IS DOWN BUT NOT OUT. OPEN TO ALL PATIENTS AS USUAL.

Customary routine, he thought, recalling his first impression of the great, solid, sprawling hospital as a Victorian mausoleum, not merely untouched by but unaware of the war, and unprepared for its realities. He felt again the chill, even on that hot afternoon, on the five flights of stone stairs, and saw the pretty flushed face of the helpful kid, and Ann, when he turned from the office window, standing behind him, a tallish, slenderly pretty Victorian figurine, made of porcelain. Then he saw Ann's tired face smiling and her hand raising her mug to him in an instinctive gesture of triumph last Monday morning, evoking Mackinlay's 'That has to be her! You lucky son of a bitch!'

Don't I know it, he thought carefully, not daring to dwell too closely on luck now that, for him also, life had become frighteningly precious – and always in the background hovered the memory of Pete Burness and thoughts of Joan Burness and her little son too young ever to remember his father. The possibility of the same, or worse, happening to Ann, had – as she had guessed – been one of the reasons he had bought the most expensive engagement ring he could afford to offer her, financially and aesthetically. And on this last Tuesday he had paid another visit to the US Embassy and left there the will he had made in Ann's favour and had had drawn up and witnessed by a firm of London solicitors. During Tuesday night's raid he had written to Michael Marlowe, just as he would have done to Ann's father, requesting approval for his marriage to Ann, giving a succinct account of his professional, financial and personal situation. He had had Michael's address from Lefty Smith, and had posted the letter on Wednesday morning before leaving for return visits to Birmingham and Bristol, and after getting from Ann a letter he would treasure for life.

He had not mentioned the will, nor that he had written to Michael, in the letter he had brought over this afternoon to let Ann know he was back and, above all, to reassure himself that she was safe. He had come over in the passionate hope, but with no great expectation, of seeing her for the first time since Monday morning, when he had had no chance to talk to her. The Luftwaffe's activities had ruled that out for the rest of the week. Yesterday morning, after another night in a train in a tunnel, he had only had time to shave, shower and change before going back to east Kent and Sussex to see the consequences on seaside towns of the recent spate of daytime attacks by enemy fighters and fighter-bombers.

He had gone down in an RAF car with Gus Mackinlay and two Swedish correspondents. The latter were reasonably convinced they owed their inclusion to the complaint by one of their number, recently published

257

in a London national paper, that American journalists in London were almost daily given – and other foreign journalists were denied – the favour of seeing and hearing with their own eyes and ears. 'To speak truthfully, boys,' said one Swede, 'we are not too impressed with British fair play.'

Josh, in the front, exchanged grins with the youngish WAAF driver, and after she refused his offered cigarettes, held them out to the three in the back of the small, elderly Ford. 'Not to worry, Olaf. If the British don't love you, Jerry must. First empty skies we've seen all week. I guess he heard you were coming and stayed home to bake a cake.'

'You must be joking, Josh!'

Mackinlay drawled, 'Just once a week, bud. Coming from Boston.'

'They do not joke in Boston?'

Josh said gravely, 'Only on the anniversary of the Tea Party: 16 December 1773.'

'To speak truthfully, boys, you Americans are as crazy as the British who still think they can win this war.'

'So I've been told.' Josh turned forward again and caught the driver's derisive smile before she erased it from her pugnaciously homely face.

He lit his cigarette and gazed out at the quiet wintry countryside under the wide, pale-pewter sky. The evergreens were more black than green; the hedges, washed yellowish-brown round the roots, mid-brown higher up, were spiky and petrified as if no green leaf could grow on them again. The telegraph poles and armless signposts lurched at odd angles after the now frequent gales hurtling down from the North Sea and meeting no opposition over the flat rich Kentish farmland until the gently rolling North Downs thirty miles back from the coast. The omnipresent sheep were grey against the green and greenish-brown fields; the hop-gardens were forests of bare poles; the leafless trees in the apple and cherry orchards, as petrified as the hedges. The harvest was in, the last autumn bonfires were out, the first winter ploughing was done, and in the little villages the half-timbered houses clustered round grey, square-towered Norman churches, the white wood smoke rose from the chimneys but no longer from the white or black-coned oast houses, and the few villagers in sight had the leisurely air of those taking it easy now winter had come and the land was resting.

'Could be another world, Mr Adams,' the driver said.

'Certainly looks that way, corporal,' he replied, seeing in memory the golden glows and smoke-smudged skies of autumn and the brilliant blues, fading greens, and angry skies of last summer. And hearing in memory 'This is one real old country, brother . . . seen it all before . . . tomorrow is another day . . press on regardless . . .'

On the return journey the four men were more silent. Since Pete Burness had been killed with all the occupants of an ARP wardens' post in Fulham by the direct hit that simultaneously demolished his Morris Oxford parked outside, two more foreign journalists had been killed in London, one in Bristol, and another in Birmingham. Before they were over Wrotham Hill, the highest in Kent, the smoke of last night's new fires in London blackened the sky ahead and began darkening the short afternoon twilight. The driver discreetly increased speed and her passengers chain-smoked, lost in their own thoughts.

Josh roused himself to glance at his watch. 'Making pretty good time, corporal.'

'If I don't get you back before tonight's Alert I'll get torn off a strip.'

'That'll be too bad.'

She smiled. 'Won't be the first time. I'll survive.'

Long after their return London's sirens remained silent, and no news had yet begun trickling in of attacks elsewhere. 'One'll get you ten,' said Mackinlay, deftly dealing a fresh hand of poker, 'the Apache have gotten the Pony Express one more time.'

Josh checked his watch against the gunmetal clock. Half-two on both. Maybe just late off? Give it more time. He pulled out and opened his *Times*. Miss Smithers heard the rustle of newspaper, glanced at her desk clock and reached for her internal telephone. She had a piercing telephone voice but Josh didn't hear her talking to Dacey. His attention was focused on a small column on an inner page that he already knew by heart. It concerned an article in the issue of *Life* magazine out today in the United States, with an account of a speech made in early May by Richard Walther Darre, the German Minister of Agriculture, to a small, inner group of Nazi officials. He was reported as saying that after the German victory England would be destroyed as Carthage was destroyed, and her punishment would be made a lesson to all other nations of the western hemisphere which might venture to oppose the Germans.

Mental vision blotted out physical sight, flicking over pictures like movie stills: the uncontrollable forest fires, the river itself blazing, and Ann's white, implacable face; convoys of red buses packed with homeless and real and makeshift ambulances crawling through smoke; figures packed like sardines under old rugs or open newspapers on Underground platforms; a thin, elderly Sister, eyes red-rimmed and glazed with grief, accepting a letter; Coventry on a mid-November night; Coventry in the last days of November, still flattened, bleeding, smelling of sewage and death, binding its wounds; Birmingham, hit three times as hard as Coventry; Bristol, Southampton, their city centres devastated like Coventry's. Pictures of faces, thousands of faces: stunned, exhausted, terrified, grieving, resigned, but, the overwhelming majority of them, savagely angry faces.

He heard the voices, thousands of individual voices, shaking with shock, or fear, or pain, or grief, but again, overwhelmingly, with ugly anger. But he had still to hear one English voice suggesting surrender. And when he tentatively put that question, still the same response in the varying provincial accents, as still in London's voice: 'After what he's doing to us? You got to be joking! We can take it – and we'll give it back! Licked him last time, didn't we? Down we may be, but not out, not by a long chalk we aren't – and you can bung that down on your bit of paper, guv!'

Pictures of Folkestone, Dover, Deal and Hastings, yesterday, the pebbled and sandy beaches mined, seafront promenades bristling with barbed wire and sandbagged gun-emplacements; omnipresent gaps or semi-ruins of homes, hotels, boarding-houses, shops, offices, hospitals; the populations down to one-third, for from late spring the Government posters had requested that all adult civilians that could, should evacuate themselves to assist the Army's anti-invasion tactics. 'Yes, these tip-and-runs are keeping us busy. We've got used to 'em. Not crossed the Channel yet, has he? Old Boney never got here either. Last one over was old William in 1066. Used to waiting for them to come, we are, round here.'

Was it the antiquity of England, he wondered – as he had done constantly during these past weeks of travelling round the country – or some inheritance from their feudal past that he had found offensively obvious in their class system until the blitz pounded them into a single entity, that gave them their totally unexpected strength, tenacity, resilience, and the flexibility to adapt that was the fount of their near-genius for improvisation? 'Whatever or the lot, brother . . . sure as hell nothing, repeat, nothing, sends their morale sky high like having their backs to the wall . . .'

The sound of quick steps broke his abstraction and

lightened his face with hope, but when Ann came in quickly, pulling the door to behind her, he felt as if an icy hand had clutched his stomach. Her face, rising like a pale flower above the upturned collar of her long cloak, had the rainwashed quality only the young can achieve after tears. She said huskily, 'I should have known you'd be here. You're always around when I most need you. I didn't know. I didn't dare think of you either.'

He went to her at once and drew her into his arms, and was unbearably moved by her shuddering sigh as she rested one side of her face against his shoulder. 'Michael, dearest?' he asked gently.

She raised her head to look up into his distressed face. 'Thank God, not what you're thinking. He's gone overseas. Thursday. He wrote to me on Tuesday saying he'd suddenly been posted with only twenty-four hours' embarkation leave as there's some flap on somewhere. No time to make London, even if he had managed to pull strings, as we're still off-limits, but he said he'd try and ring me from Aunt Maud's. Obviously, he couldn't. Our outside lines have been down all week till today. Our posts are still days late. Michael's letter only came this morning. I found it on the way to last lunch and went straight out on the terrace. I've just been walking up and down not daring to think of him, or you. I haven't heard from you all week.'

'I posted you a letter from London, Monday, and Dorchester, Wednesday.'

'I knew you would if you could.' She rested her face back against him. 'But you're here. Here! Thank God.' She closed her eyes. 'I don't know where Michael's gone. He couldn't say. I imagine, Africa. Just about everyone I know in the Army's now there fighting the Italians, and from the patients' gen the RAF keep making strikes on Benghazi and Tobruk, wherever they are. I'll have to start looking at the maps in the papers. He's probably there, don't you think?'

'Probably,' he lied, thinking of Michael's experience as a fighter-pilot. Last month Mussolini had invaded Greece, to which country the British had promised support, and the RAF had begun setting up stations in Crete to help the Greeks in their efforts to repel the Italian Army which was forcing its way down through the valleys of northern Greece. Time enough when she had to know, he thought, holding her closer and tenderly kissing her exposed cheek. 'He'll come back at least a Wing Commander. You'll see.'

She looked up at him, then drew down his face and kissed his lips.

A few minutes later she unstudded her dogcollar, unclasped and removed the silver chain, handed him his ring and showed him her father's. 'Michael's letter said I should hold on to this until the whole show's over, as on past form it's doing a better job with me.' She replaced the chain, and he saw in her downcast face that she was fighting the thought that she might never be able to return the signet ring. But when she looked up, her wet eyes smiled for the first time since she had come in. 'Did you get my letter about leaving this to – '

'I did! I just can't tell you how much – ' He kissed her passionately, then slid the ring on the third finger of her left hand, and for about a minute they stood, close together, holding hands and looking at each other with a love that went too deep for words, and with a wonder neither dared risk putting into words, because the surrounding shadows were too close and too threatening.

Cruising taxis had become rarities, but they picked one up a few yards from the Home that took them to the little restaurant off St Martin's Lane that served late lunches and was cheerfully willing to follow with afternoon tea and provide a sanctuary from the cold as long as they wished. They spent most of their time holding one conversation with their eyes, another with their voices, bringing each other up to date on their individual war news, but saying no more of Michael. They said nothing of their personal future either, until another jubilant waiter had announced a waiting taxi and they were in the darkness of the back, and she was again in his arms.

'How soon, Ann?' There was a tremor in his quiet voice. 'Please – can't you make it soon?'

'I wish it could be tomorrow. But till the blitz stops – ' She paused suddenly. 'It might be quite soon! Because of the weather – like last Sunday night.'

This time her optimism appealed to his head and heart. 'You get rough January weather?'

'January and February. Always our winter worst – and now I think of it, this must be why the top brass have timed our exodus for then. If Jerry does have to lay off, it's then I'll get my owed days off in a lump. Matron's determined we'll all have them in relays – I'm already due three weeks. If you could get some time off then, we could see Aunt Maud and do some – some thinking.'

It was only then that Josh recognised how much more than just his previous attitudes to the English had been altered by the last three months. Altered, or just blasted clean of the overlays, he wondered, knowing he was about to make the most vital pitch of his life in a blazing, irrational hope. 'I have a better idea, sweetheart. Why don't I stand by with a special licence and we can use your vacation as a honeymoon?' He heard her sharp intake of breath, and went on urgently, 'I appreciate this will hand you a pretty difficult professional problem, but knowing you, I can't see you not coming up with the right answer. Any girl who, under violent air attack for the first time when stuck five flights up, calmly appreciates that the answer is a poker game, has one hell of a lot more where that came from. And as you're determined to stay in London – why don't we start married life in my hotel? I'll get us a bigger room and a sitting-room and – er – it has a pretty good shelter. What do you say?'

For a few moments Ann felt too ill to say anything. She knew that this afternoon on the terrace she had come close to breaking-point, and that the thought of Michael going overseas without their having the chance even to say 'cheerio' over the telephone, had disinterred long-buried memories of a six-year-old forced to face the fact that the worst could, and had, happened. This last week of raids, drying out, repairing, restocking, readmitting, had drained her physically as much as Josh's silence had drained her emotionally. Even her instincts had failed her on the terrace. I've lost contact with him too, she had thought, and a cold sense of desolation had enveloped her far more effectively than her cloak. Then a student had touched her shoulder and handed her Dacey's note with Miss Smithers' message.

Suddenly she knew what she must do, as clearly as she had once known that she and Sue Hardy must run from the OPD. She said only, 'Can you afford this?'

His heart seemed to turn over. He knew he had won. 'I guess.' He told her quickly about writing to Michael and what he had said. 'Do you mind my writing?'

'Mind?' she whispered. 'If I could now love you more, I would. Michael will be so bucked. He's an old-fashioned type too – like Aunt Maud – '

'Let me have her address fast, will you?' he asked, but gave her no time to answer. They had begun crossing the river, which was visible even in the blackout as the water was always darker than the sky. There was so much more to be said, but their parting was a few minutes off at the most, and words must wait.

The taxi was drawing up at the Home and they were reluctantly drawing apart, when the sirens started wailing.

The driver called out indignantly, 'What's he thinking of to come this early of an evening?'

'Want to drop me off too?'

'Not unless you wants, guv. After all this time I'm not packing it in just as Jerry's paying the call till I knows where's he dropping his card. I'll fetch you near as I can to your Piccadilly number.'

'Thanks. I'll just see the lady indoors and – '

'No! Please.' Ann's fingers lightly touched his lips and then the fading scar over his right eyebrow. 'Take care, my love.'

'And you, my dearest. Okay.' He gave her hand another kiss. 'Be seeing you.'

'You will!' She jumped out and vanished in the December blackout before she was on the front steps, or the sirens stopped sounding the earliest after-dark Alert of the war.

Josh ducked his head between his knees to flick the guarded flame to the cigarette clamped between tightened lips, whilst his mind mechanically recorded this further demonstration of the helplessness of those caught up in an air war to shape even the next few hours of their own lives. Even though he, Ann, and millions of others had grown so accustomed to deadly danger, he reflected, custom neither lessened the danger, nor heightened his chances of seeing Ann again. The taxi drove on, and sitting back on the seat, guarding the pin-point light of his cigarette, he was acutely conscious of the sense of foreboding he had experienced three months ago to the day and within forty-five minutes of the same hour.

Again events proved his instincts right. That night saw another of London's heaviest raids, and the start of a repetition of the previous week in London, and a considerable intensification of the Luftwaffe's attacks upon the Midlands, Merseyside, the North-east, North-west, and western England. Before Josh saw Ann again, he had seen the consequences of the blitz upon Sheffield,

266

Leeds, Manchester, Plymouth, the renewed attacks upon Liverpool, and, as always, upon London. In London he had seen the Christmas decorations go up in shops, offices, ARP posts, fire stations, hotels, hospitals, private houses, council houses, and tenement blocks. Much of the tinsel was old and tarnished, many of the paper-chains and paper bells were faded; most of the cotton-wool snowballs were greyed by smoke the day after they appeared; fairylights were forbidden, but a new rash of classily painted or chalked boards came out with the message WISHING ALL OUR CUSTOMERS THE COMPLIMENTS OF THE SEASON; and new rashes of tatty little Union Jacks sprouted from new rubble, new ruins, new bomb-sites.

In the third week of December London had three quiet nights, but Ann's brief off-duty was wholly taken up by rehearsals and dress-making for the show. As always over Christmas in Martha's, as in all English hospitals, no nursing or resident staff took off-duty for anything but sleep. On Christmas Day and Boxing Day there was so little air activity that on the morning of Friday, 27 December, the London national newspapers described Christmas as raid-free in Britain.

'One'll get you ten, bud, they're taking a short break before moving right in for the kill.'

'Uh-huh.'

That night the Luftwaffe returned in force to London, and in Martha's the dress rehearsal was cancelled one hour before it was due to start. But on Saturday night, though the post-performance party had to be postponed to Sunday, the show was put on as planned for London was raid-free. Miss Dewly's delight in the occasion was heightened by her being able to use the room in Josh's hotel that he had provisionally booked, and given a final gilding when Sir Joshua Levy, Martha's most senior and renowned honorary surgeon, drove them back to the hotel in his Rolls-Royce.

Sir Joshua courteously refused Josh's invitation to come in for a nightcap. 'Many thanks, m'boy, but working day ahead. Glad you both enjoyed tonight's highly diverting revelries – most enjoyable night off for us all in all ways! And though the hospital's so busy, tonight's quiet should allow more than a token resident to show up at tomorrow's party. Nine-fifteen to eleven, Antenatal Clinic, as tonight – has to end by eleven for the night rounds. Look forward to seeing you both . . . Goodnight, goodnight!'

It was nearly midnight when Josh got to his room and immediately sat down in an armchair, lighting a cigarette with one hand, uncovering his old portable with the other, for he needed to write as an alcoholic needs alcohol. The rooms on both sides and across the corridor were empty and his hands fed in the first sheet and began typing rapidly, as if of their own volition, and in direct communication with the machine in his mind simultaneously dictating and flicking out pictures without his conscious choice or control of the words, or the mental photographs, some stills, others moving pictures.

A large underground bunker in a semi-ruined hospital, the rows of chairs facing a low, portable stage leaving just enough room for an upright piano on its right. The chairs packed with a uniformly smiling crowd in uniforms, black jackets, white coats, tweed jackets, navy battledress, and in all the faces a uniformly etched tiredness. The pianist smiling shyly, blushing with excitement, in a gold lamé matinée jacket and black velvet semi-evening dress; then another picture of her in uniform, her frightened white face fixed in a painful smile, laying her cards face down on a bare mattress and clasping her hands in her lap to control the shaking. The whole cast opening the show with 'Doing the Lambeth Walk', the make-up concealing the fatigue in the smiling faces, singing as they went into the eponymous dance, wearing 'pearly' costers' caps and

268

jackets made from scarlet, yellow and bright blue crêpe paper embellished with glued-on small circles of silver cigarette paper, the men in black trousers, the girls in short flared black skirts made from the blackout curtains salvaged from the bombed boardroom that had opened off the first landing above Central Hall. Ann, gracefully bobbing a curtsy to the applause, smiling in his direction, looking devastatingly pretty and happy and young. Ann in close-up, the bright blue cap on one side of her head and blue jacket enhancing the blue in her eyes. Then a black and white still, taken tonight on the way in, of a great empty hall, a wooden wall blocking off the right-hand side, bustless pedestals lining the cracked stone wall on the left, the marks of charring on the bare marble staircase, and hidden on either side great craters that had been graves. Another close-up: a grim-faced police sergeant, 'I am sure . . . Just the four young staff nurses . . . Found . . . identified by the Matron herself.'

The Matron tonight, her pretty, worn face smiling serenely. The Matron on an early morning in September, white, calm, eyes sunken with anxiety, and keen: 'Are you feeling quite well, young man?'

Ann in navy sitting on an office chair, pale, sad, and appealing to Miss Dewly: 'I want to ask you both a straight favour . . .' Ann, in a travesty of a nurse's uniform with an upturned crêpe-paper lily for a cap, clowning deliciously with the gangling black-haired Irishman in the skit 'The Lily of Cas' that brought the house down for the first time and had young male voices yelling from the back rows, 'Stand by for blasting when you first step into Cas as JHP next week, Paddy!'

The same guy later playing an aggrieved patient: 'Come over all of a cruel tremble, I have, doctor, 'cause I been done down me four penn'orth! Never promised me that, did old Winnie. Promised me blood, me toil, me tears, me sweat – and I've had me lot – and not one tremble! But he didn't promise nothing of knocking the civvy meat ration down from the two-and-tuppence to the one-and-ten's worth the week just afore Christmas and doing me down four penn'orth of scrag-end what's fetched on me cruel trembles . . .'

Another of the guy with Ann in another place, both unrecognisable under the caking of plaster, heaving stones not like but in a chain-gang. Then a different plaster-caked face with bloodshot blue eyes blazing with anger: 'After a good story, Mr Adams?' That picture superimposed by the same face, well-groomed, compassionate-eyed: 'Ed Laurings was a damned fine chap. Damnable waste . . .' Then a long-shot of a tall, golden-haired figure alone on stage, lowered guitar in one hand, the other upraised for silence: 'Ladies and gentlemen, by general request, "Eight Nice Wardblocks" –' Pausing for the roar of approval. 'For the benefit only of the medical riffraff at the back I repeat, "Eight – Nice – Wardblocks". Thank you.' And then singing only the first line before the audience joined in for all eight verses.

More of Ann: standing in an endless corridor, starchy, composed, eyes empty: 'I am so sorry, Mr Adams . . .' Bending over a white bed smiling into sunken eyes above an ugly green rubber oxygen mask: 'Just going to give you something to give you a little kip.' Ann, straight-backed against closed balcony doors, her eyes as steady as her voice: 'If you are going to chance it up here there are things you must know . . .'

Ann tonight, alone on stage, in a Sister's uniform and steel-rimmed spectacles, fluting authoritatively into a telephone: 'Office Sister for Mr Billings, Repairs and Works, please . . . Good evening, Mr Billings, I am afraid we have a little problem for your department to sort out. St Martha's has no gas, electricity, water coming out of taps, the Theatre Block is a little overheated and the basement a trifle damp . . . Oh, you know the basement's damp? Swimming, Mr Billings? Such a healthy exercise! I'm sure

all in Repairs and Works are excellent swimmers . . .' and
bringing the house down for the second time. Ann later,
singing with the whole cast, their crossed hands linked, a
girl next to each man, swaying to the gentle slow waltz of
the tune 'South of the Border', to which they had written
the words that ended the show at two minutes to eleven.
Words that Josh had scribbled in shorthand on the back
of an envelope but his mind recalled without needing the
reference:

> South of the river –
> Back five hundred year,
> Little King Henry gave us the charter –
> That brought us all here,
> For this is our London –
> And this is our firm –
> And here Martha's is staying –
> As Jerry will learn.

> And when the war's over,
> We'll still be right here,
> South of the river where we've been –
> For five hundred years.
> For this is our London –
> And this is our firm –
> And here Martha's is staying –
> As the future will learn.

He stopped typing and looked at the empty armchair
across the low coffee table, and visualised the bulky,
red-haired Kentuckian so clearly that one of his hands
moved involuntarily towards the full untouched whisky
bottle he had put on the floor without knowing. '. . .
One real old country, brother . . . seen it all before . . .
tomorrow is another day . . . press on regardless . . .'

He indented a new paragraph, and wrote: 'Only right
now have I seen that that last, incessantly used, corny

idiom that has so riled me, contains common sense and hope. The vital element is the hope, for when that goes it takes all else with it. Last summer France lost hope, and so Paris surrendered without firing one shot in her own defence. London and England still possess hope in abundance, and whether this hope is based upon insularity, ignorance, stupidity, arrogance, myopia, or a combination, is immaterial to the fact that it is powering one of the greatest triumphs of the human spirit over disaster in recorded history. And because this is a fact, though this last Friday night was London's seventy-fifth night raid since 7 September, and just three days left in 1940, I am writing this in the early hours of Sunday, 29 December, in London, England, unconquered.'

He released the page, clipped it with the rest, covered up the portable, then sat back, thinking of Ann, listening to the gentle hum of the sparse traffic and feeling a sense of peace he had not known all this year. He recognised that it was a purely personal peace and that its source was Ann, and that recognition gave him such joy that a few minutes later he fell asleep in the chair, smiling. He was still smiling when the room-maid woke him after his best night's sleep since 6 September.

His first waking thought recalled Ann saying last night, 'If Jerry lays off tomorrow, Matron's given all cast nurses off from five-forty-five. Okay for you to collect me at six? Lovely! I'll be changed and we'll have three hours before we pick up Miss Dewly at Waterloo and come back to the party.' And then he recalled another event scheduled for tonight – and Hitler's talent for timing.

On that night of Sunday, 29 December, President Roosevelt broadcast to his country his eighth State of the Union message and final Fireside Chat of 1940. The broadcast went out from the White House in the late evening, Washington time. And before President

Roosevelt was on the air explaining to the United States – and the world – that his proposal to help the British war effort with what he termed 'lend-lease' was akin to lending a garden hose to a neighbour whose house was burning down, the City of London was burning down.

They had left the Home and were nearing the bridge approach when the Alert began. When it died away they had skirted the ruins of the Junior Home and were making for the temporary shelter of one of the shallow, arched recesses in the riverside wall on either side of the terrace doors of Stanley Parker on the ground floor of Block 3. 'Our rule when caught out,' said Ann, 'is take shelter, stay put till the All Clear, then report back fast. If we go inside now, we're stuck till it's over. It's automatically written off the party, so let's stooge around till we see who's for it. If our zone, we dive into Stanley P. Okay?'

'Okay.' Josh tightened his grip on her hand at the recollection of some of his thoughts this morning.

The evening was as dark as midnight, cold, blustery, and the air on the terrace smelt of salt, tar and sour mud as the Thames was at low tide. Ann led the way, giving a wide berth to the looming, uneven-edged black shadows of the first two ruined blocks. They heard the distant heavy droning and the first barrage of the guns far down river as they reached the cliff-like black shadow of Block 3.

'I think it should just clear you, but watch your head, Josh.'

'Sure.' He reached up and around, touching cold solid stone above, on both sides and about a yard back. He straightened. 'These things just ornamental?'

'I'm not sure if that was the original idea. Before the war in summer they were used to back in the beds. There used to be beds and wheelchairs all over the terrace on summer days. Patients loved it. So did we.' She paused to shut out the past and control her fear of the present, aware that her delaying tactics could endanger him. 'Here they come.'

His arm went round her as they backed against the rear wall, and he bent his head over hers, ready to protect her face with his trilby as rapidly as he had seen her cover a dying, masked face with a bare mattress when she had been a strange English girl he had begun reluctantly to admire but was determined to keep out of his life. He had then seen no alternative to chancing his life; now he would gladly give it to save her life, and the knowledge of their equal danger caused him to hear the first incoming formation with the most acute fear he had yet experienced.

The guns roared and a battery of searchlights probed the black sky, but the Luftwaffe flew in too low for flak or moving white fingers and on the block roofs the hospital firemen dived face down, gasping in unison, 'Diving! We're for it!' but the thundering black cloud had streaked over the river. Suddenly the blackness was illuminated by what could have been hundreds of shining oranges cascading down, and in the heart of the golden downpour the great dome of St Paul's Cathedral, surmounted with its lantern and cross, glimmered with light.

'The City! Thank God it's Sunday and empty, but – 'Ann's voice was drowned by the next formation. Josh folded his other arm around her and she gripped his wrists as more and more deadly golden fruit rained down, and from both sides of the river they heard the jangling bells of racing fire engines laden with men clinging on with one hand. A strange pinkish glow began floodlighting the City and turning the sky directly above it the pinkish black of a summer dawn.

Ann said icily, 'Were this not so hideous, it would be beautiful. I'll have to stay, Josh.'

'I guess you must,' he said quietly, reliving nightmare, recognising the identical pattern of experts concentrating with ruthless precision on one compact target – the packed square mile of the City, the financial heart of England and the British Empire, made-to-measure for what, in view of the stormy weather forecast for the next few days, could prove to be the Luftwaffe's final attack on England this year. Already the strength of the westerly wind at ground level must be causing considerable air turbulence, but one after another the formations flew in steadily, superbly skilled and trained, the crews undoubtedly hand-picked for their expertise that had been honed to a fine edge on Coventry and other English cities. In those other cities he had seen the consequences of this kind of concentrated attack; all the innumerable attacks upon London he had watched had been far more diffuse; only in Coventry had he seen this in action. Having seen it, and though he knew that, for the present, Ann and he were in no danger, he felt the cold sweat on his tightened face.

The City was now alive with hundreds of little tongues of flames, leaping higher, rippling together, fanned by the westerly wind, dimming the searchlights and bursting stars of flak, nudging the black from the deeper pink sky above. Identical, he thought again. Starting up more fires than any fire service can handle, and then the kill.

Ann asked icily, 'Is this how it was in Coventry?'

'Uh-huh.'

She could not drag her gaze from the merging flames but pulled off a glove and reached up to stroke his face and felt the cold dampness on his lean cheek. 'HE's next. We must get ins – ' She swallowed the rest of the word at the sudden glimpse of the black shapes of bombs raining down. Though too distant even for blast waves, they swung instinctively to face the back wall, and she felt Josh's trilby being jammed over her face. A few seconds later they turned and raced for the terrace doors, seeing them clearly in the new brightness of the flames shooting up from the sites of the explosions. She had his hat in her left hand when they flopped breathlessly against the inside of the closed doors in the total darkness of the emptied, brick-windowed ward that smelt of illness, carbolic, antiseptics, wax polish, stale tobacco smoke and the fish pie the patients had been about to have for supper and were now having in the basement.

The powerful beam of a torch pierced the darkness and a man's voice called, 'Who's there?'

She knew the voice and called back, 'Mr Henty, it's Nurse Marlowe and a guest, Mr Adams. We got caught out.'

The charge hand of Repairs and Works came up the long ward, briefly playing the light over them then directing it to the floor. "Evening, nurse – sir. Wouldn't say you've picked the best time to stroll by the river.' He thumbed the tin hat to the back of his head to peer more closely up at Josh's shadowy face. 'Good show last night, wasn't it, sir? Brought your cards along again?'

Now Josh was able to place him. 'Not this time, Mr Henty.'

'I reckon I can scrounge you a pack if wanted.' Mr Henty glanced up and down the ward. The beam of his torch revealed the shadowy outlines of the five clean, made beds on either side of the doors, but not the eight on either side of the entrance with bared springs and unnaturally untidy locker-tops after the grabbing of snapshots of wives, children, girlfriends, and pipes, tobacco pouches and squashed packets of Woodbines. 'All tucked up below, and last I heard, Cas empty as Stan P. The cops don't reckon we'll have many, if any in, being a Sunday and the City still on its Christmas holidays.' He paused to listen to the continuing roar of aircraft and explosions only faintly muffled by stone walls, bricked-up windows and four empty floors above. 'He's having himself a smashing time, is Jerry, and not missing a trick. Westerly wind, low tide, yards of mud on both banks. Fire boats'll not be able to get close enough, and the lads'll have to lug their hoses in over the mud. Aye,' he mused laconically, 'knows his trade, does Jerry. Best get moving, nurse. If I'm not back to my blower up in old Tom, sharpish, the lads up top'll be sending out search parties.'

'Yes, of course, Mr Henty,' said Ann and as they walked down the ward she explained to Josh that the block's ARP post was in the inner corridor of Thomas Holtsmoor, the ward directly above. 'On past form, first floors are as safe as the ground floor, only much more convenient being closed.'

'Your young lady's not far wrong, sir.' Mr Henty closed the ward entrance doors and swung his light around the short wide inner corridor leading to the closed mahogany doors to the main corridor. 'Handy not having to shift our gear between shifts. Sorry if this puts the kibosh on your party, nurse.'

Ann shrugged. 'Trust Jerry, though actually here he could be doing us a good turn. Matron said this morning – ' She had to wait to be heard, and in the pause she thought of what else Matron had said this morning that she had not yet had time to tell Josh. Private conversation would be difficult once she reported for duty and had to leave him with others in the basement whilst she got back into uniform, and then, even if she could sit this out with him, they couldn't touch each other. She knew he was back in nightmare and needed her nearness as she needed his. If he weren't here I'd now be going round the bend about him and the City, she thought. And when she could, she added, 'Matron said if tonight's had to be called off we could have it New Year's Eve with – imagine this! – an extension to 1 a.m. to see in the New Year!'

'That'll be a bit of all right, Nurse Marlowe!'

'Won't it just!' She turned to Josh's silent shadowy figure. 'Do tell Miss Dewly that guest beds will be laid on as usual. I don't imagine she, or anyone else from outside, will turn up tonight.'

'I guess not.' Josh, breathing carefully, packed a smile into his voice. 'I'll certainly tell Miss Dewly.'

'Good show.' Ann sighed. 'I suppose I should report – '
Again she had to wait, and Josh moved closer and reached for her hand.

Mr Henty watched them thoughtfully. He had heard the anxiety in her unfinished sentence and he minded when he'd been courting: once she reported back, that put the kibosh on her evening off. But he'd lay five bob to a tanner she'd be twiddling her thumbs to the All Clear, and most like after. When he'd heard them coming in he had just come down from the roof and he agreed with the lads up there that no Jerry apprentices were up tonight. Craftsmen all, and a good craftsman knew his trade. Mr Henty was a fitter, and a very good craftsman who spoke far more slowly than he thought. This morning – like all of Martha's – he had heard of Nurse Marlowe's interview with Matron within minutes of its ending. Down the workshop they'd been real made up for her, he reflected, waiting to be heard. Repairs and Works pin-up today, was Nurse Marlowe, after giving them the best belly-laugh of the year last night. But he'd always had a lot of time for her, particularly since the blitz. Never had much to do with any nurses – except on the job – before. Nice enough young ladies, even if most were no more than slips of girls, but none had acted up like slips of girls since. Taken it same as the lads, and at times better. Surprised many more than him, that had. No screaming, no tears when there was patients around, though at times – the good Gawd knew – he'd needed to blow his nose sharpish. He minded Nurse Marlowe – and her bloke – playing cards of a Saturday afternoon, Nurse Marlowe alongside him flat on her face of a Sunday noon, and crossing the road of an early Thursday morning and stopping to pick up an umbrella after she – same as he – had just lost good mates.

He said slowly, 'The wife's packed me tea to float the *Queen Mary* tonight. Care to come up for a cuppa, nurse – sir? Wouldn't mind one, meself.'

They spent the next two hours sitting together on one of the short, low benches, lined against the inner wall on either side of the closed kitchen door in Thomas Holtsmoor. The short corridor was double-lined with water and sand buckets, sacks of sand, and stirrup-pumps. They sat on the bench nearest the landing; drawn up to the other was the small deal table from the empty kitchen, and on it the ward telephone extended from the dutyroom, an emergency set connected to the roof, two unlit hurricane lamps, a red hardbacked open warden's log-book, a small battery of old vacuum flasks and four clean, chipped china mugs. The one ceiling light on was still mains-powered, and repeatedly the flex swung and the bulb blinked.

'Not on our side, but he keeps up and generators'll be earning their keep.' Mr Henty handed them mugs of strong, sweet, hot tea. 'Seeing as word's out, nurse – sir' – he raised his mug – 'health and happiness to you both.'

Ann's smile so enraptured Josh that he forgot the raid for a split second. He smiled. 'Why, thank you, Mr Henty. I guess word gets round Saint Martha's pretty fast.'

Ann laughed. 'Beats radar!'

'Every day o' the week and twice Sundays, nurse. Ta, sir.' He accepted one of Josh's cigarettes, and grinned at Ann. 'Leaving us in one uniform and coming back in another, eh, nurse?'

Josh's face lit up. 'You've fixed the deal!'

Ann's blue-grey eyes laughed into his openly adoring blue ones. 'Uh-huh.' She had written to tell him the idea that had come to her in the back of a taxi three weeks ago, and turning back to Mr Henty she said, 'Martha's rules forbid married Marthas to work in London, but don't say anything about married VADs. The British Red Cross Society takes the trained and untrained, so I'll be back with a red cross on my apron bib and cap, on my bike, five days a week. Simple.'

He wagged his head. 'Like I tell the lads, nurse, if you can't do the job one way, have a go at the other. Just got to use your loaf – oh, now what's he up to?' A thunderous explosion echoed over the river.

The joy in Ann's and Josh's faces had gone out like a light. Ann asked abruptly, 'St Paul's?'

'I'd say too close to the river, honey.'

'That's my reckoning, sir.' Mr Henty picked up the emergency receiver. It was a couple of minutes before it was answered. He spoke briefly, then, 'Aye. Ta.' He put it down. 'Warehouses making a nice bonfire. Still seeing St Paul's. Ringed with fire but still there.' He glanced at them sympathetically. 'Time for the check.' He spoke into the other telephone then stood up and ambled off for the first of many occasions in those next two hours during which two-thirds of the City, the fifteenth-century Guildhall, eight Wren churches and centuries of English history were destroyed. When the still rising wind forced the premature return to base and the All Clear sounded through the roaring and crackling of hundreds of massive fires raging out of control, the whole sky over London was crimson and the blood-red glow was again visible from Oxford fifty-seven miles away.

Before Josh left the hospital they went up on the roof and stood with Mr Henty and the fireman a few yards back from the low parapet edging the riverside front. Josh had one arm around Ann's straightened shoulders and with his free hand held on to his hat, as she her beret, and their companions stood with folded arms, helmet brims nudging their noses, all their eyes narrowed against the blinding glare. The wind slapped their faces with hot air and millions of swirling cinders, and their ears ached from the elemental roaring of the great, whirling forest fires leaping up from the land on both banks down river; again, in stretches, the Thames looked as if on fire, and directly in front of the hospital it ran like molten rubies. And still visible were the dome, lantern and cross of St Paul's lapped by soaring flames.

Josh sensed Ann's anger from the tension of her muscles, and in the light of the fires saw it in her upraised face, and heard its undercurrent in the quiet Cockney voices.

'Lights a good bonfire, does Jerry.'

'Aye. Knows his trade.'

'You reckon this is how it looked from here in the Great Fire of London, Bert?'

'Reckon it did,' said Mr Henty, as if referring to yesterday.

1666, thought Josh, dragging his anguished gaze from Ann to look around at the outlines of other little groups on the roofs of the remaining blocks and those on the terrace far below.

Ann spoke for the first time since they had come up to say briskly, 'Thank God he didn't get St Paul's. I'm sure they'll save it now.'

Josh dared not comment, but the other men agreed that seeing as the wind had sent Jerry packing, the lads would be able to get on with the job and they reckoned old Paul'd still be there come morning.

'Same as us,' added Mr Henty, 'and seeing as it'll be Monday morning before we know it, best get down and clock off.'

Customary routine, thought Josh, drawing Ann's arm through his as they turned away.

Aside from the intervals to meet his deadline and listen to his President's voice crackling over the short-waves, Josh spent the rest of that night watching the City burn from as near as he was allowed in cordoned-off, furnace-hot, smoke-filled streets. In the morning he watched the crowds of office and shop workers streaming on foot over London Bridge. His trilby was singed, his overcoat scorched in patches, his eyes reddened and haggard, his unshaven face streaked with soot. A vast, rising pall of black smoke laced with scarlet and yellow engulfed the City, concealing what lay beneath, and the crowds streamed on. They had left home early to get to work on time, knowing they would have to walk from London Bridge station, but not whether they still had workplaces. All night they had seen the fires and heard the rumours, but there was no mention of the raid in the morning papers, and it was Monday morning and the City's Christmas holiday was over. From the extent of the smoke the truth was obvious, but the crowds streamed on and little groups of girl typists or junior filing clerks ran on ahead, taking from handbags or string-bags packed lunchtime sandwiches, pressing them upon the nearest of the army of firemen with blackened faces, and soaking uniforms, demanding urgently, 'Did he get St Paul's?' and at the answer smiling as if they had just heard they had won the war.

About an hour later he walked up the Strand, still cordoned off from Charing Cross, and on up Fleet Street until he was stopped halfway up Ludgate Hill. He had walked in the middle of the road, feeling the surface hot under his feet, and the thickening smoke stinging his eyes and tightening his lungs. In Ludgate Hill the roadway and pavements were littered with broken glass, rubble, smouldering chunks and charred fragments of wood, and grey ribbons of hoses steaming in the heat. Belching black smoke and yellow tongues of flames came from every side street and alley, and through smoke and flames he glimpsed men on turntable ladders, extension ladders, and clambering over still burning roofs or jagged roofless buildings. A little way down from where he was stopped was a parked WVS canteen van from which three middle-aged women in WVS green were briskly serving mugs of tea to firemen, who drank thirstily then hurried away, wiping their mouths on their cuffs and leaving smears that transformed their red-eyed, exhausted faces to those of badly made-up clowns. Higher up the hill, directly ahead through the blackish smoke spiralling into the thicker black cloud lying like a pall over Greater London, he saw, standing serenely, apparently undamaged, the west front of St Paul's.

'Just the one incendiary got through the outer dome then dropped backwards down the yard before doing more than a mite of damage,' said the Special who had stopped him. 'Bit of luck that, you might say. Mark you,' he looked around, 'more than a bit that was out of luck. But if tonight's quiet, shouldn't be anything to roast chestnuts on by morning. And now you seen the cathedral's still here, sir, I'll have to ask you to move on.'

Josh took another comprehensive look around and uphill. 'Sure, constable. Thanks very much for letting me come this far.'

There was no raid that night, nor upon the following one, the last night of the year. The morning papers carried shortish accounts of Sunday night's attack on the City, naming the Guildhall as destroyed but not the eight Wren churches either destroyed by fire or severely damaged, and adding that yesterday afternoon Mr and Mrs Churchill had spent two hours walking through the streets in the vicinity.

And that night, shortly after the party began, Ann showed Josh the cable that had come to her from the Air Ministry a few hours ago. It read, 'Fraternal approval stroke blessings written jga stop happy landings happy new year love michael.'

The New Year was fifteen minutes old when they left Sir Joshua Levy refilling Miss Dewly's glass with the champagne he had provided for the whole party. They slipped away unnoticed and went quietly along dimly lit basement passages, up to the ground, over to the stone stairs of Block 3 and then up by torchlight to the fifth floor. Ann led the way, silently opening and closing behind them the unlocked doors of the top-floor ward, long stripped of all movable equipment, the remains of jagged glass in the gaping windows. The icy air in the dark ward still reeked of trapped smoke, and cordite, but on the balcony the air was fresher and slightly salty, as a strong south-easter was blowing up the river.

The strength of the wind had broken the black man-made overcast into scurrying clouds, and between the clouds the starlight and that of the waning half-moon laid moving streaks of pale light upon the blacked-out city which was celebrating the birth of the New Year underground in cellars and shelters, the vaults of churches and on Tube platforms, and in converted ballrooms, restaurants and hospital basements. As always the blackout softened with purple-black shadows the gaps, the mounds, the jagged outlines, the wide patches of flattened bombsites, and the new land-based sea of ruins across the river and on the right of that high balcony. And immediately their eyes grew acclimatised to the darkness, they saw the shadowy outline of the great dome that seemed to float above the new sea of destruction.

As so often before – and as would happen far more often in their future – they had no need for words as they stood, their arms around each other, looking out into the darkness and listening to Big Ben chiming the first half-hour of 1941.